The Author

MORLEY CALLAGHAN was born in Toronto, Ontario, in 1903. A graduate of the University of Toronto and Osgoode Law School, he was called to the bar in 1928, the same year that his first novel, *Strange Fugitive,* was published. Fiction commanded his attention, and he never practised law.

While in university, Callaghan had taken a summer position at the *Toronto Star* when Ernest Hemingway was a reporter there. In April 1929, he travelled with his wife to Paris, where their literary circle of friends included Hemingway, Fitzgerald, and Joyce. *That Summer in Paris* is his memoir of the time. The following autumn, Callaghan returned to Toronto.

Callaghan was among the first writers in Canada to earn his livelihood exclusively from writing. In a career that spans more than six decades, he published sixteen novels and more than a hundred shorter works of fiction. Usually set in the modern city, his fiction captures the drama of ordinary lives as people struggle against a background of often hostile social forces.

Morley Callaghan died in Toronto, Ontario, in 1990.

THE NEW CANADIAN LIBRARY

General Editor: David Staines

Morley Callaghan

THEY SHALL
INHERIT
THE EARTH

With an Afterword by Ray Ellenwood

The following dedication appeared in the original edition:

FOR LORETTO

First published in Canada in 1935 by
The Macmillan Company of Canada Limited
Copyright © 1992 by the Estate of Morley Callaghan
Afterword copyright © 1992 by Ray Ellenwood

Reprinted 1992

Canadian Cataloguing in Publication Data

Callaghan, Morley, 1903-1990
They shall inherit the earth

(New Canadian library)
ISBN 0-7710-9881-2

I. Title. II. Series.

PS8505.44T54 1992   C813'.52   C91-095248-5
PR9199.3.C35T54 1992

Typesetting by M&S, Toronto
Printed and bound in Canada

McClelland & Stewart Inc.
The Canadian Publishers
481 University Avenue
Toronto, Ontario
M5G 2E9

They Shall Inherit the Earth

One

I N T H E early summer evening Andrew Aikenhead, of the firm
of Hillquist and Aikenhead, had gone out seeking his son.
He had crossed slowly through the traffic with an eager expression on his upturned florid face. He was there on the sidewalk
in the crowd, in the way of the passing people, looking up at the
rooming house where his son lived, and he was full of delight, as
though he had at last taken a necessary step that would bring joy
again into his life.

He went into the house, and when he stood in the hall and
saw by the names on the wall that his son was on the third
floor, he began to climb the red-carpeted stairs, puffing and
sighing at every fifth step. On the second floor, where the light
was brighter, he saw a small, neat man with such delicate fea-
tures and such fair wavy hair parted in the middle that he
looked like a pretty boy, except that his blue eyes were red-
rimmed and shrewd, and this man was tiptoeing along the
hall carrying a basket of fruit in both hands. The light overhead shone on the blue grapes, the yellow pears and the glossy
peaches as he stooped and placed the basket of fruit on the carpet by the door of a room.

"Could you tell me where Michael Aikenhead lives?"
Andrew Aikenhead asked.

"Mike Aikenhead," the man said, straightening up and

looking embarrassed. "Sure, I can tell you. Go on upstairs. The last room on the right at the back. He's in there." Andrew Aikenhead went on climbing the stairs again, while the fair-haired young man looked doubtfully at the basket of fruit he had placed like an offering outside that door.

In the little hall at the top, where there were only two doors, Andrew Aikenhead coughed, and then he began to clear his throat like a man who is about to make an important speech and offers a few preliminary sounds as a friendly gesture. Then he stood still, looking at the brown-painted door while his heart fluttered strangely and there was a yearning in him that his son might remember and know his voice that had sounded so loud. And when he rapped and his son's voice called carelessly, "Come in," he was full of gladness; and as he opened the door he thought, "That's a good omen. Things will go well."

His son, Michael, was sitting at a desk with his feet curled around the legs of the chair, and because the light on the desk was one of those lamps that students use which throw the rays of light in a pyramid shape full upon the desk, the father could not quite see the face in the shadow. The long fingers of one of his son's big hands crossed quickly through the light and spread through his hair, and then he got up awkwardly. He was a big dark fellow, and he came across the room slowly, his hand stretched out to his smiling father. "Hello, I hardly knew you. I mean I was surprised to see you," he said.

"Didn't you hear me cough in the hall, Michael?"

"No, I was reading."

"I knew you'd be surprised. I guess you didn't expect me at all," the father said, and then he sat down on the bed, for he was out of breath from climbing the stairs, and he looked around the room while he rested. It was one of those attic rooms with sloping ceilings. There was only a bed, an old golden-oak dresser, a heavy desk with one end of it piled high with books, the long window, with a radiator under it, and a worn green carpet on the floor. At one end of the room was a little alcove that could be used as a kitchenette, for there was a gas stove there and a kettle and a coffee pot. And when Andrew Aikenhead saw how poor his son was and that he lived in this plain room, he sighed, and he was deeply embarrassed and he could not look up, even though he knew his son preferred this poverty to the comfort of his father's house.

Michael was a graduate civil engineer who was waiting for some development in the industrial life of the city that would give him work. He had left his father's house when he started at the university. He hadn't been able to get along with his father the last ten years. The hostility between them had begun at the time of the father's second marriage; it had begun on the day when he had brought his second wife to the house, and day after day it grew, with the father helpless and wondering, until it was time for Michael to go to the university, and then he had said he would live alone and be independent and support himself. At the university he had waited on table, he had pressed trousers and taken out ashes, and he had sold magazines around the country in the summer.

Andrew Aikenhead remembered all this as he smiled humbly and looked at his son who was standing there holding his body tense, ready to retreat. He saw how calm his son's face was and he felt the firmness in him, and then he began to fear timidly that Michael would not need him now at all. He wanted to say, "You don't need me now, Michael, but don't be hostile. I could hardly bear it when you left us. I never really knew why you disliked me. I never really knew till this day. Many men marry the second time. Their sons go on living with them." But his head drooped and a hurt expression came into his eyes that made him look lost and helpless in that attic room, for the more he remembered the more he longed to make one sincere and friendly remark that would break the silence that was embarrassing both of them. "This place isn't very comfortable to have a chat in, is it?" he said.

"I'll go out and have a drink with you, if you want to," Michael said.

"Have a drink with me?"

"Sure. There's a place around the corner."

"That's splendid," he said, and he picked up his hat quickly, for the simple words of the speech he had planned to use for this occasion would not come to him, and his face was reddening. They were just going out when they heard someone knocking, and when Michael opened the door his father saw a fair girl with big candid blue eyes and thick yellow hair in a long bob and a round high-cheek-boned face. She was wearing a light-blue knitted sweater that was tight at her waist. When she smiled at Michael, his father thought it was the warmest and friendliest smile he had ever seen. She was carrying the basket of fruit the little fair man had placed outside her door. "I was wondering if you rapped on my door a little while ago, Mike," she said. "I wondered if you left this basket there." And by the way she spoke she seemed to be pleading that he should nod his head and tell her she had guessed the truth.

"I'd like to, Anna, but where would I get a lot of fruit like that?"

"I didn't know. Somebody knocked at the door. I thought it might have been you. Do you want it?"

"I'd eat it anyway, if I were you, Anna. What do you say if we don't ask where it came from, we'll both eat it anyway, eh?"

"All right, if you take the blame," she said.

"Sure, come on," he said, and bent over the basket she held out to him and picked out a shining red apple and offered it to her. "I don't like to take it," she said. "You know what I mean."

"I'll bite it first then," he said, and he bit the apple solemnly and grinned at her while that bright friendliness was shining in her face. And his father, who was standing just behind him, loved the way his son had so warmly welcomed the girl; he loved the way they stood there together making a kind of sudden free happiness between them over a trifle, and while he watched his son's red lips moving as he solemnly chewed the apple, he began to feel apologetic, as though he were an intruder. He said, "I could tell you both where the basket came from."

Michael said to Anna a little awkwardly, "This is my father, Anna. He just came in to see me," and he seemed to be embarrassed by his father's fine expensive clothes, as if Anna might be wondering what such an important-looking and well-dressed man was doing in that attic room.

Andrew Aikenhead was humiliated by the way their natural free happiness left them as they, becoming aware of him, offered him the politeness they would have offered a stranger, but he said, "I was coming upstairs and I saw a fellow, a dapper little fellow. He might have been a boy he was so nice-looking, only he looked pretty hard-headed, and he was putting that basket of fruit down outside your door as if it might have been an offering."

"That sounds like Huck Farr, Anna."

"I thought it was Huck Farr," she said soberly.

"Take it anyway, Anna. Don't you want to? All right, maybe you'd better not if you don't want to," Michael said, for the girl was putting the basket on the floor. "Maybe you'd give it back to him, eh, Mike?" she said. She straightened up then and the father saw that her face when she was not smiling was full of worry. "I'm glad I met your father, Mike," she said. "I'll run along, now. Good-bye, Mr. Aikenhead. Good-bye, Mike."

But when she smiled like that Michael's father suddenly found the flow of friendly words that had been eluding him, and beaming, he said, "I came around to ask Mike to go on a little trip up in the country with us for about a week. Don't you think it would be a good idea?" He spoke rapidly, so he could get it all out of him before she left; he spoke as though he felt sure that her presence there would persuade Michael to go with him.

"You certainly ought to go, Mike," she said. "Imagine

getting out of the city for a week. I'd love to," and that warm smile that had startled Andrew Aikenhead at first made her face glow again. "Good-bye," she said, and she went, and then they heard her going downstairs.

"My, she's an odd girl, Michael. It's the way she smiles, I think."

"Isn't she really lovely?"

"What nationality is she? I can usually tell but I couldn't make up my mind."

"She said once her parents were Ukrainians. I don't know much about her but she's having a pretty tough time around here. She's just about walking on her uppers. She's out of a job and everybody around here's watching her. Huck Farr, Miss Gray, the lecturer on the next floor and the electrician on the ground floor. Soon they'll be making bets on how long it'll be before Huck lands her."

"Quite an idea putting the basket of fruit outside her door. A pretty effective fellow in such matters, I must say."

"Sure, Huck Farr's a smart guy and he knows she'll get hungry sooner or later. He doesn't bother her; he just waits around like that. I certainly wish something would turn up for her."

By this time they were outside on the street, talking earnestly like this amid all the murmuring city noises, the cries of little kids playing on the sidewalk in the summer evening, the newsboys shouting on the corners and the shrill cries of little girls alleeooing to each other up the streets, and Andrew Aikenhead was delighted that they were talking so casually; he wanted his son to see how he shared his concern for the girl, Anna, and as they walked along, silent for a while, thinking of the girl, he thought he felt a warm and silent communion growing between them.

The tavern they went into was full of working men from the neighborhood, and after they had sat in a corner by themselves, the father looked around at the whitewashed walls, the faked beamed ceilings – to make it look like an old inn – the table crowded with working men and fancy women who laughed in high-pitched voices, and bums who opened wide wet-moustached mouths and wiped them with their sleeves, and he said, "Do you come here much, Michael?"

"All the time. It's my favorite hangout. Let's hoist a few," Michael said, and he called the cauliflower-eared waiter with the square jaw. "Jake, a couple of beers," he said, and by the way he winked at the waiter his father felt suddenly that Michael was making their meeting, which he had wanted to be so important to both of them, a light and casual matter. Leaning forward he said, "Is there any chance of steady work for you, Michael?"

"None at all that I can see. There are too many engineers around. I've been trying for months to get into the Lake City Light, Heat and Power Company, but there's nothing doing."

"Wouldn't you like to come and work for us in the advertising agency?"

"Me? I'm an engineer," Mike said, and he grinned at his father, as he repeated, "An engineer. I like engineering. I wouldn't like the advertising business."

Moving his glass in little circles on the table, Andrew Aikenhead said, "It's hard to begin to talk … a man doesn't know where to begin. I don't know why you feel hostile to me, son. I never knew in the beginning. I know when it started. It started when your mother died and I married the second time, didn't it, son? But lots of men marry the second time, and besides that, that was nearly eight years ago and you just kept growing away from me. I respect you wanting to go your own way. You understand that? I respect you putting yourself through college. I can't help respecting that, but you're not hostile now, are you?"

"Not in the slightest," Michael said. "I'm not a kid now. I just feel I can get along all right by myself. All I want is a job."

"You don't dislike my wife now?"

"I don't think much about her at all, if you don't mind me saying so."

"That's fine, son," the father said. He was hardly able to bear it the way his son had become so detached from him, yet he thought, "There's a fine direct way in him, but I don't know how he thinks about things. I don't know what to say to him. The way he thinks and feels is now so much different than mine. He makes me feel older. He's a direct practical man, he's a scientific man and I just run a business that he doesn't like," and he said urgently, "Look here, Michael, I know I've hardly done a damn thing for you, but that's the way you wanted it, isn't it, Michael? There comes a time in a man's life when he feels he can't live without being close to someone he belongs to…."

"Sure, I know what you mean," Michael said, for there was such a fretfulness in his father's voice as he went on pleading that he couldn't help but be a little touched. He was not drawn close to his father; he simply had begun to feel some of his father's eagerness. "I'm not asking much out of the way, Michael. I just thought you might want to come up to the country with your sister, Sheila, and Ross Hillquist. That's all." He had to raise his voice a little because of the hum of conversation around them; bits of conversation came to them in bright little snatches and drifted away and were lost in the brightness of louder words from other tables – "I said nothing doing, big boy, but I'll give you a proposition of my own." "As God is my witness I haven't seen nor heard of her in three years. You've got to believe it" – and then the sudden, high-piping laugh of a half-drunken woman. Sometimes Michael could hardly hear his father, but out of that haze of smoke in the room loomed larger and larger his father's face. It was a shrewd, clean-shaven, pink-and-white face with almost white hair; the shrewdness was mixed in with a deceptive amiability. There was not much mildness or innocence in such a face, yet there was so much warmth and eagerness in it tonight that it had become something more than the face of Andrew Aikenhead who was one of the shrewdest advertising men in the city. There was something desperate now and baffled in it. Andrew Aikenhead had got to a point where success in business no longer satisfied him. He had come out seeking his son because nothing in his business life could any longer give him much joy. The advertising business had often begun to make him feel a little weary and this surely was not the way for one of the partners of the agency of Hillquist and Aikenhead to be feeling after fifteen years in business. It was a terrible thing for a man to feel suddenly that he had devoted his life to convincing people they wanted things they really did not want, that he had created imaginary passions and lusts in the breasts of millions just to provide them with imaginary satisfaction, and to have this feeling every time he picked up the newspapers and read the advertising of a thousand commodities that went into the lives of millions of people. As he leaned across the table, pleading with the son who had left him and groping to express his desire for a new feeling between them, his eyes glowed, and Michael, who had always thought of his father as a glib, plausible man, with a million easy words, felt very strongly his yearning and his new eagerness. "It's not much to ask, Michael. It's just a little thing. You know, we might be good friends yet. You can't tell. But don't start thinking of it like that. I mean, just say you'll come along."

And Andrew Aikenhead began to nod his head as if he could still hear his own fumbling and apologetic words flowing within him while he put out his hand and touched Michael's arm. His words, the tone of his voice, his eager, excited face went underneath any resentment there was between them, and touched some deeper experience they had once shared together; it went back to the time when one had been a boy and the other a young man and they had been father and son and close together, to that time when Michael's mother had been alive. So Michael said softly, "Sure, I'll go up with you," and when he had said this he laughed suddenly. "I don't know a single reason why I shouldn't go," he said.

"That's fine. Sheila and Ross Hillquist'll be delighted."

"I'll go up with Ross. Tell him to call for me, will you?" and Michael laughed in such a careless yielding way that his father, who was glowing with delight, felt uneasily that his son was so strong in his independence of him that he thought he could afford to humor him. But his face wrinkled up with pleasure and he said, "Thanks, son. I've got to hurry back to the house. Jay Hillquist and I are having a party for a client. Thanks again, son. I'll look forward to seeing you. What are you going to do now?

"I'll stay here a while."

"Many thanks then, my boy," and as Andrew Aikenhead left his son and walked through the tables, he walked a little stiffly, so no one would notice how pleased he was. He saw Huck Farr, the little fellow who had put the basket of fruit outside Anna Prychoda's door, sitting palefaced and alone at a table by the door, and as he went out, he saw Michael beckoning to Huck Farr.

Outside in the fine spring night he walked a few blocks through that section of the city that was near the university, through streets of old houses and restaurants where he was often crowded off the sidewalk by young people with dark foreign faces, walking alone like this that he might feel all his joy before he called a taxi and drove across the city to his fine home in the new residential part of the city.

Two

WHEN Andrew Aikenhead, dreaming and smiling to himself, went into his house he met Dave Choate, his wife's boy by a first marriage, coming downstairs on the way out. From that distance, Dave, who was twenty, was tall and good-looking with the kind of lean, fresh face you expect to see on a college athlete, but when he was closer to you, you noticed the wild laughing crazy clownishness in his face. Dave had left the university a little while ago to go into the advertising business with his stepfather, but he had quit that job because they had insisted that he take it seriously. There had been no particular quarrel with his stepfather over that incident, for the truth was they all would have been surprised if he settled down to hard work so soon. But there had been a noisy family row only last night. Dave had had a party in the house that lasted all night, and in the early morning he had rushed down to the cellar and brought up six bottles of champagne and had invited the party to go upstairs to the bathroom with him and wash their teeth in the champagne, and when Andrew Aikenhead woke up and found Dave alone and saw what he had been doing he waved his fists around in the air and shouted that Dave was a good-for-nothing blockhead and he would like nothing better than to beat him with his own hands.

And as Dave passed his stepfather, who looked up at him so

mildly, he was ashamed and he hardly knew what to say, for when he was sober he was friendly and quiet, and the drinking escapades and the silly parties and the cheap and willing girls who took up his nights and days bothered him a little. So as he passed he said now, "I'm sorry about last night."

"Oh, that's all right, don't bother thinking about it," Andrew Aikenhead said quickly.

"I'm really sorry for the trouble we had."

"We'd better forget it. Don't bother thinking about it at all," he said, and he was deeply embarrassed for a reason he did not then understand. When Dave went out hesitantly without looking back, he only knew that he felt utterly free of him; he felt it would never be necessary to worry about him again. It was almost like watching someone who was harsh and relentless being pushed out of his life by someone he loved, and when the door was closed and Dave was gone there was a leap of gladness in him.

His wife, who had heard him come in, had stood at the top of the stairs and had heard the few awkward but yielding words he had had with her son, and delighted to see that he was without bitterness, she said, "I heard you talking to Dave. You were nice to him. You were very good-humored. Are you feeling good, thinking about the party?"

"I had almost forgotten about the party, Marthe."

"What were you thinking about?" she asked.

She was about forty-five and still black-haired, and when she wore the low-cut black crepe dinner gown she had on tonight she looked deep-breasted and warm with a kind of rich opulence that was half concealed by a natural passivity or stillness within her.

Marthe had been a nurse in a hospital at the time of the Great War in Europe. She had been in love with a young interne, William Choate, who was in the same hospital. There had been a wildness and excitement in the young people in those days and Marthe and William Choate decided to get married when they couldn't afford it at all. They had lived together for a year, and then the young interne decided it was absolutely necessary that he go to the war along with his comrades. It wasn't long before he was killed and Marthe was left with her son, Dave. She had to support herself and Dave by nursing again. She lived very frugally and was often weary, and it became a passion with her to gain some security for herself and her son. Nurses, who were pretty and were connected with the hospital, were always being asked to parties, and at one of these parties, an entertainment for a leather manufacturer from New York, she had met Andrew Aikenhead. Marthe had fine shoulders and her skin was soft and milky, and she looked like a woman who would never grow old, and at that time Andrew Aikenhead's wife was sick, and he was lonely and unhappy. He got into the habit of coming to see Marthe in her flat. When his wife finally died, and he asked Marthe to marry him, she felt for the first time that she was close to some security for herself and her son.

When Marthe held her head on one side, as she was doing now, and watched him with her abnormally large and soft dark eyes, she looked meditative and quietly wise, and yet she was never very calm about anything. "I saw my son, Michael, today," he began to explain slowly. The uneasiness within him alarmed him, for it was as though he were really crying out that he had betrayed her, as though he were admitting at last that he was restless and no longer stirred by her in the old way. For ten years, even before his first wife died, he had been helpless against his passion for her. She had bit by bit made his life her life and his ways her ways and she had tried very hard to be attractive to his friends, so they would forgive him for loving her, but now with nothing left between them but what there might be of a deeper love and concern for each other, and with the warmth all gone, he knew he had turned away from her and was reaching back deep into the life he had loved before he had ever met her. "Yes, I saw Michael tonight," was all he said.

"Why did you want to see Michael, Andrew? Did you go out for him?"

"I'd been thinking about him the last little while," he said, and he felt ashamed to see the wonder growing in her incredibly dark eyes.

Then she said to him gently, almost pleading that he should not be offended, "He didn't come near us, did he? He always wanted to keep away from us. You didn't worry much about him either while we were feeling close together."

"Did you say while we were feeling close together, Marthe?"

She nodded her head and said almost shyly, "I could feel this growing in you, Andrew. I knew you were getting restless." And when he turned away from her without saying anything and went into his room she followed him and said anxiously, "Don't you see what I mean?"

"No, I don't. Surely I have a right to see my own son," he said irritably.

"I didn't say not to see him."

"You're trying to imply that I'm a scamp for seeing him," he said.

While he sat down and began to jerk off his shoes, and while the blood rushing to his face as he bent over made him look dreadfully angry, she tried hard to express her fear in a way that would seem reasonable. There was such an agitation showing in her face and such a groping for the right, intimate words in her voice that he was startled. She looked as if she felt she were being pushed away from him, and while he listened to her low, murmuring voice he was filled with shameful doubts of his own honesty, and he pondered it in this way to himself: "I'm not irresponsible. I'm not planning anything. Why is she alarmed? Isn't my way of life her way?" These thoughts steadied him and he smiled and said, "It was just a simple little thing, my talk with Michael. I asked him to the country so he could be with us for a week."

"All right. I just meant that he never liked us," she said. "I meant you've been quarrelling a lot with Dave and I've often wondered if you wanted your own boy back. Sometimes you seem to hate Dave. I think he drives you crazy just being in the house."

"That's silly talk, Marthe, and it doesn't do anybody any good."

"You mean you don't know how I feel about it, yet you used to know my thoughts so well."

"I don't know how you're feeling. I don't know what you're hinting at."

"Just as a favor to me, don't let Michael come with us."

"Don't let my own son come?"

"No. I'm afraid."

"Afraid of what?"

"I don't know," she said, and the urgent pleading tone left her voice. "I guess it's just that I don't want anything to be disturbed. I guess I'm just selfish and want everything to go on the way it's been going. I'll run along now because I hadn't finished dressing." Then she smiled as she turned to go, and still really coaxing him she said softly, "It was just that when you said you saw Michael I felt everything breaking up. Maybe it was just the way you said it. More likely it was because I've been worrying so much about Dave," she said.

And when he should have been dressing he sat there holding one of his shoes in his hand still pondering the doubt that had come into his mind a few moments ago. With sudden shame he remembered the leap of gladness he had felt within him as Dave went out and closed the door, and he wondered why he had felt that way, and as he got up he was deeply troubled, for he wanted to be honest with himself.

Then he heard someone calling, "Dad, dad, may I come in? I'm in a hurry." It was his daughter, Sheila, who was going out, and she was standing at the door with her face flushed, as though she had been hurrying. She was a slender dark girl with blue eyes that always looked a little feverish and made her father worry and wonder if she might be tubercular. Tonight her young face was full of joy. By the way she kept smiling and showing her teeth, which were small, white and even except for two tiny visible spaces between the front upper ones, he knew she expected to be very happy that night with her lover, Ross Hillquist, the young doctor. Her happiness touched him so powerfully that he sat up straight, feeling free at last to show all his delight, and he said, "I saw Michael, Sheila. He's coming up to the country with us for a week. Imagine that!"

"Isn't that swell! Isn't that lovely!" she said, and they began to laugh and talk and whisper together.

"I told Michael Ross would call for him and drive him up, is that all right, do you think?"

"You better tell Ross yourself."

"Is he down there waiting for you?"

"He was talking to his father who just came in."

"Good Lord, and me not dressed. I've been sitting here dreaming."

Andrew Aikenhead put on his black and white plaid dressing-gown and went to the head of the stairs with Sheila and waited while she ran down the stairs so lightly that in her bright dress she seemed to slant away from him like a path of light. He heard her calling into the drawing-room, "Ross, Ross, just a moment." He heard her whispering to the young doctor; he heard them laugh, and then the two of them began to come up the stairs arm in arm, their faces lifted up together, smiling and coming toward him. The young doctor's warm, dark face was full of friendliness. The father loved the way those two faces together rose up the stairs to him. Ross

Hillquist was neither tall nor very short, nor fat nor hungry-looking, but he had very solid shoulders. He never struck you as being a remarkably clever man, but he always did seem to possess his own soul in a remarkable and magnificently simple way. Full of gladness to see that his daughter would surely find security in a marriage with the young doctor, Andrew Aikenhead called out eagerly, "Come on up a minute, Ross. I wanted to tell you I saw Michael. I want to have a talk with you about him."

Three

ACROWD of advertising men from the office of Hillquist and Aikenhead and their wives and a few musicians, a few successful painters who might be called celebrities and a doctor and a lawyer had come in. The men from the office were all jolly and full of loud friendly laughter; their more domestic wives were glad of the party but looked a little alarmed at knowing they would have to stay up half the night. Their distinguished guest, Stewart Roebuck, who controlled the Minerva Cheese account, had come in with them and was standing a little shyly to one side, very happy and full of wonder that he, a polite little man with a hesitant way of speaking and a pair of large thick glasses, should arouse such warmth in the women and such bursting joviality in the men.

Andrew Aikenhead went up to him and took him by the arm and whispered with a warm graciousness, "Follow me into the kitchen, Stewart, where we can be alone. All week I've been saving you a thimbleful of the neatest brandy you ever tasted." And with Roebuck blushing with rosy good humor they went into the kitchen to have a drink together. Shyly leaning close to Aikenhead Roebuck said, "I've taken your advice seriously. I'm really trying my hand at a little painting. Next time I come here I want you to see my daubings. I do hope you won't be disappointed."

"Be sure and let me see them. I'll take them around and let some painters see them," Aikenhead said. He was more amiable than ever tonight. His face shone with joyful good humor. He held the Minerva Cheese account for his agency not because he knew how to talk business with Roebuck, for business was only a perfunctory aspect of their relationship, but because he made Roebuck feel that his secret and intimate longings flowered more beautifully when he was with him than with anyone else in the world. "I haven't really showed you anything in the way of art. Tomorrow I'll get one of the art men to go to a gallery with us and give you some of the technical aspects of the thing," he said encouragingly. "We can talk business later, eh?" And Roebuck with his blue eyes shining brightly behind his glasses and full of gratitude that they weren't to talk business tonight kept saying, "Lovely, lovely, lovely." There was nothing Aikenhead wouldn't have done for Roebuck tonight, for much of the joyfulness that had come from meeting Michael was still with him and it gave him a kind of pity for this shy business man who was so full of secret and inarticulate longing.

Arm in arm they went in to join the party. Aikenhead beamed and waved his hand at his partner, Jay Hillquist, who was standing in the middle of the floor with the wife of one of his minor executives holding his salad plate in both her hands for him while he went on talking to another wife who had just brought him a cup of coffee. Hillquist was a towering man with heavy shoulders and a brick-red complexion and cheeks that were sunken because he had recently had his teeth out. Though the restless nervousness that had been in him the last two years made him sometimes blink his eyes in a rapid and astonishing way and left the impression that he was a worried man, he was really a man of simple and profound faith. If he and his company were telling the wide world that Roebuck's cheese was incomparable among the cheeses of all nations, then he and his wife and his household and the households of his employees would eat no other cheese. It was the same with milk, razors, toilet accessories, radios and pickles; he took them into his home and believed in them before he asked others to use them, so that his home was littered with countless gadgets that he never had time to touch. He filled his stomach with the condiments of his clients and then took the purges of other clients and was soon made whole again. So he, the man of faith, was the one, and not Aikenhead, that all the employees looked to with such hope to restore their security and their salaries and the faith of the old boom-time days.

As soon as he saw Andrew Aikenhead standing beside him he whispered, "Have you been talking to Roebuck?"

"He's feeling fine, Jay."

"How much does he plan to spend?"

"I didn't rush him into it. I'm letting him sell it to himself."

"It would be wonderful if you could persuade him to double his account. A thing like that in these times would jack us all up. Sell it to him. You can make him want to do it. He ought to know that when his sales start to drop he's got to do more advertising."

"He knows you can't sell cheese to people if they haven't got the money to spend, Jay."

"God help us, Andy. What's the matter with you? I don't know what's got into you these days. You talk as though you were licked. When you talk like that you just make things worse. As far as I'm concerned, there isn't any depression," he said, and he thrust out his jaw. But after blurting out his fear like that he smiled, for he knew he couldn't really get on without his old friend.

"I was feeling pretty good. I wasn't feeling licked at all," Aikenhead said. "I heard some good news tonight."

"From Roebuck?"

"No. I saw my boy, Michael."

"How's he doing? Is he working yet? He wanted to get into

the Lake City Light, Heat and Power Company, my boy, Ross, was saying."

"No, he's not working, but he's going to come up to the country with us and I feel pretty good about it."

"So that's what's been spreading the smile all over your face, eh? I'm mighty glad, Andrew, you know I would be," and he put his big hand on his partner's shoulder and gave him an affectionate push, and they smiled at each other, two old friends thinking of times many years ago when they were happy in a more innocent way, when they were both poor and their children were growing, when they were both in love with their wives.

The men had gathered around the piano and had begun to sing, and two of them had rushed to Mrs. Aikenhead, wanting her to be at the piano with them, wanting her to be there at the piano because of her soft, handsome, warm way among them. The wives of other men sat around the room watching Mrs. Aikenhead and resenting her and wondering why men wanted her to be with them. And when Andrew Aikenhead, leaning alone against the mantel, saw how his wife smiled and heard her deep voice, he felt foolish to have been disturbed a little while ago by what he had thought had been anguish in her. "Why did I feel so dreadfully uneasy when she spoke to me? She doesn't care at all. Look at her there," he thought, and he felt free again, and his florid face began to shine rosily above his gleaming white shirtfront.

But he began to feel tired, and he left the room quietly, going out to the hall and opening the front door to let the cool air in from the street, and he sat on the stairs mopping his head and listening.

Twenty years ago Andrew Aikenhead had been selling printing in the city for a newspaper press. He was married and in love with his wife, and he had two little children. In his eagerness to get rich he had joined all the good business clubs in the city, he went to a good church and he was very conservative in political matters. At this time his friend, Jay Hillquist, was the manager in the advertising department of the newspaper, and at night the two of them used to walk home from their office together sharing each other's ambition to make money, and feeling triumphant and sure of themselves and close together. They had both discovered that a lot of easy money was made in the advertising agency business out of accounts that only went to an agency for personal reasons. They both had a lot of friends and they walked along together at night wondering how to make money out of all these friendships they had made with business men in the city. They excited each other with plans to leave their jobs and join different advertising agencies and then, as soon as they each had two or three fine accounts, to quit and start an agency of their own. Andrew Aikenhead had naturally a good feeling for people, for he was friendly and warmhearted, and people liked confiding in him. Jay and he used to go to each other's homes, and while their wives and children were sitting chatting animatedly, or they were all having a game of cards or eating a late supper, Jay used to say, "The trouble with you, Andrew, is you don't use your friends. What good are your friends if you don't use them? You should go right after them and put it up to them." They both agreed heartily. When they got their own agency going they went on making friends, they kept on scheming and using their friends, and they kept on making money year after year.

A wild hoarse singing was coming from the drawing-room. It grew steadily into a desperate bawling that echoed in the hall, floated out to the street and then crashed into a burst of high hysterical laughter. And Andrew Aikenhead thought, "The contract with Roebuck is being cemented," and he smiled. It seemed to him when the voices rose again, half drunken now in a quivering gayety, that they were all afraid;

they were shrieking because the foundations they had thought timeless were collapsing. "They're all acting. They're saying that nothing has happened," he thought. "They're saying to Roebuck, 'Look, it's the same with us as it always was,' but they're all afraid the office'll fail tomorrow and they'll be on the street, and their wives are in there twiddling their fingers and full of fear, too."

And he knew that he, like a traitor, was the only one who had admitted to himself that he had actually lost his faith. There came a burst of louder song and wilder high-pitched laughter, and he thought in a panic, "It sounds like a death rattle. I've devoted most of my life to business and now that's going." He had let many of the good, timeless, simple things slip away from him and had missed much real joy. And that part of his life of twenty years ago was crying out for life against that contrived and hollow gayety he heard in the other room, and that early time of his life now seemed the most like home.

Four

SO MICHAEL was driving into the country with Ross
Hillquist, his sister's lover. They had been driving all afternoon through a country that was rolling farm land with the
road dipping down through long smooth hills and then rising
to high crests, from where you could see the country spreading
out for miles with the sun glistening on ripening fields and
gleaming on small blue lakes in every wide valley, and always
beyond the low rolling hills and the great dark clumps of wood-
land was the misty skyline, so you had the feeling of rising and
falling and always going deeper into that gray misty country
beyond the hills.

"Your old man was mighty glad when you said you'd come
up here, Mike," Ross said. "I was talking to him last night."

"It's pretty embarrassing, just the same."

"It needn't be, unless you make it."

"I don't know why I'm coming. I've got nothing against my
father now, and when he was so eager I just said sure I'll come,
but now I feel like a nut."

"You're only meeting him half way."

"I know, but you know how awkward it gets when you're
thrown close to a person you haven't been friendly with for a
year. I was a sucker to say I'd come," Michael said, but he

laughed, for though he had always felt that Ross in his thinking was all wrong about everything, he knew that if he ever needed him he was always available. Even when you were talking to Ross it was the whole of his receptive nature that was so available to whatever you had to say. Ross and Michael had gone through college together. Ross and Sheila had often come to see Michael and in that way they always kept him within reach of his family.

They were driving into clouds that got thicker on the skyline, and when they were still an hour away, a light thin rain began to fall, although if they looked over their shoulders they could still see a patch of bright blue sky left far behind, and the light thin rain fell so softly it could not be heard upon the fields. It was a very warm light rain that made the country glow softly, and whenever the rain touched Michael's face he felt more alive. From the hill they looked down into the valley at the little village of Jason and the brick hotel by the narrow stream, and on the other side of the stream was the old lumber mill with the mist hanging over the flat pastureland sloping up from the stream. They stopped the car to have a drink. Ross had a bottle of whiskey. Ross held the bottle high in his hand, but there was no glow from it in that misty light. While they were drinking they looked far down the valley where the stream broadened a little and emptied into the narrow lake, trying to see the Aikenhead house from that hill, but they could only see the roofs of houses and a church steeple away over on the other side of the lake. All this country of small lakes and streams sloped down to the Great Lakes, and sometimes on a very clear day you could almost see a water line glowing away off against the duller sky, and beyond that were the lake ports and the boats carrying grain to Chicago and Cleveland.

They crossed the bridge over the stream where big yellow pond lilies were shining on the water, and they got out of the car eagerly opposite the red brick hotel. There was a fishing party at the hotel, for some young fellows, with giddy, laughing faces, were leaning from the windows. Ross and Michael stood on the road in the light rain, with men from the village sitting on the verandas of houses along the road watching them earnestly, waving their hands at those who crowded at the window. Someone was trying to push his way through and put his head out, for they could see the others resisting and laughing and pushing him back, and then this one head suddenly shot out, a head half covered with a ridiculous, English tweed shooting cap with a bow on the top that was twisted sideways like a Napoleonic hat. Leaning far out of the window in his tweed jacket, the man in the shooting cap shouted, "Hillo, hilloo, hilloo, tally-ho, tally-ho, tally-ho. Welcome little strangers," and then he was so delighted with his own clowning that he burst into laughter.

"For the love of God," Mike said, "There's that …"

"What's the matter?"

"That's Dave Choate."

"Sure it is. You knew he'd be here."

"I didn't realize it," Michael said, and his voice became flat and lifeless and he stood in the middle of the road, his face sullen, while the clowning boy kept shouting good-naturedly, "Heh, Mike. How you doing, Ross?"

"Why did that guy have to be here?" Michael said. They were crossing over to the little old hotel that was used mainly by fishing parties in these days, for there was no reason why anyone should actually stay there when the village was so close to the larger towns. Upstairs, the floor boards were sunken and creaked badly. When Michael went into Dave Choate's room he hung back shyly. There were two bright-faced and rosy-cheeked boys, who were in the bond business, in the room with Dave Choate. They were all a little drunk. The two bond boys were still dressed in their good, smartly tailored clothes with the well-cut, square shoulders and the wasp waist, and they both had on the same neat small felt hats that all bond boys and the young brokers around town were wearing at that time. As Michael came in there was a burst of laughter, for one of the boys, the one with the hard yet childish face, had grabbed hold of his short, dark, dissipated friend by the neck and had started gouging his eye with his thumb, while he smacked him over the head with a newspaper that was tightly rolled like a club. They had both seen a vaudeville team doing something like this once, and now they took turns using each other as a stooge. They both had badly gouged and swollen red eyes, yet they both looked happy. They all looked a little drunk and very happy. But when Michael came in and hung behind and was shy and so sober, they were embarrassed, and one of the boys said to Dave, "Our act doesn't seem to go over so big with the big guy, does it?"

Taking off his absurd hunting cap and bowing low Dave said, "Welcome the prodigal. The lost one has returned. Boys, this is Mike Aikenhead. Mike to you. And, Mike, the dark guy is Mr. James T. Finn and the other guy is Henry Swinerton Phelan. They're both men of talent and you ought to like them even if they're not quite up your alley."

"Sit down, Dave," Dr. Hillquist said. "Don't be so noisy."

"What's the matter with you, Ross? Mike understands. We're pals."

"Go on and do your stuff. Don't let me put a wet blanket on the party," Michael said, but he was so obviously unwilling to be there and he was so much like a stranger among them that the two bond boys and Dave were silent, watching Michael's dark and sober face, from which the shy smile had passed so quickly. They watched him as if they expected a startling remark to burst out from him, some sharp remark that would be dreadfully hostile, and Dave Choate, whose own flushed face had a strangely innocent expression as he stared at Mike, was trying desperately to think of something smooth and bright and beautiful to say that would make them all laugh and be comrades there in the hotel room in the little village.

Michael was looking around the bedroom that was littered with elegant and expensive pig-skin bags, and he saw the neat piles of fine clothes laid out on the bed, the elaborate fishing tackle in one corner of the room, the little dressing table already decked out as a bar and covered with bottles of scotch and rye and gin, and the three big stacks of beer bottles piled behind the open door, all looking like a lot of money tossed around very freely; and the bond boys wore their clothes smartly like uniforms, with their double-breasted coats so tight at the waist and with their shirts all having the same tab collars, and they stared at him in such a way that he was sure they were noticing his own gray flannel trousers and his worn blue jacket and his battered old felt hat with a brim so much larger and more old fashioned than theirs. There were many times when Michael wanted to wear such fine, smart clothes.

While Dave began to shout and clown again, Michael, feeling he was being mocked, began to think of all the times when he had lain awake at night in his attic room with the little kitchenette, wondering if there ever would come a time when people would say to him that there was work to do and they wanted him to work for them.

He began to feel so hostile that he couldn't understand that these boys were clowning like that because he had made them feel uncomfortable. They had turned away from him and were laughing in a jolly way among themselves. So Michael stood back by the window, pretending to be looking down at the road and the rain and the veranda, where the storekeeper and his wife were looking up with such animation at the hotel, and he tried to smile apologetically whenever one of the boys looked at him, and he really thought, "If Dave says another word about the prodigal son I'll smack him right here in this room."

Then Dave said to him, "Come on and have a drink, Mike. We ought to all get along together."

"Sure I'll have a drink," Mike said.

"It's pretty hard to figure you out, Mike," Dave said. "You can't really be as sour as you look. Now don't misunderstand me, wait a minute now."

"You mean you want me to look like you guys, like the cats that just ate the canary."

"Not at all. I just want to know what you've got against me. It's not my fault if you don't want to live with your old man, is it? He's your old man, not mine, isn't he? You can't expect me to live like an orphan because you do."

"Go on, tell us, what have you got against us?" the red-cheeked bond boy, James T. Finn, said, looking very worried.

"Who said I had anything against you?"

"We don't ask you to like us, you know, but you seem so damn superior. I don't suppose we amount to much in the world, but then whoever heard of you?" the bond boy said politely.

"All right, baby face," Michael said. "You feel pretty cocky, eh? What do you guys stand for anyway? Your fathers got you jobs in the bond business, didn't they? You're a couple of big financial men, aren't you? Your fathers stuck you there because they didn't know what the hell to do with you and keep you out of trouble."

"What are you sore about, as long as we're out of trouble?"

"Because you're so damned patronizing."

"All right, go ahead. Tell us what you stand for."

"I'm an engineer. I've been getting ready for it for six years and I want to work at it. That's something you guys won't understand."

"You'd think you were all ten years old. Sit down and have a drink," the doctor said. They all laughed a little foolishly. They felt ashamed of the hostility that had come among them. Dave alone went on explaining in his shy, fumbling and half drunken way that he was willing to be friendly. Yet they were all really watching Michael's pale face that was still so full of resentment; he was wishing that he had never come to this place; he was wishing he was back in the city. As he listened to this boy pleading with him to be friendly and saw all their smooth, young, spoiled and dissipated faces turning to him, from hidden places in his memory, there rose up all the old forgotten hatreds that came from feeling he had been dispossessed, and he thought of his life in the city, of the grave and sometimes worried face of Anna Prychoda, who was always so eager to smile; of Huck Farr, following her so patiently; of all the young fellows who spent the afternoon sitting around Bolton's restaurant, waiting for something to turn up, and those that he thought of in this way, who were really a part of his life, seemed so far away from these fellows in this room.

But Dave said to him, "Mike, the trouble with you is you don't drink enough."

"I can drink more than you can standing on my head," Michael said, showing his contempt by grinning broadly.

"That's a bet, Mike," Dave said, and he took a bottle of rye off the bureau and he got down on his knees on the floor and he tried to put his head down against the floor and support his upraised legs against the bureau while he tilted up the bottle.

"You're like a couple of kids," the doctor said. "I'm going. Are you coming, Mike?"

And Michael felt ashamed that he had been so childish among them. He looked at them all apologetically; he laughed, and then he said, "There's no use talking like this. Forget it, Dave. Come on, Ross."

Dave called out to Ross as Ross was going down the stairs that he would not go up to the house for dinner; he was staying there with his friends.

Out on the road, Dr. Hillquist said, wondering, "I never saw you like that before, Mike. I never saw you so self-conscious with people before. I wouldn't have known it was you."

His round earnest face was full of surprise. He was so disturbed that he actually began to look very unhappy.

"Sure it was me," Mike said. "They were trying to insult me, weren't they?"

"No, they weren't. They were just trying to be friendly and you wouldn't let them."

"I felt like giving them all a push in the puss."

"Dave was playing up to you, Mike. He wanted you to like him."

"There never was anything to that guy to like. He never had anything, not even a prayer."

"He certainly had enough in there to get you swinging like a barn door, mister. If you didn't feel like coming, why did you come?"

"My old man got talking and it started me remembering and I got soft and sympathetic."

"As long as you know you didn't come up here to pick a fight with him, too."

"I don't see why you should harp on the fact that I don't get along with my father when you haven't got a thing in common with your own."

"I don't have to start fighting with him to let him know it. It's the same with me as it is with you, Mike. He knows I can't stand the way he's devoted his whole life to buttering his own bread. You and me, we feel there's something else in the world. Neither one of us wanted what our fathers had to give us because we felt there was real work to do in the world, so you went ahead and became an engineer and I became a doctor. That's our way of saying what we think, isn't it?"

But Michael, who was only half listening, blurted out, "I'm sorry, Ross. Here I am trying to take it out on you. Anyway, I had no right to start rubbing it in on those kids like that." He began to look truly miserable now, and his eyes which had softened shifted restlessly, and he stood on the road, looking back at the hotel as though full of remorse.

The doctor began to laugh at him, for when Michael was like this, with his face so troubled and solemn, and so full of passionate regret over a very little thing, the doctor loved him; he loved the way his hate passed so swiftly, leaving him penitent as a girl. "I'm going back there and make it right with those fellows," Michael said, turning around.

"You can't do that," the doctor laughed, pulling at his arm.

"I'm only going to apologize to them."

"Do it the next time you see them. It'll only embarrass them now."

"I feel lousy about picking on those bond boys like that. They were just a couple of good kids trying to have a good time in their own way," he said.

Going along the old dirt side road off the highway, Michael was silent, for he was craning his neck, trying anxiously to see past the turn in the road where it started to curve around the lake. Many times since he had left his home in this country he had awakened in the night, in some drab room in a cheap boarding house, thinking of home, and whenever he had thought of this road and the lake and the sky, he had been full of remorse at the separation between him and his people and this country, no matter how right and good that separation had been.

Then he heard the little river on the other side of the trees, and then they came suddenly to the turn, and there was the lake, and beyond the lake the wet low hills. An unpremeditated flow of gladness swept through him to be there again in his own country, and he looked eagerly across the narrow lake, which was only a mile and a half wide at this point, and he was silent, watching the rain falling thinly and wavering over the water and sometimes becoming transparent so you could see the humps and shadows of hills clear on the other side.

A little farther along the road was the old stone house with the blue shutters and the white woodwork, and the green lawn sloping down to the dock at the water. To one side of the house was the old apple orchard, and the trees were in blossom, and the fragrance of the blossoms was still in the heavy air. No matter where he would go, or how poor he would be, or the love or hate that would be in him, this bit of remembered landscape, the soil and the tang of the air and the color of the country would be always calling to him and bringing that swift longing to recapture it again.

Andrew Aikenhead was at the door, watching them coming up the path to the house. When they were still some distance off, he left his wife and Sheila and Jay Hillquist who had come out to stand beside him, and he rushed down the path to join his son. He put his arm under Michael's; he waved his hand at the house and cried, "Here they are." And he said to Michael, "We heard the car coming. And here we all are waiting."

Sheila was the first one to welcome Michael when he reached the house, and she kissed him, and her face, which had such a dark softness and warmth, began to glow as she laughed excitedly and whispered, "You were a darling to come, Mike. We'll have a grand time. Be nice to Mrs. Aikenhead. She's really not a bad soul at all."

"You're not really worrying about that," he whispered, and he laughed.

"No, but I think she is," she whispered. "Look at her over there."

Mrs. Aikenhead was standing a little to one side as though apart from them all now, after coming for years to this house. Her face was full of uncertain eagerness. She stood there alone, plump, soft, handsome and anxious, as though she were about to be pushed aside and did not know how to defend herself. "I want you to have a good time here, Michael," she said. "Just as good a time as you ever had."

"I saw Dave down at the hotel," he said. "He was with some friends. He won't be home for dinner."

Then she touched him gently on the arm and said, "I'm

sure your father wants to talk to you, Michael. You'll want to have a chat together," and she turned and smiled at her husband. She went away and she did not look back. She walked straight and even, and her head never turned, yet Michael, as he watched her, felt that her anxiety had become desolation, and he was so disturbed he began to feel like an intruder.

But his father was saying, "Ah, Michael, it does me good to see you here." His joy had begun to confuse him, and he hardly knew how to express himself in warm, simple words. Clearing his throat, he said, "You may be sure, my boy, that we all join together in welcoming you," and then he stuttered and looked quite bewildered, for he realized that in spite of his good feeling he was talking pompously. He was startled to find that the bland manner of a lifetime had made it hard for him to tell now of the fullness of the welcome that was in his heart, and his speech, even while he tried to stop it, became a glib flow of words, as though he were trying to sell something to someone. His deep embarrassment began to show in his flushed face. He couldn't understand what had happened to him, and so as he fumbled he longed to find a few warm, welcoming words.

Michael understood that his father did not want to sound like a greeter in a hotel, or a man swinging a big deal; he knew he merely wanted to show how eager he was, and so he, himself, was touched. Michael would have liked to have made some, easy, gentle, affectionate remark to his father that would have drawn them close together, but it was very hard to do it, for his father was talking desperately, as if he dared not stop. And Michael began to think, "Maybe he's wondering why he asked me to come. There doesn't seem to be any real warmth between us," and he was dreadfully disappointed, for his joy at being back with his own people was slipping away.

Sighing, his father said, "It's hard to explain how pleased I am." He had wanted Michael to come, and he had come, and now he knew that he, himself, in some way had failed, and so he was silent.

Some of his dignity was restored by his silence and he said gravely, "I wonder if we could have a whiskey and soda, Michael?"

"I'd like to very much."

"Come over here then," he said, leading the way over to an old chest by the window. There he poured two drinks. They looked at each other and nodded their heads and they said together, "Here's to you. Happy days." That was all. But while they were sipping their whiskey it made Michael sad to realize how he and his father had tried to come together and meet warmly with some of the dignity of two human beings, and how they had had to struggle so hard and then fail to express the humanity that was in them both. They were standing there together at the window, but he felt there had been no reunion, and he regretted that he had come.

Five

BUT WHEN Michael was in the room that had once been his, looking out at the unruffled lake after the rain, with the gray light all over the water, except for one path of pale light that would soon be swept by the full light of the moon, the longing to rediscover his home rose in him again. A rowboat was bumping gently against the little dock. The apple orchard was there on that soft slope down to the lake, and the trees were in blossom. Then the moon came out and the blossoms began to glow. Across the lake were a few lights in houses on the other shore. Then it all began to come closer, the whole soft countryside he had always loved, and it began to make him a part of it again. "The lake looks exactly the same as it always did. Maybe nothing has changed. My mother is dead, but maybe in some way she's still around here because she used to love this place so much. She used to love the smell of the blossoms on a spring night like this. Maybe every stick and stone and tree around here holds something that belonged to her," he thought. And all the days of his boyhood were alive in him as he stood there at the window; he heard the sound of the voices of children who had come there to play; he heard the eager, childish voice of his sister; they were all laughing and shrieking as they watched the dog churning around in the water after the stick they kept throwing; then he heard his mother's voice calling from the house.

A slow excitement and a kind of grudging love were rising in him as he stood there, and then he saw two figures out there walking in the shadow, and he heard a soft laugh. Sheila and Ross Hillquist, who were walking arm and arm along the path, stopped just before they left the lawn, and her light dress and the doctor's dark clothes became like one thick tree trunk touched by light.

Michael began to unpack his bag and look around the room. In one corner, put there for him, was fishing tackle, a bamboo rod for the trout pools and the stream, and a short steel rod for the bass up in the reeds at the point. As he sat down on his bed he had a great longing to go alone in the morning and fish for the bass in that swell place in the reeds. He smiled and rubbed his hands through his thick black hair.

He was still sitting like this when he heard voices coming from the other side of the house, Dave's voice and his father's voice rising and being carried out over the lake. Dave had returned alone from the hotel to get some more money and he wanted to hurry back to the hotel. "If I lost the money, I have to pay the guys, haven't I?" he was saying. "Good God, you're getting tighter and tighter. What's the matter with you? You're not broke." And the other voice, jerky and loud, said, "Not another cent, not another red cent. You can go back to the city and go to work tomorrow." The voices suggested the passion, the gesture, the faces of both of them. While they all were listening, the grocer from the village who was just leaving, the farmer from the next farm whose car had stalled out there on the road, the voices rose sharply or were silent abruptly, and Andrew Aikenhead was saying in a hard, pitiless reasonable voice, "Not another word. What did you say? Would you care to repeat it? I'm not too old to thrash a young pup like you with these two hands. You're good to no one in the world.

You'd be better dead than alive." He sounded free and strong. But the young voice, full of contempt came, "Aw, I'm tired of that crap. Why don't you hire a hall?"

While Michael listened, excited and wondering, he heard Mrs. Aikenhead calling from the house, "Dave, come here."

"What do you want?"

"Come here."

"I'm on my way back to the hotel."

"Come here, Dave. It'll be all right," she said.

Six

In the morning Andrew Aikenhead waited a long time for Michael to come down and go fishing. As he sat on the veranda and watched Sheila and Dr. Hillquist going down the road together in the early morning sunlight he began to think of the quarrel he had had last night with Dave Choate, but as soon as he found himself muttering irritably he quickly put all such thoughts out of his head, for after all it had been just such a commonplace quarrel as they had had many times. He didn't want to be bothered with such thoughts on such a morning when every bird call delighted him and the noises from the water were so familiar and so good. He could see Jay Hillquist at the living-room window with his head lowered and turned so that just one red ear showed. Jay Hillquist was scribbling in his note-book, making a plan to get the Credit Clothiers account for the agency. Andrew Aikenhead, sighing happily, felt that at last he was surrounded by his own people.

When Michael came out carrying the steel bass rod, he looked surprised to see his father sitting there in a brown tweed jacket with an old felt hat on his head and a pipe in his mouth. From Michael's line dangled the red and white minnow the bass went for in that section of the country. His father saw that Michael was disappointed to find him waiting, for there was a wary look in his eyes, and when the father saw this look in his son's eyes he, too, was dreadfully disappointed. Last night he had really decided that their meeting had not gone very well because of the natural shyness in Michael.

"I thought you'd likely want to go up to that spot in the reeds, Michael. Is that right?" he said.

"I was thinking of it. But maybe it's a little late now. Maybe I'll wait and go tonight."

"No, it isn't too late. I never believed in this five-o'clock-in-the-morning stuff. The best bass ever caught around here were caught just before noon. You remember the big beauties we used to catch up there at the point? I'll row you. Come on."

"No, I'll row you," Michael said. "I don't want you to row me."

"All right. Let's go."

They walked down to the little dock and they bent down together and grabbed hold of the boat, and because they were both so aware of pulling the boat out in the way they used to do it, they were silent and shy. When they were in the boat with Michael rowing, heading toward the point that jutted out a mile up the shore, and with the land just the way it had always been, and the sun just as bright and the very blue water just as unruffled, the father, wondering how he might break this silence, suddenly pointed over the water at the tall elm that was in the field sloping up from the water, and he said, "There's still an oriole's nest there. They seem to have been nesting there for years. Maybe we'll see one now," and he put his fingers up to his lips and made a very accurate bird call, for he could mock the call of nearly every bird that nested in that section of the country, and they waited, the boat resting on the water, till finally they saw the sunlight glint on the bright red breast of the bird that darted out of the elm, hovering high, and then swerved away.

"There you are," Michael said.

"Didn't I tell you?"

"You were right," Michael said.

The father was quite pleased, and he sat there so content-edly that Michael began to think, "Why did he have to come along and spoil this one bit of fun I planned? I feel him looking at me. He wants to be sentimental. My God, why does he seem so patient and so contented?" As they passed little bits of remembered landscape, one familiar object after another on the land, he felt his father watching him steadily. The fields sloping up from the water were bright with white daisies and yellow buttercups, in places there were rice beds in the water, and often there was the familiar but still startling sudden tin-kling of a cow bell beyond the trees. It was as though the father were soothing the son with these trees and the familiar noises and this water, pleading only that his son accept his presence there. But finally, when he began to feel that Michael had almost forgotten that he was in the boat with him, and he, himself, was remembering that night in the tavern when he thought he had touched Michael, he said a little helplessly, "Do you like it up here, Michael?"

"It's all right. I'll have to go back in a day or so, though," Michael said in a matter of fact, unfeeling way.

"There's nothing you have to attend to in the city, is there?"

"It's awfully nice here, but, well, you know what I mean. Now that I'm up here, I might as well say it frankly, I don't quite see why I came. It just isn't the same. I'm a lot older. This place isn't my place. What was mine has gone. I can remember it, but I can't find it again here."

Then it seemed to the father that he was being rebuffed arrogantly, and growing full of resentment, himself, he said sharply, "After all, Michael, no one has the plague here. You don't expect to be contaminated if you stay here, do you?"

"I didn't say I did."

"But it's what you're implying and I resent it a little," he said, and then his face got red because his son continued to watch him calmly. "You're being pretty selfish, aren't you,

Michael? You're pretty determined about going your own way. How anybody else feels doesn't seem to matter much to you."

"So you're telling me I'm selfish, eh?"

"About this you are."

"That's pretty rich and lovely. I never knew it mattered so much to you how other people felt," Michael said, almost jeering at his father. There on the quiet water in the morning sunlight, and hearing only the light splash of the oars from time to time, they looked at each other and were eager to oppose each other sharply in some struggle old and long forgotten in its beginning that went back to the beginning of their life together, to the wife and mother, and their own growth and then their separation; they were thrust powerfully against each other; they both liked it and wanted to struggle. Then Michael smiled very calmly, and the father sighed and was ashamed. Michael said, "We're around the point, there are the reeds."

"I had no intention of being hostile, Michael."

"Forget it," Michael said freely, with that casual independence that so discouraged his father.

In the shallow bay were green and brownish weeds sticking up in clusters and getting thicker as they went in till it was difficult to row the boat and they could hardly see the water at all, just a pool here and there, darker colored and shallow, with the weeds and the shallow water gradually becoming a swampland at the limit of the bay. And there was no movement in that bay, no stir on the water. A kind of haze of misty vapor hung over the swampland. They both were conscious of taking that sharp old struggle between them into this stillness and misty light and unstirring water. Over the reeds flew a young crane, its great feet hanging; there was suddenly the chattering of many birds, and the swamp was suddenly full of life. Michael stood up in the boat flicking his line out and his father kept the boat steadily in the one spot by a little pool so that he could have some play for his line in a stretch of water.

The father sat watching his son's face steadily, for as soon as Michael flicked out his line and the plug came twisting back to the boat there was eagerness in Michael's face; then there came, too, that quiet passion of the hunter or fisherman that took Michael cleanly out of himself.

The water was very warm and the bass were fat, heavy and sluggish and too well fed. They were used to having their own way and so they bit quickly at the plug. Michael reeled in two small ones in a perfunctory way. There was no struggle. They just swam, and gave a final kick when he hoisted them in. But his father, watching Michael's face, grew full of hope, for sometimes Michael smiled and he kept making little comments like, "That one had no guts at all, eh," just as though they were pals. And the father's hope grew because he knew it was hard to fish with someone you disliked and he knew that Michael was looking as if he liked the fishing there. With his face beginning to glow Michael turned to his father and said, "Are you getting much of a kick out of being here?"

"I certainly am, son."

"Why did you want to come?"

"I was looking forward to it a long time."

"Why don't you fish?"

"I'm fine sitting here watching. I gets lots of it," the father said apologetically.

At first the eagerness and the apology that were so clear in his father's face puzzled Michael, and then he grinned.

By now the sun was directly overhead, and so they started to go back, and when they had gone over half the distance they saw people waving at them through a break in a ridge of trees along the bank. Dr. Hillquist was there and Sheila and Dave's two friends from the hotel, and Dave, wildly waving a wine bottle, was calling, "Come on over here, Mike."

"Why don't you go over there, Michael?"

"Sure I will. Let's get over close to the stump stretching out there and I'll get out," he said. Then that warm generous smile that his father loved to see came on Michael's face and he said awkwardly, "We had a pretty good time up there in the reeds, didn't we?"

"We sure did. We'll go a hundred times, eh?"

"Sure we will," Michael said, and while his father held the boat against the log, and steadied the log, too, Michael stepped out and jumped to the shore. He went striding up the bank that rose from the beach to the meadowland. The sun was shining on his dark, handsome face. And his father, bending over the oars, watching him, felt that this was what he had been waiting for for such a long time, to have heard the way he had spoken, to watch him stride eagerly along the beach, to see the light shining on his face.

Seven

CLIMBING up the bank, Michael waved his hand and his face was full of friendliness. The two bond boys who had been squatting in the grass beside Sheila and vying with each other to make her soft eyes turn lazily to them, now turned and watched Michael earnestly. When they saw how eager he was to be with them they relaxed and smiled awkwardly, and the dark one, James T. Finn, called, "Here, stranger, have a drink." In the shade of a little bush was a wicker basket and eight bottles of red wine. Two tin cups were being passed around.

Dave, the only one who had got up, said, "Do you want to wait for a turn at the cup, or do you want to pick up a bottle?"

"Give him the bottle," James T. Finn said.

"Give me the bottle."

"Here you are, Mike. Go ahead, and happy days to you," Dave said, hurrying a bit elaborately to pick up the bottle like a man who wants another man to see that he's anxious to please him.

They all watched Mike tilting the bottle; they silently watched his Adam's apple bobbing a little, and they watched the sunlight shining on the bottle and on his dark hair. They were feeling that everything was going to go very well.

"What kind of wine is it?" Mike asked, wiping his lips with the back of his hand.

"Burgundy," they said together.

"It's news to me that fishermen drink wine," Michael said. "I always thought fishermen were a hard-drinking lot. Nothing but kegs of whiskey."

"We used to drink whiskey all the time," Dave said. "We found it didn't work."

"They got tight too quickly," the doctor said.

"That's right. We got tight and then we forgot that we were fishing, and then we found we could bring a good Burgundy along and you could keep on drinking it all day and still have some respect for the fish. The fish want to be considered. Wine takes the interest of the fish into account; it's not thoughtless and selfish like whiskey. It took us a long time to find out about wine for fishing, didn't it, gentlemen?" Dave said to his friends.

It was very pleasant drinking wine like that in the sunlight, not saying much, but laughing sometimes and feeling friendly. They all seemed glad to be there together. And Michael, realizing how anxious Dave's friends were to show their good will, said, "I don't know what you guys thought was wrong with me down at the hotel yesterday. I certainly tried to throw a little sand in the machinery, didn't I?"

"It was nothing," James T. Finn insisted. "You shouldn't mention it. We all get that way at times."

"I mean if I had been working at my job," Mike insisted, "and doing pretty well at engineering, I'd have thought you were having the best time in the world. When you're feeling right yourself you feel the other guy has a right to his own good time in the way he likes to take it, but if you're out of work, you feel on the defensive. You get your fur up and you think people are insulting you and you feel persecuted. That's only on the very bad days, of course."

"There's no use mentioning it; it was nothing."

"Did I tell you guys Mike was all right?" Dave asked.

"Thanks, gentlemen. But just the same I know you wondered what in hell was the matter with me. Put it down to me running amuck a bit because I had discovered a little while back that the world wasn't going to be just my oyster."

"That's right. Everything is economics," Ross laughed.

"Sex and economics," Dave said.

"All right, here's to your little pals, sex and economics," Mike said.

And Sheila laughed because James T. Finn, squatting on the ground before her, was looking at her so lovingly with his sad banjo eyes. Her hands were linked behind her head, and her legs were crossed at the ankles, and the weight of her body on the grass had pulled the line of dress tight against her breast. She was laughing softly, and teasing the boys, and wondering from time to time, whenever she looked over at Ross Hillquist, if he wasn't a little jealous. She was wanting to see his head turn sharply, or have him sit up and look at her. And Dave was saying to James T. Finn, "Isn't she lovely, Jimmie? The Aikenheads between them seem to get everything. Sheila's got so much sex and Mike's got so much economics. Remember, Jimmie, I saw her first."

They lay there in the sunlight with the blue sky overhead. The sunlight sparkled on the smooth water, and they drank the red wine and talked lazily. With his knees hunched up, Michael was flat on his back, his face was turned up to the sky and his eyes were closed. In his right hand he held a wine bottle, and he was letting the wine trickle into his mouth, and when it flowed too fast he stopped it with his tongue and let it roll around in his cheeks and then trickle down his throat. He was warm inside and he spread his arm wide on the grass as if he would hold the field down under him, and the laughter and the lapping water, the sound of birds and the friendly voices flowed into him and made him very happy, for it all seemed very good, and it seemed to be what he had wanted so much when he thought of it at night in his bed before he left the city. Then it got that he could not quite hear what they were saying. Blinking his eyes in the strong sunlight, he rolled over on his side and he saw Sheila running across the grass and she was laughing shrilly and dodging in a frantic way, and at first he thought it was Ross who was chasing her, only when he looked on the other side Ross was there on the grass beside him breathing heavily and sometimes making deep, peaceful sounds like a man falling asleep. He heard Sheila laugh as she was caught and held, and her eyes, as she passed close to him, had that feverish excitement in them that used to worry him when he saw it. But his own head was swimming and he couldn't be sure it was Dave who was holding her. "Ross, Ross," she called, half laughing, and Mike stirred, and wanted to sit up and watch her protectively, but the figures dodging across the green field in the strong sunlight of high noon blurred and came together, and they became one with the sloping field and the brilliant blueness of the cloudless sky, and he spread both hands wide, holding himself there, so the field wouldn't slope away from him too suddenly.

Eight

SHEILA Aikenhead, who looked in so many ways like her father, had a head shaped like his, only smaller; she had her father's grave, deep-set eyes and his hands with the longer slender fingers. But underneath this striking physical resemblance to her father she had the entirely different, eager, simpler nature of her mother. She had to be always with people, always yielding, and showing her intense interest in the longings of others. At college she had never been able to bear being alone; like her mother she never wanted to be left out of anything; she expressed her ardent nature with the greatest fullness in her warm and her passionate conviction in the rightness of the causes of her friends. To Ross Hillquist she had abandoned bit by bit all of her interests; she wanted only that he should become a fine doctor and be happy in his work, and she was just the way with him her own mother had been with Andrew Aikenhead. Ross Hillquist found his life growing and being enriched in hers; when she was with him all of his life became more important, for there was something in her, maybe just her ardent, sympathetic, willing nature that stirred and warmed him.

The third day they were in the country Sheila and Ross were alone up the stream where it passed the hotel, and near the old mill where the banks of the stream were laden with a heavy brown rotting sawdust; there the surface of the stream was covered with bright yellow pond lilies. They lay on the bank for a while listening to the water thrush and the stirring in the tall sedge along the bank, and then Ross, rising to get her some of the pond lilies, had taken off his shoes and rolled up his trousers and had gone wading out with a rapt expression on his dark and serious face; he had bent down, dipping his sleeve in the water and had picked one lily after another. It was a ridiculous but lovely thing to do for her, and he made it seem the most natural and simple gesture in the world. As she sat there with her hands folded in her lap it seemed wonderful to have him wade out in the stream like a child just to please her. When he turned and smiled, with his sleeves wet and the running water wetting his rolled-up trousers and with his bare legs showing in the clear water, she felt an ache of love for him, and when he came carefully back to the bank clenching the long stalks with the yellow lilies in a big bunch in his hands, there were no spoken words but just this silent aching happiness between them to be there in the shade, with the bright sunlight shining everywhere else, with the water running and the birds calling, and further up the stream a duck quacking and the sounds sometimes of a cow blundering through the logs by the bank to drink in the stream.

This subdued ecstasy that made her silent and made her face lovely with a fine stillness was in her all day, and it was in her, too, that evening when she went into the village with Dave Choate to get the mail from the city.

Dave was walking beside her, and once, when he glanced at her, there was a brooding sincerity in his blue eyes. He seemed to be afraid to speak. They were coming down the gravel road together. They both had picked long stems of grass from the road and had them in their mouths. They both had their own separate thoughts. It was just twilight. Across the meadowland the mist was gathering, a long line of mist above the ground, with shapes of cows in a line with this mist and beyond that the lake and the sunset. When they were at the bottom of the hill Dave took her by the arm and said, "Let's sit down by the tree, Sheila. I want to talk before we go in."

"Can't we talk as we go along?"

"No. I wouldn't get finished before we got there," he said.

They sat down on a little ledge by the road, looking across a farmer's pastureland at the woods. The pastureland was all yellow with buttercups spread out like golden cloths before the deep woods looming behind with the magnificently straight trunks of towering elms. Further down the pasture the farmer's dog began an angry barking, herding the cows, with their bells tinkling, out of the pasture, across the road to the barn.

Dave Choate was sitting beside Sheila with strange humility in him and that gentleness in his eyes as he clasped and unclasped his hand. Yet he could not speak. Finally he touched her knee with his hand, as if he hardly expected her to be really within his reach, and he said, "You've never believed anything I said, Sheila. You've never had to believe. In a way we've grown up together. We're the same age and in one way I'm like a brother, but I'm not a brother. I'm more like a stranger. I'm a stranger to your father and your brother hates me, but you'd never let me love you because I'm close to you."

"Dave, please don't hold me like that."

"If you marry Ross Hillquist, I just can't go on," he said, his voice fretful; he was so agitated, he was pleading with so much of his whole being that she began to tremble. She grew afraid. The passion she felt in him excited her all the more when she looked at him because she knew this tremendous hurt was in him that came out of knowing he must seem ridiculous to her and that her father had come to despise him. He was looking away off to the lake. So she said with a gentleness that made her voice soft, and showing more feeling than she had ever shown for him before, "Don't talk about that, Dave." Then her voice broke because she didn't know what to say that would soothe out of him the fear she knew was breaking in him and making him desperate. So she got up and began to walk away while he watched her with that longing, beaten look. "Sheila," he called. And she grew more afraid and began to run a little along the road. "Sheila," he called, and in that cry she felt how much he had always been alone among them; she felt how his mother had failed to bring him into their family; she knew he was old enough now to feel ashamed when sober of things he had done when drunk. "If only he wasn't so humble now," she thought, and she began to run. And again he called. "Sheila, come back." And he came running after her and he caught up to her and, pulling her down, he began to kiss her as if he knew that what he could get at that one moment would be all he would ever have of her, and there was such a trembling passion in him that her arms and her legs were numb and she could not struggle and she fell back on the damp grass; her body was being pressed heavily into the cool, hard ground, and he was pulling at her clothes. There was one moment when he just held her tight and was motionless, waiting to see if she, too, would be still. And they both were still till she cried out, "Dave, what are you doing to me?" and she began to beat him with her fists. But he would not let her go. His breath was hot on her throat and she gasped and then she began to sob. And he said, "Sheila, darling, my God."

"You've hurt me."

"I didn't mean to hurt you."

"You hurt me with your knee and your elbow."

"Where did I hurt you?"

"Here," she said, touching her breast. She bent her head and bit her lip and tried not to cry. "You can't be that rough with a girl," she said.

"I didn't mean to," he pleaded.

She started to walk away, her face grim and stubborn, and as he hurried after her, he kept saying rapidly, "I know I'm a fool, Sheila, but I love you so much, and I can't go on like this. I can't watch you just go out of my life like that." He blurted the words out of him while they went along the road, sometimes stumbling in the ruts. It got darker and they could only see a thin, white line of light on the lake. And then she felt a pleading in him that was like a wild muttering. The power of this silent pleading seemed to come out of every growing night noise; it was just a desperate whispering, "I love you. I don't know what to say. Oh, if I could only say something, if I only was different. I wish so much everything hadn't been this way. Don't you think I'd like to be a man everybody respected? I'd like to be like Ross Hillquist."

Then she stopped on the road and she couldn't help crying again, for it seemed at that moment that never again in her life would she feel such an ardent, desperate love for her as she felt in his pleading, helpless voice.

"Why are you crying now, Sheila?"

"I don't know."

"Please tell me, Sheila."

"I don't really know. I shouldn't go on in this way, and you must forgive me, but you seemed to feel everything you said so much."

"Sheila," he said, pulling at her arm and growing full of hope. "Sit down again. Just let me talk. Please, just let me talk."

"You won't try and touch me?"

"No, I'll do anything you say, but don't go in just yet." And he pulled her down on the grass beside him. She was sitting about a foot away from him and she heard him sigh. It was almost dark and he was leaning forward, then rocking back, leaning forward again, and rocking back. He did not want to speak; he just wanted to go rocking back and forth like that while he stared out at the lake. He had always been alone when he was in their home, she thought, and now he was alone, too, out here, and he merely wanted her to remain there with him because it would soon be night time, and if they began to talk quietly in the dark, they would not seem to be quite the same people as they were in the day. It was the darkness he was waiting for, for when night really came on, his clowning and his spoiled boyishness would almost be forgotten; he would not have to be ashamed or humble, and he could be simple and natural. He began to speak quietly, his voice still coaxing and hesitant, "I don't blame you for feeling the way you do about me, Sheila. It would be pretty hard to take me seriously, wouldn't it? I know what I'm like, Sheila. We've always had enough money to make me a bum and I never had to stick at anything. I could play around at college and get thrown out on my ear and I knew it would be all right. Me and my friends always knew we'd be looked after. That's the trouble, Sheila. It's just the same when we start to work. Nothing is expected of us, and somebody's got to fix it for us so that we'll be looked after, but we've got to try and be something, so we try to be funny men. Nearly everybody I know and hang around with clowns like that, but I could be different. You can't tell what I'd be like. You don't know me. It's not me you have no use for. You've got nothing against me. It's just that you can't take seriously what the whole bunch of us in the city stand for. That's what Mike said down at the hotel. He said, 'What do you guys stand for?' That was pretty good. That worried me."

"Mike doesn't hate you, Dave."

"He's got no use for me, but that's all right. Sheila, darling, does what I'm saying seem to touch you at all?"

"You know I love Ross Hillquist, Dave."

For a long time he was silent, fumbling with some thought that was agitating him and making him dreadfully ashamed. "Supposing you couldn't get married," he said finally.

"Ah, but I'm going to, Dave," she said.

"Supposing there was some reason, some good reason why Ross wouldn't want to marry you."

"I'd know about that by now, wouldn't I, Dave?" she said patiently.

"I mean supposing there was something he didn't know."

"What could there be that be didn't know?"

"He might think he oughtn't to marry you because of, because…"

"Because of what?"

"Because of insanity in the family."

"In whose family?"

"Yours," he whispered, not looking at her. His head was down as if he could not bear to look at her. When she sat there unanswering, silent and stiff beside him, waiting, he said "Ross Hillquist won't want to marry you if he knows your mother was out of her mind before she died. Not many men would want to marry you."

"There was nothing the matter with my mother," she whispered.

"I know about it. It was right here. Right down there at the house. My mother told me about it. They'll have to know that. I've known for months. But listen, Sheila, darling, it would never matter to me. It would never stop me."

"You're lying, I tell you. Leave me alone. Go away from me. You liar."

"No, it's true," he said softly. "God knows it's true."

"It can't be true, Dave. My mother was just sick. I remember my mother. Why did you say such a thing to me?" she said, and she was leaning close to him, pleading like a little girl that she should not be hurt. For a while they both became a part of the silence, and then he heard her whisper, "I was so very very happy and I wanted it to go on. It was so beautiful. Oh, Dave, what's the matter? Why do you have to say such things?"

She did not know how long she sat there. Maybe at first he

coaxed her and begged her to go into the house, and maybe he could not bear it sitting there silent beside her, but he left her. When she began to feel cold, she looked around and she was alone, and as she sat there and heard the twanging croak of the bull frogs over in the swamp by the bay she felt that from now on she would always be separate and alone. Then she got up, thinking, "No, no, no, it isn't true; it can't be true because it was too beautiful the way it was. I know better. I'll soon find out. I'll tell him he was lying."

She got up and began to run to the house. There was a light burning in only one room, the light in Michael's room.

Nine

MICHAEL, who was sitting on the bed in his pyjamas with his thick dark hair tousled all over his head, had the eager smile of welcome for his sister that she always loved to see, and as soon as she came into his room she felt so close to him that she just stood there at the door trembling and shaking her head and chewing the end of her handkerchief, unable to speak. Michael had hardly ever seen his sister helpless like this. Towering over her, he put his arm around her and held her so gently, while his soft voice caressed her, that she blurted out, "Oh, Michael, I know it isn't true. I shouldn't even be asking it, but I want to talk to you about mother."

"I'll tell you anything in the world."

"Before mother died, what was the matter with her?"

"I don't really know," he said.

The brother and sister stared at each other and their voices grew soft, as though they were afraid someone might overhear them. The little wind from the lake blew through the window, and as it touched him, Michael put his hand up to his bare throat. Then he smiled, for they were so silent, trying to remember every moment of their childhood, and he said, "This is silly, Sheila. There's nothing to it. You remember, don't you?"

"I hardly remember. I remember only that mother was

alone a lot in the house here, and at the end I hardly saw her at all."

"Why are you thinking about it now?"

"I've got to think about it. I'm marrying Ross. Why should he want to marry me if mother was out of her mind?"

"Who said that?"

"Dave Choate said it."

"What did he tell you?"

"That's all he told me. We were walking together. He kept pleading with me not to marry Ross, then he told me …"

"So Dave Choate told you," he whispered.

"Yes, Dave told me."

"What would he know?"

"Wouldn't his mother know? Why would she tell him if she didn't know?"

"Speak softly. I heard someone moving. Maybe it was the wind in the tree."

"Maybe it was just the water lapping on the shore."

"Can't you see him and his mother, the two of them, sitting there talking it all over? Going over and over it, and talking about us all the time?"

"Oh, Michael, never mind them. Just listen to me, because I was so happy, and now I'm afraid everything that was so beautiful may be spoiled. Don't sit there muttering like that. Listen to me. It isn't true. Dave was lying, wasn't he?"

"Our mother had a child very late in life. The child died and mother was melancholy for a while before she died. Many women have gone melancholy like that after childbirth. She was around here with us but we didn't see much of her. That was when Mrs. Choate first came here like a housekeeper."

"Then mother really was out of her mind … mother was quite mad, mad … Michael?"

"She was ill, she was sick, she was sad about everything. Don't say mad. It was nothing like that, Sheila."

"Then why are you whispering? Why don't you talk out loud?"

"The house is so quiet now. Everybody is asleep."

"Maybe Dave'll go and talk to Ross. No matter what Ross says he'll have the same feeling of dread that I did. It would always be there, that fear; it would always be there to destroy us. I want to have children, I don't want to be alone. I'm not a career woman. I want to make Ross happy. I want to give him a home."

"I'll talk to Ross, Sheila. How do you know he doesn't know? There's nothing to worry about at all. Don't you see, Sheila? It's not like something in the family. It's a very simple matter, something that was apt to happen to any woman," and he stood there in his bare feet with a kind of tight smile on his face that looked so white in the moonlight, and he put his arm around her and was so gentle and persuasive and so close to her that she no longer trembled and she said, "I'm glad we talked about it. I had forgotten all about that time. It's better to know and then you're not afraid. I'll go to bed now."

But for a while he would not let her go; while he held her arm he was thinking, "What can I do for her? What will become of her happiness now if this fear grows in her? They were so happy together. I could tell by the way they laughed the other night. What can I do for my sister?" but he only said, "Remember, it was nothing, Sheila. You shouldn't listen to anything that silly kid says. He probably was half drunk when he said it."

"I won't worry about it at all."

"Good night," he whispered, and he knew by the way she clutched at his arm that she would think of it; he knew that she would lie awake; he knew she would have the loneliest and most desolate night she had ever had.

He sat alone on the bed for a long time. There was a shaft of moonlight whitening the wide floor boards and touching the foot of the bed. Far along the lake was the wild and lonely mocking cry of a loon. He sat alone, remembering the time in their lives before his mother died, when they were really kids and they used to come to this house every summer. In those days they did not have so much money, but his mother had seemed very happy. She had a laughing eager face, more like his own than Sheila's, except that there was none of his moodiness in it. She was a small woman, and she was eager and friendly like Sheila, but the gentleness that went with her eagerness gave her a lovely dignity. She was full of willingness to go the way of those she loved. She had a simple unpretentious acceptance of her husband's ambitions. She was not a particularly shrewd woman, for indeed there were times when she seemed to have no particular ambition except that they might preserve their domestic happiness.

When she got sick she stayed in one part of this house and usually in her own room. Michael at that time was fourteen and his sister was twelve years old. Michael used to sit outside on the lawn, on the little slope by the orchard, looking up at his mother's window and wondering why he could not go to her room when he wanted to; why he had to wait for those few times, that were often so far apart, when she would come downstairs and be dressed and look lovely, and eat with them and be something like his mother. Sometimes Sheila and Michael used to sit together on the grassy bank at the turn of the road, waiting for their father to come from the city. At that time their father was marvelously gentle with them; they used to run down the road to meet him; he used to sit with them down at the dock when the sun was going down and watch the sunlight glittering on the lake, and usually they would laugh, but sometimes he would look worried and pat Michael on the head and say, "You're a big fellow now. I don't have to worry about you. But Sheila's still pretty young," and then he would look grave again and they would know that he would be thinking of their mother.

In the afternoons, Michael used to think he heard his mother weeping softly in her room. One day he ran out of the house and looked all around, looking up at the window and over the lake, a tall, gangling, wild-eyed kid with uncombed hair, and then he saw Sheila coming up the path from the orchard. He did not want her to hear the soft weeping of their mother. He ran into the house and up to his mother's room and he rapped on the door calling, "Mother, mother, mother, please open the door." There was a long silence, and then he heard her say in a kind of innocent, wondering way, as if she had just remembered his voice, "Is that you, Michael?" "It's Michael, mother," he said. "Why don't you come in and see me?" she said. He tried the door and then he began to tremble, for he knew then it was not locked from the inside, as they had always thought. It was locked from the outside and he had no key. As he stood there in the hall, his face pressed against the door, his heart was thumping and he held his hands stiff at his sides. He was very frightened. He went downstairs quietly, thinking, "No one must ever know. No one in the world must ever know."

That night, when his father came home, his mother was with them for a while. His father watched her gravely. But that night she seemed very much like herself and Michael was full of the strangest secret happiness.

Near the end of that year their father told them they needed a woman to act as housekeeper, and he brought Mrs. Choate, a young widow of about thirty, who was dark and sensuous and very shrewd with a kind of mysterious awareness. She came with her son David, who was about eleven years old, and they lived in the house. The way this dark, vivid, quiet woman was so sure of herself with his father made Michael resentful, and he didn't like it, either, the way the boy, David, came into the house and made it his home and was so very independent of him and Sheila; he didn't like how David often tried to keep Sheila with him late in the afternoon, and it was often late for dinner when they got home. Michael was always taking his sister away, so they could be by themselves and together, and Dave would not be able to follow them. Dave ran after them down the road once, calling, "Heh, you two, you've got to let me come. My mother said you had to."

"You go and tell your old lady she wants you," Michael called back.

"You'd better not come back unless you let me come," David threatened.

"I guess I can come back to my own house. I guess I can go home whenever I want to. It's not your place at all," Michael said.

"It's my house as much as it is yours. My mother said so."

"It is, eh. I'll make you eat dirt. I'll make you say it isn't, " Michael said, and he jumped on Dave and beat him with his fists. He was taller and stronger than Dave, and though Dave struggled bravely and would not quit, Michael got on his back and rubbed his face steadily in the dirt, while Sheila kept jumping around there in the sunlight, yelling, "Let him up, Michael. Let him up. You're hurting him."

One day Michael heard loud voices coming from his mother's room. Then there was a period of silence and then there was a heartbreaking, helpless weeping. Running along the hall, Michael saw his mother, in a dressing-gown, trying to go along to the stair, but Mrs. Choate, who was red-faced and angry, kept holding her back and saying, "You'll have to go back. That's enough of that, my lady." "Let me go. You're a foolish, malicious woman to be standing there holding me. Let me go to my home and children," the sick woman pleaded. Her eyes were bright and shining with hope. But Mrs. Choate would not budge, and the sick woman, who was being firmly pushed back into her room, tried to dart forward, and when she was held she began to weep and struggle till at last Mrs. Choate, using all her strength, took hold of her by the shoulders and pushed her back in the room and slammed the door and then stood there grimly in the hall, breathing hard and smoothing her black hair. She looked like a woman who had been badly shaken. But Michael, who was watching her, did not understand that she might have found it necessary to struggle with his sick mother. He only knew that he had never felt as much hatred for anyone in the world as he felt for her. He could not understand how he had stood there stiffly, afraid and helpless, as he watched her, and now he began to follow her along the hall and downstairs, silently stalking her on his tiptoes, watching her with his dark eyes half closed, and hate growing in his heart. He followed her around the house silently like that all afternoon. When his father came home, Michael kept close to him and took him by the arm and longed to be able to tell him what he had seen, but before his father had time to put his bag down and take off his coat, Mrs. Choate began to complain. "I can't stand it any longer. Furthermore, I won't. It will ruin my nerves. Another struggle like this and I'm through. Something desperate will happen in a situation like this. I don't know why you persuaded me to come." Michael was amazed to see that she wanted his father to know about the struggle she had had with his mother. He thought she would be too scared. He thought she would pretend nothing had happened. Michael was half hiding at the door of the room, with his heart full of joy that his father was hearing the story of what had happened. He watched his father rub his hand over the side of his troubled face. He wouldn't have been surprised if his father had grabbed hold of the woman roughly by the shoulder, and he felt like yelling out in glee. "Now you're going to get it. Now you're going to get thrown out on your ear. The only reason you told about it was you knew I saw you. Now you'll get it." But then his father went up to Mrs. Choate and put his arm under hers and said in a voice astonishingly soft and coaxing. "Marthe, don't be angry. What in the world can we do? You must be very, very patient. We have to do it. There's nothing else for us to do, is there?"

"You ought to put her in an institution," she said irritably.

"I couldn't do that. God knows it might be better, but I could not do it. Be patient for a while, for my sake. I know you have to put up with a lot, but do it for my sake, Marthe. Try and get used to it, won't you?" and he went on caressing her with his voice in this way, as if he was terribly afraid of losing her, as if she was the only one in the house that was very close to him and had his love and knew his secret thoughts.

Michael looked a long time at his father's head and his familiar face, and he was full of wonder, and then gradually the sound of his father's voice became utterly meaningless. He had such a contempt for his father and so much disgust that he felt almost sick at his stomach. He felt he could never bear to be near him again or ever hear that voice speaking in that caressing way to himself, his mother or his sister, or anyone in the world. Still his father stood there pleading with that woman, and he loathed him so that he turned and ran out of the house to be free and be alone with his sister. He looked all around outside for Sheila and then out over the water, thinking she might be in the boat, and then he wandered through the orchard and found her at the edge of the water. Every little thing she did reminded him of his mother. The way she looked at him that afternoon as he hurried up to her was just like their mother.

Sitting alone on his bed, now, years afterwards, he was thinking again of how much Sheila was like his mother, and wondering fearfully if that madness could possibly be in her too. And while it was so silent out, as if this one night in this place still held whatever pain they had ever felt there, and whatever suffering and sadness his mother had endured, he began to feel such love for Sheila, such a desperate eagerness to help her that he thought, "Isn't it terrible that that woman and Dave should be doing this again? Isn't it terrible that they would hurt Sheila in this way?" and then it seemed that that very room, the noise of the water, the light wind stirring the trees in the orchard, the whole silent house was giving back to him all the hatred he had ever had for David and his mother. Feeling the depth of his hatred surging through him, stiffening him, then exhausting him whenever he tried to be rational, he thought, "She always was a cold, shrewd, hard, knowing woman. She's crazy about Dave. It's all her fault. She'd be ruthless for Dave's sake. I'd like to watch the two of them squirm for a change. Nothing ever happens to them. It always comes out right for them. I'm not a child now. I'm not going to let them bother Sheila again with that nonsense."

Without lighting the light, and still in his bare feet and pyjamas, he went out to the hall and along in the dark to Dave's room. He opened the door and went over to the bed, and when his eyes got accustomed to the light, he saw that the bed was empty, though the covers had been thrown back and Dave's shoes were there beside the bed. "He must be in the house. I'll wait here," he thought, and while he waited, he began to tremble, and he thought he was cold, so he moved around the room in the dark. When he was by the window, he heard a sound down by the dock, and when he looked out he saw Dave sitting in the row boat by the side of the dock. It was bright and clear out and it was easy to see him. He was in his pyjamas and a sweater he had pulled on, and he was leaning forward, motionless, staring out over the water.

Michael tiptoed downstairs in his bare feet, and made no sound, and Dave did not hear him till he was on the dock.

"What do you want?" Dave asked.

"I've got to talk to you."

"What do you want?"

"We're going to talk a few things over, Dave."

"I don't feel like talking. I came out because I couldn't sleep. I was going to row myself around a bit."

Dave had lain in his bed feeling his sorrow and regret

getting mixed up with his stubborn longing for Sheila and he had grown bewildered. Whenever he began to make a plan that would show her clearly how much he loved her, and that would persuade her to listen to him and think of him, he seemed to hear her cry out brokenly, and he was more wretched and confused than he had ever been in his life.

"I'll sit in the boat with you," Mike said.

"Suit yourself."

Mike got into the boat and sat opposite Dave, facing him. The lake was softly lapping the beach. Across the lake there were no lights at all, only the darkness, but there were many stars out and a fine, clear light in shimmering streams on the water.

"This is what I want to say, Dave. You were talking to Sheila tonight, weren't you? What were you telling her? She's all broken up about it."

"I told her I was crazy about her, that's all. What's the matter with that?"

"You did, eh? But you had to be pretty mean and nasty about it, didn't you? If she didn't want you hanging around her, then you were going to do your best to make her unhappy," Michael said. He expected Dave to be apologetic and afraid, but instead Dave said simply, "I guess it was pretty terrible to make Sheila unhappy, but I'd do anything in the world if it would only make her want me." He spoke as if this was the one honest emotion in his life, the one experience of which he could be unashamed. "You don't understand it at all, Mike. The way I feel doesn't mean a damn thing to you. My God, what do you expect me to do anyway?"

"I'd like you to tell her you were kidding her, Dave. That won't cost you anything. Tell her you were a little drunk."

"That would fix it fine then, eh? Just say I'm a little drunk and then they all begin to understand me. Sheila's not a nitwit, Mike. She knows I was never more serious in my life."

"I'm only asking you to say you were kidding her and you'll leave her alone and won't worry her."

"If you don't mind me saying it, Mike, I'd be just as satisfied if you minded your own business."

"Why are you talking so loud? What's the matter with you?"

"I'm not going to keep on whispering."

"I want this to be just between us."

"So do I."

"The whole country could hear you when you were out here the other night quarrelling with my father."

"Then let's call it off and go in the house."

"No, I want to settle it."

"All right. That's all right with me," Dave said, and he went on, "If I was just kidding about Sheila it would be different, wouldn't it? Then you'd be having a legitimate complaint and I'd expect you to be beefing like this. But when you've hung on to one pretty decent emotion for years … I mean I just couldn't bear to see her going away from me like that even if it was with a pretty good guy like Ross Hillquist. I never got in her way at all. I just watched her. Then it got that I couldn't sit back and watch her go away. It was all right when we were both living together in the same house. You don't know the way I feel. I don't know why I'm talking to you like this. You don't know a damn thing about it." After pleading so earnestly, Dave began to feel shy, and he put his head down, and to say something, he said, "Do you want me to row around a bit?"

"I'll row," Michael said.

"All right, I might as well go on talking now I started. You know you never would give me a break, Mike. That's all right with me as long as you understand now that I don't want to be pushed around like a bum. This is really the first time … What's the matter? Don't you want to listen to me? It doesn't mean a god-damn thing to you, does it, Mike?"

While Michael rowed aimlessly in the quiet water he heard Dave's voice, but the words meant nothing to him at all. It only filled him with more contempt to hear Dave pleading and expecting to be taken seriously; he seemed to be really saying, in spite of his words, "I hurt your sister and made her very unhappy and I'm sorry, but it looks as if I'll have to do it again because it's good for me." And he began to feel, as Dave leaned closer to him in the boat, that this love in Dave's life, like every hope he had ever had, was selfish, perverted and useless, but it was necessary to be patient because Dave, like the two young financial men who had been with him in the hotel and all the other young fellows in the country who had been pampered and given loafing jobs, was incapable of a disinterested feeling for anyone on earth. Michael rowed the boat steadily, and he was troubled, for he began to think that possibly Dave would never understand his own selfishness, and then he began to pity him as he might have pitied anyone who was absolutely helpless against a lust for self-indulgence.

"What you feel in the matter, Dave, is one thing, but what you're going to do is another," he said quietly. "You know how Sheila feels and you're not going to hurt her any more. I'm telling you to go and tell her you acted like a fool."

"So that's all you think, is it, Mike?"

"That's what you're going to do."

As Dave jerked his head back his young face showed the contempt he felt for Michael, and yet at the same time he was full of shame that he should have tried to explain his most secret longing with so much sincerity. He wasn't afraid of Michael at all. "What are you going to do about it, Mike?" he asked.

"We're going to stay here till I persuade you to have that little talk with Sheila."

Dave laughed and said, "That's fine. Go ahead," and he leaned back, letting his hand trail in the water, then he laughed, a soft laugh sounding extraordinarily loud and mocking on the water. "All I want you to do, Dave, is to tell Sheila you were mistaken. Just leave her alone, don't you see?" Michael coaxed him. But Dave just trailed his hand in the water as they rowed out in the lake. From time to time he laughed in that soft, mocking way till Michael began to feel desperately that there was nothing he could say, nothing he could do except row on steadily mile after mile till his arms got tired. Maybe then it would be morning and they both would be too tired to talk, yet Dave, in the meantime, was there leaning back resting and laughing to himself.

Dave said, "I'm tired of this. Turn back. I'm getting cold. It's all right for you. You're rowing and enjoying yourself but I'm cold."

"I won't turn back till we settle this."

"Settle what you idiot? You're talking like a bum actor."

"I won't turn back till we make it different, God damn you," Michael shouted at him. He rested the oars trembling with eagerness to grab him and start beating him. He looked around the water, longing to be on shore. They were almost in the middle of the narrow lake. The block shape of a white frame house on the other side was extraordinarily light; it was high on the hill alone. "I always hated your guts," he said to Dave. "I hated everything you ever stood for. I hated your soft useless life. I hated you because you were a bum and got away with it and I had to work. I hated you because you didn't have a spark of pride in you. I hated your guts because you never believed in anything but your balls and your belly. I know all about you. Guys like you are all around, just vomited up by a sick class in society. You just make a stench for the rest of us."

"Imagine you of all people discovering a social conscience."

"It wasn't hard to discover a lot of guys like you."

"Don't mind if I think it funny, because you're the kind of

an unhappy sour-faced egg that everybody always leaves alone. Yet what do I discover?"

"Tell me. What do you discover?"

"That you don't like me. I'm still a bit mixed up because I can't get over my surprise. Imagine it. Listen, it's chilly, are you going back? You're getting nowhere. Are you going back?"

"No, and you're not going back either."

Then David stood up, laughing again, and he moved his arms up and down several times, warming himself while Michael watched him, and then he suddenly dove off the end of the boat, a clean effortless dive into the smooth dark water. He was only under a moment, and he came up to the surface treading water and grinning as he pushed his hair back out of his eyes, with the ripples widening all around him and glinting in the moonlight. He called out, "The water's warm. Have a good time. Cool off. Talk to the stars. There are a lot of stars and they won't get tired or cold," and then he took a deep breath and began to swim with a fine crawl stroke, rolling his head up from the water for air.

But Michael shouted, "Like hell you do, come back here, you bastard," and he began to row after Dave, putting his back into it, and when he was alongside, he leaned over, grabbed him by the sweater and tried to pull him into the boat. David swung with his hands. The boat might have tipped, but the sweater ripped, and Dave was free, and he swam off the other way.

Again Michael rowed after him, but in a hopeless, wild way, and this time he kept heading him off by cutting across Dave's path whichever way he turned. Soon he had Dave swimming in a circle. Once he was very close to him. Dave was treading water and Michael took the oar and tried to hook him with it saying, "Come on, quit, you little fool." But Dave kept pushing the oar away with his hands so Michael jabbed at him with it and pushed him under longing all the time that Dave would quit and plead with him, longing to see his upturned, helpless face in that light as he pleaded. Yet Dave, time after time, got free of the oar. Then suddenly he turned and began to swim away from the boat, heading rapidly for the other shore, and this time Michael, desperate and beaten, let him go, watching him heading surely for the other side. Once he cried out, "Come on back, Dave." His heart was pounding so heavily and he was so full of hate that he sat there rigidly till he could no longer see anything on the water.

He did not know how long he sat there motionless like that; he began to imagine he heard someone calling. Then he actually did hear, coming over the water, that one pleading cry that he had wanted to hear before, "Help, help." It rose out of the lake. Standing up in the boat Michael shouted, "Swim, you bastard. You wanted to swim, now why don't you swim?" He stared in the darkness, unable to hear or see anything because he was so numbed and blinded by the surge within him of all the hatred of Dave he had ever had and all the hate of Dave's mother too. Little waves rapped against the side of the boat and rocked it and nursed his hate till it mounted in him as if it had to be free. His hands were clenching the oars. Then he began to breathe more evenly, and bit by bit he grew afraid. Grabbing the oars he began to row steadily to the place where the cry had come from and when he was rowing around the place that seemed so indefinite on the smooth water not far away from the other shore, rowing around in patches of smooth dark water and looking eagerly all the time at the shore and beginning to see shadows rising and falling on the beach as if someone were crawling out of the water, it was the loneliest job he had ever done. He kept thinking, "He got there all right. He's a real good swimmer. Just like him to yell like that. Just like him to keep me out here all night looking for him. I wonder if he can see me from there."

And when he could hardly row any longer he began to row

slowly back to the house. He would not let himself think of anything and he was terribly eager to see the little dock. The way the moonlight touched the apple orchard gladdened him. As he tied the boat to the dock his fingers trembled. He went noiselessly up over the lawn in his bare feet. The night light shone brightly on his pyjamas. He went quietly into the house and tiptoed upstairs to his room and threw himself on the bed and lay there listening, longing desperately for some consoling sound to come from the water that never did come.

Ten

THE SUN was shining strongly in his room, and there were voices coming from the lake when Michael woke in the morning. Full of hope as he listened, he heard his father's voice, and then he jumped up and looked out the window to see whom he was talking to down there, and he saw "Windy" Hilliard, the noisy and boastful neighbor, who lived along the shore, standing up in his outboard motor boat and holding at the length of his short fat arm a fine big green bass he had caught trolling. He was shouting that he had been trolling all morning and was now on his way up to the reeds. "I'll bet you a dollar it weighs four pounds," he was shouting as he took off his panama hat. "Easily that," Michael heard his father humor the boastful neighbor, who had stopped to show him the fish. Then the neighbor waved farewell and started his engine that fluttered momentarily and then began to put put put as the boat was turned in a graceful arc, heading out over the water and up toward the reeds.

Michael watched his father coming lazily up the path with his hands in the pockets of his gray flannel trousers; his sport shirt was open at the throat which looked so ruddy and healthy and his face shone with good humor. He looked like an indulgent country gentleman, a little plump, and slowing up, who was having a very good time on his holidays. Looking up, he saw Michael, and he called, "Did you see Dave at all last night, Michael?"

"Early in the evening I did. Not later, though."

"He didn't show up this morning."

"Is anybody worried? What do they make of it?"

"I don't make anything out of it. Trying to make anything out of it would be just a waste of time. I know I'm not alarmed. By this time, I fancy, I ought to know something about that young man's erratic behavior. Did you sleep well?"

"Like a top. What time is it?"

"Ten o'clock. Get dressed and come on down, why don't you?" he said, and he went on his way across the lawn, humming cheerfully to himself.

He hummed as he passed under the window, and Michael resented the sound of that humming so much he wanted to shout out at him, "Why don't you whistle? You're not touched at all, are you? You're really the cause of this whole dirty mess. You brought us up here because you wanted to make yourself feel good. You never did anything in your life but try and make yourself feel good." It seemed incredible to Michael that he had ever believed that his father had found the things he had always thought important were really unimportant, that at last his father had begun a search for what was truly valuable. Whatever his father looked for, he would never be disinterested, he would never be magnanimous in his search. Even talking to the neighbor down at the dock a moment ago, he had sounded like a glad-handing alderman, a right hand of the board of trade, consolation of the manufacturers, comforter of the rich. He was the true source of all Dave's little comforts and soft ways. "I've been trying all my life to get away from you and you bring me up here, and then you think we've all forgotten, and it'll just go the way you want it," he thought, and he shouted across the lawn at his father, "Heh," but his father, not hearing, went on his way.

Michael felt such a passion within him as he tried to stand there looking out over the lake, that his legs began to feel unsteady, and he had to sit down on the bed. He sat there with his head in his hands, listening for every noise they made in the house. There was not much to hear. Dave's mother kept on going up and down stairs to his room. Once she called out, "His slippers are gone," and she hurried downstairs, and Michael was remembering how much he had wanted to hurt her and make her suffer years ago.

When he was dressed he went downstairs timidly, and Mrs. Aikenhead came up to him and said eagerly, "Have you any idea where Dave might be, Michael? Do you know of any places where he might go?" She spoke like this because Michael had been friendly the other day, and he was Dave's age, and might understand where Dave would go.

"The chances are he'll come walking in any minute," he said.

"That's what I keep thinking, too," she said.

"He'll be back. He'll have to come back," he said emphatically.

"You really think so?"

"He's got to," he said.

But it was terrible for him to have to be around the house with her as the afternoon passed and the restlessness in her grew. Gradually she stopped asking her husband and Jay Hillquist and Sheila and Ross where Dave might have gone. She moved from one room to another in the house, waiting. Her plump, dark face grew troubled and then very tired. And Michael had to keep watching her. She repeated many times that Dave had slept in his bed; at dinner time she looked from one to the other as she repeated this and she was stunned that no one was as worried as she, and it was only when she saw the solemn wondering look on Michael's face that she smiled at him gratefully.

But when it began to get dark and she was still sitting at the window, quiet now, with her hands folded in her lap and the unopened newspaper from the city in the chair beside her, Michael knew that he could not stand it there with her, and he said to his father, who was smoking by himself out on the porch that faced the lake, "Where did Ross and Sheila go?"

"They walked into the hotel."

"This is getting to look pretty bad."

"I don't see that it is."

"You ought to have had more sense than to have brought us along up here," Michael said sharply. His father put down his pipe and looked after him as he went out to the road.

As soon as he started to go along that road in the dark Michael felt such a sudden dread of being alone that he started to hurry and broke into a little trot. He began to feel separated from nearly everyone on earth. The tall shrubs that lined the road closed in on him and were part of the darkness when there was a turn in the road. Back on the hill there was a lighted farm house, and as he trotted along, he kept looking at that light, but he knew all the time that he was scared of seeing anyone, that the only people in the world he could bear to be with and to talk to now were those he loved, and yet there were so few that he loved that when he tried to think of them he felt alone in that country; he hurried along the road so he could be with his sister and Ross Hillquist.

When he got to the village he hurried into the hotel without noticing that men, sitting on the veranda, were watching him curiously, and he went into the beverage room and looked around, and when he saw his sister and the doctor sitting together at the table in the corner and having a beer, his face lit up with a smile that was full of warmth and relief. The doctor and Sheila were whispering together seriously. The light overhead lit up their faces as they whispered in that easy, effortless, intimate way.

Michael noticed that his sister's face at one moment was full of a deep sadness as she listened and nodded her head, and then at another moment it would change and show immense relief. Yet he couldn't help grinning, when they saw him, as if he felt that it was a piece of incredible good luck to be there with them. "How are you doing?" he said, and he sat down and called to the proprietor, Jake Sanderson, who had followed him to the table, "How about a beer?"

"Sure. One beer. Is there any word of that boy, Dave?"

"Nothing new, why?"

"I ask only because his mother and father were around this morning inquiring for him. His friends, the young gentlemen, left late last night."

"Do you think he motored back with them?" Ross asked.

"I understand he was in his pyjamas."

"Who has been telling you this?"

"It is common property around the village. I don't want you to think I am not minding my own business. I'm sorry I gave you that impression."

"You mean it makes quite a good story?" Ross asked.

"That's it, exactly," the proprietor said. "We haven't much to talk about around here, and this helps, that's all," and he smiled and left them.

"What were you whispering about?" Michael asked them.

"We were having a little council of war," Ross said. "Your little sister told me coming along that maybe we oughtn't to get married because her mother had gone melancholy before she died. She was pretty worried. You ought to have heard her. But I have just persuaded her we will get married. Am I not right, darling?"

"You are right," she said, and she nodded her head and now her face showed how relieved she was. A little while ago she had come along the road with Ross and she had tried to tell him her fear of ever having a child. She had insisted with extraordinary vehemence that if he wanted to marry her he would have to agree that they would not have children. And as he told her earnestly that he had known a long time ago about her mother's illness, he in no way revealed his own deep disappointment that she should want to remain childless. Joy had risen so swiftly in her that he was surprised, for he was unable to guess the depth of the sadness in her and her melancholy fear that something was buried in her that would always set her a little apart from other people; she had clutched his arm and talked about living for each other as they walked along the road in the dark.

"I told her she was foolish bothering about it at all," Michael said, and leaning across the table he added gravely, as if this one question alone disturbed him, "I think it bothers her that they kept our mother in a room and locked the door on her. Maybe Sheila thinks our mother had homicidal tendencies, Ross."

"It's very simple," Ross said. "Many women have gone melancholy after childbirth, particularly if they lose the child. They just sit around overwhelmed by sadness. There's some danger of them destroying themselves, not much danger of them bothering with anyone else. People have absurd notions about insanity. Any kind of a nervous sickness that touches the mind is called insanity and then it becomes mysterious and people are afraid. You'd be surprised how many of our best citizens spend a few weeks a year in mental hospitals." He talked with such assurance that both brother and sister listened eagerly and nodded their heads at each other.

"It never bothered me in the slightest. Nothing like that bothers me," Michael said, and he smiled at them innocently.

"Did you see Dave at all last night?" Sheila asked him. Michael knew she was meaning, "Did you speak to Dave after I saw you last night?" and she was leaning forward watching him intently.

"I didn't see Dave at all," he said easily.

"He probably has a lady friend up the line," Sheila said.

"He wouldn't go calling on her in his bare feet and pyjamas, would he?" Ross said.

"Why wouldn't he?" Michael asked. "Why should you ever be surprised at anything that guy ever did?" He asked this question with such emphasis as he glared into their faces that they smiled and shrugged their shoulders and he was embarrassed and merely sat back listening to them.

The young doctor began to tell them what he planned to do. "I don't expect to make a lot of money in the first couple of years, but if I get to know how to work with people and understand them, that'll be enough. In a small town you get to know everybody."

Dr. Hillquist had some kind of a collective notion in his head that had made him reject his father's vigorous individualism and all his ideas and ready catch phrases about human liberty and personal rights. His father was frankly a little bewildered by this opposition to his own ideas; he liked his son and thought he had a good mind. He simply couldn't understand his son when they got talking seriously about such matters. It was as though the young doctor had thought a long time about freedom and liberty and had kept asking himself when he was actually free among people.

And as Michael listened, too timid to say much for fear of reminding them that he was there when they were talking so intimately, he kept watching the eagerness and the love that grew in his sister's face; he began to wonder that anyone could feel as close to and as free among simple people as Ross did, and with all his soul, as he listened, and felt the desolation and sickness possessing him he yearned to be as free and un-self-conscious among human beings as Ross was. He listened and wondered as he heard these two voices which were the only voices he could think of that would soothe him and sound so dear to him tonight. But Sheila was saying, "It's time we were going, isn't it?"

"No, don't go," Michael said excitedly.

"What's the matter?"

"I haven't finished my beer."

"Go ahead then. We'll watch you."

"I'd like to hear you go on with what you were saying about people, Ross. I'd like to go into it deeper. Why can't I feel that way?"

"You, Mike? Don't kid us, you haven't enough faith in anything."

"What should I have faith in?"

"In life on the earth," the doctor laughed.

"Me? You've got me all wrong," Michael said, full of eagerness to defend himself and explain that people did not understand him. "I don't know what gave you such a notion. You've known me a long time, Ross. I won't say I'm the most believing man in the world. I know I've often told you you were naïve. I know you think I'm suspicious about people. You've often told me to occasionally give someone a break. I know that and it's true, but I don't want to be a hermit. That's where you get me wrong. I like being with people. I love sitting here tonight. I like all kinds of people. It's probably unfortunate that I have a suspicious look about me, but I haven't any grudge against the world. I don't seem to have any faith and I can't recite a creed of any kind and don't go to any church and I seem to be pretty cynical but you know how easy it is for people to kid me and sell me something I don't want. That's because I'm a believing man. Besides, I'm pretty impulsive and you can't be impulsive and be of a completely cynical nature. I often do a thing and am very sorry for it. I'm always full of remorse. I suffer for doing things, simple things."

"What's the matter with you, Mike?"

"Nothing at all. Why did you say that?"

"You seem pretty excited."

"I'm excited because I hate being taken for a malicious person. I'm the most gregarious man you ever knew. I don't know why people think I like being alone. I can't stand being alone. I like hearing simple people talk and laugh. I know I haven't many friends but that's because I'm not a good mixer. I get shy.

I keep thinking people won't like me. I know I should stop thinking about myself and everybody would like me. If I could suddenly find that I liked a great many people I'd never be uncomfortable with people again, would I? It's funny, but the more I worry about myself, the more I reject the whole world. I get blue. I wonder if there is actually anything but what's blue in me. It's terrible to feel this way when you really want to be friendly with everybody. Why are you going? Are you going to leave me sitting here, Sheila?"

"We're going to hire a hall for the friend of the people."

"You've got a better notion of yourself than I thought you had. Come on and walk back with us, Mike," the doctor said.

Michael was a little ashamed, for he knew his sister wanted to be alone with her lover. "Are you sure you don't mind?" he said lamely. "Are you sure you don't want to be alone?"

"Come on along, Mike," Sheila said.

So he went with them gladly and they walked back very slowly and when they got up on the hill they stopped and looked at the moon shining over the fields and at the lake down there in the valley which was like a brilliant white strip of light in the darkness of the valley. Sheila kept saying, "It's lovely here; isn't it beautiful from the hill here?" but Michael could not bear to look down at the lake in the hills. Sheila's young voice sounded loud and eager in the night and Michael knew that she and the doctor wanted to sit down there by the road and show their love for each other. He knew they were waiting for him to say, "I'll leave you and run along to the house." There was the curious silence of waiting among them. As he tried to think of something to say that would make them want to keep him with them, Michael felt miserably that he could not go, for he could not bear to be alone in his own room waiting.

Eleven

T HEY ALL saw the old Ford car come swaying up the road and stop jerkily with a gasp and a shiver in front of the house. For a while no one got out of the car. The trailing cloud of dust on the road settled down; the old car might have been always there in the sunlight like the trees and the bees that droned in the clover by the side of the road and the green pastureland beyond. At last a tall heavily moustached country policeman swung his legs from the front seat and got down and he was followed by the farmer, Joel Hilton, who owned the car and lived in the house on the other side of the lake, and who was dressed in his best blue-serge suit. For some reason they both took off their hats and came up the path to the house.

It must have been the way they had taken off their hats that alarmed her, for Mrs. Aikenhead left those who were watching at the window and she ran out with her thick and heavy black hair flopping up and down on the nape of her neck and coming loose, and she cried out, "What is it? Where is he?" and then in a softer more pitiable tone they all could hear, she said, "Ah, I knew it. I felt it all last night and the night before."

Dave's body had been found on the other side of the lake, the policeman said. It looked as if he had been hurt before he was drowned because there were bruises on his shoulders made by some heavy instrument and his sweater and pyjamas were torn.

"Do you see? Do you see? What do you think of that?" Mrs. Aikenhead said. "God in heaven, help me. What do you think of that? How did I know? Why was I so sure, tell me that," and she clutched her husband by the arm and swung him around so he was facing her. He looked much older, standing beside her because there was much worry and a pallor in his face instead of his usual ruddy-faced good humor.

"I don't know what to make of it, Marthe," he said.

"You don't, eh? Well, I do," she said.

The farmer and the policeman were hemmed in by Jay Hillquist and Ross and Sheila who answered questions and asked them excitedly, and for some reason they all kept their voices low, almost in a whisper. But Michael remained where he was, standing behind Mrs. Aikenhead, who was sitting stiffly in a rocking chair and mumbling to herself. Sometimes she stared earnestly into her husband's face and looked wonderingly at the hand he had put lightly on her shoulder, and then she suddenly began to rock back and forth in the chair, back and forth monotonously with a loose floor board creaking a little. Twice she stopped and looked up at her husband again, remembering how she had insisted two nights ago before they had gone to bed that he did not want Dave in the house. Moving her lips as if she were getting ready to shout, she grew bewildered, then she sighed and said quietly, "Now you're free. Absolutely free."

Michael heard his father whisper softly to her, "I know how you feel, Marthe, but don't say anything you'll be sorry for. I did everything in the world for Dave. I put him ahead of my own boy, Marthe. I put him ahead of my own son. I did everything I could for him because I loved you so much, Marthe. I let him bully me, Marthe. I was afraid to be like a strict father with him for fear you'd think I was against him. Marthe…"

But as he listened to his father's urgent, anxious, fearful pleading it got so that Michael could hardly hear the whispering voices; he had begun to remember how he had sat rigid in the boat, full of hate. And sounding so dreadfully clear within him he heard Dave's cry for help, then he heard his own voice crying, "Swim, you bastard," and he knew then that he had let Dave drown and he began to feel all the misery and desolation of his guilt, even though he would not accept it. When he saw Mrs. Aikenhead shake her head savagely he thought, "She knows he's to blame and in a way she's right. It started years ago and he was to blame. He arranged the whole thing."

Then Jay Hillquist, who was standing at the window, said, "There they go. There's to be an inquest. We'll all have to be there. They figure they can have it in two days over at Barrie."

"Have they gone already?" Mrs. Aikenhead said. "Aren't they going to do anything?" and rushing to the window she called over Jay Hillquist's shoulder, "Officer, come back, come back here a minute," and she watched them returning to the house.

When the officer and the farmer had come to her she began to say very earnestly, "There's a good deal that you ought to know about this matter and I don't know why you hurried away. Didn't you wonder how it might have been for my boy around here? That's what I want to tell you. Nobody liked him. Maybe I shouldn't say that because the girl, Sheila, there, she always got along all right with him and they grew up together, and Michael, over there, he and Dave hardly knew each other or had much to say to each other in the last ten years. It's my husband that knew Dave." So far she had not wept at all and now she paused and made an effort to sound reasonable, and then she went on in that earnest worried way, "My husband didn't want the boy around at all. You should have heard them quarrelling the other night, the first night they got here. You should have heard the way he talked to Dave and you should have heard the contempt and hatred in his voice. You certainly ought to know about that. Why didn't you ask about it instead of running off the way you did?"

The policeman was embarrassed by the passion he felt in her voice; the farmer was staring with simple unconcealed curiosity at Andrew Aikenhead whom he had known for fifteen years.

"She's very upset," Andrew Aikenhead said. "God help her, I don't wonder."

"Did you and the boy have a quarrel, Mr. Aikenhead?" the policeman asked.

"We had a little quarrel about money matters. Maybe I should call it a routine quarrel. There was a good deal of smoke but no fire," he said, and he smiled his extraordinarily persuasive smile. "You'll have a chance to hear all about it if you want to."

But as soon as the men had gone for the second time Mrs. Aikenhead began to talk again in that restless, passionate way, as though she were alone with her husband. "Why did you want to come up here?" she asked. "What did you have in mind?"

"We come every year," he said patiently.

"There was something different about it this year because you planned it for weeks ahead and I often saw you smiling to yourself. I wondered what was in your mind and now I know. Andrew, you wanted that boy to go; you wanted to get rid of him; you wanted him to die. You said he'd have more dignity dead than alive. I can remember how you promised me over and over again that you'd make him like your own son and yet the more you tried the more you hated him till it got so you couldn't stand the sight of him around the house. He had to die just because he was my son. That was the only reason; he was my son, and you didn't want me to have a son. I can remember when he was a child he wasn't spoiled at all, and if he changed it was your money and your ways that spoiled him and then you couldn't stand him. What did you do to him, Andrew?"

"Marthe, be quiet!"

"I can tell by the way you look at me that you know what happened," she said. "Dave's dead and he wouldn't be dead if I had never brought him near you. He wouldn't be stretched out and found drowned, if it weren't for you. For months there's been guilt in your heart," she said, her voice rising sharply. And it seemed to Michael, who listened and watched her and got more excited himself that she was getting at the truth with an uncanny penetration, that every word she said was absolutely true, that it was a much higher truth than could be got at in the simple fact that he, himself, had let Dave drown; it went behind that fact and included it and went beyond it. Her words were pouring out of her in a wild way that made them all think she was telling of things she had often discussed with her husband, who stood beside her trying to soothe her, yet showing so clearly by his helpless gestures, that no matter how much he might have loved her at one time he could not hold her now. She had stopped for breath, and her eyes had a glazed wild look in them, and suddenly she shrugged her shoulders in an all-embracing gesture of disgust and walked swiftly away from them and out of the house.

Michael was the only one who followed her, and he followed timidly a few paces behind her, still hearing her muttering to herself. She went down to the dock and she stood there in the brilliant sunshine looking over the smooth water. One hand was up to shade her eyes as she looked far over at the other shore. And with his heart pounding and fearing to intrude, Michael hung back, mumbling, "God help her. What's she going to do?" and he was timid and wondering, watching her motionless figure.

Then she stepped off the dock to the beach and she began to walk as fast as she could in the sand, and she never stopped watching the other shore. It was such a clear day that you could see the color of the oat fields and the wheat and the light tin roof on the farmer's barn over there. Michael followed her on the sand. A little way out on the water a kingfisher was hovering, beating its wings, almost standing still, then swooping down close to the water. And while he noticed all these things Michael had the feeling that he had to watch every awkward movement she made as she stumbled along in the sand, growing tired, her feet slipping and tripping sometimes as she stepped over fallen boughs from the overhanging trees, but when she came to a little inlet where the water was shallow and where the surface was littered with bark and bits of brown rotting logs she stopped and she began to wade out in the shallow water. Soon the water was up to her knees and her skirt was bellied up by the water, but she kept the one hard, rigid expression on her face as she went farther out.

Then Michael could bear it no longer, and he cried out, "Come back, please, please come back," and he went splashing out in the water after her. He grabbed her by the arm but it was hard to make her realize he was there beside her, and when he began to lead her back to the beach, he might just as well have been leading a little child, for she looked at him innocently, and tried to smile. "You aren't much older than my boy, Dave, are you, Mike?" she asked. "You would have got to like Dave if you had known him better. It was good to have the two of you together up here."

She stumbled in the water and went down above her waist, and when the water dripped off her, and she leaned so close to him, and her eyes were so frightened, Michael felt more sorrow for her than he had ever felt for anyone. He tried to carry her, but she was heavy, yet he stumbled up to the sand, and then he laid her down in the shade of an overhanging willow. With his wet handkerchief, he bathed her head, and he tried not to hear her saying, "Maybe it was a mistake. Maybe it wasn't Dave at all. They wouldn't know. I would be the only one who would know for sure. I want to see him. I want to look at his face. Oh, Jesus, he was my only son. Doesn't that matter to You? Doesn't it matter how much I loved him? Isn't the love for him what really mattered, dear Jesus? He was my only son...."

But Michael, trembling, left her there and ran back to the house, and they all came back with him and carried her among them. They thought she had fainted, for her eyes were closed. They carried her into the house and put her on a couch. They were in a half circle around her, all watching her. The young doctor had his fingers on her pulse. Jay Hillquist, who was on one knee on the floor beside her, was saying, "It's all right, Marthe. It's all right now. We're all here with you." Her wet clothes were clinging tight to her, and they all saw that her body no longer had its youthful firmness, and the flesh was soft and slack. When Jay repeated, "We're all here with you, Marthe," she startled them by saying quietly, "No, you're not all here, Jay."

"Look, Marthe, we're here, look, Marthe."

"Your wife isn't here, Jay," she whispered.

"My wife?"

"Your wife never came here since I've been here. She never asked me to her house either, Jay," she said.

And as Michael watched her wild, frightened eyes turning from one to the other and turning to him, he was full of wonder that he had ever wanted to hurt her and make her cry out in her wretchedness, for now her suffering, and his own desolation, was so much deeper than any desire he had ever had to hurt her.

Twelve

Driving into the village to get the mail late in the afternoon, Andrew Aikenhead said, "You don't really think, Jay, that people will blame me, do you?" His old friend, who was driving the car, said gruffly, "I wouldn't give the thing a moment's thought," but as he spoke he looked straight ahead along the dry dirt side road and he could not conceal the concern he had begun to feel for his friend.

Andrew Aikenhead said earnestly, "Just tell me what you, yourself, think. Honestly, Jay, you don't think I know anything about it, do you?"

"I don't think you had anything to do with it."

"But you don't laugh, or think it's funny at all, do you?"

"Nobody likes being talked about the way they were talking about you this afternoon."

"It was just idle talk, Jay, a whole lot of idle talk."

"They decided Dave was drowned by someone unknown and that leaves it open for them to go on hunting. That talk was terrible, the talk of the messenger boys who heard you quarrelling with Dave, and Marthe's story the way that cop told it. It certainly won't help business if the city papers take it up."

"Do you really think they'll talk about it in the city?" Aikenhead asked, staring out over the ploughed field by the side of the road. All afternoon, since they had been questioned in town, he had felt like stopping people, shaking hands and saying heartily, "What ridiculous stories they're telling about me," and yet as soon as he saw anyone he knew he found himself wanting to say earnestly, "You don't really think …" Instead of speaking he had turned away, looking stern and unfriendly.

In the village everybody was sitting in the shade of the verandas, waiting for the sun to go down; there was the sound of birds in the trees, or a voice, raised a little, drifting out to the road. The odor of baking biscuits and rich, slow-cooking stews came from the row of open doors. In the stone cottage opposite the hotel the door was open, and Mrs. Riggs Ross, who had just come in after having a cup of tea with three of her neighbors, saw Andrew Aikenhead getting out of the car and she stood with her hands on her hips, and called back into the house in a voice so distinct it could be heard out on the road, "There he is now, Ned. My goodness, right under our noses."

The muttering among the men sitting there in their row of chairs stopped as Andrew Aikenhead crossed the road. No voice was raised above a whisper. One by one these old acquaintances nodded their heads at him with what he felt sure were stern, unfriendly wondering faces. The smile left his face, he flushed, and he didn't call out their names, but lowered his head and went into the hotel.

He asked Jake Sanderson for his mail. He watched Jake finger the letters and stop from time to time to wet his thumb meditatively. "It's a great day out, Jake," he said eagerly. "The first of the really warm summer days, eh?"

"It's sure warm enough here. How was it over in Barrie?"

"Just as warm as here, you may be sure."

"A few of the boys out there went over to the inquest."

"How did they think it went?"

"It doesn't matter the slightest to me how they think it went, Mr. Aikenhead. I knew you and your kids and your first wife, too." The proprietor spoke with such loyalty and candor that Andrew Aikenhead was touched, and he muttered, "Thanks, Jake, thanks a lot." And he took his letters and went out.

But no one called out to him in the old way from the veranda as he got into the car beside his partner. He had always thought of this country of soft-rolling, cultivated hills and fields ploughed brown in the springtime, and of woods, small blue lakes, ponds and trout streams as his own country. Whenever he came here he felt he was coming home. As he thought of Jake Sanderson saying, "I've known you and your kids and your first wife, too," he felt very surely that the most intimate part of his life had been close to this country and these people, who knew him better, he often thought, than his business friends in the city. Yet now the same people were all joining together to gossip about him; and whether they believed this gossip or not, they had separated themselves from him. Sitting silent in the car, driving back to his house on the lake, the thought of his separation from this country he had loved began to fill him with desolation.

"Go a little faster, Jay," he said. "We said we'd get back in time to say good-bye to Ross and Michael."

"They'll wait for us."

"Not when they want to get back to the city before dark. I don't want to miss them," he said.

When they were a little way off they saw Ross and Michael putting their bags in the car and Sheila was with them. It was much cooler here by the lake. A little breeze, blowing the scent of apple blossoms to the house, was ruffling Sheila's hair. When the boys were in the car Michael stood to one side watching his sister and Ross like a curious child, and he turned his head and listened first to Ross and then to Sheila as if he must not miss anything they said.

Going up to his son, Andrew Aikenhead smiled in a shy eager way. "I'm sorry it turned out like this," he began, taking

Michael by the arm. But when he saw his son's unfriendly face and felt his arm hanging like a dead weight, he withdrew his hand. "I'm glad you came anyway," he said awkwardly. Mumbling something, Michael nodded and seemed anxious to go. His father longed to say to him, "What did you mean, son, when you said the other day that I had brought on this mess?" but the withdrawal from him he felt in Michael hurt him so much he only said in a simple, dignified way, "Did you say goodbye to Marthe, son?"

"She didn't come down. I didn't know if she felt well," Michael said.

"We can't let you go like that. Can you delay just a moment?" he said, and he left them in the way a gracious host hastens to correct some little oversight on his part that might have offended an honored guest. He hurried into the house and went up to his wife's room.

"Marthe," he called to his wife who was lying down on a couch by the window. "Michael's going."

Her eyes were swollen from weeping and her cheeks were flabby. "Your son's going, is he?" She spoke in a flat dull tone that filled him with pity, though he knew by the way she looked at him that he had become like a stranger to her. As he watched her it began to seem terrible that she should no longer want to live with him when he had had such a helpless love for her for so many years. At night in his bed, such a few years ago, he had sought out her face, longing for her soft opulent ways as if his soul loved her. Such a little while ago he had gone slinking out at night, full of guilt, to visit her in her little flat. Day after day he had become more helplessly aware that the only part of his life that had warmth and mystery were those times when he hurried along the street in the city, thinking, "What will become of me? What will become of her and my wife and my children?" It had got that he could not bear the loneliness that grew in him when he was leaving her in her flat in the city. His longing for Marthe had grown stronger than his scruples and when his wife got sick he coaxed Marthe to come to his house in the country with her son. After their marriage he had rejoiced in any little social success she had had; he had whispered often to her that she was the kind of a woman he needed badly to attract people to his house. All these longings, out of which he had gradually built quite a different life, were recovered in him now as he waited for her to say simply that she would go downstairs and say good-bye to his son.

"Why shouldn't I say good-bye to your son? I have nothing against him," she said.

"I know that. I know you've nothing against any of us, Marthe. Dave's buried now, and we're here with each other."

"I don't belong here. I won't live here. I never should have come here. I wanted Dave to have a chance to get on, that was why I came. I knew you could give him such a chance, but that's gone and I don't want anything you ever gave me. I wish I could give it back to you. I wish I could give back every little joy I ever shared with you. I want to be alone. I won't go over it because you know it and you needn't look at me as if I'm getting hysterical, because I'm not. I'm through, that's all. I knew the way it was getting between us and I told you about it before we came up here. Is that the sound of the car going? I'll call to them from the window," she said. She went to the window and called out firmly, "Good-bye, Michael. Good-bye, Ross." Her husband was standing beside her, waving his hand, so they were joining, at least, in this farewell.

Ross was sitting in the car with the door open and Michael was kissing Sheila, but they all waved up to the window. Then Michael got into the car and it turned away from the house.

Maybe it was standing beside Marthe at the window that made Andrew Aikenhead feel that Michael, going away again, was rejecting him the second time. He began to think of that time when Michael had gone away before, years ago, taking Sheila with him, away from this house. Sheila had given him an account of it months after it had happened.

The day after he had married Marthe and had brought her to the house for the first time as his wife Michael had gone out of the house after dinner looking for Sheila, and had found her picking raspberries in the bushes near the woods a little way along the lake. Her eyes had looked big with wonder when he said savagely, "Come on, Sheila. Come on with me."

"Come on where?"

"Down to the village and along the highway."

"I don't want to. Look, I've hardly got any berries," and she showed him her straw hat with a few berries in it.

"We've got to, Sheila. You go in and get a bag and take some food from the pantry and put on a coat. I'll tell you why as we go along."

She was used to doing what he told her. Besides, it occurred to her that it might be fun going along the road like this with him in the evening. She left him standing there, waiting, and she went into the house.

When they started along the road, with him carrying the bag, it was twilight, and the farmers were bringing in the cows from the pastureland. It was calm on the lake and there were the dark shapes of a few boats going out to troll till sundown. As they went along the dirt road to the highway he tried to tell her how full of hate he was for his father and the woman he had now married. Sheila began to cry. She stood in the middle of the road crying, and he had to pull her along by the arm, and as he pulled her stubbornly with a fierce unyielding look on his face, she began to catch some of his feeling. She grew full of enthusiasm. Her eyes glowed and she said, "We'll go. You're right, Michael. They don't want us, do they? I'll go wherever you say. That'll be fine, that's the thing for us to do, Michael. Where'll we go?" "I thought we might get a ride on the highway. I thought we might go on up to Lakewood and get on a grain boat and go to Chicago." Her spirit soared and she walked along beside him eagerly, with her head up, but he took those long strides that were almost too swift for her. His head was down and he was almost sick with hate of his father and his father's wife and her son and everything that belonged to their life.

While it was twilight, walking along the highway the brother and sister did not ask for a lift, for with the light in the sky they preferred to keep on going and they were shy of standing out on the road and waving their hands. A little later a farmer gave them a lift for four miles. A salesman picked them up and carried them along another twelve and then, when they wouldn't talk to him, he got scared of the eager, ecstatic-eyed girl, who kept wetting her lips, and the morose lanky boy who stared along the road and would not open his mouth. Getting worried, the salesman put them out of the car, and he drove on wondering where they had come from and where they were going. They walked along the highway, and cars passing at a high rate of speed swept them with their headlights, threw gigantic shadows momentarily across the fields, and then swept on. The fields became awfully silent. The ditches teemed with night noises. Sheila kept hold of Michael's hand. She was walking slower and Michael, too, was a little afraid, but he kept on striding along till the stars came out in a brilliant night sky, and it was far colder than they had expected. For three miles they trudged on like this and gradually that splendid enthusiasm went out of Sheila, and she became like any other scared little girl with her feet hurting her, with her legs dreadfully tired, chilled by the night air, appalled by the silence of the fields and sure the road would never end. "Michael, Michael," she kept saying, but he pretended he did not hear her.

"I can't go on, Michael," she said.

"You've got to," he said.

"My legs are so tired, Michael, my legs are very, very tired."

"No they're not. You've got no spunk, that's all, Sheila."

"Yes, I have. I have, really," she pleaded, but he would not listen to her and he kept on going along, with her pulling at his arm sometimes, for she was too frightened to stay there while he went and yet too tired really to keep up with him. When he shook himself free of her hand in disgust, she began to whimper. There was nothing for her to do but trail after him, crying softly, "I can't go farther. Just sit down a little while, Michael. I can't go farther. Please sit down a little while."

At last he agreed to rest by the road, and she sat beside him with her head against his shoulder, sighing and trembling, while he stared in a kind of solemn wonder at the dark shapes of barns in the fields. The longing to close her eyes and go to sleep was strong in her and she clutched his arm desperately with both her hands so he could not leave her, and she let her weight fall against him. Soon she was sound asleep. He was not afraid, sitting there alone by the road. By this time he knew he could not go on, and he was thinking of Lakewood and the grain boats, and Chicago. He was very glad he had got this far. But he, too, was tired and his head began to droop. The lonely cry of a bird scared him a little, and he tried to hold his eyes open. Then he dozed and soon was asleep. They were found there in the morning, there on the highway some thirty miles from home.

And Andrew Aikenhead, standing beside his wife at the window and full of this memory, saw Michael turn and look not up at the window, but out at the lake. He looked for a long time far out on the lake to the other shore, where on such a clear day there shone the separate colored patches of ploughed earth, trees and ripening fields. The father was frightened, and he began to tremble, feeling the fullness of Michael's withdrawal, and thinking, "What does it mean? Why is he going? Why is Marthe going? What is happening? When we were fishing up there in the reeds he seemed so close to me. What's happening to me?"

Thirteen

THE NIGHT Michael returned to the city he looked around the room with a kind of love; everything was there, just as he had left it, the coffee pot on the end of the gas stove, the pile of books on his desk, the golden-oak bureau, and the branch of the tree stretching across the window. Nothing had happened there at all.

Then someone called, "Are you there, Mike?"

"Who's that?" he said.

"Huck Farr."

"Come on in, Huck," he said.

The little runt of a man, with the bright blue eyes that looked a bit puffy, and the friendly grin of a comrade of men, came in and sat down and said, "Boy, you must have had some time of it up there in the country. What was it all about?"

"Who was telling you about it?"

"Don't you think I read the papers," he said.

Michael was glad to have this delicate-featured little man with the hard eyes there smiling at him, for he began to feel as he stared at Huck's pretty face and was full of friendliness himself that no matter what he might have done on earth he could be sure Huck Farr would not hold it against him. Huck was beyond any moral law or loathing. He believed only that men ought to be comrades, that they ought to drink together and fornicate often and understand and admit they were all liars and petty thieves.

When he had entered college five years ago Mike had worked in the summer with Huck selling magazines around the country. In those days, Huck, who was the crew manager, used to say he had a line of crap as high as a telegraph pole. As he sold magazines from house to house he got the notion it didn't matter what you were selling as long as you were selling it to women and selling it in the right way; he posed as one thing after another till bit by bit he began to believe, himself, that he was a veteran of the Great War. Again and again he told his story of wading in mud and blood in Flanders' fields, and if the women standing at the doors got impatient, he cursed them with all the passion of an old soldier who had once shed his blood for them and was being rejected by them now; the women were terrified and pleaded that he forgive them; they wanted to be gentle with him because his pretty little face was so full of passion. Huck never tried to sell anything to men; he thought all men ought to understand each other. As he grew older he began to devote all his time to his own fake veteran organization, selling calendars at fancy prices to wealthy women who wanted to help old soldiers on the memorial days of all the great battles they had fought in France.

It seemed to Michael that Huck Farr could give him warmth and comradeship when no one else could, that Huck's tolerance was so vast it was like an infinite charity for the mistakes of all men, and he smiled at him warmly and asked, "What about the good Anna? Have you got to first base with her yet?"

"All the money around here is on me, bozo."

"Any progress?"

"On all fronts. It's what the boys in the trenches used to call a war of attrition. How about coming out for a drink and telling me all about the monkey business up in the country?"

"Where'll we go?"

"Any place you say. Listen, Mike, was that your old man that came here one night? I bumped into him in the hall and he asked me where you lived."

"Maybe it was. What about it?"

"Your old man's in a jam, take it from me. His picture is in every paper. But they haven't really got anything on him at all, have they? Are they going to pin it on him?"

"What's it got to do with my father? Why do you keep talking about him?"

"Because they put his picture in the paper, didn't they? They'll soon have everybody swearing your old man had a hand in it. If you don't want to talk about it I'll lay off."

"There's nothing to talk about. How can he help what they put in the papers?"

"That's right. But I'll tell you something. I could tell it was your old man when I first saw him in the hall. He looks a lot like you around the forehead."

"Nobody ever said I looked like him before."

"All right, maybe not, but you won't get sore if I say you do?"

"Who said I was sore? What do I care if I look like my old man?"

"You just looked a little sore, that's all. Are you coming out for a drink?"

"I don't feel much like a drink. I don't feel like it right now," Michael mumbled.

"I'll go along then," Huck Farr said, and when he was at the door he said earnestly, "It's none of my business," then he looked worried and went out.

And Michael stood there thinking, "Why did he have to start talking about my father? I guess they're talking about him all over the city," and he began to remember the way his father had stood at the window looking after him the day he was leaving, looking after him with a baffled, wondering expression on his worried face, and as he thought of this he felt in him the beginning of such a sadness he could hardly bear it, and he sighed and got up and hurried after Huck Farr.

At the corner he stopped to buy a paper, and he was holding the paper up to the light so he could see the account of the inquest when he saw Anna Prychoda hurrying across the road to meet him. It was a fine summer evening and she had on a light print dress. When she got close to Michael that marvelous warm smile was on her face and she called, "Are you just back?"

"I came in late this afternoon," he said.

"You didn't stay long, did you, Mike?" she said. "It's awfully good to see you. You seem to have been away for about a month," she laughed.

Her joy at seeing him was so unrestrained that she began to feel a bit ridiculous. But it hadn't been going very well with her in the city. Day after day she was becoming more and more like a lost girl in the city. It happened this way: When she had a job as a fashion designer she seemed to know people and there were many places where she could go, and the city seemed to belong to her and she was at home there; but when she lost that job and took one in the dress department of a store, she got very little money and work for only a few days a week, and the city seemed to get much smaller because her experience became more and more restricted and her life more secluded. She had moved from place to place till she hardly knew anyone where she lived. After she had been out of work for some time it got that there was no place for her to go and no one she could borrow money from, and finally when she was completely separated from whatever life she had known in the city, she realized that she was lost. She had only that summer dress and a black silk one, trimmed with white, left. She had that pair of stockings with the little run in one of them carefully sewn, and that pair of shoes turned at the heels. When she had left the house that evening the electrical appliance salesman in the front apartment had said to his wife, "There she goes in that dress and those shoes. It's getting funny watching her," and the elderly Miss Gray, who gave a course of lectures on world affairs to young ladies who would come to her apartment on Friday evenings and pay twenty-five cents, hugged her starving gentility to her withered breast and whispered, "That little man who puts the food in the basket outside her door will get her and turn this place into a brothel and I won't stand for that." Yet on that warm summer night, when Anna put out her hand and touched Michael's arm her smile was warm and beautiful and at the moment she was content.

"I don't really know you at all, Mike," she said, "And yet as soon as I saw you going along the street and knew you were back I seemed to have known you a long time." But when Michael stood there stupidly waiting for her to say something about his father, she added awkwardly, "I guess I missed seeing you around."

"I wasn't away long enough for anything to change around here," he said, showing no friendliness, but just being polite, for he was anxious to catch up to Huck Farr and have a drink with him.

"Some things have changed," she said. "The little lady in the blue dress is gone."

"I don't know any little lady in a blue dress."

"You know the squat little one we watched one evening. She used to walk around the square and she wore the same light blue dress all the time."

"I never watched her. You told me about her."

"That's right. I'm the one who was watching her. I only saw her pick a man up once and that was only after she argued with him for about ten minutes. Maybe the police took her away."

At night from her window at the front of the apartment house she could see a bit of the square under the street light. On the good nights men out of work and wandering sat on the benches with newspapers beside them, and when they lay down on the benches they put the newspapers under their coats for warmth. Often they sang a kind of mocking hymn, then they laughed, and the hymn and the laughter held them all together there in the square, but if they made too much noise the policeman on the beat came along and chased them away. Whenever Anna heard that singing, or the burst of laughter, or the voice of the policeman drifting up to her window, it all seemed to become like the wail of the utterly lost, and then she was full of fear. Yet in the morning, if someone only spoke pleasantly to her, her natural gladness and dignity and joy were restored to her.

"Are you coming back to the house?" she asked.

"I'm in a hurry, Anna. Did you see Huck Farr pass this way?"

"I saw him at the corner."

"Which way was he going?"

"He was walking slow and he crossed the street."

"I promised to have a drink with him," he said, and he turned away and seemed ready to forget her so quickly that she stood there puzzled, watching him hurry away, and wondering if he had ever really liked her.

He went to the tavern on the corner where he had talked with his father that night, and through the haze of smoke he looked around for Huck Farr. He could hardly believe that he had let a friendly and tolerant man like Huck get away from him on such a night.

Someone was calling, "Michael, heh, Mike, over here." A round-faced young man with untidy hair and thick glasses and an air of personal loneliness was beckoning eagerly. He was a young Jew, Nathaniel Benjamin, who had just written his doctor's thesis in philosophy at the university and was waiting for a call to some great college. He lived across the road from Michael and was the loneliest young man in the neighborhood. In his time Nathaniel Benjamin had been at two minor universities, he had gone to France after a year at Harvard, because he had read the symbolist poets, and had become a disciple of T. S. Eliot. He got to France just in time to announce his conversion to the church. That was in 1928 when young intellectuals in America and England, but mainly in France, were announcing their conversions on all sides. His return to America was a kind of triumph, and his friends were desolate, for he was obviously two or three steps ahead of them in feeling the spirit of his time. But in two or three years times got very bad. There were newer and just as passionate conversions among the young men, only now they were all announcing their conversions to communism; and they jeered at Nathaniel, assuring him his intellectual position was as out of date now as knee breeches. They expected him to become an apostate. But that was where they were mistaken; they only made him unhappy; he had found something that had soothed his soul and made him more joyful than ever before, and he intended to fight savagely before he gave it up. Again and again he rushed to the attack, for he loved disputation, but unfortunately he was lost in the new intellectual world of economics. There was one night with Michael, at the time of the Dollfuss liquidation of the socialists in Austria, when Nathaniel was for the first part of the evening an ardent royalist, then as he was attacked, a fascist, and then, when his heart began to be touched by the plight of the socialists and he almost wept, he was a socialist. By intellectual conviction, however, he was really a royalist, even though he was from Detroit. His friends all called him the Detroit royalist. After one of those long wrangling disputes with Michael, or anybody else, he used to go home and feel dreadfully alone, wondering, as he knelt down and prayed in his room, why the hand of God did not reach down and caress him. He would get into bed and go over and over the argument. For many hours he lay awake, trying to be patient as he waited for day to come so he could rush out and crush his antagonist with a vicious, but much more carefully prepared, intellectual attack. It seemed really that no one on earth would give him a chance to show the real tenderness and longing for love that was in his nature.

Making a little bow he said to Michael, "Won't you sit down at my table? I want to say at the start I don't think for a moment your father would have a hand in that fellow's death."

"Thanks. I didn't know you knew anything about my father."

"I've known you a long while, though, and your father looks like you in his pictures. I don't believe those stories at all. He looks like a fine man."

"Thanks, thanks, Nathaniel. I think I'll have a drink. Do you want another drink?"

"All right. But I wasn't just making a perfunctory remark. I say to everybody what I just said to you." He spoke with that softness and concern that Mike had sometimes felt in him when they were talking and sharing the same enthusiasm for anything. Behind his glasses his eyes shone brightly, his voice was as soft and tender as a woman's, and no one would have believed at that moment that the slightest statement of an intellectual difference of opinion would have started him roaring like a mad bull with the barbs in its neck. With Nathaniel speaking softly and slowly, and with the warm friendly voices of working men all around him, Michael was eager for consolation, and he said, "I feel terrible about the way it turned out up there in the country. We were all so friendly. I'm talking like this to you, Nathaniel, because you seem to feel so sympathetic about it. It just happened that way, as though no one had anything whatever to do with it." But even while he spoke eagerly a desolation grew in him that he could hardly stand, and he stopped, and for a long time he stared at Nathaniel, resenting the way Nathaniel wanted to soothe him and sympathize with him. Then he blurted out, "The trouble with Christians like you is that you're never happy unless you have someone to pity. You want to be sur-rounded by wretched people so you can exhibit in full swing the tenderness in your nature and the love you think you ought to have for people. There's no use talking about the way I feel about that drowning with a guy like you because you wouldn't understand it. You're a guy who believes in free will and the responsibility of the individual soul, and the soul's destiny, and all that crap, aren't you?"

Nathaniel's face got white. "Yes, I do," he said politely. It had not occurred to him that he would have to wrangle again tonight, but he got ready to defend himself by leaning across the table belligerently. "I believe in those things," he said.

"Sure you do. You're the perfect fall guy for any obsolete Christian theologian."

"If you had even the faintest conception of what the words meant you wouldn't talk like that."

"I'm willing to discuss it. I'm willing to listen to whatever you have to say. You're the old logician, go on now, start telling me about it." Michael was full of glee because he had noticed that Nathaniel's lower lip was beginning to tremble. "I ask you, Nathaniel, old socks, because you know all the answers and I don't. I'm just an engineer."

"Ah yes, a roll of drums and then the trumpets, tata tata taa, tata tata taaaa. Gentlemen, I give you Mr. Aikenhead, the modern man."

"Sure, that's me."

"The modern man, no hope in anything, no faith in anything. Just immersed in matter. The young modern …"

"Listen, what do you want me to be? An antique like you are? Just something to put on the mantelpiece? Let it pass. I'm not insulting you. I just want to know if you believe there's usually a chain of causes going way back that shape the most trivial event."

"I don't choose to discuss it with you."

"Why?"

"Since you started the insulting, I'll tell you. There's no use talking about it because you wouldn't understand me.

Frankly, I've always regarded you as my intellectual inferior. Your scientific point of view … Don't make me snicker. You and your priests of science! You want to know anything about life and you ask some little guy who has been looking at a bit of rock all his life with his nose pressed against it, and he blinks his eyes in the sunlight and answers and then shuts himself up in his test tube again and everybody shouts that science has spoken." Nathaniel took a deep breath and looked as if he wanted to pound Michael with his words.

"I didn't want to quarrel," Michael said. "Why can't any-body talk to you for two minutes without starting to quarrel? I just wanted to ask you a few questions I thought were up your alley. You were talking about Dave Choate's death, and it occurred to me that it must have been accidental. Things like that don't happen because people want them to happen. Now don't get sore. I'm just saying you can't sit in judgment of any act unless you know the circumstances surrounding it. We're all conditioned, aren't we? If one man has money and the other hasn't, they can't look at anything in the same way. Look at Dave that was drowned and look at a guy like me. He had lots of ready money and a good time, but I sit around in one-horse rooming houses waiting for something to turn up. We don't play in the same league. We never meet. That's what I felt up there in the country. My father and Dave belonged in another world than mine and they have their own problems and their own drownings and it's hard for me to understand them. I don't want to, either. It doesn't touch me at all. Of course it doesn't mean the same to you. A guy like you can sit back and make absolute judgments about human beings. Here's what I mean. I know everyone of us went up there with the best intentions in the world and look at the way it turned out; all by itself it turned into a mess. You mean to say there was anything the matter with us wanting to go up there? Nobody wanted it to happen? Was it the will of God? If it wasn't anybody's choosing why do we have to take it? Nobody wanted that from your God. We'd like to hand it back. It's not good. You know why bastards like you talk about God's plan and free will … This just occurred to me and you can have it for nothing. Nothing ever happened to you. That's why you want to pity everybody. You've got to get in somehow but not close enough to get hurt."

"Why do you talk to me as though I were a swine?" Nathaniel muttered.

"I was just stating your point of view and trying to state it correctly."

"You've never tried to understand my position. I never said anybody was ever absolutely free to make any kind of a choice. If the passions overwhelm you you can hardly be free. That's what St. Thomas Aquinas would say."

"Then you'd hardly ever be responsible for anything you did when you were worked up?"

"You might be just free enough to have just a little influence on whatever happened. I think St. Thomas would say that."

"But I'm asking you what you'd say?"

"That's what I'd say."

"You're just a talking machine and I have to sit here listening to your favorite records, Nathan, my love."

"I'll fix that for you. I'll go. You're an ignorant uneducated bully with your smug smiling face immersed in matter. You're just anti-semitic and I despise you."

"Why am I anti-semitic? I've got more Jewish friends than you have yourself."

"Then why did you call me Nathan?"

"Isn't that your name?"

"You called me Nathaniel up to that point. It's your sly way of trying to be insulting."

"Baby, baby, bunting, Nathan's gone a hunting."

"I don't care to see you again. Remember that. You're

incapable of grasping a single idea. You can't stop thinking about yourself. I don't want to listen." Nathaniel, feeling wretched, got up and left Michael sitting alone at the table.

Smirking to himself, Michael sat there remembering Nathaniel's white, quivering face, remembering how he had looked so hurt, and he thought proudly, "I put it all over him. He bleeds easily. That'll do him good. Imagine a guy like that, the greatest egotist in the world, telling me to stop thinking of myself. He knew that I wiped the floor with him intellectually. I wish I could have told him that the real cause of Dave's death could be found way back in my father's life, and that I was full of economic resentment. He might see that. Sometimes he's sharp." As he sat there he was so pleased with himself that his face lit up and was like the face of a man in an audience who is applauding a persuasive and eloquent speaker, and he thought, "I like this dump here," and he grinned at the waiter and wanted to wave his hand at the customers. A stout blonde girl who was with a man who had quaint handlebar moustaches, nodded to him, liking his eager, smiling face. Charmed by such friendliness, Michael raised his beer glass to her as though enjoying a personal triumph.

When he left the tavern he walked home like a man who has a strong conviction of his own simple dignity. He sat on the bed and took off his shoes and looked at them together on the floor. It had been a fine thing to look at his shoes in that way night after night. When he got into bed it was splendid to find himself falling into the quick justified sleep of one who is very tired.

But he began to dream, and his sleep was light, and then there was a kind of half sleep where he was trying not to dream and for a while it was as though he were awake, with an extraordinary series of pictures of unfamiliar places running through his mind, and behind each one of these unrecognizable pictures was the sound of faintly lapping water, the lapping sound always getting a little louder, like the sound of small waves striking the boat in a lake in which the water was getting rougher, and then there was just the darkness of night and the vast immeasurable expanse of water. Then there was nothing to see but night, nothing but night upon the water, nothing to look at but the loneliness of night on the wide water, nothing but night, then nothing but dark water. Michael was sure he was dreaming, but when he heard that cry, "Help, Mike," rising right out of the water, "Help, Mike," rising and sinking into the water he sat up in bed and was full of terror, and he trembled. "I was dreaming," he said, but the feeling of dread was so strong he could not lie down again; he let his head sink down slowly on the pillow, yet he was crouching, ready to spring up if he heard anyone cry out again. While he was wide awake his fear was so magnified by the night, and his terror so deepened by his abandonment to his desolation, and his guilt so deeply implanted in him that he tried desperately to remember his eloquent conviction of a few hours ago when he had been sitting in the tavern. Then he thought he saw his father's face looking at him, and he was nodding his head, nodding so sadly that Michael began to hate the sight of him; and so that he wouldn't think of anything he began to repeat with a kind of firm childishness, "One, two, three, four, five, six, seven, all good niggers go to heaven. One, two, three, four, five, six, seven…." But the night was very long. "One, two, button my shoe. Three, four, knock at the door," the easiest, the most childish, the most formidably simple things to say. The most welcome sound he ever heard was the sound of the milkman running along the alley and rattling his bottles, and the sound of the horse jogging and the shod hoofs clattering on the road, for it meant it was nearly dawn, and there was an end and soon it would be light.

Fourteen

Day after day as he sat in his room in the mornings reading the newspapers that would not let the country forget the drowning and his father, he began to feel that soon they would have to turn and seek someone else. Soon they might even start whispering about him. But by now he felt very crafty. He went over and over a plan he had made to leave the city. There was about one hundred and ten dollars he had saved working in the summers in good times and he withdrew this money from the bank and hid it in his room in the mattress of his bed so it would be always there for his security if ever he had to go. When he was reading the papers he sometimes heard footsteps outside the door, and there would be a soft rapping, and when he did not answer and did not move, the footsteps would go away. Once his disputatious friend, Nathaniel Benjamin, came to the door and called out mildly, "Are you there, Mike?" and while Michael was thinking, "If he comes in here arguing with me again I'll kill him," he heard him going slowly down the stairs.

Sometimes he longed to be in the company of old friends, but when he met men he had known at the university on the street, and they stopped and shook hands warmly and swore they would come and see him he was sure they would never come, for they knew he wasn't working and would be unable to do anything they wanted to do. If he stood on the street talking with them he became embarrassed and he stuttered and felt ashamed, for he seemed to have no dignity. It got so that he wanted to pass by without seeing them.

The wretched meals he was eating so he wouldn't spend too much of his little hoard of money, the utterly exhausting night thoughts he had before sleeping, and the dreams that were so vivid, precise and so perfectly memorable that they often continued to flow through his thoughts when he was awake had begun to make him a bit light-headed during the daytime. Once when he was on the street looking at a tree in the square and at an old man who was sitting on a bench and rubbing one knee, this sudden light-headedness came, and it was accompanied by a kind of taut brilliance in his vision that made the bench and the square shift and waver uncertainly, as though someone wiggling the slide in a magic lantern had caused the image on the screen to go like that; he wondered if the whole world wasn't like that, just something inside him like the slide in a magic lantern. At night once, when he was in his room, he had another one of those brilliant and erratic moments, and he felt that he had an intimation of his destiny; he felt he could follow clearly his predestined movements on the earth. But he resisted this notion so strongly that he cried out, "Sure, I can see what's expected of me. I don't intend letting anybody find out anything. Am I to let the whole city know I'm to blame for Dave's death just because I didn't like him or his mother? Oh, yes, like hell I will," he mocked himself.

In his long, half-waking dream he saw the lake again. Men and women rose up out of the water, and they kept rising up and he had to keep watching till he recognized his mother, a sad-eyed mother sorrowing over all those men and women who were rising up like the race of men on Judgment Day; she had received them and sorrowed over them and then there was nothing left but the lapping water. It got so that Michael would lie there waiting till he could see the water in the night.

There were never any stars or a shore or a single sound. When he couldn't sleep and was so tired he was dizzy, he got up and sat rigidly at his desk recalling again and again the moment when his father had come into that room for the first time. Starting with his father's return into his life he began to build, in the most precise detail, an entirely different sequence of events that might have followed that return. Again he saw the two of them, shaking hands warmly there in the room, and then it was the next day, quickly like that, and he was driving to the country with Ross Hillquist, just as they had done except that it wasn't a rainy day; they didn't even stop at the hotel in the village; he never even saw Dave's face at the window and they drove past the hotel, through the village and on to the house; in the morning they had gone fishing.

Sitting there at his desk with the city noises coming in through the window, with the old scraping sounds on the stairs, and with someone sometimes knocking at his door, he even began to hear long beautiful sentences he might have spoken to his father, and his father's long answers pleased him immensely. So bright and intense were the pictures he made in his mind and so clear the words he imagined he heard that in his great longing he began to believe that this actually was the way it had been. Such a yearning for these things that might just as easily have happened swept through him that he sat there tired and rigid, neither hearing nor feeling anything and refusing to let himself live outside those imagined scenes. Then he got up and whispered, "That was the way it should have been. Oh, why couldn't it have gone along like that when it started so well? Didn't the good will in me mean anything?" As he looked out the window he felt such anguish in his soul he cried out, "It's always been rotten for me. I've never had anything but bad luck. I just wanted to work and be prosperous. Am I never going to get a break? I leave them all because I want to be alone. I wait on tables at college. That's all right, you understand. I'm satisfied to look after myself, but afterwards I can't get a job. I spend four years getting ready, then I can't get a job. If I had had a job I never would have gone up there. I would never have wanted my father to do anything for me. Who the hell asked him to come near me? I didn't ask him for a cent. What brought him here then? It was his own fault. Blame whatever brought him here, don't blame me. I didn't want to hurt anybody, do you hear? Leave me alone, leave me alone. God Almighty, leave me alone."

He pressed his face hard against the window, as though crying out to all that crowded part of the city on that spring night. Breathless and full of bitterness, he wondered whom he was crying out to. He listened and heard that snatch of bawdy song coming up from a bench on the square, where a few men would sit nearly all night because it was such a good night, and opening the window wider, he shouted out, "For Christ's sake, shut up! Can't you let a guy sleep? Get out of there! Leave me alone!" His voice sounded weak, helpless and frantic against the surge of city noise. He cried out only against the meaningless confusion of living, and was impatient of the existence of all other people.

Then he listened, hearing someone knocking on the door, listening with that feverish, dangerous brightness in his head again. His heart was fluttering as if he were very hungry or very weak. With immense gladness he realized that whoever had been there had gone away.

He heard the tapping on his door again the following night when he was very tired and wanted to go to bed early. At first he was quiet, with his heart pounding, and then he called out sharply, "Come on in."

Anna Prychoda, whom he could not remember having seen for days, was there, with a hesitant, shy expression on her face. Instead of coming in she looked at him doubtfully for a long time. She had on her one good dress, a black dress with a shining white satin collar, which gave her fair hair a startling bright golden shade. People in the apartment house were watching Anna Prychoda with a growing excitement now. It was as though they were all in a little circle around her, kneeling down with excited faces, watching her crawling like an insect to some place where there was security, and always stumbling and falling back. Miss Gray, the lecturer, said, "She's deliberately egging that little man on. I know girls like that. She's just a little rat trap all set to catch him. She ought to be told to get out of here."

"She owes two months' rent, but I'll bet anybody two dollars that Huck Farr doesn't lay a hand on her," the janitor said.

"I'll bet two dollars she's with Huck inside of a week," the electrician said.

"He'll never get her. If he was going to get her he'd have got her before this, wouldn't he?" his wife said.

"I'll make it five to three they're together in a week."

"I'll tell the owner what's going on here."

"I'd take it as an even-money bet."

"She doesn't even speak to the guy."

"That don't matter. They get a little closer together all the time." They watched her like this, and sometimes thought about her while they worked. She waited at Michael's door, testing the words she was going to use, watching him all the time in that shy, wondering way. Finally she said, "Hello, Mike."

"Hello, Anna," he said. "Where have you been?"

"I've been around. I've looked for you but I haven't seen you," she said. "I tapped on the door a couple of times but I guess you were out or asleep. Do you sleep during the day?"

"No, I go out. Do you want to know where I go?"

"Not now. I wanted to ask you something."

"Why don't you ask, Anna? Why are you so shy?"

"I don't know. You just don't look the same, Mike."

"So I don't look the same, eh? What looks so different about me?" he asked irritably.

"You look excited."

"I'm not excited in the slightest. You mean you've tapped on my door just to tell me I look excited. As a matter of fact, I'm bored, Anna. Vastly and stupidly bored. What did you want to ask me?"

"I wanted to ask you about Mr. Farr."

"I can tell you all about him. An honest, industrious, conscientious young man who always manages to get along in the world without having anyone tread on his toes. He never butts into anybody's business. Can I say anything more than that?" The half-mocking way he answered her disappointed her, and she turned and stared down at the worn bit of green carpet on the floor, and then with the toe of her brown and badly scuffed shoe she began to make a little pattern on the carpet, going over and over this little pattern while he watched her in a rapt way, as if she were making a sign on the floor that would last forever. Tonight her neck looked very beautiful, for she had curled up the ends of her fair hair into a bunch of tiny curls. When she looked up from the carpet she was beseeching him to be aware of what was in her thoughts. Then she said, "I didn't know much about Mr. Farr. Tonight he asked me to go out with him. I didn't know what to do, because I don't really know him and there's something about him I don't like." Taking a deep breath, she watched him with that shy earnestness, then she said jerkily, "I thought I'd ask you if Huck Farr was all right. You were the only one I'd rely on because you know him and you know me, and we've been friendly." Her face was beginning to light up with a desperate hope while she waited and saw that he was hesitating.

Then he said, "He's a grand guy. Huck's as steady as the Rock of Ages," for he was remembering how he had longed for the consolation of Huck's company the other night in the tavern; while Anna stood there with the hope going out of her eyes, he was achieving in his mind an astonishingly simple relationship with someone; Huck and he were two men together, and Anna was a woman. So he said in the way any man might help out another man, who was testing out a woman, "Huck's a pretty good guy, Anna."

"If he wanted me to be his girl …"

"Sure he does. We all know he does."

"Would you go out with him if you were me?"

"I'd go out with him. He's ace high with me."

"I just wanted to ask you, that's all," she said, but she did not go, and for a long time she stood there studying that pattern she had made with the toe of her shoe on the floor, and by her persistence making him watch it too, as if she hoped, by having them both concentrate on the same thing, to make him feel what was in her. But he only wondered what she was trying so hard to avoid saying. Then she went reluctantly, turning her fair head at the door, with the eagerness all gone from her face, and she said lifelessly, "Thanks, Mike," and then she was gone.

Feeling like any ordinary man who had helped another commonplace man, Michael went into Huck's apartment where Huck, standing before the dresser mirror, was adjusting his elegant striped tie. "Huck, I'm your little pal," he said.

"All right, pal. Where have you been these days?"

"I've been sitting around, thinking. It's extraordinary how it makes you feel. You just sit there and never see your friends. Who do you think was in my place now? Your little Anna."

"What did she want with you? I thought I was the one making a play for her."

"She wanted to get the simple low-down on you. You know what I said? I said you were the Rock of Ages and all she had to do was cling to you."

"You should have told her she was my Rock of Ages because she's sure cleft for me," Huck said, holding out his small and lovely hands and contemplating his manicured nails. He couldn't stop smiling; whichever way he turned, he smiled his knowing little grin, and he got a bottle of beer and put it down in front of Michael and said, "Drink it while I go on dressing."

As he stood in front of the mirror he looked a little like a chorus boy, for he loved fine flashy clothes, and he was really pretty when he had some sleep and was rested. "There's something about a girl like Anna that makes it pretty hard to keep your hands off her," he said. "I love them when they're soft like that. I mean bright faced and firm and eager on the surface with a lot of spirit, but with something very soft underneath in them that makes you follow them along the street longing to push them over. By God, when they look like that they haven't got a chance of getting away …"

"Oh, sure, you step in there and take your cut at the ball just like we all do. It doesn't cost anything to make a pass at them."

"I get to first base every time. I bust them right on the nose every time. And they got to be good to play in my league. I'll tell you something, and no kidding, Mike. Anybody can get them. You just got to be nice to them. Show them little attentions. I mean when you're crossing the road with them take them by the arm like you cared a lot, and then help them on the street cars, see? And once you get them feeling soft for you they're easy to push over."

"I've seen you with some awful little tarts just the same."

"Why pass up any of them? I'd go for a snake if someone would hold its hips," Huck said.

They talked about women and both wanted the same thing; they liked each other; and Michael began to remember, one by one, the names of all the little chippies he had ever known, names sounding soft and warm and lovely now, names like Margaret and Irma and Mary and Frankie, and that high yellow girl, Estelle, who kept cutting her wrists and wanting to die; he longed to lose himself again in the warmth of their easy ways. His face brightened, and his voice was soft and lazy, because he had this delightful feeling of comradeship in him, but when he looked over at Huck, who was all dressed now, he felt suddenly that it was like watching a man eating a splendid, shiny, rosy, red apple while you waited for the core.

He didn't like this feeling at all, and he said awkwardly, "Thanks for the beer, Huck, I'm going."

"See me in the morning and I'll tell you how she went," he said.

When he was alone, Michael remembered how Anna had looked back, pleading with him, and he muttered, "She's nothing to me. I don't see why I think about her at all," yet he paced up and down, listening intently for the sound of her feet on the stairs, or the sound of Huck coming out to meet her. At last he heard Huck's footsteps in the hall, then stopping to wait at the head of the stair, and then there was the light slow measured footstep coming along the hall, and then the broken tread of two people who were not in step at all clattering down the stairs.

Rushing to the window, Michael waited for them to come along the sidewalk in front of the square. There they came, passing under the light, with Huck's shoulders swaying, with him no taller than Anna and his head low on his shoulders. He was holding her arm protectively and his face kept turning to her, and for a magical moment their bodies swayed together in the light and then swayed out into the shadow, and the light just touched her ankle, and then they were gone. "I wonder where he's taking her," Michael thought, remembering how much like a stranger she had looked when she came into the room, a stranger in great trouble, and he had sent her away to go crossing through the square, a human being too tired to resist any longer. She was passing the benches where so many men sat around waiting hopelessly. "She's nothing to me," he repeated, resenting the sadness he felt within him. Then he grabbed his hat and hurried out to the street.

Crossing the square, he could not see them and he began to run, and with each echoing footfall he kept hearing himself say, "You go with Huck. He's all right," as if he would hear it forever and ever. The words and his footfalls beat into his heart, yet he insisted, even as he ran, "I've got enough to worry about. Why couldn't she leave me alone? I don't want to inter-fere with anything."

At Oakley's cafeteria he caught up with them, and he stood outside pressing his face against the window, watching Anna look up at Huck from time to time as if she were puzzled by his marvelous politeness. The waiter had brought a plate of ham and eggs and toast for her and Huck was just having a sand-wich.

When he went into the restaurant he sat down solemnly beside them, and Huck, a little surprised to see him, said, "Hello, are you going to have something to eat?" in his bright, hard way. Anna only looked up once, then her mouth opened in wonder and she turned away sullenly.

"I don't want to eat anything. I don't feel well," Michael said, and he smiled at them like an innocent boy who was glad to be there and tremendously interested in anything they might say. His childish interest was so persistent it was hard for Huck to make any intimate gesture to Anna, for if he whispered or stroked her hand, Michael leaned over, full of profound curiosity, waiting to hear the slightest whispered word.

At last Huck said sharply, "Why don't you go home, Mike? What are you hanging around for? We've got things to do."

"I just wanted company, that's all," Mike said.

Anna's face was sullen, and whenever she looked at him she sneered a little, and he knew that she had become one with Huck Farr in despising him. If Michael glanced at her inno-cently, she glared at him, and once she leaned over and said very softly, "Why don't you go away? Why do you sit there like that staring at us? I don't want you with us." She was sure he was trying to humiliate her; her face was full of shame, but her blue eyes were hardening with hatred of him. "Don't you understand what we say? Go 'way," she whispered.

"What's the matter with him, Anna?" Huck asked.

"What do I know about him? He's your friend."

"That's right. Heh, Mike, you're giving me the jitters," Huck said, and when he leaned close to Mike his pretty face was hard, his soft, sensual mouth was twisted to one side and his eyes had a bright, restless look in them. As he waved his head jerkily from side to side he looked like a little guy getting ready to step up and smack a big guy on the jaw. "Don't start getting me sore, Mike," he said. "You know how it'll go if I get sore. What are you trying to do, hand me the bird?"

"I never met such people. I just sit here with you because I want company and …"

"You're lousy company, Mike."

"I haven't got started yet. For all you know I may have a mouth organ in my pocket and I might be good with it and then you'd roll into the aisle there…."

"Close your hand quick, Mike. Now open it. There, you've got it now. Put your hat on it and take it home."

"What have I got?"

"The bird you've been handing me," Huck said.

Michael felt Anna's sullen hatred in the way she watched him, as though he were obscene, and when she smiled at Huck, he knew she was mocking him, but he just sat there enduring this humiliation when really he longed to go.

In a little while Huck nodded at Anna and told her to get up. She looked terribly ashamed as he took her firmly by the arm and led her out of the cafeteria. Michael sat there alone and thought, "They can't fool me. I know where he'll take her. They've gone around to the Brunswick Arms to have a drink. He'll try and get her a bit tipsy," and he, himself, went out to the street. When he was with the crowd on the sidewalk where hundreds of round-faced, swarthy men and women were lazily strolling on this warm summer evening, where under the street lights boys and girls were standing close together with their elbows pressing into each other and sometimes laughing softly, he said to himself, "I wanted so much to get up and leave them, yet I sat there helplessly. It was terrible sitting there. It got so I couldn't move. It was just like dying there." He hurried along to the Brunswick Arms, dodging people who walked in groups, longing to know why he had let himself be humiliated, wondering how he could ever bear to be with them again, yet knowing by the beating of his heart that if he did not see them in the tavern, he would be weak with disappointment.

They were sitting together at a table in the corner of this gaudily decorated tavern where most of the neighborhood street sluts found a man for the evening, and Huck was leaning against Anna, who looked soft, lovely and unresisting, and he was whispering as if he wanted to put out his hand and feel the tips of his fingers sinking into her flesh, just that, and then draw away contented.

They looked at him, and their faces were dead for him, but he smiled and sat down and ordered a drink, for he no longer cared whether they wanted him there or not. He drank three beers rapidly, one after the other. And Huck, who was getting frantic, leaned over and whispered to him, "Can't you see I've got work to do? Am I carrying you around like a watch charm?" His whispering voice quavered a little because the longing for Anna in him was very great, and he went on, "What kind of a mug are you turning out to be, letting me down like this? Are you stupid, Mike, you bastard? Go over there by yourself, and cut yourself a nice paper doll."

"I thought you were fond of me. Haven't you got any influence with your man, Anna? Don't you want me here?" Mike said.

"I think you've gone crazy," she said. The strength that had led her from Michael's place, to Farr's room, and to the street and this tavern, that kind of strength that had grown as her despair and her hunger and her loneliness deepened day after day, could not carry her much further, and she half got up as she spoke, and her eyes were wild, but she only shook her head, and they thought she was going to cry. While Huck was pulling at her arm, Michael grew frightened, and he said, "If you don't want me, all right. I'm on my way," and he left them, looking for some place to sit where he could watch them.

Near the door he saw his old friend, William Johnson, sitting alone, staring at an empty beer glass, and he was full of joy, and he went over and sat down at his friend's table.

William Johnson, who had been a dentist, was a thin, tall fellow with a thick blond moustache. At one time Michael had thought him the wittiest fellow he had ever known, but in the last few years, especially after he had married a rigid-minded girl, he had become serious and studious, he had given up dentistry and had become a Marxian economist, and now he wanted to get into newspaper work. He and his wife talked about nothing but politics and whenever he disagreed with her she threatened to leave him.

Last week, before going up to the country, Michael and Mr. and Mrs. William Johnson had sat in this tavern discussing the class war, and the Johnsons, leaning across the table ardently, had repeated over and over the one important question, "Are you with us? You're an engineer. There'll be work for you to do. You're important to us. Are you willing to work for a classless society? If not, then say so, and to hell with you." And as Michael sat down with William Johnson he remembered how he and his wife had been so passionately concerned the other night that the poor and the exploited should be given justice, he remembered their concern for the happiness of many humble and simple people, and now his own face lit up warmly, and he said, "You're just the man I want to see tonight, Bill." But William Johnson nodded coolly and said nothing.

"What's the matter, Bill, don't you want me to sit with you?"

"Not particularly, Mike. We know how we feel after our discussion last week."

"You're not still thinking of that, surely? I was just kidding, Bill. I was kidding about what I thought were your excesses.

You can be funny one night, can't you? You can have a comic aspect like anybody else, can't you? I didn't disagree with you, either. I thought it was funny when your wife said that Stravinsky was just another manifestation of the breakdown of the bourgeois spirit and there'd be no sad songs after the revolution. I said nuts to that. I thought it was excessive when the pair of you insisted all people would begin to think alike then. Just a little excessive. But I wasn't laughing at you and your wife. I don't know what made you think I was."

"It's all right, Mike. I've nothing against you except that you're an individualist and you date horribly."

"But I wasn't laughing at you, Bill."

"Why argue about it? I'm for drawing the lines sharp and clear."

"What lines?"

"You're an individualist; you're immersed in your own petty problems, and you'd be a social fascist."

"I'm nothing of the sort. I'm an ordinary human being," Michael insisted, almost pleading with his friend, his voice rising. For a long time he looked at his friend till he began to see more than his thin face with the nervous eyes; he began to see his friend as a man who had succeeded in giving order and dignity to his own life. He began to feel a strong surge of new life in his friend, and it was not just a power that was in his friend's savage, emphatic words, or the strength in the economic theory that had changed his life; it seemed to Michael that the history of all men, through the faith of men like William Johnson, was given at last a splendid meaning, that there in their own time such men were directing it toward a goal. Bewildered people like himself, Michael thought, found only silliness and confusion in their lives, yet there was William Johnson proclaiming that a human being could find dignity carrying on the struggle of all the humble people who ever lived on the earth. There was such a faith in Johnson, such a feeling for the flow of time, Michael thought, that he, himself, began to feel humble, and he longed to free himself from his distress by losing himself in his friend's disinterested hope for the poor of the world.

He looked over at Anna, who sat there in her black and white dress, solemn and wondering, and he smiled eagerly; then he thought of the men in the square whose voices drifted up to him at night; they might all go forward together, moving along together with William Johnson to the reward of the dispossessed, the fruits of the earth. And he thought, too, "Dave Choate's death would be simply an economic matter for Bill Johnson. I resented Dave's useless, parasitical life, but any passion or dislike we had for each other was just an unimportant, individual passion. The only thing that is really important is that all of us in this room and people like us all over keep together and get some security."

Michael pleaded with his friend, "Why should we quarrel, Bill? I'm not working and you're not doing too well either. I feel lousy these days. We ought to stick together, no matter what we think. Do you get what I'm driving at, Bill?"

Bill was worried, for he was thinking of the intellectual ardor of his young wife, and he said at last, "It's no good, Mike. You're my political enemy. It's hard to say that because you're not a bad guy. But there'll be even harder things than that to do." And because he was of a warm and friendly nature he added, "Please don't start reducing it to a matter of personal friendships."

And Michael, feeling terribly disappointed, looked over at Anna, whose face now showed a dogged desire to make herself attractive to Huck. "See that girl over there in the black dress with the white collar?" Michael said to Bill.

"You mean the blonde?"

"That's right. See the little guy? He's trying to make her."

"So are ten other guys with ten other women here."

"But that one, Anna – her name's Anna Prychoda – she's letting that guy push her over just because she's broke and sort of punch drunk from being pushed around in the city here. She's on her uppers and there's nothing for her to do but let that guy push her over because he's got a little money to feed her. It's pretty ordinary, but it's pretty tough, isn't it?"

"She's a sweet-looking little customer. She's got swell eyes. She's got a good shape too."

"But what about it?"

"That's easy. It's a perfect example of what goes on in society. It's a perfect example of economic necessity on her part. That's what's going on all over. It could all be settled by an economic adjustment. Don't you see, Mike, it's just an illustration of everything I've tried to tell you?"

"But what about the girl? Doesn't she worry you?"

"She's just an individual. What's happening to her may be tragic. I don't deny it, although even our conception of tragedy may have to change. She's an illustration of a larger issue and you can't stop to worry about her."

"Listen to me, Bill."

"Go ahead."

"You're not a fake, but you're dry and unfeeling. Your head's so full of abstractions and logical necessities you can't be touched by anything that's happening to a simple human being."

"It's all right with me, Mike, if that's what you think," Bill laughed.

"If you're as hard boiled as all that then I'm damned proud to be your political enemy," Michael said, and getting up angrily, and full of sympathy for Anna, he walked over and sat down beside her, and he was so silent that neither she nor Huck Farr knew what to say to him.

The curl was coming out of her hair and there was a stubborn look in her eyes that already seemed shrewder and wiser. While Huck had been whispering to her and squeezing her, she had been trying to show him some of the warmth and eagerness she knew he wanted. She was willing to give him whatever he wanted, only whenever she looked around the room a wondering desolation was in her eyes, as though she were thinking "It doesn't matter what becomes of me. Nothing at all can become of me. Nothing. Nothing." And there was such darkness in her that her eyes at times seemed to be closed and she could hardly see the faces, or hear the voices of men and women around her.

All evening, while Michael had mocked himself doing the things he did not want to do, there had been growing in him a deep concern for Anna which he could not feel strongly because he had so much pity for himself, but now the desolation he saw so clearly in her face, and the words of William Johnson, shocked him. There she was beside him, twenty-three years on the earth, maybe with good luck forty years more to go, and already they all were crushing the humanity in her; and while he had these thoughts, and watched her trying to give herself fully to Huck Farr, his concern at last became a surge of love.

Huck was sneering at him. "Back again, you bum?" he said.

"Sure, back again," Michael said. In the way he smiled Huck felt his contempt, and his own smooth pink and pretty face hardened and he became tense with a vicious, fearless fury. His lips looked as though they were rubbed and swollen and there was a reckless crazy look in his hard blue eyes. It was hard to believe such a smooth, small face could show so much passion. "I warned you once, Aikenhead," he said, shaking his finger like a towering big fellow who was bossing a job. "I won't warn you again."

Michael was toying with Anna's beer glass while he and Huck stared at each other; and then he picked up the glass and held it up against the light, and then he swung the glass in an arc and the beer, spilling out, splashed over Huck's head and over his shirt. Huck jumped up and screeched and made everybody in the tavern stand up. "I'll kick your guts out,

Aikenhead," he yelled as he grew frantic trying to wipe the beer off his shirt.

In a wondering, fumbling way Michael said, "I don't know why I did that. I never threw a glass like that in my life. I never thought of hitting you. I don't know what happened."

People from other tables and two waiters were standing there listening. One waiter was down on the floor wiping up the beer. "Why don't you say you meant it, you big yellow bastard, and then I'll break a bottle over your head?" Huck said.

"I'm not yellow. You know you're a little guy and can't get hurt, that's why you call me yellow."

"You haven't got the guts to say you meant it," Huck shouted, and then foul, vivid and startling words flowed out of him. "If you want this bitch here, why don't you say so? She's been sitting staring at you all night with her tongue out anyway. Go ahead, you push her over," and he grabbed his hat and pushed his way through the waiters and rushed out without looking back.

As everyone stared at Anna her face showed the shame she could not bear, and lowering her head, she hurried out, with Michael following a little way behind her.

On the street Michael tried to take Anna's arm, but she pushed him away; so he slowed down a little while she hurried ahead. Then he caught up to her again and took her arm, and again she pushed him away without speaking at all. She had been half running, and now she was tiring, and though she wouldn't let him touch her, she had to let him walk beside her. It was a beautiful, soft spring night, and they might have been out for a walk on such a night, walking along silent and thinking of each other and aware of no one else in the world, for that was the way the relief flowing through him made him feel; it filled him with gladness, no matter what she said, and he wanted only to be able to see the side of her face, or to reach out his hand and touch her arm as they walked through the city streets with the noise of traffic and the sharply rising and fading cries in the murmur of city life in the soft night air around them. It was hard for her to go on walking like that on the way back to the square, sometimes half running, without feeling the tenderness in him, yet when he tried to stop her under the light, when he tried to speak, she said sullenly, "Why are you following me? You must be out of your head, and you've got to leave me alone."

"It's all right just walking with you, isn't it?" he asked.

"You can walk where you want to, only don't touch me," she snapped at him.

"We'll go home together anyway," he said.

He tried to soothe her with soft words and break her sullen resentment. "It was terrible to have you go off with a guy like Huck," he said. "Why don't you pick on someone who'll give you a break? In some ways you don't seem to have any sense at all. You're just like a little girl." He tried to laugh but she wouldn't look at him.

When they were going up the stairs in the apartment house, with her ahead and him following, she didn't even turn and look back till she got to the top, and then with one hand on her hip, she said, "Will you please stop following me around like a dog? This has been going on all night and I'm tired now." But he stood at her door while she opened it, and then he stepped in quickly.

"You better get out of here and stop your clowning. I want to go to bed," she said. She sat there on the couch beaten, staring at him and waiting, and he felt her contempt and her desire to abuse him, but he only smiled and then sighed when she said, "I'll give you two minutes to get out of here."

"You couldn't have understood what being Huck's girl would amount to in the long run," he said.

"You stupid, stupid, stupid man, you've got no feeling. Anyway Huck really wanted me. That was something. That was something, you understand. I'm grateful to him for that.

As long as someone wanted me I could feel I was alive. I could feel I was a human being."

"Ah, so you're boasting."

"He'd have given me anything he could have got and I'd have a place to stay and something to eat."

"You think so, do you? You'd be surprised if I told you it was just that Huck could see you were a round heel."

"What's that?"

"A girl that anybody can push over. A girl that just flops over."

"All right. That's the way it was," she said sullenly. "What have you got to say about it?"

"Everybody around here knew it," he went on calmly. "They were all betting against you. The electrician downstairs and the sour lady who gives lectures and even the janitor who's a pretty good guy were all betting on Huck. I was the only one, the only one, mind you, who was backing you. You certainly let me down."

"You'd think I was a horse. You make a game of me. You're all the same." And then when he hesitated, she whispered, "If you don't get out of here quick I'll open the door and shout. I can't sit here any longer listening. I can't stand it. I can't stand it, I tell you."

"Just a minute now. Wait just a minute," he insisted. "I watched you going across the square. I went out and ran after you. You see how much it mattered to me?" and he looked so dreadfully sad that she began to believe he really cared for her. The consolation she found in his few words was already driving the hardness out of her. She remembered all the friendly little conversations they had ever had in the hall or on the street in the evenings. But she whispered suspiciously, "I don't believe you."

"Why are we whispering?"

"Because I don't want anyone to hear us here."

"I'm not making any noise, am I? I just kept dogging you

around. I was following you like a dog. Why do you think I was so worried?"

"What were you worrying about?" she asked, showing a little curiosity.

"I knew you didn't know what you were picking up in Huck. But he's a grand fellow in many ways, I've got to say that, only with women he's just like a mink and you've got a better chance of catching anything that's going around with him than with anybody else I know."

"Catch what?"

"What a little innocent you are! If there's anything you can catch from making the rounds of all the little tarts in the neighborhood you may be sure Huck's caught it and worked his way through and is ready to pass it along. He's a little mink, I'm telling you. I remember when I was a kid we used to all want to pick up a little street girl, but we were all scared, and we were scared no matter how much we wanted it. And look at you. Not scared at all. I could have gone up to Huck and just asked him if he was able to get around now and the chances are he would have thrown a fit. I say the chances are. In God's name, woman, you've got to watch who you hook up with. Don't you understand that? I guess you think it's just like catching a cold and no worse."

"I don't know anything about it."

"It didn't worry you at all, did it?"

"I know there are words for it, but they don't mean much to me."

"Good God, why do you think the city is full of clinics and the clinics are full of patients and the patients taking one painful treatment after another and limping around?"

"Girls don't think much about that," she said, and she began to cry softly.

"Do you want me to tell you about it so you'll be wiser next time?"

"No, please don't, it's too horrible. I was just crazy."

"There's something soft about you, Anna. It's lovely but it's soft, as if you always wanted to be giving something to people. You can't keep looking at everybody as if you want to hug them without getting hugged and then getting hurt. Men can feel whatever it is that's lovely and soft in you. They can tell as soon as they set eyes on you."

"Why didn't you warn me when I asked you about him?"

"Things have been going pretty bad for me. My life is pretty mixed up. I think of things, but then it's too late."

"I'm a dunce, I guess," she said humbly, and she was so grateful because he was earnest and worried.

"You certainly were helping yourself to a nice prize package. That's why I couldn't bear to let you out of my sight."

"I didn't know you were watching me," she whispered. "That was what..." The bit of gladness that had only touched her swiftly while he was speaking now began to flow through her. "Oh, Mike, I didn't know you felt like this. I didn't know you'd be so disappointed in me."

"I've been pretty mixed up these days. I could feel everything you were doing, but I couldn't think about it," he said.

His reverence for her showed in the way he touched her; he put his arm around her while she cried a little and her body trembled. Yet even while he was kissing her he kept looking at her sorrowfully. "She's very lovely. How soft and white and desperate she looks when she's crying," he thought. He tried to make her lift her head, and when he couldn't, he muttered, "It was terrible to see a fine girl like you getting hurt like that."

Looking up at him, she asked, "Were you sore, Mike, when you saw me with him?"

"I felt dreadfully unhappy watching you going down the street."

"I would have felt so different if I could have known you were there watching me and worrying a little. I knocked on your door twice last week," she said. In her wondering earnestness the words poured out of her, and sometimes she was mixed up, and sometimes, when he comforted her, there was a surge of hope in her. "I wasn't trying to provoke you. I wasn't trying to get you sore or be nasty," she said. "I didn't know how you felt, so I want you to forgive me. I wasn't trying to offend you, I just didn't care. Won't you forgive me?" she pleaded.

They lay close together, with their arms around each other, like two people who were scared of getting lost again. Her eyes were closed, and there was a little shadow on her full and lovely white throat. For a long time he looked at her, then he pushed at the shoulder strap of her black dress, and it came away easily from her white shoulder, and he felt the smoothness of her shoulder, and he kissed her breast. He kissed her breast three times. Then he put his head against her, and he felt so bewildered, he closed his eyes. They both seemed to need each other's love so much. His head was against her, and it was silent, and someone passed outside on the street, and a door closed downstairs, and the window shade rustled once, but while they lay there and it was silent, he began to hear the beating of her heart against his head, and soon he could hear nothing else but the beating of her heart, and it grew stronger, and it seemed to get louder and louder.

Fifteen

B UT IN THE morning, when he was at the corner restaurant getting a cup of coffee, he saw Huck Farr staring at him and smirking. Then he knew that Huck despised him as a man and as a comrade. He knew then that he was at last beyond even the infinite tolerance of Huck Farr.

"I had no right to get in Huck's way," he thought. "I was trying to tell Anna about him, but supposing he was able to tell her about me. He's free to do anything he wants. I'm not free. It's all a mess," and he strode by Huck without even glancing at him. When he was outside and striding along the street he was so disgusted with himself he couldn't bear to remember the words he had used to lecture her. All day long he kept away from his place so he wouldn't meet her.

Early in the evening someone knocked on his door, and when he opened it, there was Anna, waiting candidly, as if she were presenting herself to him. He resented the way she did not look shy at all. The little fair curls were on the back of her neck and she had on her black and white dress again. "I looked for you earlier in the day, Mike," she said, "but I couldn't find you." She smiled with such a fine, warm, unembarrassed gladness that he had to turn away from her. "Aren't you feeling well this morning?" she asked doubtfully. The way he had talked to her last night, the love she thought she had felt in him had given her at last a feeling of security. But while she waited and grew a little shy, he began to hear again the ridiculous words he had spoken last night, and now they not only sounded stupid, but mocking and hypocritical. "I wish you'd forgive me for talking to you the way I did last night," he blurted out. "I had no right to talk to you like that."

"Why do you need to be forgiven? You felt like saying it and maybe it had to be said because it was terribly true."

"But I didn't feel like saying it. Don't you understand? I didn't mean to lecture you like that and interfere with you. I don't know how I got started."

"I loved hearing you say it the way you did. I wish you wouldn't apologize."

"Why didn't you start laughing at me and then I would have stopped? I made a fool of myself," he muttered, "You should have stopped me."

"I felt more like crying than laughing," she said, coming right into the room. Then her face shone with joy and she threw her arms impulsively around his neck and began to rub her nose into his cheek. "Last night I was so very unhappy. Tonight I am happy. Don't you understand that?" she asked.

"Anna, Anna, you must not misunderstand me. I apologize to you. I didn't mean to make you feel that way. I was talking like an actor, like a ham actor, just for the sake of talking so I wouldn't have to think of anything."

"Then you didn't mean what you said at all?"

"I don't really know what I said. God knows what I said that I ought to be ashamed of. I just know it was false and I wanted to impress you, and now I apologize because I respect you."

"You weren't scolding me? You weren't disappointed in me?"

"No, why should I be disappointed in you, Anna? You know yourself it was like listening to a Sunday school teacher and really you're laughing at me now. I'll bet you've got your tongue in your cheek," he said, trying to be lively and gay.

"You mean it was like a joke?"

"It's a wonder you didn't throw me out on my ear. I'm terribly sorry, Anna. Isn't it all right now?" he said.

She looked as if she could never express her hatred of him, but she was so humiliated, she was unable to move. "I shouldn't have come here again," she whispered. Then she cried out, "You miserable smart alec," and she ran out of the room and downstairs.

In a panic he ran after her, chattering, "A guy can get talking like that. You just keep going on and then you get drunk with the sounds and you like it and you can't stop." But she had gone into her own apartment and the door was locked. "I can explain it to you, Anna," he said. "I was foolish talking like that, and now it's terrible to have to tell you I was foolish. But it's better to be honest about it, isn't it? I'm honest because I respect you."

But he heard no sound in the room, and he stood there, knowing he would never forget the way the life and the hope had gone out of her face.

He went out to the street, but wherever he went he kept thinking of that look of despair on her face, and when he began to feel he would never see her again, he knew how deeply he had hurt himself.

When he came across the square much later there were only a few lights in the windows of the apartment house. He was walking boldly, for by this time he had decided that he had to explain fully why he had insulted her, no matter what happened to him. Hurrying up the stairs to her place, he rapped on the door, and when she did not answer he pounded more urgently, pacing up and down the hall, feeling if he did not see her he would have to shout out her name.

Then the door was opened just a few inches in a guarded way, as if she had known by the impulsiveness of the knocking that he was there, and he saw just her mouth and her nose and her angry eyes. "Don't close that door. Please, Anna, you've got to listen. I don't know what I've been doing...." But that was all he had a chance to say, for she slammed the door, and he heard above the slamming noise a snatch of her words "loathsome mortal ... never ... my sight." And he was standing there in the hall staring at the solid brown door. So he would be able to think of something overwhelmingly persuasive, he looked away from the door and stared instead at the green carpet in the hall leading to the door. There was just that door between them, and when he listened he felt her on the other side, listening, too, and wanting to beat him. Then he began to mutter, "Anna, please open the door, Anna. If you just open the door for two minutes I'll not come in. Just listen to me and I'll go quietly. I think of you all the time, Anna. I know what I'm saying now. Did you hear that? I think of you all the time. Please, please, please, forgive me. All I ask is that you say you forgive me because I insulted you. I see very clearly how it turned out last night, but you must understand, Anna, that I did not want it to be like that."

"Please go 'way. It's late," he heard her mumble.

More urgently, for he was sure she was listening now, he said, "I must apologize if I never do another thing in this world. Don't you see how ridiculous I am? If you could only forgive me and see that I was funny, very, very funny. Then you would laugh. I was astonished that you did not laugh at me, for I'm nearly always funny. Sometimes I don't intend to be funny but it's better to assume that I want to be comical because it will turn out to be funny. You remember you called me a clown yourself last night, Anna. You said 'Stop clowning.'"

And Anna, who was on the other side of the door, must have felt the despair that was destroying him, for he became inarticulate, and for a moment he could not go on. It was then that she opened the door a little again. She was terrified by his wild words. She felt other people would stand out in the hall listening to him.

As soon as he saw her he got his breath and went on in a monotonous, almost reasonable way, "It's not just because I'm ridiculous that you ought to laugh at me, Anna. There's much more to it than that. You've got to know that nothing I've done in a long time, weeks and weeks, maybe all my life, has any meaning to it, so even if I insulted you it didn't mean anything, did it? Nothing I do means anything and it gets terrible, it gets terrible going on like that and you've got to pretend. That's why I told you I was acting last night and that was very true. I know how bad you felt last night, but it seemed funny. I can't stop it seeming funny."

Leaning close, with his palms pressed against the door as he tried to push it open, he thought surely she would hear the beating of his heart. She put out her hand to stop him, but she was frightened. She had begun to pity him so much that she could hardly speak. "I beg you to forgive me, Anna," he said. "And I just want you to understand that my life takes these ridiculous twists. For God's sake, forgive me."

He was pleading with such despair that she forgot her own pain, and she forgot, too, how he had hurt her. All that warm and lovely softness was in her face as she put out her hand compassionately and touched him on the arm and whispered, "Please don't go on like that, Mike. There's nothing the matter."

"I'm not going on," he said, and he smiled as though he were trying to recover whatever inherent dignity he might have possessed once; but he was so bewildered that he only stared at her when the smile had gone. Full of pity, she tried to take him by the arm and lead him into the apartment, but then he suddenly brushed her arm aside and cried in a frantic voice, "Don't touch me. Leave me alone. I tell you I'm a funny man." He turned away and started to run down the stairs. Anna called out softly, "Mike, Mike, come here," and he stopped once and looked up at her, and then he laughed a little and shouted, "I'm a funny man. At last I see what I amount to in life. I'm a clown. Why don't you smile at me? You ought to all smile at me."

He stood out on the street looking across the square. A fine summer rain had just begun to fall in a very mild drizzle. He felt the softness of the summer rain on his forehead, soft and gentle, and making no noise as it fell in the night on the city. But his body felt hot and he turned up his coat collar and shivered as he walked along the street with his head down. Water trickled down from his hair and ran in little streams down his cheeks. He kept on walking and he did not know where he went. He did not know how he got home. He only knew it was very late and he was in his own place and was too tired to undress and he had fallen on the bed with his body burning, and he was thinking, "I often get the flu like this. I got it every year when I was a kid. If I just had a little quinine it would be all right."

Sixteen

THAT EARLY afternoon when Michael woke up, blinking his eyes in the strong sunlight, he saw Anna Prychoda standing over by the little kitchenette. For a long time he looked earnestly at her slim ankles and at her waist and at the fair curls on her neck, and he was puzzled and wondering, and when he was sure that she was really there, he sat up in the bed and leaned forward, hardly daring to breathe for fear she might hear him. While he was watching her so solemnly, she turned, and when she saw that he was awake, she said simply, "So you're all better. All better. Isn't that fine, Mike?"

"How long have you been here?"

"I've been coming in and out the last two days."

"Then why didn't I see you before? I got up a couple of times and I never saw anybody here."

"I just kept coming in to see you were all right. I tried to fix you up a little, Mike." And as though she had gained some kind of dominance over him during the last few days that gave her assurance and security, she came over to the bed and put her hand on his head and looked at his eyes to see if they were clear. He kept watching her with a frightened shame, remembering, and waiting for her to remember that night when he had pounded on her door. He put out his hand and touched her dress, afraid that she might go, and then he moved his fingers slowly up and down the cloth of the dress while she wondered what was in his mind. "I'm sorry about the other night. I'm very, very sorry. You'll forget about it, won't you?" he asked.

"I've forgotten about it now, Mike. I haven't thought about it at all," she said. "I believe you're all right now. Your head feels cool. You were pretty feverish the other night though. Now you're fine. It was like the flu. You got hot and cold and kept mumbling while you were sleeping." Then she began to laugh. "Isn't it fine that you're all right now?" she said. Her laughter was so free and happy and so much like a young girl's laughter that his shame and his shyness and his fear that she might go all left him, and he smiled and began to look at her with more curiosity. She had on some kind of a white smock instead of that black and white dress she had worn so much; her hair was combed carelessly and her lips were far too red, but there was something else about her he had never felt before; and whatever this was, it was as though he had been trying to see it that night when he pounded on her door, that night in the tavern, all through that night when he had sought her, and now he saw it truly for the first time; he simply saw her by herself in her own natural brightness, and he was so delighted that he said, "I never thought it would make me feel so good just to see someone."

"Would you like me to go now?"

"Please, please don't go."

"I'll have to go soon anyway."

"You don't have to go now, though," he insisted, for as she bent over him he had felt he had never been close to anyone who had been so full of disinterested goodness. Yet even while he looked at her with such reverence he was thinking, "I shouldn't ask her to stay here with me, but I want her to stay so much."

"What's bothering you, Mike?" she asked.

"It seems terrible to hear you say you have to go."

"But why are you looking at me like that?"

"I seem to find out everything about you just looking at you, where you came from, where you are going, as though we had known each other a long time."

"Isn't that lovely? Please tell me where I'm going."

"I know why you've been coming up here looking after me."

"My, the things you know today. Yet you won't tell me anything. You just nod your head and look wise."

"It doesn't matter how much anybody hurts you; as soon as you feel other people are hurt you want to give all of yourself to help them." As he spoke very softly and smiled, it began to seem an extraordinary thing that this girl who had been full of such despair a few nights ago, with no money for rent and hardly a stitch to wear, and her face sullen, and her eyes shrewd and wise as she sat with Huck Farr in the tavern, should have become so happy that her face simply glowed, just because she was there waiting on him when he was sick. It seemed a terrible thing that poverty and worry and bitterness should have ever obscured her natural brightness.

"You're an awfully fine girl, Anna," he whispered.

But she was made shy by the new reverence she felt in him and she said, "I'm not like that, Mike. You feel upset about the way things have been going for you, and that makes you think I'm so much nicer than I am. I know what's the matter with you."

"You know?"

"Sure I do. You're worried about your father. I didn't read it in the papers, but Mac, the janitor, told me about it. Wasn't it terrible, wasn't it such a pity? You expected to have such a good time when you went away."

"Did Mac say anything else?"

"Just that it looked bad for your father, but they hadn't arrested him. I didn't believe such nonsense."

"You can't know anything about it," he said uneasily.

"I saw him here with you that night and he looked so eager, and he was very friendly."

"You can't tell much by a man's face," he said. "I never knew what was going on in my father's head," but as soon as he had realized that he was speaking out of the old desire to lash out vindictively at his father, he grew ashamed, for he knew that she was startled, and so he said awkwardly, "If only the newspapers would leave him alone and people would forget about him he'd be all right."

"I know how you feel. I know how your father must feel and how it's been worrying you. Poor man," she said, and the fact that she had discovered this private sorrow in Mike made her much more eager to show her tenderness. The compassion and the charity he felt in her made him long to lose his identity in love for her. He had become so silent that she felt she was intruding, so she smiled brightly and went over to the little kitchenette and pretended to be busy with something.

And while she was there she knew he was still watching her, and perhaps it was because she suddenly realized that this was the first time they had spoken to each other since he had rejected her the other night that she grew shy. Though her face reddened and she busied herself earnestly at whatever she was doing, she would not let herself glance over her shoulder at him. Then something far stronger than her shyness and her suspicion began to pull her to him; turning, she looked sideways a little timidly, watching for some impatient or impulsive gesture from him that might offend her. She saw only a yearning and an absolute stillness in his wondering, thin, white face.

"How have you been eating, Anna?" he asked.

"I took some money. I suppose you might say I stole it."

"Who did you steal it from?"

"I got it out of your pocket," she said. She picked up his trousers that she had folded neatly and hung over the back of the chair. "I got it out of one of these pockets," she said. For the first time he noticed that everything in the room was in its place; his clothes were hanging on the pegs on the back of the door, his books were piled neatly on his desk, and his brown shoes were there on the piece of carpet beside the bed. Grinning at her, he said, "You didn't find much in that pocket."

"I've been eating on you just the same, and there's still some left in the pocket."

"When do we eat again?"

"Right now, Mr. Aikenhead, but all the cans are empty. There's nothing to eat."

"Maybe it's time Anna hurried out to the store to do the family shopping."

"That's true. I should have had it done before this but I wanted very much that you should wake up and we could have our lunch together." She picked up his trousers and with a serious face she thrust her hand into his pocket and he could see her fingers moving under the cloth.

"Who undressed me, Anna?"

"What a silly question. I did. Who else in the world would take the trouble to undress a big fellow like you?"

"That's right. And you'd better keep on looking after me. You'd better hurry right down to the store. This is the first time in weeks that I've been hungry."

"Are you really going to get up, Mike?"

"I'll be dressed when you come back," he said.

With a few silver coins clutched in her hand, she hurried over to the golden-oak dresser and leaned close to the mirror and fussed at her hair a little. Then she slipped off her white smock and hung it on the back of the door and throwing him a kiss, she rushed out, leaving him there alone, holding on to an eager happiness.

But as soon as he realized that she had gone he grew full of worry and he jumped up and hurried to the window to watch her going along the street. There she was on the pavement right below, without her hat, with her feet moving rapidly as if soon she would break into a little run. The afternoon sunlight shone on her fair head, and she sometimes disappeared momentarily in the noonday crowd. He hunted eagerly, as though she were really lost, and caught a glimpse of her head. He began to think there was something special about her among all those people down there going to work or returning home, or meeting, or parting and going ahead into an uncertain future. She was distinct among all those city people because she had such a little feeling of security inside her and she was going along with such hope in her face. And when he could no longer follow her he knew how he longed to have her back there in the room with him. Even while he muttered, "I mustn't let her stay here with me. When she comes back I'll tell her to leave me alone. Sooner or later she'd get into trouble with me. Something will happen to me to destroy me sooner or later and it would touch her too," he knew how necessary it was for him that she return and stay with him. If that hope and little security she had found should be destroyed, he knew how she would be hurt, and he could not bear to hurt her again. And he sat on the bed with his fear and his sorrow and his new marvelous concern for her all so mixed up within him that he was bewildered, and the only thing he was sure of was that he was waiting very eagerly for the sound of her footfall on the stair.

When she came in with her parcels, and with her face flushed from hurrying, he jumped up and said, "You took an awful long time."

"I wasn't gone ten minutes. I hurried so that I banged into people and they thought I was crazy."

"I had a feeling you might never come back. That's why it seemed so long."

"Oh, Mike, you're so silly. Where on earth would I go?"

"Wherever you'll go when you say it's time to leave here."

"Then you don't want me to stay?"

"It just can't be done," he said, looking very worried.

But she knew his concern was all for her and she began to laugh. "I was in here nearly all last night anyway," she said. "I had to get out of my own place last night. The janitor was pretty good about it. He was told to put me out long ago and he let me stay on. He'd let me stay there yet, but the owner managed to rent the place the other day."

"Haven't you got a home anywhere, Anna?"

"Sure I have."

"Then why don't you go home?"

"My people live in Detroit," she said. "That's where I was born. I guess that's as far as my father and mother got in their wandering."

"Then why don't they help you?"

"Up to eight months ago I was trying to help them. I've got three sisters and a brother, all younger than I, and right now with the world the way it is and my father not working, I guess they have a hard time eating. I'm certainly not going to worry them any more. I won't get in your way, Mike. I can live in the corner over there and look after you, Mike."

"We'll see," he said rather weakly.

While she was opening the parcels on the table her hands began to tremble. "I never could figure out how you felt about me, Mike," she said.

"I never had such a fine feeling for anyone," he said, and he spoke with such an earnest conviction that she began to laugh.

"You're telling lies, you know you are, Mike. Why do you lie to me? Oh, Mike."

When she repeated his name her voice rose eagerly, as if she were calling him and half laughing. Growing excited, he insisted, "When you keep watching someone and worry about them and start brooding over them and want to help them, isn't that when you're in love? That night when I watched you and Huck Farr going along the street together and could not bear it when I thought I mightn't ever see you again, wasn't I really loving you then?"

"Maybe," she said doubtfully. "It was hard for me to understand. There's no use talking about that now, though, Mike. We'll wait and see what happens, eh, Mike?"

With a fine free assurance, as if at last she were in her own home, she began to move briskly around the room, and as he watched the competent movements of her hands, and the little, regular swing of her hips whenever she took a few steps, he began to feel that she was really free now because she was there in that room with him. He felt such joy and such security, himself, that he started to follow her around, smiling apologetically whenever she stopped and frowned at him.

Early that evening she made him lie down and rest, and she sat beside him and found an incredible number of interesting little things to say. He listened eagerly, and she did not know that every time she finished a sentence he tried to bring himself to tell her to leave him. She could not know this because he kept asking her questions about herself that always led to longer answers. She talked to him about her family and the city where she was born.

Her father and mother had come to America at the beginning of the Great War and had settled in Detroit. Her father had been a carpenter in his own country, but in Detroit he had got a job with good wages in an automobile factory. Anna had been their first child born in America. At the picnics the Ukrainian-born people used to hold outside the city limits in the summer time, her father used to sing the native songs, and when she was still very small he taught her to play the mandolin and accompany him. Her father was a friend of the new Russia, and when those of his people who were religious started having their own picnics, he began to take Anna and his two boys with him to the labor study groups on Sunday afternoons. Anna was never very happy at her childish class in economics because she knew her mother was at home, wishing she was at the picnics where the children would be doing the native dances and where they would all be drinking and singing songs.

When she was at high school, and in love, and dancing, her father used to beg her at least to wear a red revolutionary button on May Day; sometimes just to please him, she used to sit with him in the evenings and listen to him talking economics. He had failed to interest his two boys in the labor movement and they wanted to become professional baseball players. His disappointment in his sons made him love Anna all the more, and he gave the money, when she was finished high school, to go to New York and study fashion designing in women's clothes.

"Were you very good at it?" Mike asked her.

"I loved it. I loved clothes. I worked at it for a department store here for two years, but when things got pretty bad in the business they let me go. I mean they let me take a job in the factory."

"That wasn't so good?"

"Maybe I wasn't so good."

"Why didn't you go home?"

"I started writing them lovely letters a couple of years ago because I really felt full of joy then to be working at something I loved and to find so suddenly there were such beautiful things all around me. I kept on writing these letters and I kept writing them right up to the end because my father was on city relief and they were having a lot of trouble of their own."

"Didn't you have a lover at all to look after you?"

"I had two of them. One of them was just ready to start practicing law and the other boy worked in a broker's office."

"They couldn't have loved you so much."

"Sure they did, Mike. They were crazy about me, but the young lawyer had nowhere to go, times were so bad, and his mother bought half of a small practice for him out of town, and the boy in the broker's office… Well, it wasn't his fault they shut up the shop. You know the way it was, Mike."

Every time she answered a question he showed his great satisfaction with a wide smile, as if his life was being enriched by these little bits of information he was getting from her. And if the silence grew when there seemed to be nothing further to ask, he grew alarmed, and another question came eagerly.

"Oh, Mike, I haven't even asked you one single question," she laughed.

"It's like getting more and more of you," he said. "Everything seems to make you a little more beautiful. It gives me such a feeling of joy just to listen to you telling me about yourself. I don't know what to say. I don't want you to go. Just go on talking. I don't care what you say. I know how good you are, I know how very, very good you are, Anna."

Then they were quiet. And these moments in the dark and the quiet of the room began to seem the most precious of all. She was crouched beside him on the bed. Through the open window all the noises of the city came humming into the room like the murmur of everlasting life, and there were flashes of city light against the night sky that illuminated the room. His hand went out and touched her breast timidly, and then he began to hold her very tight, holding her desperately, and making her a little afraid because she knew, when he would not raise his head from her breast, that he was crying to himself. "You really ought to go, Anna," he muttered, "but don't let me tell you to go." And then the anguish that had been so mixed with his relief, passed out of him, and there was just the one surge of joy. When her voice, soft and gentle, came out of the darkness, saying, "I don't want to go. What makes you think I'd want to go?" it was the most intimate and caressing sound he had ever heard. She kept telling him he should go to sleep, and he did begin to doze, huddled close to her, and he had no sudden waking moment of vast doubt, for their room now had such a splendid silence, the profound and comforting silence of home.

Seventeen

THAT HIS wife should have left him had filled Andrew Aikenhead with sorrow, yet he understood how desperately necessary it was for her to do it. He had agreed to pay her an allowance once a month; he had settled on her one half of his property, mainly his government bonds, and he had kept for himself his house in the country and his city house, both of which had been mortgaged for years because he had never been a wealthy man. His business was of such a nature that he had to live with an ostentatious lavishness that made his home and his social life an expensive bay window for the advertising business. Marthe had not wanted this settlement from him, but when he insisted that she take it, she had found in herself a feverish desire to be free of the places where she had worked and hoped and failed. She went to Chicago. The last time he heard of her she was in New York and planning to go to Europe.

Day after day the city papers printed Andrew Aikenhead's picture, and without ever saying it openly, they made a great many people feel certain that he had been actually guilty of Dave Choate's death.

One day, as he sat in his office tapping the glass top of his big desk with his pink finger tips, he began to wonder if Michael would ever come and see him again. It seemed such a little while ago that he had gone out seeking him, and he could remember so vividly the first time they had really been together. Willing and warm friendliness that had given him joy had shone in Michael's face that time they had gone fishing together. It had been the one time for both of them when there had been swift recognition of the intimacy there might have been between them; it had been what he had waited for for such a long time and now, as far as Michael was concerned, it was unimportant that they had ever been together, for he still kept away from him.

Jay Hillquist, who had been ill with what the doctors thought was poison in his system left from his abscessed teeth, came to the office only three days a week. One after the other came turbulent conferences on those days as they all schemed to hold advertising accounts that were slipping away. Though he was a sick, worried man, Jay Hillquist's sunken-cheeked face was bursting red with energy and he shouted at them all, at Aikenhead, at the copy writers, at the art director, and at Henry Huston, the contact man, who mopped his bald head and tried to show by his desolate expression that his concern for the business was even greater than his chief's. They were planning a program which would be so attractive to Roebuck, the cheese manufacturer from the Middle West, that he wouldn't hesitate at all to enlarge his advertising appropriation. Hillquist had just finished shouting, and they all were silent, looking eagerly at Aikenhead and longing to hear his smooth, plausible healing words. They were waiting for him to balance his partner's rowdy, irritating eloquence with his own glib advice.

Yet he only sat there among them, looking out the big office window, pondering his own secret thoughts with his blue eyes wondering and innocent. Sometimes he leaned over as though trying to look beyond the great gaps between rising surfaces of the city skyscrapers and catch a glimpse of blue sky.

Then Henry Huston cleared his throat and said, "What do you think, Mr. Aikenhead?"

Andrew Aikenhead looked at them all shrewdly for a moment, then he began to smile broadly. "This argument is just a big waste of time," he said. "You all know as well as I do how we got that Roebuck account in the first place. You never really got it by selling him a plan. There are at least ten agencies in the city that can equal or surpass any service we can give Roebuck. He's got to be charmed into wanting all we can give him. Gentlemen, I suggest you continue to leave him in my hands. I'll see him tonight and fix it up." He smiled and looked so shrewd they sighed with relief.

"That fixes that. Thank the Lord for that," Jay Hillquist said, but he was disgusted with his partner. For hours he had been waiting for him to speak like that; he had watched him stubbornly and had seen how detached from them he was and he had wanted to shout, "Doesn't it mean a thing to you the way business is dropping? How long do you think we can stand this? Agencies are going out of business all over the city and you're sitting there dreaming day after day. You haven't been any help to us for weeks. The way you go around makes people gossip about you all the more." And he hurried out of the office, so they would all feel they had been wasting a lot of time.

After the conference, Henry Huston, the contact man, came into Aikenhead's office. He was a tall man with large protruding front teeth, who was always grinning with excessive friendliness, and his hand went shooting out with a vigor that never left anyone unimpressed. Henry Huston was proud of knowing nothing whatever about the advertising business and he used to boast about it, and then explain with just as much pride that he did know every important business man in the city. In a way he was like a bird dog for the agency, who galloped along in advance, and then stood still, sniffing, making them all watch alertly while he pointed gracefully at the business quarry and waited for Aikenhead and Hillquist to hurry up and bag the game. He said to Aikenhead that afternoon, "I just wanted to say, chief, that there's a lot of talk around town that's pretty silly. You know the way people talk after they read anything in the papers. I just want to say I don't believe a word of it. I know you had nothing whatever to do with such a mess. That's all, Mr. Aikenhead." He stood there stiffly with a kind of military loyalty.

"There is a lot of talk, and I'm glad you mentioned it, Huston. I'm glad you don't believe it."

"Not a word of it, sir."

"Do you really hear much talk?" Aikenhead asked anxiously.

"In one place and another. No one would say anything to me directly, of course, for they know of my admiration for you."

"Why, thank you, thank you, Huston," Aikenhead said, and he was deeply touched and he kept nodding his head up and down. He was so very glad that Huston, the lanky bird dog, was uneasy and he made his little bow and went out.

With his face flushing, Andrew Aikenhead sat there thinking, "There's nothing of any importance whispered in any club room that Huston does not hear. It means they're asking him about me at luncheons and in the gymnasium, where they all take their exercise, and when he's out at night too. I can hear them having their little whispering conversations." If Huston had actually spoken to him like that it means there was a growing conviction all over the city that the police at least should arrest him. "Maybe that's why Jay looks at me steadily, then shifts his eyes when I smile at him. Why shouldn't I smile?" he asked himself.

He put on his hat and coat and went hurrying out, as if this was his first intimation that such whispering might destroy him, and on the way up the avenue, walking through the noonday crowd in the brilliant warm sunshine in his light gray double-breasted suit with the red rosebud in his button-hole, and his gray moustache trimmed sharply and his white hair shining under the line of his black bowler hat, he thought, "I'll keep my eyes open and listen a bit too and find out for myself." He was so troubled he crossed the road against the red traffic light, yet when he got to the entrance of the old Richmond Club where elderly well-dressed men were getting out of cars and striding up the steps with impressive dignity, he, too, went in with as much assurance as any of them.

It was in the lounging room where many of the members were having a glass of sherry before lunch and where the light was poor but the furnishings heavy, sombre, and enormously comfortable that he noticed when he entered a few heads sliding up and jutting over the backs of the leather chairs, white heads and gray ones and bald ones rising out of the depths of those massive, comfortable chairs to turn to him and then swing unobtrusively away. At noon time, for two hours at least, those important and influential heads were in repose while the owners meditated on the basic business structure of the nation, yet today a few of those heads actually swayed out of their separate places and came together and remained together while there was, Andrew Aikenhead felt sure, a little malicious gossip. He had intended to go among them, smiling in his easy way, and ask one of them to have lunch with him. Instead, an unaccustomed shyness made him turn, and he sighed and went into the dining-room alone. When he had first come back from the country they had asked him about the drowning of Dave Choate and had shown a little sympathy, but now they never mentioned it to him at all. As he ate his lunch alone he never once smiled, for he was thinking, "I'll not come back here again for a while. It's stuffy in here after the sunlight anyway."

When he was on the street again and feeling a little freedom and enjoying it after the dark solemnity of the club, he felt resentment against his helplessness surging in him. "Why don't they arrest me and then maybe everybody would feel better and I'd have a chance to say something? I can't say anything if they won't openly accuse me," he thought. "This is dreadful. It can't go on like this. It's getting worse all the time and I thought it would die down." He began to walk faster and he was red cheeked and fierce looking and puffing with indignation when he got back to the office.

That night he went to the Buckingham Hotel to have a persuasive conversation with Stewart Roebuck, the cheese manufacturer, who was in town again. From the time he walked into the lobby he began to think of all the arguments he might have to use to make Roebuck believe he ought to double his account with them, yet when he was in the elevator, he suddenly realized that underneath these arguments he was ticking off in his head, there was another plan he was working on far more earnestly; he was trying to think of something he might do, some simple honest gesture he might make that everybody in the city would understand and that would end the gossip about him forever.

Stewart Roebuck's eyes were shining brightly behind his glasses, because he was overjoyed that Aikenhead had come alone to talk with him. The Hillquist agency had insisted that he stay as their guest in the most expensive suite in the Buckingham Hotel while he was in the city, and as he sat there that evening in the suite that would have had to satisfy the Prince of Wales, or the late Rudolf Valentino, he was childishly eager to have Aikenhead come alone to see him. In the last month Roebuck had begun to paint pictures with great earnestness, and he had really come all this way from Chicago because he knew of no one in the world, neither his wife, nor his employees, nor any of his old friends, who would look at his paintings with as much sympathy as Aikenhead.

But Aikenhead came in gloomily and sat down with his hat in his hands, almost forgetting why he had come. While Roebuck was smiling and rubbing his hands together and saying eagerly, "I've been waiting to show you something," Aikenhead smiled patiently. "You remember you took me to the art gallery here about a month ago?" he went on. "You remember how much we talked about painting that day?"

"I remember it well."

"No one would ever believe a manufacturer of cheese would ever go in for anything like that, particularly anything in the modern manner, would they? I mean in these days you wouldn't expect me to be wasting my time at it when everybody's got so much to think of, would you? It's different with you because you have commercial artists around you all the time, but with me, well …"

"Well, Stewart …"

"Look here," Roebuck said shyly. From a leather brief bag he took three pieces of very stiff cardboard which had become oil paintings, each one a still life, apples beside a jar, apples and a bag, apples and an old hat, and everything he had painted had an innocent quality, as if he had been much happier with his box of paints on Sunday afternoons than he had ever been in his life before. "As soon as I got home last time I started right in to paint and I could hardly wait to get up here again to show them to you. I wanted you to see them first and if you liked them, then I would show them to other people. What do you think?"

Striding boldly across the room, he placed the three pieces of cardboard against the legs of the chairs, moving them a little to the right or to the left, so he would get the proper lighting on them from the ceiling. He seemed to dance around them, turning continually and grinning at Andrew Aikenhead like a school kid.

Andrew Aikenhead leaned forward mechanically, knowing what he was expected to say, for the whole Roebuck account with the agency had been built by him around Roebuck's wistful love of painting; they had given him a tender encouragement; an understanding of his wistfulness that no other agency could have possessed, and now Aikenhead was to say, "There's real talent there, by Jove, a strong, primitive, resourceful talent," or something like that that Roebuck had come all the way from Chicago to hear. But after he had said, "Very nice, very nice," Aikenhead only tapped the top of his head restlessly, and his florid face took on that detached expression they had come to know so well at the office. His thoughts were not of Roebuck, nor the painting, nor of business at all. And while Roebuck waited, Aikenhead said, "You've probably heard a lot of talk about me since I saw you last, haven't you?"

"I know you've had some trouble and I'm sorry, but I didn't pay any attention to any talk I heard. It all seemed pretty absurd, so I wasn't even going to mention it."

"You're sure you didn't believe it?"

"I just said I didn't put any stock in it at all, didn't I?"

"Then you don't really think I had anything to do with it?"

Roebuck began to look worried, for he couldn't understand why Aikenhead was pleading with him for belief in his innocence. He had honestly never suspected him at all, and the gossip he had heard he had thought pretty stupid, and now he was impatient that Aikenhead should be so serious about it. "I don't go in for gossip at all," he said impatiently. Then he turned determinedly back to his painting, again adjusted one against the chair and looked up at the lighting and shook his head professionally.

Still detached and anxious, Aikenhead watched him, and when he heard Roebuck saying mildly, "What do you really think?" it seemed a terrible thing that he should have to abandon his own deep grief and immerse himself in Roebuck's hopes and praise his daubing; it seemed despicable that a business contract should be based on such a relationship and he said a little irritably, "I can't make much out of it."

"Then you don't like it, is that it?"

"I just can't make much out of it," Aikenhead said. But as soon as he had spoken he was in a panic, and in his longing to show that false enthusiasm that always came to him so easily, he began to mutter, "It's remarkable to see you going on like that. It certainly is. I must have some of our local painters see your work."

But there was a grim, defeated expression on Roebuck's face as he picked up his paintings like a rejected salesman. Andrew Aikenhead knew then that the Roebuck cheese account was slipping away from his agency. He grabbed Roebuck by the arm, he went on talking eagerly, but Roebuck only blinked his eyes. Roebuck knew there was no true enthusiasm in the speech he was hearing; he felt that as far as Aikenhead was concerned he might just as well have not shown him the paintings at all.

They went on talking, they drank together, they even made a few stiff jokes and smiled a little, yet Aikenhead felt more and more that Roebuck had grown cold and had lost all confidence in him. Once he insisted on trying to talk business, and Roebuck only looked at him with a childish curiosity. When he saw Roebuck watching him like that Aikenhead lost all confidence in himself.

That night in his home he began to ponder over what was happening to him. He wondered bravely if he might not have actually done something he could be truly blamed for. In his black and white dressing-gown he had gone to his bedroom with a bottle of scotch and a siphon of soda, and he had sat there sipping the scotch, pondering and letting the hours go by. When he heard Sheila come in he called, "Sheila, I want to ask you something."

There was no joy in Sheila Aikenhead's face these days, but there was no anguish either for she had begun to look more self-possessed, more aloof and more truly superior among people than ever before in her life. No one who knew her expected her to admit in any way that there had been any disgraceful publicity for the Aikenhead family. Her own feeling was hidden in her heart.

"What was it?" she asked.

"I was wondering if you had seen Michael at all these days."

"I haven't seen him at all."

"Has Ross seen him?"

"Not that I know of."

"That's odd, very odd."

"What's odd about it?"

"Nothing, nothing really. I was just talking to myself," he said hastily.

She was going, but she turned and said impatiently, "Why do you sit there night after night like that? What's the matter with you? Why don't you go to bed?"

"I was just thinking."

"You should stop thinking. You'll sit there thinking and you'll take one drink after another till you fall asleep. It's very foolish."

"I'll go to bed now," he said, very anxious to mollify her. He began to feel that if he argued with her a passionate indignation would show in her face and voice, and he was afraid of what might be said.

But he stayed there sipping his whiskey, and soon he forgot all about Sheila, as he tried hard to grasp the significance of Michael's rejection of him. The more he thought of it, the more excited he got. His hand trembled a little as he lifted his glass, for it now seemed possible that Michael, too, believed him guilty. His thoughts kept going back to that evening when he had gone out seeking Michael, and he had found him, and had returned home and had met Dave Choate in the hall. As he remembered feeling that he was pushing Dave out of his life, and had been glad it could be done so easily, he began to feel an ache of remorse, for he knew that the will to be rid of Dave had actually been in him that night. Maybe Dave's mother had known it when she looked at him that night; she must have known it, for she had pleaded so earnestly that he do nothing to disturb their life together. Listening to her, he had felt full of secret guilt. And now she, too, was gone.

His face had got flushed and his head was nodding up and down, and he had to hold his glass very steady, but the awareness of his secret guilt was growing so rapidly that now it was flooding through him and overwhelming him; it reached back into his life and dragged out his unfaithfulness to his first wife; it touched all the uneasiness and the doubt that had gone with his love for his second one; but it stayed most powerfully with the longing he had once had to be free of Dave.

When he got up in his excitement, he walked unsteadily, yet he was welcoming this realization of his own guilt, for it gave him something at last that he could understand, it explained in a way what had been happening to him and it made it seem almost just. "I always got away with everything I wanted," he thought. "Nobody really resisted me. They had to come my way. Dave wouldn't be dead if it weren't for my doing. I'm sure of that." He leaned against the window and swung the curtain aside and looked down at the quiet street. He grew bewildered. He wished he could see over to the other, noisier part of the city, and he wondered where Michael was and what he was doing.

Eighteen

JAY HILLQUIST listened patiently to everything his wife had to say, he nodded his head in agreement, and sometimes he even looked miserable, yet he kept on repeating, "It's business. It's got nothing to do with friendship. He'll understand that."

"Are you sure you have to do it?"

"You can't interest the man in the business. Look at the way he handled that Roebuck business. We lost that account simply because he didn't care enough to hold it. I'm not going to stand for that."

"You can't break up like that after fifteen years together," she said.

"God knows I don't want to, but it's you and Ross I'm thinking of, and our home and the bit we have. We haven't been able to save anything to speak of and we can't stand a terrific slump. Sometimes I think you have to spend more money to get business than you ever get out of the business. We now do about a quarter of the business we were doing a couple of years ago. We're not quite covering the overhead," he almost shouted.

It bothered him to have his wife watching him like that as he moved uneasily around the room because he knew she was noticing his sunken cheeks and the way his clothes hung loose on him. She went on watching him with that patient sadness that he could hardly stand. She was a quiet gray-haired woman, who at one time, years ago, had stood for everything he had ever wanted; when he was poor and working in the business office of the newspaper, she had a little money; when he had been boisterous and blustering in his way with people, she had been quiet and well educated. At that time he used to dream of making her love him and taking her to dinner in the crystal ball room of a hotel and paying a lot of money for the dinner, and then sitting back and sighing with satisfaction as he looked at her and lit a fifteen-cent cigar. But as they grew older, he had left her many times for other women. You could see him any night at his club. Sometimes he seemed to think his club was his home. In a way, he and his wife no longer had a life together except during those times when he was worried, or deeply stirred, or thought someone had betrayed him; then he returned to her and they began to feel again that they had always been close together.

"It's pretty much a question of simple faith, isn't it?" she was asking him. "You and Andrew were poor together. I'm not saying you're rich now, you may even fail, but if you end the partnership now, when he's in trouble, it's like a betrayal of him." In her patient, quiet way she was saying everything he, himself, felt most deeply. "God knows we have nothing against him," she went on. "You, yourself, have as much faith in his integrity as you ever had. Jay, dear, can't you see that he belongs to the best part of our life together. We still share our affection for him. We have that left at least out of our life and our early hopes, and what we once loved most. He was always at our home. Even when he got married the second time and he knew I didn't want to know his Marthe, he didn't let that separate us. When we look back, our life seems to have had so many separations in it, separations, I mean, from things we love, one broken attachment after the other, separations we once thought we couldn't stand and that we've almost forgotten now. Something is always happening to wrench us away from the things we love. Everybody knows it. Andrew, too, must have felt it when he kept coming alone to our house, yet he kept coming. Sometimes I used to think that he thought our place was really his home."

"That's true, that's true, but why do we have to talk about that? All I'm saying is that he's no longer interested in the business."

"That's because of the way people are talking about him."

"Supposing they arrest him?"

"If they could have arrested him they would have done it long ago."

"Maybe they're only waiting."

"It's the way people make stories up. You know it's all nonsense, don't you, Jay?"

"We always get talking about the wrong things when we have this discussion, Alice. I share such thoughts with you. I agree with you. But if I don't end the partnership it will bust up into pieces. Can't I be his friend without being tied to him in business?"

"I don't see how you can now."

"Oh, dear, that point of view makes me wild. I never in my life mixed up business and friendship and I'm not going to do it now. Andrew Aikenhead's going to cost us thousands of dollars. I can't understand his attitude anyway. Why doesn't he quit? He does nothing but mope in the office day after day. He feels persecuted. He expects people to be talking about him when they don't even know he exists. That isn't all though. He doesn't want to do business; that's what burns me up. He's betraying us; I'm not betraying him." Jay Hillquist had begun to shout because he resented the sorrowful expression on his wife's face. She was sitting there, ready to weep, with her hands folded in her lap. Though Jay resented her sorrow, he really had far more resentment for his own sentiment and what he was sure was the softness in his own heart. As he muttered, "To think I'd ever see the day when I'd let a personal relationship interfere with business," his heart was troubled and he was full of secret shame. Yet he would not let himself respond to the urge from the deeper part of his nature, for he felt it would be a betrayal of everything he stood for in his daily life.

As he mumbled uncertainly to himself, his wife couldn't help thinking of the time when he and Aikenhead had been young men and they had gone for long walks together in the evenings and had made such ardent plans to make money; she remembered the time when Ross and Sheila and Michael were little; and the early jealousies that had developed between the two families over every precocious move made by either one of the boys. After his second marriage Aikenhead still kept coming to the house, and sometimes he stayed very late, sitting with them, saying nothing, but thinking the old thoughts with them, and they never asked what was worrying him, but were just simple and friendly. And now Ross and Sheila were going to get married.

"What on earth have these questions to do with a simple business transaction?" Jay said aloud. "My business judgment built up over a period of years tells me there's only one thing to do. If he's sensible and in his right mind, he'll agree with me. As a matter of fact, I'd be ashamed of Andrew Aikenhead if he ever tried to turn the matter into a sentimental human relationship. I'll bet all the tea in China that he won't."

"Then you insist on going to see him tonight?"

"I'm going right now while it's fresh in my mind." They looked at each other with worried faces and were silent. They looked at each other like two people who were growing old and were afraid of what was happening around them.

Then Jay Hillquist put on his hat and coat and went out to his car and drove through the streets to his old friend's house. It was only when he had stopped the car on the road in front of the house, and was looking up at the door and at the unlighted windows that he felt hesitant. As he bent over the wheel and made no move to get out, he seemed to hear on that summer night air the sound of laughing voices hovering over the steps to the door. "Good night, good night, my dear, a lovely time. It was wonderful to have you. Please come soon again." And he heard, too, the hoarser, heavier, rollicking sound of boisterous drinking men leaving the house after the party, and then the voice of the first Mrs. Aikenhead calling from the steps, her voice drifting down to the curb, "Jay, you forgot to tell us what time you were having dinner," and then her husband calling from the door, "You'll get your death of cold, dear, come on in." Her laugh had been very clear on the crisp, frosty air of that winter night. And Jay, who was a little ill and gaunt and aching, found himself longing for those times again. Then he jerked his body out of the car, for he despised his weakness, and he said to himself, "What's all this to do with it anyway? I'm getting it all mixed up." As he hurried up the walk and rapped on the door he looked very stern.

Andrew Aikenhead, himself, came to the door, and he was delighted to see his partner; and, putting his hand on his shoulder, he led him into the drawing-room and said, "Well, well, well, Jay, you haven't come around like this in some time." He was alone in the house. He had been reading. His eyes looked very tired. But the sight of his old friend gave him such a warm excitement that his hand actually began to tremble a little as he handed him a cigarette case.

When they were sitting down, Jay said awkwardly, "I'm afraid this is just a little business visit, Andy."

"That doesn't matter, Jay. I'm awfully glad to have you come here anyway."

"I know, I know, but tonight I'm going to get right down to brass tacks. Have you been thinking of the way the agency has been going?"

"Why, yes. I've often thought about it," Aikenhead said earnestly. "Things are pretty bad with us, but are they worse for us than they are for other agencies in the city? I think you'll find we're doing as well as anybody else." There was a kind of pleading reticence in the way he spoke, as if he might have gone on and elaborated upon his explanation of the collapse of other agencies in the city, but his pride prevented him from doing it. The slow, uneasy smile that came on his face made Jay realize suddenly that his partner knew intuitively everything that was about to be said between them. And that smile was so patient and friendly and such a plea for faith that Jay grew impatient and he said gruffly, "I don't know whether or not it's entered your head, but I don't think we can go on any further the way we've been going. With the overhead what it is, there's not enough there for the two of us. I'm putting my cards right out on the table for you. You probably have your own opinion about it, but I know I'm not licked, not by a damned sight. I'd like to clear the decks and plunge right in."

"You mean that you'd like to end the partnership?"

"I didn't say I'd like to. I think we'll have to."

"You feel you ought to?"

"I want to do the sensible thing."

"And that seems the most sensible thing?"

"There are two or three reasons why I'm talking like this, and the main one is that I've been unable to understand for a long time just how you felt about this business. A while back you seemed fed up. You got some kind of a new slant, and whatever it is I don't like the philosophy. For all I know, you may have fallen for this crap about the collapse of capitalism, like my son Ross. I'm not saying you did. I said maybe you have. When you get thinking like that about business and wondering whether the profit system is right, you might as well quit. You've got to quit before you can start thinking like that. For ten thousand years men have fought with each other to make a little money and it's only when they get tired that they lay down and start talking about feeding each other and not looking after themselves. This business depression doesn't mean a damn thing to me. I think it can be licked as we've licked every other depression, but when a man who has a stake in a community feels like throwing up his hands and getting out, that's betrayal of the sacred right to hold private property, and he's either very tired, or he's a little mad. I've told that to Ross, and he laughs, because he never had to work for it like we've had to, and now I'm telling it to you, just to remind you of it." Jay was honestly indignant, for he could not imagine a society among men where there was not a ruthless struggle for profit, where man did not stand alone, and where a man did not have a sacred right to demand that he be left alone to conduct his own business in his own way.

"Why are you talking like this to me tonight, Jay?"

"Because I've been thinking of my wife and my home and not just of myself." But Andrew Aikenhead was listening with such a polite gravity that Jay had to strive desperately to find just the words he wanted to use. "To put it mildly, you don't seem as interested as you used to. In a way you've turned against the business. You know what I mean. We've got to remember that we're business men. We've got to be sensible. There, I've given you the thought right in the hollow of your hand. You can't despise an organization and give service to it. You've got to live your daily life in terms of your organization or you betray it every day...." Jay had begun to talk in this badgering, bullying tone with which he was so familiar and in which he felt most free, when he realized that his old friend was just listening and saying nothing and watching him with a terrible, unsurprised gravity. Jay's fine flow of words was broken, the harsh, bullying tone went out of his voice, and he said slowly and anxiously, "I mean I think we ought to quit, Andrew. Christ, I hate to do it, but I think we've got to do it."

As the two old friends waited for each other to speak there was a hushed silence between them. They were leaning close to each other in the most intimate way. And Andrew Aikenhead, rubbing his fingers over his chin, said mildly, "You're sure, Jay, that you're not really thinking all the time that

that talk about me and the boy, Dave, isn't going to ruin the business?"

"I know how harmful it is. I won't say I don't. It's terrible publicity. But aside from that, I don't agree with your judgment recently about anything. It's been erratic and it's costing us a lot of money."

"Tell me just one thing, Jay."

"Go ahead."

"Do you believe I had anything to do with that boy's death?"

"I'd swear to God you didn't," Jay said, and he stood up, and he was so glad the business matter had been disposed of so easily that his confidence returned and his face began to show all his enthusiastic conviction. Now that the separation from his old friend had been made, he was able to give his full assent to such a simple question. "The talk around town was all pretty ridiculous but people are forgetting all about it. It makes my wife laugh. The only thing we don't like is the way you took it. It got you down, it got you licked. Sometimes it even shows in your eyes. Forget it," and Jay hoped he would be able to go on with this encouragement, and then he could leave the house without having shown his shame.

Aikenhead only said, "Thanks, Jay. Let's have a drink on that, if you don't mind." He went over to the tray on the little table by the mantel and he poured two stiff drinks of scotch and handed one to Jay. Then he clicked his own heels together, and standing erect, as they used to do when younger and they were duck hunting in the fall and had come into the cabin after hours on the water in the chill of the morning among the reeds, he said, "The best time in the world, Jay. Happy days."

"Happy days," Jay repeated mechanically, "here she goes."

"Down the creek."

"Bottoms up," Jay said.

While Aikenhead stood there with the empty glass in his

hand, Jay was more uncomfortable than he had ever been in his life. He longed to know what his old friend had been really thinking of that he should have given that old toast of their youth.

But Aikenhead was only thinking that Jay's home and his wife had always been a link with that part of his own life that belonged to his first marriage, to the mother of Michael and Sheila, and he was thinking that whenever he had gone to Jay's house after his second marriage, he had been keeping that early part of his life fresh and alive in him. He was simply thinking it was not likely he would go many times more to the Hillquist house.

Nineteen

IT OFTEN seemed to Anna a most astonishing thing that she should always be able to return in the evenings to the place of someone she loved. After shopping in the Jewish section, where the food was cheaper, she walked along the crowded avenue with her parcels held against her, and she was always certain, as she passed the lighted stores and the bakeshops with their open doors and their odors of fresh baking bread, and the delicatessen shops crowded on that summer evening with jabbering, gesturing young men and girls, that Michael would be waiting to welcome her and would seek out some fresh way of showing his admiration. As she walked slowly, with her face glowing, she hardly saw anyone who jostled against her that night; she was thinking that Michael was completely in her keeping; she knew how grateful he was to her for her love. It gave her such joy to realize that his worry was often only for her, that she began to smile, and as she caught a glimpse of the face of a frowning girl, passing with her lover among all those that drifted by under the lights, she began to think she knew what the young man was whispering; he was saying, "You and me, we're here together on this evening, we're together and walking and we should be so much closer together. Please stay with me. Please come with me," and then she began to believe she could hear the whispering of a thousand city lovers there on the street, and at the lunch counters, and coming from behind those darkened windows; the young men were softly begging, and the girls, growing more and more uneasy, looked doubtful, and yet listened. It seemed incredible to Anna that only a little while ago she had gone through those same streets, looking up at the lighted windows, longing to be loved, longing to be drawn into the life in those houses whether for joy, or weeping, or a worried waiting, for it had been terrible to feel alone where everyone was attached to someone. Yet tonight, with the little breeze touching her and blowing the rich smells of food from the restaurants, there was nothing human going on in that city block that she did not understand, the weeping of a girl deserted, the joy of a woman knowing love for the first time, the wail of a sick wife full of despair, the young man brutally beaten in that room over the poolroom on the corner, the lustful old man coaxing the innocent little girl to sit on his knee; she felt the surge of that complicated life that she could not see, just as she heard the noises on the street, smelt the gas and the oil from the cars, and then looked up, full of joy, at the dark sweep of city sky. Her heart beat a little faster; she hurried; her love grew as she hurried and she felt that if she did not soon get home to Michael, she would be smiling so broadly people would stop her and question her.

At the apartment house, Mac, the janitor, with his small bright eyes, his egg-shaped head, his one kidney and his heart trouble, was opening the door for her. Mac wanted to talk, for he was by nature a friend of the people, but Anna only said, "It's the nicest evening we've had, Mac," and clutched her parcels tighter and hurried up the stairs.

Mike was sitting at his desk by the window, making figures on a pad, and when she came in, he smiled in that gentle worried way she had come to love. His face was thin, and he was pale, but there was a quietness in him he had never had before. Putting her parcels down on an end of the desk, she cried out,

"Be honest, Mike. Tell me exactly what you were thinking of ten minutes ago."

"I was adding and subtracting," he said.

"I was sure you were thinking of me. I sort of felt it. I was sure you would say you were."

"Thinking of you gets in the way of my arithmetic," he said. "Look what you've done; I've hardly figured out anything."

"What were you adding?"

"We've got thirty-four dollars left," he said.

"But we just paid our rent."

"That's true, but we owe a month's grocery bill at the store on the corner."

"We can give them seven dollars on account and they'll carry us for another month."

"All right. That leaves twenty-seven dollars, and you've got to have some kind of a dress."

"I can get a dress in a basement of a store for four dollars and make it look as good on me as something you'd pay twenty-four for," she insisted.

"That'd be grand, and that leaves us twenty-three dollars to be tucked under my head at night."

"Why, that's splendid, Mike. I had no idea we'd get along so well on so little. I'm actually getting fatter, Mike. Wasn't it funny I was so sure you were thinking of me?"

"Oh, it was only for a minute," he teased her. "I just stopped once with my pencil in my mouth, and wondered where you'd be at about that time."

"I knew it," she said. "It was terribly exciting knowing it."

"Ah, my little Anna is so easily excited these days."

"I'm not. But I was coming along the streets looking up at the lighted windows, and then suddenly I felt very much in love. It just swept through me and I had to hurry."

From day to day his gravity had increased his gentleness, and now he was so touched by what she had said that he could hardly speak. And when she came over and put her head down against his neck, he held her close to him, and his hands began to caress her hesitantly. "Do you think you'll always come home like this, Anna?" he said.

"I'll hurry even faster," she said.

"No matter what happens, you'll always be as eager as this?"

"We'll keep it this way so nothing can happen."

His head was still pressed against her, and he was murmuring like this when they heard a knock on the door. They were both very still. He did not even lift his head, but he whispered, "Who do you think it is?"

"I don't know."

"It wouldn't be Huck Farr. He's not that friendly yet."

"I'll go. Why are you holding me?"

"I don't want to see anybody."

"I'd better see who's there anyway," she said.

She opened the door, and there was Nathaniel Benjamin, the young Christian professor, beaming with good humor, and he came waltzing into the room joyfully and threw out his arms and announced, "Salute me. I've got a job. I got a wire today. I'm going to teach metaphysics to the ladies in a college near Boston." As he strode up and down the room he was so innocently happy no one could help liking him.

"That's wonderful, Nathaniel," Mike said. "Yet look what it means. It means you'll be leaving us."

"I'll go, but I'll never leave you. I belong here with you people," he said. Then he turned and said to Anna, "What would you like, flowers, candy, wine, music? Whatever you want, just ask for it now. Don't you understand? It's Benjamin speaking. Benjamin, your affluent friend." Looking at them both as though he would love them forever, he sighed in contentment and sat down beside Mike.

Anna got the coffee percolator and lit the gas and started to make the coffee, for she knew Mike and Nathaniel would sit there for hours till it was long past midnight, drinking coffee and making stimulating conversation. Mike was so tender with Nathaniel on such nights as these that Nathaniel actually glowed. Anna couldn't understand how the two of them could talk for so long about notions and things; she couldn't understand how they could speak so softly and be full of wonder, how they both grew eager, as it got later, to express the warmth and willingness in them. In the old days Mike used to smile and bait Nathaniel till he roared and rushed out, and now Nathaniel was content to sit there hour after hour, never wanting to go home, loving the way Mike listened to him. Anna, hearing every word they said as she stood apart, making sandwiches, was disturbed, for she could not understand this change in her lover. Even though she loved the way his gentleness brought out the tenderness in Nathaniel's nature and permitted him to feel free and happy in this one place in the world, she was baffled by Mike's own humility. He let Nathaniel say things to him that would have made him ironic and amusing in the old days. It irritated her even more deeply that Nathaniel's wondering, eager, talkative, boisterous happiness never reached out to include her.

The coffee was percolating, and she had placed the three cups on the table, when she heard the young professor talking about women and chastity. His wide face was full of innocent enthusiasm for his spiritual life as he said casually, "Women aren't really necessary to me. I can lust after them, and thank God, think they're lovely, but I have the will to leave them alone. Fornication is the death of the spirit, you know. Is it T. S. Eliot who speaks about the modern attitude, mere animal couplings?"

As the words sifted through Anna's thoughts she remembered that time when Michael had said so earnestly, "Do you feel I ought to marry you, Anna?" and she had answered honestly, "I've thought about it, Mike," and he had persisted, "Wouldn't you be much happier?" and in her candid way she had declared, "Not unless it made you easier in your own mind." And now, leaning against the table, and listening to Nathaniel, she remembered Mike's voice, and her longing for security with him quickened, and there was an eager stirring inside her as she stared over at his thin, peaceful face. "When his head was pressed against my breast a little while ago when I came in from the street, I wanted him. I went on wanting him. Right now that feeling of wanting him is all I can remember, and it's so strong in me it's funny it doesn't reach out and touch him," she thought. But Mike was still listening to Nathaniel with an eager smile on his face as if he loved the warmth of his friend's words. In her disappointment, Anna thought, "Why don't you tell him to go home, Mike? I still feel your hands touching me, Mike. I still see your face against me. You don't need to marry me, Mike, not unless you really want to. But I want you so much, Mike. I'll wait such a long time and then maybe you'll always want me to be with you. Why don't you send him away?"

The young professor, in his passionate conviction, raised his voice a little, because Mike had mildly disagreed with him. "If you'll be honest, you know yourself, you often get a better feeling out of a poem or a picture than you can get out of copulation." Then he turned, and when he saw how Anna's face had reddened, he smiled apologetically. She was quiet, hating him, and waiting for Mike to laugh at him, and yet Mike only said, "I'm afraid you're a bit nuts on the subject of women, Nathaniel."

"I think you're really a pretty cold-blooded fish," Anna said sharply.

"I cold-blooded? I, Benjamin, cold-blooded? Ah, madam, you don't realize how you slander me and all the ladies who've loved me," he laughed. "They used to beg me to love them."

"I know you're quite a firecracker, all right," Anna said. "You often hit the ceiling, but the excitement's all in your head and not in your heart."

Anna did not know how she had hurt Nathaniel by suggesting there was a difference between the things he thought and the things he felt. It created a dualism in his nature that terrified him; and he looked at her unhappily, and then he struck out, "You're a woman, Anna, and therefore you can't imagine a passion that isn't purely physical. Would you believe this? Would you believe it," he said vehemently, "if I told you that six hundred years ago in Europe there were monks who would tear the skin off each other's backs with pliers, just for the sake of an idea? You can't understand that, can you?"

"I know I can't understand it. But I know, too, that that's what you'd like to be doing. Then you'd be really happy."

"What's the use?" he said, shrugging. "You're a woman. You've no choice. You've got to feel that way. I'm talking about a kind of joy and passion far different from any you know. There's a French poet, Max Jacob, and he gets up early in the morning and goes out to church and goes along singing at the top of his voice, and all the little middle-class people are shocked. What would you think of his kind of joy?"

"I'd say he was acting like a cheap show-off, parading before everybody."

"I'll write him and tell him and he'll worry himself sick," he sneered.

So Anna said nothing more; she only listened, her face sullen, wondering that Michael should be able to like Nathaniel's conversation, wondering what there was in it that sometimes pleased him so much. She assured herself it was only a mental excitement, and that was why she did not understand it, and yet she grew fearful as she listened, for she began to realize that Michael was getting a pleasure from Nathaniel's company that he could not get from her. While Michael was smiling at Nathaniel, as if he was sure he had found at last the one true bright and good part of his friend's nature, Anna was feeling more and more separated from them. A dreadful discontent

began to overwhelm her; she wished she had had a fine education; she wished she could enjoy such intellectual conversation; she longed to be able to take delight in fine ideas and not
to have to talk always about things she could feel and see, and
then it would never be necessary for Mike to turn away from
her to another for a satisfaction she had been unable to give
him. So she leaned forward and listened, her chin thrust out,
and as she wondered, and hated the young professor, and was
hardly able to follow him, she began to feel very humble.

When Nathaniel had gone she said to Mike, "Why do you
like him so much? You used to bait him."

"I like his enthusiasm. It's simple and wonderful. He was
pretty happy tonight. It makes me feel good when he's so
happy. He makes everybody feel good."

"He isn't simple. He throws himself around at everything.
He's like a street girl. He wants the whole world to go to bed
with him. You used to bait him."

"I know I did. That was because he used to get so mad, and
then he'd lead with his chin, and the temptation to take a sock
at him was terrible."

While they stood by the window, they heard a lusty voice
singing below in the street, and they looked out together and
saw Nathaniel Benjamin cutting across the square; they saw
that his hands were in his pockets as he passed under the light;
they heard him singing at the top of his voice. It was a bit startling to hear him singing alone like that in the city square. He
was singing the hymn, "Adeste Fidelis."

"There, didn't I tell you. He's a phony," Anna said. "He's
singing like that so we'll be sure and hear him. He knows we'll
be at the window. He's singing like that to make us think he's
like that French poet he talked about."

"Supposing he feels that way."

"If he saw a Salvation Army man singing on the way to
church on Sunday he'd laugh his head off."

"Nonsense. He's just feeling good."

"He'd turn you into a monk with his crazy ideas," she said passionately.

"I don't agree with you about him at all. I know he makes people feel like fighting with him. When you don't know him well, or have just met him, you only notice the things about him that separate him from you and everybody else. They're the easiest things to see, and then you're not really seeing him at all, because the part of him that's the deepest part of him is soft and gentle and he's terribly unhappy when he can't be gentle. If you just see him as God's angry man and think he's rambunctious and irritable, you don't see what really makes him a person at all. And when you see him like that the chances are that it's just the part of you that wants to be different from people that is seeing him; you're not seeing him with your whole person, you…"

"It's hard to see what you're getting at, Mike."

"Maybe I mean people just see him with their heads and not with their hearts at all. I distrust my head now. I don't want ever to be aware again of the things that separate me from other human beings." Then he smiled, and was quiet.

She tried earnestly to grasp what he was saying, but it was not clear to her, and she was humble; she only knew that she was in some way being pushed further away from him. "I don't think you understand Nathaniel at all, that's why I disagree with you so utterly," he was saying. "There's so much strife and chaos in him it often makes him feel wretched. His Jewish arrogance and his Christian humility make such a conflict in him that he's got the jitters half the time. Didn't you see how hurt he looked when you said that what went on in his heart and what went on in his head were two different things? But he's fine if people will only let him have peace. All the guy's longing is really for friendliness and goodness and peace. I don't agree with you at all."

When he had finished she was sullen. Then she got frightened at the feeling she had of being apart from him. She began to wonder what had happened to him that made him so much more patient, that had made him a bit timid, that gave him sometimes a shy and frightened look, and had filled him with a vast willingness to have charity for nearly everyone. And though this feeling in him, she knew, was good, she had often thought it came out of some secret grief he kept hidden from her.

"What happened to you to make you feel so different about it?" she asked suddenly.

"I don't know what you mean."

"You feel different about so many things," she said restlessly. "Sometimes you don't even look the same and you're so quiet."

"There's nothing different about me at all," he said.

Then she realized how wide and quick the separation from him might be, and the sullen discontent left her, and her wide blue eyes began to show the helplessness she felt.

And he was troubled, and he had to turn, and with neither of them speaking or moving, he felt himself being pulled toward her, so he said softly, "You were lovely when you came in with your parcels tonight, Anna. What had happened?"

When she began to say, "Nothing really happened. I was just coming along the street on the way home," he felt the magic surge of her whole being to him. "I was walking along and I began to have the feeling that everything going on all over the city touched the two of us tonight," she said. "There was only one thing …"

"What was it, Anna?"

"I hoped you'd be sitting there when I came in and you'd have your chin on your hand and you'd turn and look at me as if you'd been liking me a long time. It sometimes hurts me inside when you look at me like that. It hurts so much, but in a way it's very good, and I keep wanting to feel it for a long time."

"You can feel it all day and all night and then all eternity waits for us, you little Russian."

"Eternity can afford to wait, Mike, but we'll speed it up and have it all now. And anyway, I'm not a Russian."

"You little Litvak, then."

"You're ignorant. I'm not a Litvak."

"You little round-cheeked Pole."

"Yah, in my father's country they hated the Poles. Listen, Mr. Mike. This is my country just as much as it is yours."

He laughed a little and reached out and pushed her gently, and she loved it, but she knew there was no real gayety in his heart. Underneath the lightness of his words was the darkness she could never touch, that had been in him ever since he had been sick.

But when they went to bed, and he put his arms around her and kissed her and their bodies were together and he held her tight, there was an ecstasy between them that made her cry out brokenly in the dark of the night. Yet she felt that even in his lovemaking, even in the way he held her fast, there was a worried hurrying, as if he knew he must be quick and hard, or it would all be lost. And she lay there when they were still, wondering what was hidden under the gentleness and the lightness with which he touched her.

Once she woke up and found he had hold of her arm. He was clutching her arm so tight he was hurting her, yet he went on sleeping and dreaming and breathing with that deep and terrible steadiness. She was frightened as she lay there wondering what was in his dreams, and her arm was almost numb, yet she could have cried with joy at knowing his fear of losing her. She began to think she would simply be very patient and day after day he would feel her love for him, and his security would grow and he would laugh more and never be sad when they were together.

Twenty

I T DID NOT seem unjust to Michael that he should be free and his father should be bearing the blame for Dave Choate's death. There grew in him day after day a great hunger to find that there could be justice among human beings on earth. When he was passing through the streets among those with faces full of discontent, or passing by the long lines of men outside the soup kitchens and seeing the evictions of families of men who wanted work, or when he read the police court news in the papers and read of brutal crimes and vicious punishments, he felt that the life of the city was like a turbulent riot in which there could never be any order or justice, in which you had to hold fast to any little thing you loved or it would be snatched from you. He often had a great hunger to feel that he was making a just balance between his father's life and his own.

Yet in his heart he knew he dare not pity his father, for fear of doing something that would lead to a separation from Anna. Often when he was raising the window before going to bed and hearing the rumbling noises of the city, it was hard to believe he had found Anna and her goodness and her love in the meaningless strife of his life and in the death and corruption around him; he felt that their love was such a precarious thing that they must live very quietly and try and be alone.

He had got work for two weeks in the research department

of the Lake City Light, Heat and Power Company. This company, which supplied electricity to the city, was trying to overcome the industrial depression by stimulating people to use power in new ways in their homes, and they had established a research department where engineers worked on plans for equipping homes with electrical heaters. The work Michael did was hardly more than clerical work, but he and Anna were very joyful. It excited them to think the company might find some real work for him some day.

The night he got his first week's salary, a night in the early autumn with lights in all the store windows and the street lights lit, he did a very stupid thing: Before going home he took his thirty-two dollars and went and stood in front of the window of the little dress shop where he and Anna had often stood when they were out walking at night. He looked a long time at a black chiffon dress with wide puffed sleeves and a plain green belt at the waist. That dress had been in the window all week. It was such a simple graceful dress that it looked sophisticated and flowing with a very worldly distinction. Night after night when they had looked at the dress he had hardly noticed that it was on a manikin with a silver head, but now that he was alone, he noticed the manikin, and it was like looking at Anna's dress on someone else, and the manikin, tall and silver-haired, was very cold and lifeless. He kept looking at the dress and seeing it on Anna, and then he got excited, and he hurried into the store, smiling broadly and making a little bow to the girl, and he paid twelve dollars and fifty cents for the dress, and asked them earnestly to put it in a nice box for him. Then he rushed out, full of elation, and walked fast through the streets, among all the passing faces, with the soft cool air of the early autumn evening quickening his love.

When he had started to climb the stairs into the apartment house, he heard Mac Mackenzie calling, "Mr. Aikenhead. Mr. Aikenhead," and he stopped on the stair, holding his box in both hands.

Around the foot of the stairs came the janitor's bald head and beet-red face with the pale blue eyes, and he was breathing hard and sighing, for he had just hurried over to the corner with a few bets he had taken for his friend in the cigar store, who ran a little handbook on the races. He had just had time to sip a bit of whiskey, and then he had thought he had heard Michael's step on the stairs. Tonight the janitor looked worried and ashamed, and this was remarkable because he was so easy-going and unheroic in his own life that he had a patient gentleness for nearly everybody. "I got something to say to you, Mr. Aikenhead, that's pretty hard to say," he said.

"Did you ever find it hard to say anything to me, Mac?"

"God almighty, I never realized there were so many interfering scarecrows in the world. I never could understand why people wanted to stick their noses into other people's lives."

Michael thought someone had complained to the owner of the apartment that Mac's breath smelled of whiskey all the time, and he laughed and said, "Is someone treading on your toes again?"

"It's not my toes they're hurting this time. You know Miss Gray, the lecturer?"

"I ought to. She told me one time I was no gentleman because I didn't stop and speak cheerfully every time I saw her."

"She's complaining about Miss Prychoda living in your apartment."

"There's nothing to complain of in our place, Mac. You know that," Michael began fearfully. "Our place is a nice, quiet place. We never have any company and we never make any noise. What's the matter with her?"

"You understand, Mr. Aikenhead, it's absolutely okay with me. I know you're fine people. But that woman's nuts or I never listened to any woman that was. She's kept her screwiness inside her a mighty long time, but now she's at the age where she's going cockeyed about everything and mainly about sex. She's got a crazy look in her eyes. She hardly makes a plugged nickel on her lectures. I started to argue with her and I thought she was going to scream at me."

"Tell me what she said, Mac."

"What's the use of repeating it? She said the place was a brothel now, and you and the girl would have to get out or she would. She says everybody knows what goes on in your place with that girl not married. So she says I got to tell the owner or she will. I thought I'd tell you."

"Did she say anything about Anna?"

"That's when I thought she'd scream at me because I laughed and said, 'Lady, you're talking like a book and a pretty old one,' because she kept saying the girl was what she called a fancy girl and a joy girl, so I said with a dead pan, 'You mean she's a whore, ma'am?' and I thought her eyes would jump out of her head with excitement, but she just said the place was a brothel and then beat it." And because he was dreadfully ashamed to have to tell this to Michael, whom he liked and respected, he tried to laugh as he added, "That makes me the keeper of the brothel, doesn't it?"

But Michael only said, "Did anybody else say anything? Did Huck Farr say anything?"

"Him, I should say not," Mac said, and he shook his long forefinger and said seriously, "That man's a good guy. You'll never catch him with his finger in anybody else's pie."

"I guess there's nothing for us to do but move," Michael said. "Thanks for telling me, Mac." And as he went on up the stairs all he could remember of what had been said to him was that Anna was not married to him. It began to seem a terrible thing that he was exposing her to the wild and bitter gossip of women like Miss Gray. Each one of his footfalls on the stair sounded loud, and with each step as he mounted, his love for Anna began to grow, and he kept thinking, "This is terrible.

Why don't I marry her? How can she believe I love her? She wants me so much to marry her." And yet as soon as he felt this eagerness to marry her, he felt that fear he had known the first morning he had found her caring for him in his room, and he had known surely that he must leave her free of him. But a voice within him was crying, "Hurry, hurry and talk to her and make it right with her and give her some security," but from deeper within him, and out of the fear that was so close to his heart he heard, "You must always let her be free. It's your own selfishness that would try and tie her to you. You want to pull her along with you," and then his footsteps were much slower, as if he never wanted to get to the top of the stairs.

When he opened the door he could see Anna in the little kitchenette with a blue rubber apron on. But as she turned, she only noticed the box under his arm, and she said, "What have you got in the box, Mike?"

"It was pay day," he said.

"But it looks like something to wear, Mike."

"It's for you, Anna," he said quietly, and he put the box on the table.

She bent over the box, and she lifted out the black chiffon dress with the green belt, and she let the material of the dress slide slowly through her fingers, and she said nothing. But when she raised her head, her face was dreadfully solemn. "It's that dress we used to look at. We can't afford it, Mike. It's very lovely, but we can't afford it, darling." And it was comical to see her suddenly wrinkle her face up and then start dabbing at her eyes, and then before a moment passed, to see the different wrinkles of laughter while the tears were still in her eyes.

"Why are you crying, Anna? What's the matter? I don't want you to do anything like that. Please be happy about it, darling," he coaxed her, but his voice was so soft that it became even harder for her to be sensible.

"I'm silly, Mike. There's nothing the matter with me. Can't I cry if I want to?"

"But I wanted you to show some joy."

"Can't I show it that way if I want to?" she said.

Then she picked up the dress and pulled off her apron and rushed over to the mirror. She slipped off her old dress, and patted her hair, and put lipstick on her lips, and then put the new dress on. She was all radiant with excitement when she turned and walked slowly across the room. "How do you like me, Mr. Mike?" she said lazily, for she knew she could wear fine clothes as well as anyone in the world. And when he saw how innocently joyful she was and how she had walked across the room like someone who was proud and free, he felt he had never seen anyone who possessed such a natural, lovely dignity. And while he looked at her and was full of longing that she might remain forever like that, it began to seem terrible that the neighbors should be calling her a whore. With his face white and solemn, he tried hard to feel her gladness, and he never spoke.

She saw how worried he had become and she felt he had started fretting about having spent the money when they could not afford it, and she went over to him and put her head against him and said, "It was mean of me to make you feel I wanted the dress so much. It was selfish of me to gloat over having it on my back. I lose my head when I see anything beautiful, and my heart leaps and I want it, and I become so selfish. But I don't need it, Mike, darling. I'll send it back. You haven't had a new suit in years. I'm not your good Anna. By instinct I'm entirely selfish."

"I wasn't thinking about the dress at all," he said. "You looked lovely, and you've got to keep it. I was just thinking we've got to move."

"No, we don't. We're only a month behind in our rent."

"That's one reason why they'll let us go. I was talking to the janitor. Miss Gray was complaining about us living together here."

"What's there to complain of ? We've never bothered

anybody and we're quiet and respectable. I don't see anything wrong. I don't know why anybody would want to worry us when we're quiet and want to be alone. What did she say?"

"She said we've turned our place into a brothel."

"What did she say about me?"

"Nothing much about you, just the brothel stuff. The bitch! I'll bet she couldn't sleep at night thinking of us up here, overhead, loving each other and being content. All right. We've got to move."

"I'm a brothel girl, am I?" Anna kept saying, and her face reddened, and she was full of vigorous confidence. "I'll go and have a talk with that woman," she said. "I'll have her apologize. I'll make her ashamed. I'll bet she won't look me in the face." And she rushed out, and he heard her running downstairs.

While he waited, and listened fearfully, thinking of the thin woman's eyes snapping crazily at Anna, he could almost see the two of them facing each other, and then his own indignation became so strong he jumped up and opened the door; but while he still had his hand on the door knob, he saw Anna coming along the hall. She was white faced and subdued. "I didn't see her," was all she said. "She wasn't in."

He did not know what to say to her because she was so forlorn and quiet, and when they were sitting down in their own place, she hardly looked at him; her head was on one side and her hands were clenched together in her lap and she was frowning and wondering.

Then she said timidly, "Do you think I look like a whore, Mike?"

There was such an ache of helplessness in him, such a vivid memory of how she had looked a few moments ago as she walked across the room in the new dress, that he could say nothing. He only shook his head.

"It must just be that we're poor that would make anybody think I wanted to turn the place into a brothel."

"That's our hard luck, too, because we're just poor enough to be terribly respectable."

"Did you ever see a girl in a brothel that looked a bit like me, Mike?"

"I won't in this world, you little nut, but maybe I will in the next one," he said, trying to make it a joke.

And then, while they were looking at each other innocently, he was waiting for her to begin reproaching him, "If you had married me this would not be necessary at all. You keep saying you love me and don't want to be without me; then why don't you marry me?" Her face showed how troubled she was, and while she was silent, he felt they were both having the same thoughts, just as they were listening to the same sounds from the streets coming through the open window, the noises of brakes screeching and kids playing and shouting; and then when they both turned their heads and watched the way the night air was bellying the window curtain, he felt certain that what had just happened was truly the beginning of some degradation for her.

But when she did not reproach him at all, he said jerkily, "I didn't want anything to change. I wanted it to stay just like this for us so nothing would happen."

"Nothing much has happened, Mike. Nothing that really touches us. I've often noticed the way that poor old girl stared at me."

"There's no use trying to hold on to anything," he said. "It all gets broken in the same stupid, meaningless way. Anybody could run this god-damned universe better than it's run. No matter how you long for a thing, it doesn't matter. You get kicked around just the same. There's no order in anything human. Everything you love, everything simple like the noises on the street out there, and the bit of wind coming through the window and the sunlight on the good warm days, it's all accidental. We love each other and try to hold it, and that's just accidental. You know what I think, Anna? You know how I could show it was important and not just accidental that we love each other and want to be always together? I could die, or we both could die, and then we'd make it important. That would be absolutely final, and it could never be altered, and listen, you'd make what you died for important. They never could change your assertion of its importance. But I'm scared of dying. I'm frightened of it. Death touches you everywhere; it's on the streets, and in your mind, and it's what destroys everything we hope for and everything we try to hold. I've got it figured out, and the only way you can lick it and destroy it is by dying, but I don't want us to die. I'm scared of dying. I just want us to be able to stay together." He spoke out of the fear that had been in him for so many nights. He spoke with such a resentful bitterness that she was silent in wonder. He spoke out of his disordered dreams. For the last month he had been able to sleep and there had been almost a stillness at times in him, but the deep fear rose in him whenever they were most happy, as if their happiness was so fragile that it could not be strained by too much ecstasy, too much hoping, or any kind of despair.

And Anna was troubled by the fear she felt in him, for she remembered the time he had pounded on her door and had run down the stairs. "It's just a trifle," she said. "Do we care where we live? Doesn't it mean anything to you that we can save a month's rent? We'll leave by request and we won't pay the rent. Isn't that lovely? It just came along at the right time."

"Could you look around tomorrow?"

"I'll hunt up a place in the afternoon," she said. She seemed to be delighted. "Do you know what I've got for dinner?"

"I can smell it."

"You don't know what it is. My mother used to make it and we used to love it at home. Cheese and potatoes rolled in a batter. Wait till you taste it!"

As he watched her moving briskly around the room, her

face beginning to glow, he began to feel elated at the thought of having a new home with her. She moved faster; she lifted the lid of the pot and the steam rose up to her head, and she was entirely absorbed in tasting the bit of food on the end of her fork.

He marveled that she was able to give all of herself to each separate moment; for her there was something everlasting in each moment that took all of her life. From time to time she talked about their new place, and he watched her, and he listened, and he began to feel there might be something high and even deathless in their love for each other.

Twenty-One

ALL THAT autumn they lived in a small top-floor flat in an old-fashioned apartment house near the botanical gardens. It was a place that would never be free again of the smell of cooking food. The sunken floor boards and the stairs had been marked and worn smooth by men and women who had worked and eaten and sweated and were long since dead. Their room with the sloping ceilings and the long window across the front had held the heat on the warm nights, and so they knew it would be cold in the winter. They shared the only bathroom on the top floor with a blind old soldier and his wife, who had a small pension, and with two young men of fine continental manners and soft voices, who were through college and were carrying canes and wearing spats while their mothers kept them and they waited for the time to come for them to begin suitable careers.

In this new place where no one knew them Anna and Michael were like two lovers who were together after only a short while of love-making and wanted to remain hidden from people. Anna skimped and saved and bargained ruthlessly with the bit of money they had, and persuaded grocers to give her credit, so they were never really hungry. They ate hamburg steak and sausages and a great many potatoes, and while the fresh vegetables like cabbages and tomatoes and peas were still cheap Anna went every morning to the market, like an old experienced housewife.

On Sunday afternoons, when there was bright sunshine, they walked over to the grounds round the university and sat down underneath the trees and fed bread crumbs to the pigeons. This was only the beginning of their holiday. Instead of going home, they went to a Chinese restaurant where you could get a full-course meal for fifteen cents, and they glutted themselves, and sighed, for the food was heavy, and then they walked back to the apartment and lay down on the couch and were very quiet and attentive, for they had come to the last part of the holiday program and they did not want to miss any of it.

In the next room the two young men had put their favorite record, "The Black and Tan Blues," on their talking machine, and in a little while their friends began to come in and soon they were all talking French. They were all friends of France. No one who ever came to that room had ever been to France, but they were in love with the French tradition and what they called "French things," and on these nights no one would dare speak a word of English. It was very pleasant for Anna and Michael to lie there listening to the strange accents and the broken hesitant speeches. The night was warm outside, and they heard the familiar street sounds mixed with these strange awkward accents from the next room. Finally there was ter-rific excitement. A professor from the French department at the university had just arrived, and he was also a great friend of France, who had been there once, and better still, he was by intellectual conviction a French royalist, and he was going to talk to them in French about the Paris riots and tell them what a fine chance there was for the restoration of the French monarchy.

While it was often funny to hear the friends of France having such sport, it seemed incredible to Michael and Anna that they should be listening to such detached and lofty chatter and such passionate enthusiasm for far-away causes when their own worry was what they would have for dinner, and when Mike's own particular worry was whether he would ever feel alive and free again.

On the day the blind soldier in the next apartment got erysipelas, Anna got a letter from her parents. She had phoned for a doctor for the blind man's wife, and the doctor had come and looked at the man who had numbness growing in his arms and his tongue, and had thought it might be spinal meningitis. While they waited for the specialist to come, Anna had listened to the wife whispering her worry, and then when the specialist had come, she had gone up to her own place, and there was Mike with the letter from her parents.

It was not much of a letter, just a blunt note from her father announcing that they were coming that night on an excursion train from Detroit and would stay overnight. The letter said they were worried about her being out of work, and were wondering how she was living.

"They can't come here, Mike. What'll we do?" Anna said.

"Sure they can come here. What's the matter with us?"

"They can't see you living here, Mike."

"I don't have to live here tonight. I'll get me a little room in a third-class cheap hotel."

"But you're all around the room, dear. They'll feel you around here."

"They won't feel me around here any more than they'll feel all the pimps and pedlars and second-storey men that ever lived here with their bimbos, will they? We haven't made the faintest impression on the atmosphere of this joint."

"Anybody could see a man lives here."

"Put everything of mine in the clothes closet and lock the door. I'll come and see you when they're here, like the boy friend calling on his girl."

"They'd never forgive me, Mike," she said, looking very

worried. Then she began to laugh and she got excited. "Come on," she said. "We'll soon get rid of you around here."

They took his shoes, his slippers, his winter coat, his pyjamas, everything that was in his drawer in the bureau, and his pipe and his few books, and they dumped them all into the closet. For a moment Anna stood there with her hand on the door looking at this pile of personal property that was all Mike owned, and her face was full of wonder, and she looked as frightened as though she were losing something; then she laughed and slammed the door and locked it and gave him the key.

They had their dinner together and they made a great joke of it, as though they were separating, and this was a last supper, and then she went down to the station, and he went off to an early fifteen-cent movie. He had got into the habit of going to these movies in the afternoons in spite of his will to save the money; he could sit there in the darkness, staring blankly at the screen, all his senses dulled, forgetting that he was alive, forgetting that he would go out to walk through the streets. Anna always knew by the shamefaced look he had on his face when he came in that he had been to a movie.

At nine o'clock that evening, when he went home, there was a quickening in him, and some of the shyness that a boy feels when he is going to meet his girl's people for the first time. Yet when he had climbed the stairs and was rapping on his own door, and he heard Anna coming, he started to grin, and he was afraid he would laugh out loud, but when she opened the door wide and called, "Come in, Mike," he went in timidly and stood there, ready to bow hastily to anyone who would speak to him.

Anna's mother, a plump woman with a worn face that was wreathed in smiles, was sitting on the couch, and her hand went up and fumbled with the neck of her blue dress as Mike looked at her. The father, a short powerful working man, smoking a pipe, was sitting beside his wife. His face was wide and inscrutable, except that there was that same fierceness in his eyes that came in Anna's eyes when she was angry. Before Mike had come in they had all been sitting there chattering. The father had pushed Anna away from him and stared at her, as if she had become a woman since he had seen her. The mother had kept on talking excitedly.

But now when Anna said, "Come on, Mike. This is Mike. I want you to like him because I do," the father and mother both stood up and bowed uneasily. The laughter and the gay excitement went out of the mother, and she looked at Michael, who stood there awkwardly, almost too scared to move. She looked at him shrewdly for a long time, and then she made a little, polite deferential bow. Her husband resented the way she had bowed, and glaring at her as if he could have beaten her, he grunted sullenly. Because they were silent and watchful, Michael knew they were feeling that he was close to Anna; they were feeling there was an intimate bond between them, and that he might in some way be taking her from them. Anna, unaware of this strange hostility, beamed at them all, and included them all in her love. She was sure she was only acting like any girl who brings her sweetheart to her home, and yet by the way she slid her arm possessively under Mike's, or the way she turned her head and said eagerly, "eh, Mike?" as if she had to have his approval, and all her other possessive little gestures that were now a part of her life, she was making them feel surely that Mike was actually her lover and that he might even be living with her.

In the one long moment of silence the father and mother seemed to be trying to feel everything that had happened to Anna since they had last seen her. Then the mother, smiling apologetically at Michael, said simply, "Excuse us, please. We haven't seen our Anna in a long while. We don't know much about her."

"Sit down, mister," her father said.

"Anna has told me a lot about both of you," Michael said. But the father and mother only looked at each other as if they were wondering what Anna might have said about them to a young man who was apart from them and would not understand them, and their silence and the way they looked at each other made Mike feel he was not of their people; he felt that they loved Anna and were afraid of him and were waiting for him to say something that would justify them in despising him.

And Anna grew uneasy, for she knew Mike was really pleading with her, and she said in her direct way, "Don't you like him, Papa?"

"I don't think we'd agree about much," her father said bluntly.

"I'm sure we would, Mr. Prychoda," Michael said eagerly.

"Now, Papa, he's a nice fellow and you know it," Mrs. Prychoda said.

Anna smiled warmly at her mother, for she was grateful, and the mother, pleased with herself, said to Michael, "Anna's father worries about her. But you shouldn't let him worry you, son. Nobody knows what he's thinking. I even never knew, myself."

"It is not true. I say what I want to say. I don't try to please," the father said.

"Does something seem to be the matter with me, Mr. Prychoda?" Michael asked.

"Nothing."

"We'll be good friends then, won't we?"

"Maybe. I could not say now."

"You don't understand, Mike," Anna said. "Papa's sitting there thinking you're an enemy of the working class."

"Are you a communist?" her father asked.

"Not exactly," Michael said. "I've found it difficult to have any definite political affiliations. I'm an engineer, but I'm not working."

"You're all the same, you people," Anna's father said contemptuously. He took his pipe out of his mouth and held it out in front of him and declared firmly, "I'd like my Anna to have someone in love with her who had strong class ideas." Gruff and stubborn, he sat there, with his blue eyes unwavering. In Detroit he had three days work a week. The last two jobs he had had before that, the employees had gone on strike and the strike had failed, and he had lost his job and he had become very bitter. "I am different than you," he said. "I know how you feel, but you cannot understand how I feel. It has not touched you, but it has touched me, and I do not like to see Anna not caring much."

"I do care. I do care. It has touched us," Anna shouted, and her father looked at her and grinned.

Anna's mother had been listening earnestly while her husband talked, and when Anna shouted, and the father again began to talk rapidly to Michael, who looked bewildered, the mother chuckled, for she knew her husband was willing to talk to Michael, even though he only talked bitterly. So she sighed in relief, and she said, "You come into the kitchen and make a cup of coffee for us, and let your boy and your father talk a bit, Anna."

While Michael sat there shyly with Anna's father, finding it difficult to make an inoffensive, friendly remark, he could hear Anna and her mother talking in such a way in the kitchen that it seemed they would never have time nor words enough to tell all they had often thought and wanted to say to each other. Anna asked one question after another hardly pausing for an answer, yet listening eagerly, and then she would say, "Listen, mother, wait till I tell you ..." Words flowed out of her, words about trifling little incidents and things she had hoped for and many things she had seen. Through the open kitchen door, Michael could see her leaning against the cupboard; he could see the side of her face and part of the skirt of her black dress. And when the animation in her voice seemed to grow, he wondered why it was that she had never talked with such abandonment to him; it was hard for him to understand why she should feel so free to talk just because she was with her own people.

Then Michael realized that Anna's father, who was silent, was staring at him intently, as if he would discover in some slight change of expression on his face, his most secret thoughts. And while he watched, the father's own high-cheek-boned and impassive face had a troubled hesitancy in it. At last he said awkwardly, "You and the girl are fond of each other, eh?" and he leaned forward eagerly.

"I love her very much," Michael said simply.

"She always has her own way. She always went her own way," he said, and he smiled and showed his fine, strong, white teeth. Then the worried groping expression was on his face again as he said, "We are fond of the girl. You can see that. Listen to them out there in the kitchen." Yet Michael knew the father still had not dared to express what was in his mind; he was hoping eagerly that Michael might be betrayed into saying something that would reveal how close he was to Anna; and sometimes, when he kept watching Michael and was silent, he seemed to be begging him to tell him the things he would like to know; he seemed to have found out by Anna's intimate little gestures, and by the ease and grace and fullness of her obvious feeling for Michael, that she had given herself to him. But the delicate words that might have expressed the father's thoughts were too difficult for him, so he jerked back his head with the short gray clipped hair, and tried to see through the kitchen door, and said, looking worried, "We're poor people. Anna was not used to much when she was with us. But she's used to a certain way, and it's not your way, and I don't think it ever will be your way."

That was the only time he tried to tell Michael to leave

Anna alone. After that he sat there and was silent, as though he were trying to feel everything that had happened to Anna since she had met her lover.

Michael was so touched by the love of these two people for their daughter that he smiled warmly and began to say, "We'll get along fine together, you and me. Don't worry about that."

"Maybe so. You're an engineer. That's good. You're not a lawyer, or a broker man, or something like that. We will need engineers. Maybe you will work again and build fine things."

"Remember, I am not against you."

"You must be with us, son."

Then from the kitchen came the voice of Anna's mother saying, "Don't you bother using eggs. You keep the eggs. We'll have just the coffee. Your father is not hungry."

"The eggs are all we've got for sandwiches and I'm going to use them," Anna said.

"It is wrong, Anna. It is very wrong. You should not do it," her mother said.

"She did not use to talk like that in good times. We have to watch everything at home now," Anna's father said apologetically to Michael.

Michael felt ashamed, for he began to think of his father's house, and his father's friends and their land of plenty; it did not seem to be the land of these people at all. He began to feel very close to this taciturn, unbeaten man. He felt all his courage and his hope. "We're going to have a lot to talk about. I'm glad I've met you," he said.

"It'll suit me," the father said. "I hope you get work, son."

By the time they had had their coffee and sandwiches they were used to each other. They could all talk rapidly, or they could be silent, or they could laugh, and they could all feel close together.

When Michael was leaving, they all went to the door with him, but Anna took his arm and stepped out in the hall with him and half closed the door on the others. There they put their arms around each other and kissed each other, and she whispered, "Do you mind, darling?"

"It's great fun," he said.

"They like you. Isn't that swell?"

"I like them a lot."

"They expected me to go out here and say good-bye to my boy friend," she whispered. "We'll have to make up that dollar and a half for your room some way."

Crossing the little park by the botanical gardens, Mike looked back at the apartment house. There was a light in the room of the friends of France. There would be a light in the room where the blind man was suffering from erysipelas. As he crossed through the park he could not keep feeling he had deceived Anna's people, because the feeling they had given him was so warm and friendly. He felt close to them, and they had filled him with hope.

Twenty-Two

At the time of Sheila's wedding to Ross Hillquist, Andrew Aikenhead was living so quietly in the city that his business friends downtown hardly ever saw him. He had never gone to his club since that day when he had felt his fellow-members were staring at him uneasily, for by this time it was hard for him to feel at ease with even two or three people; there would always be one among them, he was sure, who would believe him guilty of a terrible crime and resent that he had not been punished.

Out of his interest in the advertising agency he had got a sum of money that he had put aside, so there would always be an income for Marthe while she lived. It was not very much money, for an advertising agency has little in the way of permanent assets, and an agency in decline has hardly even good will to sell. But he had decided to sell his house in the city, and collect whatever equity he had in it, and sell his country place, too, if he could find a buyer, and take a little apartment in a quiet place where he could live alone after Sheila was married and had left him.

In the mornings, when he used to wake up, it was hard to believe that they did not want him downtown at the office. He had to tell himself over and over again that Jay even did not want him, and he would get up and dress and mutter to himself, "I'm not an old man. I'll get in to something else," yet he could not think of a single human activity that interested him at all. It was the season of the musical recitals. There had been a time not long ago when he and his wife had dressed for every concert, and the people who liked music had grown used to seeing him walk down the aisle, but now he hadn't the slightest desire to listen to music. He wasn't even much interested in having his whiskey and soda after dinner and reading the meditations of Marcus Aurelius, and nodding and thinking, "Superbly civilized."

Yet he could not stop walking in the streets in the early afternoons, and sometimes he passed the Agency office and looked up at the way the sunlight shone on the big windows. When he walked away he wanted to walk proudly and bow to people, but he had become suddenly a humble man, and if he saw anybody he knew, he lowered his eyes, or maybe looked at them in a sidelong, furtive way. He had grown careless about the way he dressed, and his trousers were baggy, and his shoes dull and unpolished, and his white hair was a little too long.

But the night before his daughter's wedding, when he was sitting dstairs by himself, looking aimlessly at his empty whiskey glass, he began to realize that his own daughter was upstairs and that all week she had been full of a restless eager happiness. And some of that joy she expected to find began to touch him, as he thought of it, because he loved her and she was close to him, and his eagerness to share her happiness became so great that he couldn't sit there, and he got up and hurried upstairs in his dressing-gown, with his white hair tousled all over his head. He stood in the hall outside her door and he listened and was sure she was awake. There was no sound in the room, yet he was sure he could hear Sheila breathing, and such a marvelous gladness was in him that he actually smiled, for he began to think that away over on the other side of the city, young Dr. Hillquist was in his own room at this time, and was wide awake and having thoughts that were much the same as Sheila's. It made him remember the night before his own marriage when he was Ross Hillquist's age; he had lain awake nearly all night trying to get used to the notion that he would never have to ache with desire for his girl again, that she would be there in his bed beside him for him to love, warm and close to him in his bed, when up to that time he had always been alone.

Then he went downstairs, and when he had been sitting there a little while, looking forward eagerly to going to church with Sheila tomorrow, planning how he would dress, and how he would greet his old friends and how they would all share the same happiness, he heard Sheila coming into the room.

Her dark glossy hair was loose and brushed back from her small head, and she was in her negligée. When her father looked up, her face was full of the warmth that she wanted to express to him. "I wanted to go to sleep, but I couldn't," she said softly. "I was thinking I wouldn't be sleeping here again. My whole life seemed to be turning around this one night. I heard you moving down here, and I thought you might be thinking the same thing."

"I was sitting here thinking how happy you'd be."

"I want to be terribly happy. I want us to get lost in our own happiness. Is that selfish?" she asked.

Her intense sincerity startled him, and he said, "You're right, Sheila. Put your happiness with Ross ahead of everything in the world, and if you find your home and your happiness are with him, that'll be your garden and it'll be the most beautiful place in the world. You must be happy, Sheila. You will, I know, but remember how much I wanted you to be happy. You and your children…"

"I don't want any children, daddy," she said. "We'll let everything go for the sake of our own happiness. I'll do everything for him. I'll live for him. I know it sounds selfish, but I want us to be closed off from everything that might take us out of our love for each other."

"Ross mightn't like that, Sheila. Most men want to have children."

"But I've told him how I feel. I've told him I don't know how people can bring children into a world like this. Haven't people any sense of responsibility at all? What can you ever do for children that will justify bringing them into the world?" She spoke with such a vehement passion that he did not know what to say. Ever since her mother had died she had felt close to him, and had often talked to him as intimately as she might have talked to her mother.

But he was troubled to hear her talking like this, and he said, "You mustn't even think of such things on your wedding night. You'll feel different when you go away from here."

"Yes, soon we'll be going to Lakewood. It's a little town, and we know nobody there, and Ross will be working and he'll be happy."

"It's so hard to believe you're really going away."

"You'll be staying here," was all she said, but she looked at him as though she were caressing him with her thoughts.

"I'll stay here, though I don't know why," he said, and he sighed. Then he said, "You go to bed, Sheila. We'll all be together tomorrow and it'll be the beginning of a very great happiness for you."

"I'll go to bed, but I won't be able to sleep."

"I couldn't sleep on my wedding night either."

"Good night, dad."

"Good night, Sheila," he said.

In the early afternoon Andrew Aikenhead and Sheila drove together to St. Bartholomew's church. They were sitting together in the cab, and Sheila was delighted with the eagerness and the good humor that showed in her father's face, and with the way he had dressed for this occasion. It was the first time in months that he had tried to look confident and eager. It was to be a quiet and informal wedding and Sheila was wearing a tweed travelling suit. And as they sat close together in the cab this good eager feeling was between them, as if they both felt they were close to happiness. The only time they spoke was when Sheila turned her head and said mildly, "It looks as if it might rain." She took hold of her father's hand and held it the rest of the way.

Because it was to be such a quiet wedding they were all meeting in the vestry of the church, and when Sheila and her father went in they saw Dr. Albert Tucker talking to the young doctor and his mother and father and Michael.

Dr. Tucker was one of the most successful ministers in the city, and when he stood there, as he was doing now, with one hand clutching a prayer book, and his other hand waving as he urged everybody to be more jovial, he gave one a bewildering impression, for though his manner was so warm and encouraging, he had the shrewdest pair of half-closed blue eyes of anyone in the city. They were wise, hard, materialistic eyes, and they hardly ever changed in expression, even when he was comforting the sick, or drinking the health of a distinguished visitor to the city. But he had known the Aikenheads and the Hillquists for years, and he had baptized Sheila and now he was marrying her, and he was just saying, "I'll be there at the death of all of you, too," when Andrew Aikenhead came in.

Dr. Tucker put out his hairy, freckled hand to Andrew Aikenhead and said, "How's my old friend?" and he tried to show by the little bit of extra enthusiasm he put into his greeting that as far as he was concerned he had not tried to pass judgment on his old friend at all. The only trouble was that Dr. Tucker had exactly the same broad-minded manner and the same comforting enthusiasm when he was visiting prisons and asylums, so it was hard for Aikenhead, who knew him, to know what he was actually thinking.

They stayed in the vestry only a little while, but while they were there Andrew Aikenhead was almost jolly, he was so full of good will. He went up to Jay Hillquist and slapped him on the back, and seemed to have forgotten that they had not seen each other in a long while. It was only when he noticed the disgruntled expression on Jay's face that he felt a little shy. Jay was annoyed that it was to be such a quiet, unostentatious wedding, and, of course, he blamed Andrew for that, and, besides, he was embarrassed by the warmth and heartiness of his old friend's greeting. Such earnestness and such warm laughter seemed to him to belong to another time, and he did not know what to say, and he looked helplessly at his wife, who pitied him, and began a conversation with Andrew Aikenhead in a simple, friendly way.

"How is the business, Jay?" Aikenhead asked.

"Fine as silk," Jay said.

"Picking up at all?"

"It's not getting any worse, and from now on, damn it, it's going to get better." Jay had got noticeably older and his neck looked creased and red and stringy. He said stubbornly, "It'll get better if I have to fire everybody in the office."

"You'll probably do that very thing," Aikenhead said, and at that one moment, when he smiled and drawled his words, he was smooth and superior in the old way.

Then Michael came over and stood beside his father and smiled a little shyly as he put out his hand. Michael looked as if he had just had his hair cut and his suit pressed. He had come to this wedding eagerly, grasping at this normal relationship with his own people, and when he heard his father's voice, and saw him smile, he had said to himself. "Everything is all right. Nothing has happened to anybody. It's going fine. We're all glad to be here," and his own great willingness to be one with them all made him look flustered and excited. "Hello, dad," he said. "How have you been feeling?" and he took his father's hand.

His father was so touched by this simple gesture of friendliness that he turned hastily away from the Hillquists and said to Michael, "I feel splendid to see them getting married. It's what we always wanted for them. They'll be very happy. It's good to see you. Tell me a little about what you've been doing." His joy showed strongly in his face, and his longing to begin a gossiping conversation with his son about trivial but intimate things was so great that it made him seem childishly innocent. Michael began to talk to him. He began to talk slowly and awkwardly, but then he saw how his father's face was thin and the ruddy color all gone from it, and how his confidence had been replaced by this innocent yearning for friendliness. There was something about his father's eagerness that began to frighten him. He could see what had happened to his father, and suddenly he felt that his father's suffering and bewilderment were being thrust out at him for him to bear, and he resented it and looked impatient, and went to turn away.

"Have you just a moment, Michael?"

"I thought they were ready to go into the church?"

"Ah, so they are. That's a pity. Come and see me.

"I will," Michael said, and he left his father and went over to talk with Ross Hillquist and Dr. Tucker and Sheila.

For the first time that afternoon Andrew Aikenhead felt hurt, and he looked around nervously, and then he took hold of himself and cleared his throat and joined the Hillquists again.

The wedding was quick and simple. Andrew Aikenhead entered the church by the front door, with Sheila on his arm, and he walked solemnly up the aisle, walking slowly in step with Sheila, and feeling a pride and dignity in having her with him, because she was lovely and young. The few people who had come into the church and who were in the back seats couldn't help craning forward to get a look at her face. Ross and Michael were waiting at the front of the church by the choir stalls.

Sheila and Ross stood together, and Dr. Tucker read and prayed, and once they could all hear him whisper, "Have you the ring, doctor?" and Ross looked nervous, as if he might have forgotten it, and then his face lit up, and he handed the ring to the minister. At the moment when Ross was fumbling for the ring, Andrew Aikenhead began to wet his dry lips, and he leaned forward tensely, feeling that someone might cry out and spoil it, but then when he saw that it was finished, he couldn't stop smiling; he sighed and smiled, and stood up and shifted his weight from one leg to the other and kept on smiling. "Splendid, splendid, splendid," he kept repeating.

Sheila and her husband were going away at once. They were saying good-bye at the church door. They were taking Michael with them as far as the station.

"Good-bye, good-bye, good-bye," they all began to call to Sheila and Ross, who were getting into the taxi. Sheila's face was warm and glowing and lovely, and her eyes were moist and she was laughing and half crying in her excitement and happiness. She kept hold of her husband's arm while he leaned out and talked rapidly to his father. They all started kissing each other. "Good-bye, darling, good-bye, son, good-bye, my child, good-bye, dad," they kept saying, and then they began to throw kisses.

The Hillquists and Andrew Aikenhead were left standing on the sidewalk in front of the church in the bit of cold sunlight of that late autumn day. The three of them stood there together, looking after the cab, while the wind blew the leaves along the street. Once Sheila waved her hand out the window, and the three old people stepped forward eagerly and waved their hands. Then there was a cold gust of wind, and the rustle of more leaves, and Mrs. Hillquist put her hand up to her throat.

"There goes a good part of our life," she said.

"They've gone," Andrew Aikenhead said. "They've gone."

"Well, old friend, here we are," Mrs. Hillquist said, sighing.

"Well, Alice?"

"It does seem like the end of something for us, doesn't it?"

"They'll be very happy together, I know that."

"It was nonsense to run off like that," Jay said. "The lot of us ought to have had a wedding dinner of some kind. Why did they want to do it, anyway? Besides they ought to have had a big wedding and not such a hurried business as we had," he grumbled.

"That's all you've been thinking of, Jay," Mrs. Hillquist said impatiently.

Jay fussed with the buttons of his coat, and he blew out his breath noisily, for he wanted to restore the intimacy they had once had with Andrew Aikenhead. "How about coming along with us for dinner, Andy?" he asked gruffly.

"'Thanks, thanks, Jay. The trouble is I've got an appointment in an hour," Aikenhead said. He was really grateful. He made one of those gallant bows to Mrs. Hillquist that he so often used to make to her. But he also appeared to be a little frightened, as though they had made it clear that they regarded him as someone who was weak and had to be sheltered.

While the Hillquists were waiting gravely for him to say good-bye to them, a man in a peak cap came running up with a newspaper camera held against his chest, and when he was a few feet away from Aikenhead he lowered his head to the camera and shielded his eyes with his hand. But Andrew Aikenhead stood there smiling at the camera man, while he thought, "The pretense is that they want my picture because I am a father whose daughter has just been married. They haven't had a picture of me for some time. People mustn't be allowed to forget me. It's absolutely meaningless. But I've been happy today. It's the first time in months I've felt such happiness. They won't spoil it. They won't make it meaningless, too," and he took off his hat, and smiled broadly, and looked up so the light would be good on his face. "How's that?" he said to the camera man, as though he were an ordinary happy father who looked forward to seeing his picture on the society page. "All right, is it? Thank you," he said, and he walked away almost jauntily, preserving the day's happiness.

While he was standing at the corner waiting for the red light to change, he thought he saw the bright yellow cab that had carried Sheila and Ross away, jammed there among other cabs at the intersection. He began to wave his hand, trying to make them see him, but just then the green traffic light came on, and all the cabs moved slowly across the road, and the bright yellow cab shot forward on the other side and went farther and farther away.

Sheila and Michael were carried farther and farther away. He looked after them, as they went, and he remembered that time when Michael and Sheila had gone away years ago, of the way they had gone that day he brought Marthe to the house, and he wondered earnestly about what had actually happened that day, years ago, while he muttered, "But they're really gone now. They're really gone."

Twenty-Three

MICHAEL saw his father again one day in the early winter when he was sitting in Hilton's lunch room. There had been an early fall of wet snow, and he was sitting by the big plate-glass window, watching the heavy snow flakes drifting slowly across the steps of the City Hall which was on the other side of the street. As soon as the snow fell on the sidewalk it was trampled into black slush. Men coming into the restaurant took off their hats and shook them before going up to the counter to get their food.

In the cold weather of the winter the chairs in Hilton's restaurant were always filled with bums and petty crooks and pimps and gamblers and a great many young men who had nowhere else to go. The young men who were out of work sat in their chairs along the wall and stared blankly at the floor. Sometimes big red-faced Irish detectives, wearing hard hats, came in and sat there and looked over the customers, and everybody stared at them and knew precisely that they were big red-faced Irish detectives, wondering whom they might be lucky enough to pick up that day. The floor was filthy from wet boots, and a bus boy kept mopping it up with hot soapy water that made the air smell sweet and sickening, while a whitecoated, square-faced bouncer, collecting the coffee cups, tried to drive anybody away who had been sitting there half an hour.

Michael was wondering how it was that the bouncer knew so surely that even the decently dressed men had lost their confidence and would get up and go meekly when he ordered them to go. The bouncer was coming his way, and he ducked his head nervously into the sporting page of the newspaper. And when the bouncer had passed he looked up, and he saw Bill Johnson coming in. "Heh, Bill," he called eagerly.

Bill came over, smiling broadly with that spontaneous friendliness he could not subdue. Today he looked more boyish and handsome than ever, even though he had a big piece of sticking plaster over his right eye and a welt on his jaw. He and some of his friends had got caught in an eviction riot when they had tried to stop a bailiff from pulling the doors down from a house and lugging out a kitchen stove. When he stopped smiling, he looked white faced and wary.

"Did a Mack truck hit you?" Michael said. "It doesn't look as if the revolution is going so well."

"That's all right, Mike. You look as if you'd been pushed around too, only you've been pushed around in a different way and haven't even had the satisfaction of taking a sock at someone and getting socked. You're pale around the gills."

"I feel all right. What's the matter? I'd say go ahead and be a chopping block if you thought you were getting anywhere. But you know you're not, Bill. You know there's not going to be any revolution in America. You haven't got a chance. They've got the police and the army."

"Jesus, what am I to do? Lay down my arms at once? I didn't know you were such an authority on the technique of revolution."

"Sure I am. Ask me anything you like. I just told you what I had been thinking. Do you really think you have a chance, Bill?"

"I'm not a fool, Mike. I don't expect any revolution tomorrow. It may take years. It may take all of my life and a hundred years more, but it's coming and it's worth working for, and I know that every bit of work I do now and all the tough times we go through and the beatings you take now and then all pile up and hasten the end, and the human race goes slowly forward." In his excitement, Bill whispered, pulling at Mike's arm, "You know damn well you'd feel a lot better if you, yourself, had something to live for."

"I agree absolutely, Bill. Listen, you don't think you hate the way things are any more than I do, do you? Drive along your bandwagon and I'll get on it. I'll go with the parade right up to the big tent. But I've learned something else. I know it will help a lot to clear the land away and so it'll be easier to live, but there's more to it than that. The personal problems will begin all over again then. You seem to think that you just have to have an economic house cleaning and we'll all get justice. None of us will get justice, personal justice, and we'll start hungering for it all over again."

"You want a little private orgasm with the universe."

"That's right."

"Why don't you try prayer? You and your little pal, Nathaniel Benjamin ought to team up."

"I haven't got his faith or yours."

"Try talking about justice to these babies sitting around here and see if they speak your language," Bill said.

Michael looked around at the row of men with their white discontented faces, at the old man with the white moustache who had just dropped off to a sleep that would only last a moment, at the furtive-eyed Pole sitting by himself at the window, at the two excited, whispering little men with the battered hats, and at the Jewish newsboy from the corner who had come in and was trying to sell filthy pictures that mocked Hitler, the German. They all had the faces of human beings; they were all intended to be men.

"Don't tell me they understand your language either, Bill. You've been talking social justice to guys like these for a long time and they won't even roll over. It's personal with them.

They'd like a break, they'd like justice, but they never expect to get it."

"So they just sit around like you, doing nothing about it, waiting for justice to turn up."

"That's it. They sit around and wait."

"Waiting to inherit the earth."

"That's it."

"They don't understand their condition and what it's all about. Even if they did they wouldn't have the guts to do anything about it," Bill said.

Then they both leaned back and raised their feet, for the bus boy had swished his sopping mop at their chairs, and while they held their feet up, and were silent, Michael saw his father come in, with his coat collar turned up, and with a little crown of white snow on his hard hat. He went up to the counter and bought himself a fried-egg sandwich and coffee, and he sat down and put catsup on his sandwich. Then he began to drink his mug of coffee, and when he had finished, he sighed, and pushed the mug away and looked around mildly. He had the same hurt, unresisting expression on his face that so many men had who sat in that restaurant in the afternoon, and he was just as untidy, and he, too, had no place in particular to go.

Then Michael realized that his father was looking over at him. His heart began to beat unevenly, and he could not budge, and his face felt wooden, and finally he dropped his head, muttering, "Why doesn't he go? If I speak to him everything I've built up will fall to pieces. He'll come around and destroy it. My God, he looks terrible. I only want to hold on to what I love and nothing more. He doesn't see me. He doesn't know I'm here." And he kept his head down, his heart thumping so slowly and so loudly he was sure Bill Johnson would hear it.

As he waited miserably with his head down, he began to feel that his father, too, was waiting, and it got so that he could not stand it, feeling his father's eyes were turned on him, and he had to look up blankly, hating himself for his wooden, unseeing face.

But his father was getting up, turning up his collar around his neck, his blue eyes wavering around the place, and never quite seeing Michael again. He went down the aisle. He went out to the street and he stood a minute in front of the big window, looking up blankly at the City Hall clock, as if it might be of extraordinary importance to note the exact time. The snow melted on his thin worried face, and then he went on along the street.

"Wasn't that your old man that went out?" Bill asked.

"I didn't see my old man."

"I thought you were looking at him. I thought he was coming over here."

Bill took one quick, wondering look at Michael, and then he said, "Jesus," and he shrugged his shoulders, and it was easy to see that he had only contempt for Michael, for he thought he had rejected his father because the whole town had been talking about him and now he looked like a derelict.

So Michael said, "So long, Bill. I've got to go," and he hurried out and looked along the street. A little way along, opposite the department store, he saw his father with his shoulders stooping a little and with his hands in his pockets, going ahead aimlessly. And even as Michael insisted to himself, "He didn't see me. What makes me feel so sure he saw me?" he felt such a desolate shame within him, and such a pity for his father that he began to follow him along the street. This was the first time he had felt such shame. At the wedding he had looked at his father and had got scared suddenly. That was all. Now he followed him in the lightly falling snow, full of pity and shame and thinking only of how those blue eyes had shifted away from him when he had ducked his head in the paper.

But when they had gone a little way, and the figure of his father was getting lost among the people who were crowding out of the department store, he suddenly longed to be at home with Anna. "I know how he feels, I know everything that's happened to him. He looked so broken; but what can I do?" he thought, and as he hesitated there on the street, he grew frightened of doing something he would regret later on. The only way he had of resisting this fear was by yielding to his longing to hurry home to Anna, to think of nothing but Anna and her goodness and their peace and their security, so the shame might be shut out of his heart.

When he was going into his apartment he heard a man's voice, and he listened and was full of fear before he opened the door, but when the voice rose and he knew it was Ross Hillquist's voice, he went in gladly and stood there smiling with relief.

The young doctor was sitting at the folding table with Anna and the table was covered with parcels and cans of cooked meat, for the doctor had taken Anna out to treat her. He did this whenever he came to the city. He and Anna had already cut themselves slices of rye bread that they were eating with salami and dill pickles. The doctor's dark healthy face was beaming with the gladness he felt in being there with them.

"We couldn't wait, Mike, old boy. Your little lady got hungry."

"We intended to wait for you," Anna said, looking very ashamed. "It was all my fault. Ross wanted to wait, but I simply couldn't. I looked at the food and I just couldn't wait. I don't know what's the matter with me."

"Isn't she the guilty girl," the doctor said. "I went into a store and left her holding some bags and when I came out she was eating a cheese wafer."

"I know. I'm ashamed. I don't know why I did it. But if you hadn't come out when you did I would have eaten the whole bag."

"Ross will think you don't get enough to eat," Mike said.

"I've been like a little pig the last few days."

"How is Sheila, Ross?"

"She feels well enough, but she's too quiet. She says she loves it up in that town, but I think she hates it, and she's creating a little private world for herself, a little boudoir world. She's more elegant and more lovely than ever," he said. Then he was silent, and he was worried, but when he looked at Anna, and at Michael's thin face, he smiled warmly, for he felt there was something desperate in their love and their poverty and their eagerness to be friendly, and it made him feel that his own private worry was utterly unimportant. He really believed now that they were often hungry, and as he went on saying, "Sheila gets in with people like the high school principal and an agent's wife who once lived in New York, and they have their cocktails in the afternoon, and she talks a lot about when we'll go to New York, and she makes me feel that we're happy in such a patient, lovely, untouchable, boudoir way," he was wondering what he could do to help Mike and Anna.

"What do you want her to do?"

"I'd like her to be with people like you and Anna," the doctor said suddenly. And then he beamed, and he said eagerly, "That's why I'm here. I want you both to come up for a week. It'll be a change for you and it'll do Sheila the world of good."

"You want both of us to come?" Anna asked uneasily.

"Both of you. You especially."

"Maybe your wife would not want me to go up there with Michael."

"She's crazy to meet you. I talk all the time about you."

"The winter seems a hell of a time to go up there," Mike said.

"I'll tell you what I'll do. I'll give you a little excitement. I'll fix it for us to go on a wolf hunt when the January thaw ends."

"Wolves up your way?"

"We'd have to go about twenty miles into the hills and the bush. It's been a lean winter and they follow the food wherever it goes and this year the deer have been coming down pretty close to the settlements, and wherever the deer go the wolves will go."

Michael said excitedly to Anna, "We must go, darling. I'd do anything to get away from here for a while. I'd be awfully glad to go. Sheila will love you," and his enthusiastic words began to flow out of him so rapidly that Anna and the doctor began to laugh at him.

While they ate and drank a little beer and laughed they felt they were making plans for an excursion into a promised land where they would all feel very happy as soon as they got there. Anna tried to coax Ross to stay with them that evening, but he said he had to catch the train that left in an hour.

"You can listen to the friends of France if you stay," Michael said.

"They're good, but I can't do it, Mike."

"They're all we have to offer in the way of comic relief."

"Have you seen your old man, Mike?"

"No, I haven't seen him."

"He takes it pretty hard, doesn't he? Sheila was worrying about him. I used to get along with him fine. The last time we talked a lot was about a year ago. We had an argument about Nietzsche, and he couldn't see the notion of a superman at all. He says my father was the only superman he knew." Ross was putting on his coat.

When he had gone, Anna and Michael sat there looking at each other, and they both felt a little sad, and then they smiled at each other. Then Anna got up and took a slip of paper from her purse and said quietly, "He told me not to let you see this till he'd gone, Mike."

Mike looked at the slip of paper and saw it was a receipt from the woman who owned the apartment house for two months back rent. He looked up at Anna and his eyes filled with tears, and when he had to put his hand up to his eyes he was ashamed and could not speak.

At last he said, "I forgot to tell him I did see my father. I ran into him on the street. I don't know why I didn't tell him, Anna."

"What's the matter with you, Mike?"

"Nothing."

"What are you saying?"

"Just that. It's nothing. I just remembered," he said. When she kept on looking at him and frowning and wondering and hesitating, he was frightened and couldn't understand why he had mentioned his father.

Twenty-Four

WHEN Dr. Hillquist drove his car along the streets of Lake-wood on the winter nights and out along the silent country roads, where the trees in the winter fields were stark against the skyline, there would often be echoing in his ears the sounds, the voices, the cries of the life in the town and the farmhouses; he could still hear the angry words he had had with J. V. Holden, who owned shares in the town shipyard, and Holden's voice faded and was gone, and there were, instead, the mingled cries of the boy whose torn eye he had sewn up, the gasping whisper of the young man who had fallen asleep that night in the horse stalls and had died drunk while the terrified horses kept on kicking him. As Ross drove along with the bit of night light shining on the snow fields, while he heard all these sounds in his head of people living and dying, he would suddenly remember that his own Sheila would be sitting up waiting for him, no matter how late he would be. Then his private life began to seem aloof from the town life and untouched by its labor and misery. He began to feel that he and Sheila never did anything but nibble delicately at their own tenderness for each other, that he was given a reticent and lovely sweetness when he wanted a passionate lust. He felt this most sharply whenever he saw the sunlight flooding the faces of children coming home from school at noontime.

Grain boats from Chicago and Cleveland had once loaded grain at Lakewood, and the town had a drydock, but now there were few grain boats, and the drydock was usually empty. Whenever Ross was getting in his car near the big board fence around the shipyard, he would look up at the criss-crossing structure of the steel work and wonder how long it would be before the town heard the clattering of the riveters and the clang of steel on steel again. Then he would look out at the glint of light on the line of the cold dark water. At first he had thought he was having a little success in working with the people of the town. But then J. V. Holden had started to smirk at him when they talked about relief for the unemployed shipbuilders. The fathers of the town, too, were property holders, and very skeptical of anything Ross had to say. Even when he had gone eagerly to farmers, who had far too much unused land, and had tried to persuade them to let families from the town, who were out of work, till subsistence plots, he found the farmers suspicious and reluctant. Besides, when he talked to the poor families in the town, who were almost starving and living just on a bit of town relief, he found they had no enthusiasm at all for tilling the soil. They were town people, they said, and had a right to work in the town. Yet Ross succeeded in getting fifty families to declare they were ready to work the unused land that the farmers might let them work. "I can do nothing alone," Ross used to think when he was most depressed. "I've learned that at least. Enthusiasm is not enough. I can do nothing alone."

It was an afternoon in the last week of the January thaw when the doctor went to the station to meet Michael and Anna. The thick snow covering the streets and the roofs and the fields was melting in the strong sunlight, and the melting crust of the snow was glinting brilliantly. Long, heavy, pointed icicles were hanging from the station roof and dripping on the platform and melting into pools that were like dark patches on the snow-covered platform. An engine, shunting up and down the tracks, shot steam high into the winter air. From far down the tracks, beyond the curve by the town park, came the forlorn hooting of the train from the city, and from the street across the field a few people began to hurry across the path through the deep snow, hurrying so they could stand on the platform and watch the train stop and then go on to the next town. Farmers, wearing heavy fur caps with ear flaps, and with long wet moustaches, and old colorless blankets over their horses, and thick furs over their own knees, were sitting on their sleighs, or in battered automobiles, the tops of which were heaped with snow from being left out all night. One of the great icicles hanging from the station roof cracked and snapped off and was shattered loudly on the platform. Everybody looked up.

As the doctor waited, humped over the wheel of his car, he was worrying about a young woman and one of the town boys who had come to him last night. The young woman, who had been pregnant only a few weeks, begged him to perform a very simple operation that would abort her. She and the town boy were planning to get married in two years. It was not that they did not want to have children, but the young man wanted to study bookkeeping in the city and in two years he would be ready to marry the girl. They had both pleaded desperately with the doctor to understand that they were not selfish people, and that they would willingly have children, but if they were forced to marry now they would be very poor and he might not even get work. But the doctor, looking worried, had refused to listen to them, no matter how much they had pleaded. He had even got a little angry at the notion that anyone wouldn't want a child under any circumstances. But as he sat in his car at the station, he was muttering, "Maybe I made a mistake. Maybe it was up to me to help them. Who am I to pass judgment on how they ought to shape their lives?" Then the train bell was clanging, and he looked along the platform and saw Michael and Anna standing there, Michael tall and serious, with his arm under Anna's, and Anna looking around with that wide, eager curiosity, as if she had never seen such a place in her life. Anna said something to Michael that made them both laugh out loud, and the two boys, loafing on the platform, began to stare at her red cheeks and her fine body and the bit of fair hair that shone brightly in that brilliant afternoon sunshine.

"Mike, Mike," the doctor called.

"Heh, Ross. Don't get out. We'll be over," and they came running along the platform, and when they were at the car, Anna reached up and kissed the doctor, who was saying, "She'll have to sit on your knee, Mike."

"I felt so grand when I got off the train," she said. "I didn't know the lake was out there. You can see the ice along the shore and the water looks so awfully blue. It's lovely, isn't it?"

"We were watching the gulls out over the lake," Mike said.

"Let's go," the doctor said.

With Anna sitting on Michael's knee, they drove away from the station, and the three of them chattered rapidly, not bothering to listen to each other, for they had to express their gladness at being together.

At the house, a white frame house with green shutters, both Michael and the doctor stood back and were silent, waiting anxiously to see how Sheila would greet Anna. Sheila, who was very slender in her black tea gown, toyed with the beads around her neck with one white hand, and with the other reached out to Anna, who looked roughly dressed, bundled up in her old coat, and who was beaming and almost bursting with eagerness to be friendly. She was smiling with that astonishing, wide, eager girl's smile that always brightened her face so beautifully. The doctor saw Sheila looking shrewdly at this girl that her brother loved, this girl who had not had her education, who had nearly always been poor, who was not even expecting Michael to marry her, and yet was content. And as Anna went on smiling shyly, and was so eager to be friendly, so utterly without shame of any kind, the doctor knew his wife was a little startled, and he smiled as he saw Sheila take Anna by the arm and take her upstairs, talking all the time in an eager, wondering way.

"They're going to get along," Michael said.

"Sheila never knew anyone like her," the doctor said. "The first thing we do is to have a drink, and if you're at all hungry we'll have the girl get you a bite to eat."

"You've got a swell place here," Michael said. "This room just looks like Sheila, the way it's papered, those prints of French painters. I'll bet I can tell you just what the walls of her bedroom are like, too."

"It's all Sheila," the doctor said, feeling glad because Michael was there grinning like a boy and looking around as if for the first time in months he was in a place that was like home. While they were having the whiskey and soda the two girls came in and Sheila looked very elegant in her tea gown beside Anna, who was carelessly dressed in a brown woolen dress, and who had to keep pushing back her thick, fair hair.

The doctor at once felt the shyness and the wonder that grew between the two women as they made little bits of conversation. Anna wanted to keep looking wide-eyed around the warm room, she wanted to glance shyly, from time to time, at Sheila, and look at her clothes, and her hands, and her delicate complexion, and to wonder at her reticent, easy way. After one of those wide glances she could not help saying, "You must be very happy here. Just as soon as I came in here I felt very safe. You won't know what I mean. Just that everything would always hang together here. It must be wonderful." And then she smiled with such warmth that they all knew she wanted to say, too, that she knew of the love between the doctor and Sheila, and felt the security they had, and that it must be very comforting, especially when she remembered her own place in the city and her need of money and the dreadful uncertainty of her life and her love.

The grave-faced doctor, who was drinking his whiskey and only half listening to Michael, was glad his wife was upset by this bold, warm, eager, wondering girl. He knew Sheila could not understand how any girl could possess such enthusiasm and such a desire to laugh suddenly, and who could let her face light up like a delighted child's over the most innocently simple matters that came up in a perfunctory conversation, when her own life was drab and full of an infinite number of unfulfilled and desperate hopes. Then he heard his wife saying, "It's pretty hard to do anything with a town like this, you know, and it's got now that we just have our own little group socially. The trouble is, hardly anyone seems to realize that roads lead out of the town as well as into it," and while the doctor listened, he knew his wife was really thinking, "Anna doesn't feel shy at all. I wonder if she doesn't actually feel situations. Her life from day to day must be dreadful, with Michael not even working. Doesn't the girl know about my father?"

The doctor began to smile so broadly that Michael, who had been asking many questions about the wolf hunt they had planned, was puzzled, and he looked at the two girls and then at the doctor, but the doctor did not offer to explain his little joke. Michael went on asking about the clothes he would have to wear, and about the snow shoes and his face began to show the excitement that had been growing in him all week.

Sheila and Anna were standing by the window, looking down the long street of fenced-off houses that led beyond the town and into the country and up to the sloping, snow-capped farmland of the hills shining against the blue sky. And as she laughed easily, Sheila was saying, "Ross seems to have taken over the whole town for adoption. You get a pretty crazy picture of life, being a doctor's wife. Life becomes just a long line of limping derelicts and pregnant women and ailing old men. And nearly all the women who aren't sick want to have some private little malady that nobody in the world will understand but Ross. All the women in town who are with child beat a path up to our door. Ross just takes it all as a matter of course."

"He just naturally likes everybody, and that's why you can't help liking him," Anna said.

"I don't think it's really because he likes them. He sees a lot of confusion and disorganization around him and thinks it's up to him to straighten it out. Oddly enough he's not a tidy, precise man in his own life at all. He doesn't even know who pays him and who doesn't."

"That's just like I thought he'd be."

"He's intelligent enough to know how bad things are in town when one half lives by taking in the other half's washing. But it doesn't discourage him. He seems to like the place all the more. Sometimes I could shout at him. Don't you agree?"

"I never thought about it like that."

"You just go along from day to day."

"I guess I do," Anna said apologetically.

"I'd like to shout at the women who come here and shrug their shoulders and say they're afraid they're going to have another child, the sixth or seventh, or even the eleventh. Poor souls, they haven't any awareness at all of what's going on around them. I sometimes think you can't even breathe unless you make a little island for yourself. I wonder, if they ever stopped a moment and realized how unjust it was to bring children into a world like this, would they still come here just the same."

But Anna's face had begun to show how disappointed she was and she said timidly, "Don't you like the town at all, Sheila?"

"Of course I like it in some ways. I like being here with Ross. It's like a little island for ourselves here and we can devote ourselves to each other," Sheila said.

The doctor, hearing nothing Michael was saying, leaned

forward and was troubled, for he had felt the intensity in Sheila's low voice, and now he saw a quickening in her intelligent face, and he thought, "No matter how close I get to anybody in the town, or what I do around here, I can never make Sheila glow and forget herself and abandon herself to anything."

Then Sheila had to go and see about the dinner and Michael had a chance to whisper to Anna, "How do you like her?"

"She's cool and lovely. I think she's a darling. She makes me feel a bit noisy. Am I noisy, sweetheart?"

"She likes you."

"But Ross seems a bit different up here," she whispered. "Something troubles him. Sometimes he looks sad and patient."

But Sheila had come back, and she went over to Anna, who was looking out the window again. For a while they were both silent. Then Sheila said, "I'll say this much for it. It's not a bad-looking place, is it?"

"Ah, Sheila, I listened to everything you said a little while ago. I know what you mean, but it couldn't seem ugly like that to me. Look how lovely the street is out there with the snow banked high in the sunlight. The light on the hill is so lovely too and I never saw such a blue lake. It's the winter and the white snow and the clear sky that make it look so blue. Mike and I were mad about it as soon as we got off the train. Oh, it's a beautiful place here, Sheila, and just think, Mike and I didn't even know it was here. There must be places like that all over the country," she said. "If you only lived long enough you could go from one place to the next one, or you could stay forever at a place like this."

Twenty-Five

THE DIRECTION of the wind changed, and from the north and over the water came the snapping cold, and in the night the slush froze hard, and a thin, hard, glistening crust was laid over the melting snow.

Michael and Ross were driving down to the flour and feed store on the main street where they were meeting Jo Jamison, the Indian, who was going on the wolf hunt with them. They had their snow shoes and a box of canned food in the back seat of the car.

Michael looked like a lanky lumberjack in his high boots and red and black mackinaw and leather hat.

At noon time the sun was glistening on the brilliant surface of the snow crust. Little kids coming home from school were sliding on the ice and shouting, their faces raised in the sunlight, when Ross got out of the car at the feed shop. Ross had on a long, knee-length, white woolen, French Canadian coat, with thick red and black stripes encircling it. Ross's face was round and ruddy, and he looked almost squat as he swaggered into the store. The three old men, who were sitting on the bags of chicken feed around the wall, winked at each other and stopped chewing their tobacco when Ross came in in his bright coat of many colors, but Ross was delighted to see that they were grinning at him as though he were a comic character.

One of the old men said, "Hello, doc. There's Jo over there. He's been waiting a bit."

"We're late, but I couldn't get away," Ross said.

Out of the shadow at the end of the counter came a stocky Indian wearing a brown leather windbreaker over an old gray sweater. "It's all the same," he said. His face was as round as a ball and his hard brown skin was all wrinkled up in smiles, as if he had been doing nothing for years but chuckle to himself, and yet as soon as he stopped smiling his face became as solemn and wooden as a dead Indian's face.

"This is Mike Aikenhead, Jo. He's a mighty hunter."

"Sure," Jo said. "All of us mighty hunters."

"This is the first time I've shaken hands with a big wolf hunter," Mike said.

"Two all last year," Jo grinned. "We all have good time just the same. The deer are down at that swamp and if the wolves aren't there then there're no wolves around here. Maybe we catch a rabbit and eat it." And when they went out into the sunlight Jo was grinning as if a wolf hunt in that part of the country was pretty much of a joke.

They all crowded into the front seat, then they crossed over the tracks and out to the highway and turned south from the hills and away from the lake, heading for the black ash swamp some twenty miles south. It was good the way the three of them were huddled tight together in the front seat with the car taking the hills easily, and with Jo telling in his soft and pleasant voice about the time in the Great War when he got as far as London, England, and got lost and wished he were back in the wilderness again.

The road kept climbing steadily from the lowland and once when they were on the summit of the highest hill they stopped the car. It was by the fence of the red-brick church, the fence where the yellow briar bloomed in the spring. And they looked back over the wooded hills and the shadowed valleys and the shadowed mounds that were rocky ridges, and the undulating roll of snow fields, patterned with snake fences and stark elms, the whole country sloping down to the mist line at the lake. At times when the sun was very bright the fields shone as though under glass. Mike thought, "It's like a different world. My life's a different life. We'll never have to go back to the city. It keeps getting more exciting."

Down in the valley they turned into a sideroad. In the fields along the road were big, bare snow-capped rocks jutting out of the ground. The whole country was rocky, and here there were many snow-covered ridges.

The road ended at a farm gate, and there they got out of the car and sat on the running board and tied on their snow shoes. Then they slung the blankets on their shoulders, and Jo carried the provisions, and they began to cross the farmer's field. The crust of snow was broken easily by the weight of their bodies, but they didn't sink more than two inches in the soft snow underneath.

It was easy going down the sloping field. They climbed over snake fences. Soon they could see the black ash swamp ahead with the bush of dense spruce and cedar, and there were more rocky ridges and little gulleys.

Jo pointed, and said, "Plenty deer over there."

"Only deer?"

"No. I got a lynx there. But soon you see the deer paths. Deer yards over there. I show you," Jo said.

The fringe of the swampland did not look cold until they were out of the sunlight and close to the dense bush, and then it was desolate. Beyond one of the ridges, and by the fringe of the bush, and by a flat stretch of snow that was a great pond in the summer time, was the old shack Jo used for trapping in that country.

It was almost twilight when they got to the shack and looked back at their tracks in the snow. With the light no longer gleaming on the snow crystals it seemed terribly cold. Jo came out of the shack with a couple of axes and said, "We got to cut wood. We got to make a fire."

While they were cutting wood at the edge of the impenetrable bush Mike was alone, and when he listened, he heard only the sound of the other axe somewhere on the other side of the hut, and when the axe was silent and he still listened, he began to feel the dreadful silence and the coldness of the bush at twilight. He began to feel that in such a silence and in such a place with it so cold and the night coming on, all his hopes and the dreadful fear he sometimes felt in the city were truly unimportant. And again he listened, and again the vastness of the country and the steadiness of the bush and the darkness began to touch his mind and he thought, "If I stayed here, I'd just function like the deer or a fox or a wolf or a rabbit. I'd just be an organism, part of the living things around here; there'd be nothing distinctive about me; there'd only be the distress of my body and there'd be no distress in my soul. I never could feel separated from things here. Here my self, my soul would be lost, but it would be found because I would just be. I'd be a part of all things just being around me. I could hear the call of a winter bird and look up innocently and say, 'Brother.' I could go on day after day like the trees. My mind would grow quick from watching, my eyes would be like a hawk's eyes."

The sound of the axe came from the other side of the hut and then Jo called. Soon they had a fire in the big cast-iron stove, and while Jo opened the cans of beans, the doctor poured whiskey in tin cups. "Here we are, lads. Ready for our friend, the wolf."

"We'll be lucky to see a wolf," Jo grinned. "They never come close to me. They don't like me."

"Why are we wasting our time here looking for them, then?" Mike said.

"Sometimes you get a shot at one. They go like a bit of smoke on a windy day. Maybe you catch them in traps."

"I want to have my gun handy if I see them, anyway."

"Maybe they run from you. Wolves are all right. You hear a lot of bad stories about wolves. But they are just like you and me."

"You don't think they're the meanest things on earth?"

"If they're hungry, they kill, like you or me. They're afraid of men."

"I've read of people being thrown to the wolves. Maybe you mean that what actually happened was that the wolves got alarmed and ran away."

"I don't know. I never knew a man who was thrown to the wolves," Jo said, grinning brightly.

"If a wolf isn't just plain mean, then what among living things, in God's name, is mean?" Mike said.

"I don't know," Jo said simply.

"I'm thinking of wolves, the name wolves, like men have always thought of wolves, wolves killing and tearing and preying on weaker living things. Wolves hunting deer and hunting in packs. For God's sake, don't let's get sentimental about wolves."

"Maybe you're right," the Indian said, shrugging. "These wolves around here are small. Much further up north you get big timber wolves. Very big. Ten feet almost. One time I was trapping in the bush. I got lost. Just a big gray sky like a piece of lead. I can't go by the sun. At night I sit by the fire with my three dogs. The wolves come up at night and make a circle around. I can see their eyes shining, and my dogs howl, and run round and round the fire all night. But they don't come near me and my fire and my dogs. Then, next day, my best dog gets lost. He's my best fighter, too. He lick any two dogs. Then we find him and the wolves have torn him to pieces. Maybe they were hungry. They ate him."

"The wolf has a bad reputation, all right," the doctor said. "But maybe it's an undeserved reputation."

"Don't you see, Ross. A wolf is an individualist," Mike said.

"They kill out of the sheer lust of killing, and they kill without sense." Both the doctor and the Indian were looking at Mike and wondering why he was so excited. He was jerking his arm up and down trying to emphasize every point he was making, and there was an intense indignation in his face. "If you want it to be clear that a man is ruthless and an enemy of society you call him a wolf, don't you?" he went on. "Any enemy of the race you call a wolf because he knows no moral law, and that's why you can't organize society, because it's full of wolves, and they don't know justice, and don't want it. The financial brigands and labor exploiters and the war profiteers and the Wall Street sharks and nearly anybody who tries to put his head up in a world of private profit, what are they? Wolves I tell you."

While Mike talked like this, he was really crying out against the meaningless confusion of whatever he had known of living, and his search for peace, and he wanted most of all, even without quite knowing how much he wanted it, to justify his preservation of his own bit of happiness and his own life.

But the doctor and the Indian only looked at each other and shrugged their shoulders. They went on eating their food. When they were finished, and they had all started to smoke, the doctor said a bit irritably, "After all, you don't know much about it, Mike. What do you know about wolves? They may be all you say, just useless marauders. But I thought you were a man with a scientific education, a man full of the spirit of scientific inquiry."

"What you're asking me to do is give the wolves a break, eh?" Mike mocked him.

"I'm only saying you don't understand anything about it."

"I can feel pretty keenly about it just the same," Mike said. While the Indian listened and watched impassively and smoked, Mike and the doctor grew more irritated with each other. Mike felt that the doctor wanted to be patient and understanding about something that did not require much understanding, and he began to feel, while they sat there smoking in the shack with the woods behind them and the darkness beginning to fall on the stretch of snow they could see through the window, that he and the doctor would never truly understand each other while they lived, because the doctor had never had any experience with the tough, harsh, brutal power that was the power men used to survive. Ross was a happy man, with peace and unity in his soul, who had never been pulled and pushed close to death in the riotous struggle to live. He was a simple man and was willing to believe the wolf only wanted to live. So Mike said passionately, though he kept his voice low, "I understand the wolf better than you think. Listen to me. A little while ago when we were chopping wood I felt I might stay up here and lose my personality and become one with the silence and the woods and the natural life around here. It was a good feeling and I wanted to keep it because it made me feel peaceful, but as soon as I start talking to another human being, and I mean you, I feel how different we are, and how we can never really understand each other, and that we each have a world inside us."

"That's just because we disagree. Supposing we agreed?"

"It isn't just about the wolves. It goes a lot deeper than that," Mike said impatiently.

"The trouble with you, Mike, is that you're bogged down with a lot of nineteenth-century notions about science that have been discarded long ago."

"I'm the popular scientist, is that it?"

"Your notion of your scientific training has always been a red rag to me," the doctor said. "Sometimes I can't help thinking that scientists don't know anything. They all work their own little gardens and they all hoe their own little patches. They specialize. They refuse even to consider the relation of one thing to another. If you ask them to, they apologize and say, 'Excuse me, that isn't my field.' Yet the whole world worships them. I'll respect science that's first-hand observation, just the same as I'd respect your observation on life among the wolves if it was worth a damn, but it isn't."

"What am I to say?"

"I haven't any idea."

"You know how I felt about you, Ross. I always thought you were a swell guy, who felt everything in the right way, but was absolutely wrong in his ideas about everything."

"And knowing you felt that way never worried me in the slightest, did it?"

But then Jo said, "Listen."

And while they sat there, and felt the stillness of the night coming on, they heard a lonely, wailing howl. They got up and went outside and looked over the stretch of flat snow-covered pond and beyond that to the first ridge, and beyond that to a gulley and a second higher ridge. Over there the shadow was deeper, and the falling darkness made a misty light where it became one with the snow and the sky. "There's something moving over there on that ridge. Look over there," Jo said, pointing. "Just three specks moving in a circle, little specks." And they looked over there, and Mike was sure he could see the three specks moving, moving round and round in some kind of a dance, and then the three specks were still, as though they knew they were being watched, and then they were gone, and no one could see how they had gone. "Maybe that's as close as we get to them," Jo said.

"You're sure they were wolves?"

"Pretty sure."

But they stayed out there watching till the heavy darkness came, and the bush seemed to open up and envelop them, and the stars came out. "I keep thinking the wolves come closer like the night," Mike said. "Following the line of the night right up to the shack."

They bolted the door, and put out the light, and lay down on their blankets and tried to sleep. They were all wide awake and listening in the darkness, and Mike kept staring at the flickering light in the stove. It was not cold in the shack.

Then he heard Ross say very softly, "Mike, are you still awake?"

"Yes."

"How did Sheila look to you?"

"Pretty much the same as she always did."

"But did she seem to be the same? Didn't you notice how she had changed, how the core of her seemed to have changed?"

"She's a bit cynical in a kind of wearily wise way and maybe she's getting a bit affected."

"I'm afraid of her becoming neurotic," the doctor whispered. "She's afraid of life, afraid of letting it touch her. She only wants to protect herself. She'd like the two of us to be swayed only by the rise and fall of our own passion and never know anything but our own love for all eternity. And that feeling in her isn't a desire to abandon herself in love; it's just self-protection."

"Do you know what's the matter with her?"

"Sure I do. She feels her mother was mad, and she herself must never have children. And she's been worried about what the world thinks of her father, too."

"She's never said anything to me about it."

"She doesn't talk about it to me either. It would be better if she did. She's turned it in on herself," Ross said.

They lay there, and they were silent, and in a little while Ross whispered, "I thought I'd ask you if you'd noticed her, that's all. Good night, Mike."

"Good night, Ross."

While Mike lay there, wide awake and worrying, he heard the howl of the wolf again, and it was closer this time, and he began to tremble. On any other night, if he had been feeling good and had been among friends, the howl of the wolf might have made him snuggle down into his blanket and feel the warmth of the shack and smile in his security, but now he was full of fear, and it was not a fear of the wolf, but a fear of being alive and alone. There was just the one bit of light from the narrow window touching the floor. As he waited for the sound of the howling again, he felt he was waiting for a cry from another living thing that was alone and hostile. That moment of terror while he waited began to embrace all of his life. Quick flashes crowded into a moment that was eternity before the darkness of his despair overwhelmed him, made him dwell on his mother's madness, his sister's sorrow, his father walking through the snow, stooping and growing old and looking around with a frightened face, and the anguish in his own soul as he watched him go; and life and death kept beating in upon them all, and life brutalized them and crushed them and death awaited them, and they were living souls caught between life and death, and they resisted and longed for justice; they all became one in their common suffering. How small his own little place in the city was. There in their little place they kept their love, and it was all they had to put against life and death. "Anna, Anna, Anna," he began to mutter. If only the love between them could flow out from them and touch the world; but their love could touch no one but themselves; it could only grow more intense and become an agony, and yet how lucky, how marvelously lucky to have found it and resist with it, and deny joyously that it could perish on the earth. Then it came again, further and further away, the threatening wolf's moan, out of the night and the snow, deeper even than that, out of the core of the hostile world.

In the morning, when Michael and the doctor woke up, they were alone, and they looked out the window and saw Jo sitting outside on a log, with the white stretch of shining snow before him, smoking his pipe. Jo had been up early and he had made the fire and cooked the breakfast, but he had been too polite to waken them.

When they had eaten, they put on their snow shoes and took their rifles and started to cross the wide flat stretch of snow, heading for the ridge where they had seen the dark specks last night. The snow crust was thin, but very hard, and in places it was as hard as ice, and in other places the snow shoe broke through easily. The ridge was much farther away than it had looked last night. Jo was a little ahead of them, hurrying, with his head down, and the doctor and Mike were puffing. Mike looked at the doctor and laughed, for the doctor's nose was running a little and the cold air was making tiny little icicles on his wet moustache.

Jo kept bending down and staring at what seemed to Michael to be the utterly unmarked crust of the snow, and when they were on the ridge, he moved around in a circle, his face tense and his brown eyes half closed in the sunlight that made the snow crystals sparkle and tired the eyes. "Look," he said. "Two or three, maybe even four around here."

"I can't see anything," Mike said.

"There's nothing there," the doctor said.

"Just little scratches, that's all," Jo said. "No break in the surface. They have big pads. But little scratches there just the same."

The scratches on the ice went in a circle, and then they went off along the ridge. The doctor and Mike followed Jo, and they were tense and alert, for they were sure they were close to the wolves. There were places where the snow had drifted against the ridges, and if they stumbled, they were deep in the snow. They had turned into the fringe of the bush, and then out again, then on to another ridge. Then Jo threw out his hands and smiled. "No farther," he said. "No more tracks."

"They must have gone into the bush."

"Hard to say. Just like wisps of smoke. Gone now. They hunt along the fringe. Then vanish. No wolves today," Jo said.

On the way back to the shack, Jo was taking a short cut over ridges and gulleys, and when they came to a flat stretch of snow that was a strip of marsh in the summertime, with a gulley at one end, and the rocky ridges on the side, Jo said, "See, a deer yard. See the tracks, just like trails."

There were tracks out from the fringe and over as far as the gulley, and the snow in these trails was tramped down by the hoofs of the deer.

"There's something over there," Jo said, pointing to a mound off the tracks and out on the crust of the snow. "Let's see what it is."

They crossed the deer trails and were out on the hard crust, and when they had gone a little way they saw that the mound was really the carcass of a deer. There were many other carcasses, and blood marks, with the snow churned up, and the carcasses stuck there in the hard crust; the sharp hoofs of the deer, piercing through the crust, had impaled them in the snow. A deer stuck stiff in the snow is very dead; there is nothing quite so dead. The carcasses were slashed at the throat, or slashed on the nose, and the flesh of the tenderloin had been torn from every one of the carcasses, just the nice juicy tenderloin torn away, and the rest of the carcass left there to bleed and freeze in the snow.

"Wolves here, all right," Jo said. "Just the other day, too, since the thaw ended and the crust formed on the snow."

"Good God, I never saw such a wanton slaughter in my life," Mike said. "Look at the way they've torn off the tenderloin and not bothered with the rest."

"'The wolves hunt at the fringe and watch the deer yard here," Jo said. "Deer are all right if they keep to the paths. The wolves wait for the crust to form on the snow after the thaw, then they get the deer off the paths. The deer try to get away going across the thin hard crust. The sharp pointed hoofs of the deer break through the crust just like through thin ice. Wolves pretty lucky. They have bigger pads and go quick over the crust like we saw, making only scratches, maybe, and the deer stuck in the snow can't move their legs, stuck good and stiff. See. Snow here three feet deep. The wolves pretty swift to get them by the nose, or slash the throat, see," he said, pointing to a carcass.

"And they just tear the tenderloin," Ross said. "They don't even stop to eat them. They don't want them for food, just a little of the tenderloin. Why do they do it, Jo?"

"They like tenderloin, maybe," Jo grinned.

"There's a bit of natural justice for you, Ross," Mike said savagely. He stared out over the snow which was shining and making blue spots dance before his eyes, and he looked at the wilderness of spruce and cedar and the enormous blue sky with the heavy clouds rolling and merging and threatening to sweep over the impersonally bright sun, and then he looked down again at the slaughtered deer, stuck stiff in the snow, and he shouted, "What a god-damned useless slaughter. Useless, purposeless, wanton slaughter. You had the nerve to talk to me last night about meaning and order in life and justice and God knows what else, Ross. Look at it. Put your nose down and try and smell it. The natural history of natural justice. Don't you like that for a title to the picture? How about 'The Search for Glory'."

"I don't know what to make of it," the doctor said, looking worried.

"It's a bit of sheer wanton slaughter. Slaughter for the sake of slaughter."

"What are you getting at?"

"That's the way it goes on the earth. The deer were alive. So are we alive. And that's the way it turns out," he said, pointing to the carcasses. "Deer, I guess, can't hope and long for things and, like the psalm singer, complain to the Lord, which is just as well."

The doctor was dejected, and he kept scraping his foot on

the crust of snow and staring at the blood on the snow. "It's pretty hard to explain," he said. "But that doesn't mean I have to see it your way."

"I don't think it matters much how we see it. There it is," Mike said.

"What do you make of it, Jo?"

"You look pretty sad," Jo said. He had just lit his pipe, and the little puff of blue smoke was whisked away in the wind. Then he turned and pointed at the ridge and the bush. "Over there, there's a she wolf and a litter of pups. Over there maybe under old logs and in the rocks is the old she wolf. Pretty soon the snow begin to melt. The snow starts to go quick in the spring. It's pretty hard to catch deer when the snow goes. The wolves can't hunt them when the snow goes. Then what's going to happen to that old she wolf and her pups? They get pretty hungry by and by with no food because it's spring, and she's got to stay up there with the litter of pups. But maybe they look ahead like you and me. They kill the deer here, and they leave it here because it's not far away from the litter and the she wolf. You say cold storage, eh? They have something to eat when the snow goes. Maybe then the young don't starve. Then the she wolf looks after the pups."

"Mike, did you hear that?" the doctor said, pushing Mike by the shoulder, "Did you hear it? Doesn't it mean anything to you?" and the doctor, standing there in the snow in his coat of many colors, was beaming in his excitement.

"It's pretty hard to believe," Mike said.

"He doesn't believe it, Jo."

"Many people don't believe it," Jo said. "Many old trappers don't believe it. That's all right. I'm pretty sure. You wait. In the spring the frozen meat go pretty quick. You come up again and see. I feel pretty sure."

"Can the wolves worry months ahead about their young being hungry?" Mike asked. "They'd need a chart. Who draws up the chart for them? I'm not arguing. I'm knocked over. If what you say is right, then this useless slaughter is full of meaning. But is it justice for the deer, Ross?"

"I don't know about that, but I believe that everything that happens would have just as much meaning, if we could only see it properly," Ross said.

"Maybe we go back now," Jo said. "Look. It's cloudy and the snow and the wind come. Maybe a blizzard come soon."

They began to tramp back on the snow, and the wind was getting stronger, and the light, hard snow was driven against their faces. Sometimes the sun shone, and then it was gone again, and the snow whirled around them and it was darker over the ridges. Feeling more and more deeply stirred, Mike walked with his head lowered, thinking, "What do I know about anything? What do I know about justice? Why have I thought so much about justice? Is it justice for the wolves when the deer are slain? Is it justice for the deer to wait and be slain, and can they cry out and complain, and who would hear that cry and know what it meant? My own conception of justice spares me and kills my father. Day after day I try to balance the book so I will be justified. The old Greeks talked a lot about justice. Socrates. The giving of every man his due. What is any man entitled to?"

The sun had vanished from the sky and a vast shadow fell upon the earth, over the rocky ridges and the desolate bush, and over the frozen carcasses stuck in the snow; the snow was driven hard against their faces as they leaned into it, and it covered the deer paths, and fell on the wolves, and the lynx and the rabbit and the bear and the multiplicity of life that was preserved in the winter. The wolves had their time and their seasons, and the deer fed and fattened and died in their own time, too, and when the snow had gone and the warm weather came, their carcasses lay there and rotted, and carrion picked at them, and beasts that were hungry tore at the old bones, but still there was a little left for the she wolf and her litter. Now the gusts of snow were driving hard against the faces of all human beings who were out at that hour, in the country or in the city, but when the wind had gone down at nightfall the stars would come out in the heavens and shine impartially on the agitated and the turbulent and complaining living souls.

But there might be unity in life on the earth, and it might be only vanity to try to understand the meaning of the single parts. "Maybe justice is simply the working out of a pattern," he thought. "The deer and the wolf have their place in the pattern, and they know justice when they conform to the pattern … And there would be a justice for all things in terms of the things themselves. There would be justice in art, the justice of form, and there would be social justice, the logical necessity of preserving the pattern of society. If society was what it was today, and there was class striking at class, it was like a jungle, and there was no pattern and no unity and no justice. That's the best I can do," he thought, and he walked on.

Then he cried out within himself, "But what about justice for each single human being? That must be there too. I stink with pride when I judge my father's life, or Dave Choate's life." And as he walked on, closing his eyes against the biting snow, he became very humble, and he thought, "I know everything will have some meaning if I stop passing judgment on other people, and forget about myself, and let myself look at the world with whatever goodness there is in me."

Twenty-Six

SHEILA was trying to fit a pair of her goloshes on Anna the afternoon they were alone together. The little, thin rubbers Anna was wearing were hardly any protection crossing the road in the snow. Sheila's goloshes would not fit and Anna, bending down, red-faced, tried to push her heel in. Sheila watched earnestly for a while, then she cried, "To the devil with them. Let's go. I'll get you a pair at the store. Please let me get them." She spoke as if it were her fault that her goloshes would not fit Anna.

On the way down to the main street they sometimes crossed the road, and then Sheila took Anna's arm and helped her step from one icy spot to another. The cold wind from the lake made their cheeks glow. They held on to each other so they would not slip, and they laughed and began to feel much closer together, though they hadn't really said anything at all. When they were going into C. B. Mercer's general store to buy the goloshes, they met Mrs. Simon Seeley, the wife of the General Motors dealer for the town. She wore a mink coat, the only coat of its kind on the street that day, and when she hurried over, with her little body almost squirming in affectation, and her hard, thin face wrinkled in smiles, Anna thought she was one of the homeliest and hardest women she had ever seen. She couldn't understand how a girl like Sheila could put out her hand so eagerly to such a woman. Often, in the good weather, Mrs. Seeley and Sheila, who were good friends, drove to the country club for a cocktail and a game of golf together.

"Anna is my brother's fiancée," Sheila said.

"How lovely for both of you."

"Isn't it, darling?"

When Sheila realized that Mrs. Seeley was staring at Anna's clothes, she flushed, and she did not ask Mrs. Seeley to come home with her and have a cocktail as she had intended to do.

They went from one store to another, and there were many introductions, and it became almost exciting going along the wide street in the brilliant sunshine, holding each other so they wouldn't slip, and with the air getting crisper all the time.

But when they were at home again and alone in the house together, Sheila found herself doing little things that would keep her from feeling awkward and affected; she mixed cocktails and chatted easily about the smoothest cocktails she had had last fall at the country club, and though she knew her voice was low and pleasant, she couldn't understand why Anna listened as though everything she said deserved the attention of her whole soul. Sheila was flustered a little, for she didn't know whether Anna was instinctively very polite or truly fascinated by the sophistication of the conversation, or just naturally charming; and when Sheila grew puzzled like this she was uneasy, and she began to resent her own awkwardness; she felt she was just chattering helplessly; she resented Anna's repose, for there she, herself, was so much better dressed than Anna, her complexion a little finer, her voice a little softer, yet whenever Anna spoke, instead of listening, she simply sat there thinking of herself, as if one half of her personality had become sharply critical of the other half. Then, at last, she could not help admitting to herself how full she was of admiration for Anna's lovely simplicity, and then she grew a little shy, and was quietly eager.

That night when Sheila was alone in her bedroom, trying

to sleep, she began to listen for some sound from Anna's room. The window faced the part of the town by the lake, and the winter moonlight came into the room. There was the quietness of a town on a winter night with only the noise of someone passing and crunching the hard crisp snow. Sometimes there was the sound of the voice of someone passing, sounding loud in the dry, clear air. The thaw was ended all over the country, and the ice had come again, and it would be the coldest time of the year. There grew in Sheila a wide wonder that Anna could feel so happy when her existence itself was so precarious, when most people who were respectable would not even have her in the house. Yet Anna wanted to become nothing but what she was; she wanted only to be allowed to possess her own repose. And Sheila thought of her own restless urge to become something else and never to be still, and of her neat, private world, and of her own secret dream that Ross would be able to go to Europe and specialize. Maybe they would live in a city like Vienna or Venice, where it was said that the soft air and the water and the sunlight made lovers long to lie together and love lazily, forever. She thought of her growing distaste for anyone who did not know what she imagined to be the manners of Louis XIV, or anyone who did not feel that the thing to do was to keep amused, or anyone who did not understand all that was meant to be implied by the word "amusing." She thought of her longing to live in a beautiful city that would glow with light, and where there would be music and laughter, and languorous women, and well-dressed gentlemen with soft eyes, whispering and hoping; and all of this dream and this longed-for life was like a gorgeous upholstery for herself. And now Sheila muttered, "Oh, what a vulgar picture," and she kicked the clothes off herself and got up out of the bed and stood there, slender and tense, in her nightgown till she began to shiver with the winter air coming through the open window. Then she hurried out and rapped on Anna's door, longing that Anna might be awake. When Anna called, "Come in, Sheila," she went in so quickly that she was a little ashamed.

"It's nothing," she said. "I just felt like talking. Are you awake?"

"I couldn't get to sleep. It sounded a little strange. The noises aren't like the noises you hear in the city. I was thinking of being alone. Why don't you turn on the light?"

"I'll close the window and sit here. Would you like to talk?"

Anna sat up in the dark and clutched her hands around her knees, and they both began to talk about Michael. Anna asked one question after another; she asked about Michael's boyhood and about all his little peculiar characteristics, about the way he talked, and the quarrels he might have had with other boys at school, about the people he might have hated; and whenever she heard anything that delighted her, she held her head on one side and repeated it over slowly to herself, as if she was putting it away in her memory before assembling all these new parts of a picture of Michael she had never known. She kept saying, "No, no, that isn't Mike," when Sheila said he was hot-tempered, or self-willed, or quarrelsome, that nobody could ever manage him, that he was independent and arrogant and that she was the only one he never quarrelled with. "It doesn't sound like Mike at all," Anna said doubtfully. "It just doesn't make sense." "Then you tell me how you get along with him," Sheila said. "You don't seem to know him at all," Anna said. "You're his sister, yet you don't know him." And she began to tell about the solemn expression that was so often on Michael's face, and his gentleness and quietness, and the way he seemed to wonder about the whole world as he watched her with such love in his eyes. Then Sheila began to laugh and said, "That isn't Mike, Anna. What's the matter with the man? Being poor must upset him terribly. I'd never know him at all, darling, from your picture. We just don't know the same man."

And when they were both tired, and Sheila was yawning and getting up to go, Anna said, "Should we put on our goloshes when the sun's out tomorrow and go down and look at the ice along the lake?"

"I'd love to," Sheila said. "We'll have a lot of fun."

When she was back in her own room, Sheila lay there, still wondering, still restless, yet feeling a quickening within her.

There was still the same brilliant sunshine next day. Anna and Sheila went down to the street opposite the station and cut across the station yard by the water tower, and went along toward the dock and the grain elevator. The street leading out of town went north as far as you could see, and it became as it led deeper into the country, far beyond the town, a slowly rising slope with little clusters of houses here and there, till it merged and was lost in the blue line of snow-bound hills. Today, after the thaw and the freezing, parts of the valleys in the hills were intensely blue, and parts gleamed like magic mountains in the sunlight.

They went slowly past the old lumberyard which was close to the dock, and they stood looking at the snow-covered piles of lumber that were like ice blocks after the freezing. And beyond the lumberyard was the shoreline with the jagged ridges of gray ice, and beyond the ice was the intense blue of the water, deepening in blueness far out by the rolling banks of clouds with their deep, mysterious vaults. The two girls stood together on the road, looking over the water into the vaulted depths of the clouding sky as if they might find hidden there, beyond the blue water, some intimation of a fulfilment of a secret hope.

They were close to the shipyard before Sheila realized that Anna was hardly talking at all and was walking slowly, her head down. Then Anna put her hand up to her head.

"What's the matter, Anna? You look so pale," Sheila said.

"I don't know what's the matter. I'd like to sit down."

"Are you sick, Anna?"

"I don't know. I felt dizzy. Oh, dear, Sheila, my two fingers are numb. Look," and she held out the fingers of her right hand.

"Do you want to sit down?"

"There's no place to sit down."

"Look. Sit on the iron rail of the little bridge over the ditch. Come on," Sheila said. She helped Anna, feeling her weight against her. When they got to the little bridge she let Anna lean back on the rail, and she supported her with her arm, and coaxed her to put her head down on her shoulder. Anna closed her eyes and her lips were pale, and she kept saying, "I'm dizzy, very, very dizzy. Oh, dear, what's the matter with my hand? Sheila, I think my arm is going numb. Oh, Sheila, what could it be?"

"I don't know, darling. Oh, Anna, I don't know."

"Where we live in the city there was a man who got erysipelas. They said it started with his fingers going numb. What will happen to me if it's erysipelas? At first they thought the man had meningitis."

"Darling, darling, don't worry. I'll rub your hand. It's just numb. It's just the blood not circulating. Here, take off your glove." With her free hand Sheila began to rub Anna's fingers and thumb, and then her arm, looking earnestly from time to time at her worried, frightened, pale face, until Anna said, "I don't feel quite so bad. Let's go home if we can. I'll walk slowly."

On the way back Anna insisted that her head was clearing, and she kept working her thumb up and down, and sometimes she swung her numbed arm out from her, saying, "It's just like after your hand falls asleep. I'm not worrying, Sheila. I'm just frightened because it might be erysipelas. That's the way the man's hand went."

And then Sheila grew frightened and she longed that her husband might be home when they got there, though she knew he would not be home until night. They walked slowly, arm in arm. The rolling cloud bank they had seen across the lake was overhead and the day became gray, and by the time they got to their own street a light snow was beginning to fall, a dry, fine snow.

"I thought it was too cold for snow," Sheila said. "Let's hope they get home before the snow comes, and the roads are clear."

"I love the snow," Anna said.

"Why do you love the snow?"

"It always reminds me of my childhood. When we were kids we used to love the first fall of snow so much because we didn't know what was happening to the earth," she said, and this memory of her childhood seemed to gladden her a little and she smiled and patted Sheila's arm comfortingly. But the frightened look did not go out of her own blue eyes.

When they were home Sheila made Anna lie down on the couch in the living-room, and she knelt beside her and pulled off her goloshes and she chafed her arms and gave her a little whiskey. Then Anna cried suddenly, "I'm going hot and cold," and Sheila, growing terrified, ran for quinine, and she helped Anna upstairs to her bed and undressed her, muttering, "Maybe it's a chill. Maybe the change in the weather, the difference between the country and the city air affects you."

"Maybe, Sheila. That's what I'd think if it weren't for my arm. Maybe it was something I ate for lunch. Oh, dear, my stomach's turning over," she said, and she turned away and buried her head in the pillow and curled her body up so that she was lying crouched, her eyes closed.

Sheila kept going to the window and looking along the street to the station. It was getting dark on the street in the late winter afternoon, and already she could see a few lights coming on down by the station. By this time the snow was swirling hard against the window, hard, dry snow, whirling crazily across the street light, driven fast by the wind from the lake. "I

wonder if it snowed where Ross was," she thought. It was getting a little colder. "Maybe there's a blizzard all over. Why
don't you come home, Ross? God knows what is happening to
Anna. Is there anything in the world that has not happened to
her? Why does it have to happen to her just because she's so
much in love, and so alone, if it weren't for Mike." And though
she stayed looking out the window, it got so she could see only
the frightened face of Anna. By this time it was dark.

Then she heard them coming; she heard them shout and
start to laugh, and there came the heavy tread of their feet.
Ross was calling, "Where are you? Can't you give two lonely
hunters a drink?"

"Come up here, Ross," she called out eagerly.

"Wait till we get some of these clothes off."

"No, come up now. Hurry. Anna's sick. Hurry, quick."

There was a momentary, absolute silence, then they came
hurrying up the stairs and into the bedroom. Snow was still on
their shoulders and their faces were red, and they brought the
cold into the room with them. "What's the matter, Sheila?"
Michael said. "Anna's lying there. What's the matter with her?
Ross, what's the matter?" and he ran over to the bed and put
his cold hand on Anna's hair and started to turn her head over,
calling softly in a voice Sheila had never heard from him
before, "Anna, darling, look at me. Tell me what's the matter,
darling."

Sheila was saying, "She got very dizzy, Ross, when we were
walking. Her arm went numb. Her finger went numb. She
thinks it's erysipelas."

"My God, erysipelas. Oh, it can't be, darling," Michael
cried.

Anna turned over and looked at him and said, "It was
something like the man who had it said he felt. I don't feel so
bad now."

"Let's see your tongue. How does it feel?" Ross asked her.

"Thick and heavy and kind of numb, too."

The doctor bent over her and looked at her tongue, and then he put the short, strong fingers of his right hand on her abdomen and massaged her, and then he undid her dress and took her breast in his hand and squeezed the nipple so hard she cried out, "You're hurting me." And then he looked around at them and smiled a little, even though he was very worried, and he said, "I don't think it's erysipelas."

"What's making her go numb?" Michael said.

"That's just her nerves, I think, and circulation."

"What's the matter with her, Ross? Why don't you tell us instead of sitting there like that?"

"I think she's pregnant."

"You're sure?"

"It's the truth. There's not much room for doubt. I'm sorry, Mike."

"Oh, Mike, my sweetheart, I'm so sorry," Anna said. "I know it's my fault, honey. I ought to have been more careful."

"How long has it been like this, Ross?" Mike said.

"I wouldn't say for sure without a more thorough examination, and I don't think she wants that now, but I'd say pretty close to three months. Between two and three months."

"Anna, you poor dear, you little silly, you must have known," Mike said.

"Maybe I did think so. But today I didn't know what was wrong with me. It was different today and it seemed so strange. It wasn't at all like I thought it would be," Anna said.

Sheila kept watching her husband, who was sitting on the side of the bed with his head down; sometimes Ross glanced uneasily at Mike, as if he were waiting to be asked to help him.

Mike was grave as he looked at the doctor, and the doctor, feeling the uneasiness and the wonder in him, turned away hesitantly. Then Sheila knew that Ross was thinking of the young couple who had come to him the other night, saying,

"It would be so easy for you. Can't you do something about it for us?" and then had gone away grimly, leaving Ross muttering angrily to himself; but Sheila knew now, by the way Ross was avoiding Mike's eyes, that he would not be able to refuse this time. So she coughed, and her husband looked up at her, and she made him feel, by the way she smiled at him, that she, too, was urging him to help Anna and Mike.

These thoughts of hers were all swept away when she heard Anna asking, "Do you mind much, Mike?"

"It's all right, darling. I'm just surprised, that's all."

"You were so silent I thought maybe you were worrying."

"I was just feeling glad, and I was trying to understand why I felt glad."

"Then I'm glad too," Anna said.

The shy way Anna had whispered, "Then I'm glad too," had so impressed Sheila, that when she went downstairs to see if the dinner was ready, she felt she was dreaming. In a little while she had forgotten why she had come downstairs, and she stood at the window of the front room, looking out at the darkness of the street. "There was no fear in Anna at all," she thought. "And Mike wasn't afraid either. Yet there was everything in the world to make her afraid, and him too. They were poor, and he hadn't married her and they had no security at all, yet I know that from the beginning she has never wondered if he was entitled to have children, or whether his family was a good breeding stock. She was glad. They both want only to live."

And while she had this wonder in her she tried to make well up in her soul her own deep secret fear; she tried to think of her mother dying with a broken mind, and of her father becoming the talk of the town and acting like a hunted man; but that secret fear would not rise in her now. She pressed her face close to the window. At the corner of the pane was a widening frost line. Outside it was freezing hard, and snow was driven against the window, and the wind whirled it away under the street light. When the wind was still, the snow flakes drifted aimlessly, and then it seemed to her, while she waited for a gust of wind to blow the snow along the street, that she had wanted her love for Ross, and his love for her, to be that way too, drifting lightly this way and that, and never touching the earth.

As she looked out at the snow that had covered the earth she began to feel eager; she felt she might have anything she wanted; she felt she might find a new fullness in living. She felt she was free.

Twenty-Seven

THE NIGHT they returned to the city, and were on a street car, going to their apartment, Michael began to feel the stillness that was in Anna as she stood close beside him, and he put out his arm and touched her a little shyly. When she turned and smiled at him, there in the crowded street car, her face showed her contentment and the security she felt in being with him. The eagerness of his thoughts became like a song of gratitude as the car bumped and the bodies of men and women half rolled out of the seats and rolled heavily against each other. "I'll just let myself be free to love her. I'll follow my love for her from one step to another and it will be all right," he thought. "Nothing can really happen to us because nothing can ever separate us."

Leaning close to her, he whispered, "Let's get married tomorrow, Anna. We'll go out and get married."

Yet she only squeezed his hand and said simply, "Do you really want to, Mike?"

"I'd love to do it."

"You don't have to, Mike. It would be all right with me, if we could go along like this."

"It's necessary to me now, darling."

"Then I'm glad," she said.

It was chilly in the apartment, and they sat on the radiators, assuring each other the janitor was burning soft coal. It was the same old trouble. If the soft coal was used the radiators got hot quickly and were hot for about two hours and then, as they cooled off just as quickly, the chill came into the room and touched their blood and made them desolate. Night after night they had sat on the radiators in this way. They heard the friends of France talking in the next room. The friends of France were all right; they had a couple of electric heaters, and at this hour no doubt were swilling tea in the Russian style, the old Russian style, the holy Russian style, the little Russian style, while they talked about the tremendous impact of the Dostoyevsky novels on France.

Suddenly Mike said, "Anna, we think we're cold. We think we feel the chill of death in us here, don't we?"

"My ankles are cold," she said. "My legs are getting stiff."

"But that's nothing. We can go to bed and get warm. But death is in the next room. Listen to them. They are the dead. Listen. You didn't know death was such a nice gentleman. They're not in the world of the living at all, Anna. My darling, let's go to bed," he said.

It seemed a long time since they had been alone together, and Anna was so flushed and excited and warm that he wanted very much to make love to her. And when they were in bed, with the chill going from the sheets, they laughed, and he knew by the way she put his head on her shoulder that she wanted his love. Yet he was a bit afraid of her body now, as if whatever was growing and changing and always becoming in her, must ever be preserved. With his head on her breast, he went to put his palm on her belly, and she knew he was afraid, and she began to laugh and seemed to want him more than ever.

"It's like this, sweetheart," he said. "Maybe I shouldn't touch you at all when you're pregnant. I read that in one of

Tolstoi's essays one time. I just remembered it. Tolstoi had very definite notions on the subject. Nothing should be done to disturb the development of the child."

"How old was Tolstoi when he wrote that?"

"Getting on a bit. Certainly a bit past the first flush of youth."

"It wasn't hard for him to write it."

"No, but maybe he was right. He's put you out of circulation from now on."

"All right, it doesn't matter how I feel," she pouted. "I'll just be an incubator from now on."

"Darling, you'll get so healthy and strong and statuesque and you'll never feel better. See what good parents we are. We think only of the child."

"Mike, I don't think he'd mind much. Not right now."

"Is it going to be a boy?"

"Don't you want a boy?"

"It better be a boy, or I'll beat you."

"Then he's a boy. And listen, Mike. He's an awfully polite little boy, self-sacrificing and devoted to his mother and father, and he won't mind you loving me a little right now. He'll be very patient with us for a while."

"Maybe it'll be all right if we're very careful."

"We'll be terribly careful, Mike," she said.

But when Anna had fallen asleep beside him, and he lay there listening to her regular and contented breathing, all the hope that he had possessed so abundantly in the warmth of their love-making began to seem terribly unsubstantial now. The high brightness that had come so swiftly to them was gone now. They lay there in the chill of their small apartment, with the winter quietness of the city outside, and he began to think, "I don't feel free even now. I know I ought to tell her about Dave Choate and my father, and free my father, but it would harm her dreadfully. It would not be fair to her now. Yet if I followed the urge of whatever goodness there is in me, that's what I'd do, and I'd be free, but I couldn't bear to hurt her now. I must wait. I must wait. It would hurt her dreadfully and she could not stand it now. And while we wait nothing more can happen to my father, God help him, but I can't leave her, or part from her, or let her go." He felt that whatever he did he would do only out of love for her. When he was acting out of a fund of love, it would give him a vision of the world that would be fresh and his own, but all around him would be people who were restlessly seeking and never really finding, willing to change one vision for another, wishfully seeking the right one, and they would make it desperately hard to hold on to his own way of seeing it, yet he would have to hold on to it, no matter who rejected it, for when it was gone he would no longer be a lover and would be just as confused as anybody else.

The night they went around to the house of the minister who lived just two blocks away, they went in quietly and showed the minister their license to marry. He was a tall, thin man with an astonishingly long, sharply pointed nose. Maybe it was just the rimless glasses resting low on the bridge that accentuated the pointed tip of his nose, for when he took off the glasses, and called, "Mary, Mary," to his wife, and then peered at Anna and Michael, he looked almost benevolent, although benevolence wasn't an expression that came readily to such a sharp, hungry face.

His wife, a gray-haired, plump woman, came into the parlor, smiling cheerily in a way she must have smiled on five hundred occasions. "Now we need one other witness," the minister said. "I wonder if you could get the caretaker, Mary." And when the caretaker came in, bald-headed and beaming, he had just the right air of innocent gayety.

It did not seem to be much of a wedding. The four of them stood in the middle of the little parlor and looked terribly solemn while the minister went on reading rapidly from the Bible in his hand. Michael was thinking it was all a pretty dull business, until he turned and looked at Anna and saw how warmly she was smiling, and then he knew that no matter what she had said, or how indifferent she had wished to appear, she was really terribly glad. While she watched the long thin lips of the minister parting and coming sharply together again, there was such an ardent thankfulness in her face that Michael felt that old unending ache of love for her.

"Thank you. Thank you," Michael said to them all when it was over. There was such gratitude and sincerity in his voice, and it had come so suddenly, that the minister, who was making his low, professional bow, straightened up, and looked at his wife in surprise, and raised his eyebrows. His wife, too, began to look eager, as though aware, suddenly, of being close to some great happiness.

Then Mike gave the minister three dollars, apologizing humbly for offering such a small fee. The minister slapped him on the back and looked at Anna as if he were wondering if he dared kiss her. But Mike quickly took Anna by the arm and led her out into the cold night air.

As they walked along the street on that night late in February, that night that was deep in the cold of the winter, an elation rose so strongly in them that they could not speak. They were walking toward the brilliantly lighted avenue, keeping close together, and smiling at the red faces of people who passed with their hands up to their ears, but this extraordinary, silent shyness became such a mixture of gladness and anguish for Michael that he could not bear it, and he said, mocking her, "How does it feel to be made an honest woman?"

"I don't feel any different at all," she said. But then she took his arm and pressed it tight against her and whispered, "Oh, Mike, I shouldn't say it, but I do feel a little safer," and with his arm pressed so tight against her body, he became aware of all the relief that was flowing through her. "I know it was a funny little wedding," she said. "It was just like buying a couple of tickets for a game, I suppose. But I loved it, I loved it," she said, and her face, so white and lovely in the night, was lifted up to him in gratitude.

From that night on, whenever Mike felt any despair, he began to turn it into a longing that their child might be born. Day after day he watched Anna's body changing and growing, and her face becoming plumper and softer, and sometimes, when there was a little extra heat in the radiators in their flat, she let him put his hands on her belly to feel the stirring within her. Then she'd say, "Can't you feel him? No? What's the matter with you, Mike? Put your hand right there. Harder. You won't hurt him," and she pressed his hand deep into her flesh, and they both listened solemnly, staring intently into each other's eyes. Smiling slowly in her delight, she said, "There, there, did you feel it, Mike?"

"Maybe I did. I'm not sure," he said, a bit disappointed.

"That was it, all right," she said.

It was time for her to start wearing loose house dresses, and she ripped up her old black and white dress, and loosened it a lot; and in the daytime, working in the flat, she wore one of those aprons that could be let out or tightened. Though she was sometimes sick a little bit in the mornings, she had none of the crazy instincts that so many women have at such a time in their lives. Her skin was clear and it had begun to glow, and day after day she grew plumper and healthier. For her exercise they took long walks in the evenings. They walked along the street in the last of the winter, in the early spring, in the first sudden flood of good bright sunshine and warm weather in the city, and her shoulders were a little wider, and she was full breasted and her face kept glowing. It was an early spring in the city that year; the harbor had been open a month and the boats were coming in, and all over the city, among the merchants and the dispossessed, the ball players on the city sandlots and the little kids playing marbles on the street, the young girls walking slowly together at twilight and the boys playing indoor baseball on the road, shouting and screaming and dodging the automobiles, among them all, the dry old men and the girls wearing their little suits and swagger coats, there was rising joy in the firm belief that the good weather had come to stay. In the shopping sections of all the city neighborhoods the vegetable stores had heaped their green stuff out on the stalls, the blood-red tomatoes and the green cabbages and the clean carrots, and the Italian merchants, fat and heavy and happy-looking, stood at the doors, close to the stalls, watching for little kids to come and steal the apples.

One day Mike met Mrs. C. Wilberton Ashley, whom he had known at college, on the street, and she asked him if he could tutor her young brother in high school Latin. Mike put his arms around Mrs. Ashley and embraced her, he was so delighted. The job was only good for eight hours a week, but there was enough money in it to pay the grocery bills. Mrs. Ashley's young brother used to waste a lot of time with Mike talking about football games they had seen. Neither one of them liked Latin very much.

Anna was worried about having no proper clothes for the baby; she used to sit by herself, imagining that the baby was born and that it had no little sweaters or pretty dresses, or stockings or blankets like the babies of other women. Her shame sometimes at her inability to provide these clothes was very great, though she did not mention it to Mike, until the night he was sitting by the bed trying to read some Elizabethan love lyrics to her.

"Oh, stop," she said. "I can't be bothered listening."

"Anna, what's the matter?"

"Why do you insist on reading those poems to me?"

"I thought you'd like them."

"I haven't been listening to a word you've said. You've just been reading them to amuse yourself," she said bitterly.

"You're almost savage about it," he said. "Is there anything on earth you want?"

"Yes, I'd like some ice cream," she said.

"All right," he said. "I'll get you some."

"Never mind, Mike. You can't afford it," she said, watching him fumbling through his pockets for a dime. In the trousers of an old suit he found a dime, and he hurried over to the drug store and he came back with two ice cream cones.

"There," he said. "Now eat it."

"You eat one too."

"All right."

"Mike, darling, I was dying for some ice cream," she said.

"Why didn't you say so instead of getting so impatient and not listening to me read?"

"I wasn't thinking of ice cream at first," she said. "At first I was wondering if we'd ever have any clothes for the baby and wondering what we'd put on it, and then I felt restless and began to long for some ice cream." There were tears in her eyes as she spoke.

Two days later Sheila and Ross came to see them and Sheila brought enough clothes for two babies. Ross gave Mike the name of a young Dr. Nolan at the hospital. He said he had talked to Dr. Nolan, who had promised to look after Anna when it was time to take her to the hospital.

They wanted all the days to pass quietly now, and swiftly, too, for they felt they were doing nothing but wait. Every night, before they went to bed, Mike used to put his ear against her and listen while she complained, laughing, "He's a regular villain. He's going to be bold and strong like his father. He's rough with me, too. He's simply kicking me to pieces." But she was feeling wonderfully well, and whenever he came in in the evening and saw her sitting on the bed with her face glowing, she looked almost monolithic; she seemed to grow more radiant as life grew in her; she required more love, more peace, more joy, more sleep, and food enough to eat till she sighed. The pains that had been in her hip and her arm had gone away. She walked slowly now, with her head up, slowly, with her face lovely with its softness and contentment, and every time he looked at her Mike felt pride in her, pride in the child that was to be born, and he felt sometimes that he had no life of his own, that he need never think of Dave Choate, or his own father, or his own soul again, for his life was growing into hers.

In a happy, foolish way they began to call the baby "Abe." Every night when he came home, he said, "How's Abe?"

"He had a good deal to say today," she said.

"What does he talk like?"

"Oh, Mike, he's got a terrible East Side accent."

"Dear little Abe. We must never be anti-semitic with him," he said.

Twenty-Eight

ANDREW AIKENHEAD was living in a small, one-room bachelor apartment near the university. Sometimes he had a longing to be with friends in the crowds, he had a longing to be on the lighted avenues at night, in the beginning of the spring weather, when the crowds drifted slowly by, and he had to fight hard against this longing when he hid in the solitude of his room.

In April, the season of light rains, patches of sunlight and cloudy afternoons, he used to walk up the avenue, always hurrying. In the last month he had begun to hurry when he walked, and anyone looking at him would have thought he was desperately afraid of not getting to a particular place at a particular moment.

One afternoon he saw his old friend, Dr. Albert Tucker, of St. Bartholomew's church, ambling down the street, his big body rolling like a sailor's as he tried to favor his tender and slightly misshapen feet. He was holding his big umbrella high over his head, and he had on his black coat, which was flying open, and his sack coat underneath was open, too, and on his vest dangled freely his heavy gold watch fob.

Taking off his hat in the rain, Andrew Aikenhead said timidly, "I'm very happy to see you, Dr. Tucker. I was thinking of you the other day."

"Thinking only good things, I'm sure," Dr. Tucker began in his bland and impenetrable manner. Then he looked closely at Andrew Aikenhead, who was standing there bareheaded in the rain, with his wet clothes unpressed and his wavering blue eyes full of doubt. And when Dr. Tucker, with the hard, unspiritual face and the screw-driver eyes, saw that his friend looked as if he had been persecuted until he was quite willing to be destroyed, his own heart was touched.

Something had happened last week to Dr. Tucker that made him feel he understood Andrew Aikenhead's distress. Dr. Tucker's feet were of an awkward shape, though hardly anyone knew it. He hated his feet and tried to hide them by wearing expensive, stylish shoes, which only hurt his feet terribly and gave him his well-known sailor's roll. Last week, feeling that he could no longer endure his secret agony, he had gone to the store of J. C. Sneath, the shoemaker, and he had puffed and gasped for breath as he took off his shoes and showed the shoemaker his feet. The shoemaker, a quiet, modest man, was honored to have such a distinguished political, civic and religious leader there in his store, surrendering to him, and he put out his hand and touched Dr. Tucker's feet while Dr. Tucker watched him earnestly. "I can make you a pair of shoes that'll make you forget about your feet," the shoemaker said. "If you can, then you'll have my gratitude for all eternity," Dr. Tucker said. He was full of hope when he left the store. When he returned at the end of the week and tried the shoes on and walked gingerly up and down the carpet, his face began to light up in wonder. He wrung the shoemaker's hand and he began to crack jokes, and his big body shook with laughter, and he went out of the store with the eagerness of a boy leaving school for the summer holidays. After he had worn the shoes three or four days, he was standing on the street corner one afternoon, talking with the banker, Beverley Hill, and his wife, and in a pause in the conversation he became aware that the banker's wife was looking down and staring at his own specially constructed shoes. Now the comfort he got from these shoes was astonishing, but they did not look beautiful; they looked exactly like a pair of specially constructed shoes for a man with ungainly feet. Dr. Tucker's face reddened; he excused himself, and as he went on his way, he grew enraged and he muttered, "That woman will tell the whole town I've got deformed feet." He felt that he would become a ridiculous figure. Soon the whole town would be laughing at him, and yet up to this time, in spite of his pain, no one had ever known about his ungainly feet. From now on, no matter where he was, no matter how prominent the place, at a civic luncheon or on a platform, or even at the communion rail in his church, people would look first of all at his feet. It began to seem like a dreadful, scandalous piece of stupidity that a shoemaker should have dared to make such a shapeless pair of shoes for him. He went home and took off the shoes, and put on the painful, but stylish ones, and he hurried back to the shoemaker's store. With his gray eyes biting out at the merchant from under his heavy brows, he snapped, "I don't care for these shoes. Here they are. Thank you. Good day." The shoemaker said, "What am I to do with these shoes, Dr. Tucker?" "Do whatever you please, my good man. You've succeeded in making a laughing stock out of me," Dr. Tucker said. The shoemaker said, "Aren't they comfortable? I said they would fit," but Dr. Tucker only glared at him and turned to go. "Just a minute, Dr. Tucker. Don't you intend to pay for the shoes?" the merchant asked. "My good man, I've just told you that I'm not satisfied with them," Dr. Tucker said. "Do what you want with them, " and he kept going out. Defying the man whose life stood for all that the influential people of the city esteemed and thought most valuable, the shoemaker dared to say quietly, "You'll pay for them, Dr. Tucker … in court."

Two days later Dr. Tucker actually heard that the story of

his shoes was being whispered around the city. In panic, he sent a check to the shoemaker, with his apology. That he should ever become the talk of the town was a terrifying thought to him; it seemed horribly unjust; yet he had another feeling that he had never had before in his life, a feeling that was almost regret and shame. And that was why he was looking at Andrew Aikenhead this afternoon as if he had realized for the first time what the man had endured.

Emboldened by the sympathy he saw in Dr. Tucker's face, Andrew Aikenhead said, "I was thinking I'd like to come around to the church more often, Dr. Tucker."

"By all means do, my friend, and there's a warm welcome for you."

"I'm not really a religious man, as you know, Dr. Tucker, but when we grow older we find ourselves longing for the places of our youth." Then there was eagerness in Aikenhead's face and he said humbly, feeling his way, "I was thinking I might come around for communion on Sunday."

Dr. Tucker looked at Aikenhead shrewdly. "Andrew," he began, making Aikenhead feel full of hope by the intimate way he used the first name, "Andrew, I want to ask you one simple question, and I want you to answer it man to man."

"What is it, Dr. Tucker?"

"Did you have anything whatever to do with that boy's death? There's been a lot of talk around the church, but I'm willing to take your word for it."

"On my honor, I had nothing whatever to do with it."

"Forgive me, my friend. Forgive me, if you can, for asking. I'll rejoice to see you on Sunday." Dr. Tucker thrust out his hairy, freckled hand and smiled broadly. He went striding down the street, under his umbrella. Andrew Aikenhead, watching him go, began to nod his head in relief.

On the next Sunday morning Andrew Aikenhead came a little late to the church, for he did not want to be noticed by the prominent merchants and professional men and their wives, who had once been his friends. He wanted to be unobtrusive and quiet this morning, for his loneliness had been greater than he could bear, and now he was going to make a simple, unpretentious gesture toward the world and his God. When he went alone up the wide steps, it was comforting to remember that he was going into the church where Sheila had been married just a little while ago and where he had last known some happiness.

While the choir sang beautifully, he sat at the back of the church and began to think, "There's nothing quite so fine as to be among your own people, even when they don't know you are with them." As he looked around at the solemn, earnest faces of the great congregation he began to think it was wonderful the way they were all held fast together in one splendid, abiding communion while they worshipped God. He began to feel that he could truly lose himself among them, and, in losing himself, possess forever his own soul. The sound of the music and the sound of the ardent voices became like a caress. He, himself, longed to make a little prayer. Without any glibness, he whispered to himself, "I used to take pride in being different from other people. I used to like to think I was going my own way and that I was clever and that it was up to me to have my own way with the rest of the world. In my own way I was an enemy of the community because I was only interested in my own welfare. I know now how terrible it is to keep doing things that make people draw away from each other. I'm terribly sorry for anything I ever did that separated one man from another. I've had to feel a lot to see it that way, but now I know how dreadful it is to be put apart from people. It's not good to stand apart in your thinking and hoping. My God, I want to think and feel as all these people here think and feel. If I do that, then I know I'm closer to you, God."

He realized that people, who were not going to communion, were beginning to leave the church, but he could hardly lift his head. And when he began to go up to the front of the church, seeing no one and nothing but Dr. Tucker, his ears heard, "We do not presume to come to Thy holy table," and "Bread of heaven, on Thee we feed," words that had such a sudden, magnificent meaning, he felt he would hear them forever. Such words were the words that told of his own humility. He did not notice that the coal merchant, A. S. Grabell, who was beside him, was staring at him indignantly, nor that the furrier, Stanley Helmuth, kept nudging his wife and nodding at him, for he had forgotten that his clothes hung loosely on him and that he had a furtive way of lowering his head.

It was when he was kneeling at the communion rail, with a rapt and eager expression on his pale, thin face, that he noticed how the woman, who had been kneeling beside him, was edging away. And his shoulders sagged a little, and his head drooped lower. On the other side of him was Mrs. Mortimer Horlick, the president of the Community Women's club, a plump, high-breasted woman with a determined, handsome face. As soon as she saw Andrew Aikenhead, she straightened up and gasped. He looked very timid, but to her he looked like a man who was obviously guilty of a foul crime. "This is scandalous. It's sacrilegious," she muttered, and she turned, and went away, her face stern and her eyes proud, that all might see.

There was a crowd at communion that Sunday at St. Bartholomew's, but there was this gap among them, where Andrew Aikenhead was kneeling.

When Dr. Tucker, passing with the communion cup, came to that gap and looked at the bowed head of Andrew Aikenhead, the vivid coloring mounted to his own head, and his hand, holding the cup, trembled. He stood like that such a long time that they all turned and looked at him, and he made them feel his fury and his contempt. Then he bent down, and with a strange, clumsy tenderness showing plainly in his manner, he gave Andrew Aikenhead the bread and the wine.

Andrew Aikenhead had intended to sit for a while after communion at the back of the church and enjoy the peace and the dignity that had gladdened him when he first came in. He started to go down the aisle, and then his legs moved faster, and he wanted to run and he dared not look back, and he went right out the door and took a deep breath of the clean air, and stood there on the steps in the sunlight.

He stood there listening, as if he expected to hear them all come running out after him. Then he grew frightened. "I must never take a chance like that again," he thought, as he hurried along the street. "I was a fool to let them see me like that. I'm lucky to be here now."

When he got to his own place he thought he would feel secure, but after he had mixed himself a whiskey and soda and had sat down by the window, he didn't even lift the glass, he just sat there listening, and waiting. "What did I expect of those people, anyway?" he thought. "They're the people I've been trying to keep away from." Yet still he listened, still he waited, trying to locate the slightest noise on the street. "I might just as well have done it," he thought. "Not having done it makes it all so meaningless. Maybe I was the cause of everything? Marthe must have thought so, for she'd rather live any place in the world than beside me. Michael keeps away from me. Even my own people have rejected me. Yet I can't understand it. I want it to mean something. If I'm to blame, then it means something." The feeling of secret guilt that had been growing in him day after day flooded through him now, and he did not resist it this time; he wanted it, and accepted it and waited for it to destroy him. Yet still he listened. He forgot that it was Sunday. There were hardly any noises outside, no clatter and clang of steel, no sound of factory whistles or the hum and beat of the industrial life of the city. He began to drink his whiskey, and he filled his glass again and again. "Is nobody doing business today? The city's terribly quiet. I'm out of business. Maybe everybody I know is quitting, and the city's quiet, and our own time is dying. It's the death of our time. I want everybody to know that I accept the blame for what's happened to me. I want it to end." Again he listened, and he heard absolutely nothing, and he smiled a little, and then a deep sadness grew in him, and though he thought he was staring at the glass in his hand, he could see nothing. There was nothing. There was no desire even to see the glass, because there was nothing, and he stopped listening because there was nothing to hear. While he felt his spirit dying in the darkness and stillness and silence within him, he made no protesting stir.

Twenty-Nine

THE DAY Ross and Sheila were in the city on their way to New York, where he was going to specialize in surgery, they were as excited as two lovers in the first week of their marriage. They brought presents to Mike and Anna, and stayed the morning with them, and in the afternoon, Sheila went to see her father.

In the evening they were having dinner with the Hillquists. It was a splendid farewell dinner, with Jay Hillquist offering one pretty toast after another to Sheila, who looked lovelier, he said, than she had ever looked before. Mrs. Hillquist, too, seemed to be aware that her son was much happier and more eager than he had been since he got married, and she kept looking gratefully at Sheila. In a way it became a party that was a tribute to Sheila's youth and loveliness and high spirits, though they did not understand why it should have turned out like this, except that the Hillquists all suddenly felt free with her, and they wanted to express their love and their pride in her, feeling for the first time that it would delight her to hear it.

That night Jay Hillquist, who looked gaunt, stringy, hollow-cheeked, and feverish-eyed, had a lot of his old enthusiasm. Turning to Ross, he said, "Business is getting better. By God, I knew it would. Not much better, mind you, but it's beginning to move. What do you think of that, son?"

"It doesn't matter much in the long run," Ross said.

"Doesn't matter? It's life for all America. I can feel the blood begin to pound in the old heart of the world again," he said. He raised his freckled hand in a gesture of triumph. His sunken cheeks made his wide grin look fanatical.

Then Ross saw that his father had felt he was really fighting off death and that for him there was only one kind of death, the failure of his business.

"All that's the matter with people now is that they're jumpy," his father was saying. "They're frightened. They're listening for something to frighten them."

"They're listening and they hear it, all right," Ross said.

"I can't understand such fear. I despise fear."

"Yet they do listen," the doctor said. "All kinds of people, all classes of people are listening and wondering, and yet they do hear it. Talk to them, workers and capitalists, and priests and politicians, and they'll tell you they hear it. It's in the frightened faces of people on the streets. They're all waiting."

"If we could only get rid of that frame of mind in people, we'd shoot forward, son."

"You can't get rid of it because they do hear it, and they know it."

"Hear what?"

"The change creeping on. The new order they all know must come."

"Ah, rats, son," Jay said. "Wait till things get going again. Wait till we get working again. Put your money on me, son. It's going to go my way, or, by God, men like me will know the reason why." And then he was silent, as though thinking of the change Ross was predicting. At last he said to Sheila, "Did you see your father?"

"Yes, I did. He used to expect me to see him, and now it doesn't touch him one way or the other."

"Did you know I asked him to have dinner with us all

tonight? I thought it would have been nice if we could have all been together. I wrote him," Jay said.

"What did he say?"

"He didn't even bother to answer," Mrs. Hillquist said.

Ross saw the sadness coming in Sheila's eyes, and she kept looking over at him, and after they had looked at each other for a moment, with that surge in him to her, and her response, and the feeling of their oneness, she smiled, and he knew that she was sure he had felt what she wanted. He nodded and said, "Maybe I could run over and say good-bye to your father, Sheila. I've got time. Dad could take you to the station. Would you mind, Sheila? Would you, dad?"

"You ought to say good-bye to him, son."

"I'd like you to say good-bye to him," Sheila said. "I know he'd appreciate it."

"Tell him to come and see us. We'll get Sheila to the station on time," Jay Hillquist said.

When he left the house and was on his way in the taxi, Ross began to wonder if it was a mistake to stir up an old sorrow; earlier in the evening he and Sheila had come along the street arm in arm, and every street noise and little breeze and each passing face had kept adding to the deep excitement that came from knowing they would soon be away together making a new life in another city.

As he got out of the taxi in front of the dull-looking apartment houses that were near the university, he thought, "This is the first time I've gone to see him. He always used to come and see us."

When he rapped on the apartment door, he could hardly hear Aikenhead calling, "Come in."

As he opened the door he saw Aikenhead sitting in a leather chair by the window. The window was open and a little breeze from the street was blowing the edge of the drape against his face. He was wearing a brown dressing-gown. There was a crooked part in his hair, his iron-gray moustache was long and untidy and his eyes looked too big and frightened in their deep sockets. But what Ross noticed most was the dreadful stillness in Aikenhead's face, as if he wandered around day after day going nowhere, and that wherever he wandered death kept growing in him. Just a little over a year ago he had been a dapper business man with an easy polished manner; now he sat there with his ear to the open window and all the street noises on that early summer night came flowing into his ear to become a part of the stillness and death in him.

"Hello, Mr. Aikenhead," Ross said.

"Good evening. Won't you sit down?" he said. There was no gladness of recognition in his voice at all.

"I was going away. I just wanted to say good-bye to you."

"To me?"

"Yes."

"Oh." And then he stirred himself a little and said, "Did you say you were going away?"

"Yes."

"I hope you do well then. I hope you have some luck." He spoke with such a perfunctory politeness that Ross knew he wasn't interested at all. The still, unwavering, blue eyes of Aikenhead so upset Ross that there was panic within him; he felt he was looking at someone who not only wanted to die but had died, and he wanted to run so he would not be touched by such desolation. Then he was ashamed and he began to talk cheerfully, "I didn't want to go without saying good-bye to you," he said. "Michael doesn't live far away from you. Do you know that?"

"No, I didn't."

"Have you met his wife?"

"No, I haven't."

"You'll love her."

"Why did you want to say good-bye to me?"

"Well, when I was going, I got thinking of the way you used to come to our house and have a drink and start singing. None of us could sing. You used to stand there and shout in a terrible voice. It was funny."

"I don't know why you should have thought of that," he said fretfully.

"Sure it was a crazy thing to think of, but they're the things you think of when you're leaving a place."

"It was kind of you to think of me."

"I don't see why," Ross said awkwardly. For a moment he didn't know what to say. Aikenhead was just as detached now as he had been when he first spoke. Then Ross suddenly grinned and went right on talking cheerfully about many simple things. "I guess the last time we were together was the night we ran into each other coming home from the concert. It snowed pretty heavily that night, do you remember? There weren't many taxis so we started to walk and then we went in and had a drink. You certainly were worked up that night because you'd heard Mallory was going to run for mayor again. You talked like a blue streak."

"Did I?"

"You sure did. Here, do you want a cigarette? No? All right. I'll have one anyway. Say, listen to this; I just heard this today downtown. Mallory's going to run again this year and he'll get in. He's got the city hall so tied up it's like the old homestead for him now."

"What's that?"

"The same old city hall gang is going back into office again, and nobody of any consequence will really run against Mallory because of the way he's got the town sewn up. I guess civic politics is pretty much comic relief, and I suppose it's all right if you can look at it in that way, but I get worked up just like the way I do over a sporting event. I mean I hate the way everybody goes for the same old hypocrisy year after year, but I guess there's nothing to do but bite your nails and like it, is there?" Ross went on talking about civic politics in as natural a way as if he had just met Aikenhead on the street corner and they had started right in to talk about those things in which they had a common interest. An excitement came into Ross; he leaned forward and his eyes began to shine, and his voice rose a little. Sometimes he laughed out loud and then the words went on flowing out of him again.

In a little while, Aikenhead, who was blinking his eyes as though groping toward something he could just barely see, began to feel some of the animation in the young man's voice. For a while he hardly spoke, he only leaned forward as though loving the sound of Ross's words, and then gradually he was drawn into the discussion of municipal politics.

"Nothing I ever knew about Mallory was good," he said.

"There's certainly enough to know about him."

"But nothing much good," he said.

For a while they spoke and listened and agreed and it seemed to be very much like one of the discussions they had often had before. Then they paused and nodded their heads, as though they were both thinking of the same thing. It was one of those natural pauses that come in the conversations of people who are very friendly. Then Aikenhead looked up at Ross, as though he were pleading with him to go on talking. A flush had come into his cheeks. The animation he had felt in Ross had begun to warm him. There was an awkward, shy eagerness in his voice as he said, "What did you say you were planning to do, Ross?"

"I said we were going to New York. I'm going to specialize."

"Oh, you're going away," he said, and he looked very disappointed. "It was good to see you. I ought to have had you here with Sheila, but you're going away. That's too bad."

"I have to run along now. I can't stay a minute longer," Ross said.

But Aikenhead did not get up from the chair; he seemed to think that by remaining seated and just watching Ross he could hold him there a little longer. Yet only a little while ago he had been lifeless and detached from everything.

Ross was touched, and he stood there smiling and then he walked over to him, wanting to say good-bye affectionately. He put his hand down on Aikenhead's shoulder and said, "Good-bye for a while," and then he put both his arms around him and embraced him warmly.

Aikenhead looked up at him, wondering, and then he stood up and he was full of such delight that his face began to glow with life. His thin face was wrinkled up in smiles. He was excited and he began nodding his head up and down. "Maybe you could write to me," he said.

"Sure I'll write to you."

"Tell me what you're seeing and doing, and tell me about the concerts you'll be hearing, will you?"

"Sure I will."

"Maybe we could carry on some of our discussions in our letters. You remember the argument we had about Nietzsche? Maybe we'd both have a lot more to say. But don't forget to write. Promise you will," he said, and he reached out and held Ross by the arm, as if he dared not risk losing this new link with the warmth of life.

"I'll promise you," Ross said gravely, for he felt the man's life really depended on this promise.

"I wish you were staying, Ross."

"I can't do it. I've got to work and learn and I've got Sheila to look after."

"I know, I know. I was just wishing, that's all."

"I've got to go now."

"Good-bye. Remember to write."

"Good-bye, Mr. Aikenhead. I'll surely write."

Ross had only fifteen minutes to get to the station, and

when he was outside he ran along the sidewalk looking for a taxi. He was out of breath and worried about missing the train. He kept looking up at the big clock as he ran into the station waiting room. His father and Sheila were standing there, waiting, and watching him running toward them. Sheila, with the three bags at her feet, was smiling in relief. Before Ross reached them, his father beckoned to a redcap, and then Ross was with them, and his arm went around Sheila's waist and he began pulling her along to the train.

"How was my father? Did you see him?" Sheila asked.

"I saw him. We had a good talk. He looked much better when I left him."

"I'm so glad, Ross. I'll feel so much easier in my mind now."

"That's fine, son," Jay Hillquist said. "Now take care of yourselves, both of you."

While the father was calling, "Good-bye, good-bye," they were hurrying down the iron stairs to the train below. Soon they were on the train, and it began to move out of the station.

They smiled broadly at each other when they were sitting down in the observation car. "It's wonderful to be going away," Sheila said. It seemed extraordinary to both of them that they were there together on the train and going away.

They went to the Pullman car and got undressed and Ross lay on the inside of the berth by the window. Beyond the city the train had gathered speed, the great headlight was stabbing into the dark of the country, the coaches creaked as they rolled around a curve in the tracks, and Sheila's body lurched against Ross and they knew they had left the flat land and were passing over the low rolling hills. They were silent. Someone passing in the aisle brushed against the curtain, making a swishing, brushing noise, and then there was the bumpa bumpa bumpa bumpa bumpa, the monotonous rumble pounding into the bodies and the minds of them all, the salesmen, the chorus girls, the thief running away, the worried wife seeking her husband, and the lovers locked in each other's arms and whispering. It was then, above the rattle and the swish of the engine against the wind, that Ross began to hear the sound of Andrew Aikenhead's voice, pleading, "You'll keep in touch with me. You'll not forget me," and as Ross closed his eyes, he could see the man's face with the eagerness and hope growing in it. "He wanted to die. His spirit was dead. Yet if I could have stayed there and been friendly he would have felt that he was a human being again." Then he was deeply troubled as though he were on the bank of a river and watching someone far out sinking into death in the water. "I'll write him, all right. For a while I'll write … as long as I remember the way he looked and the sound of his voice." For that moment, when the train was on a stretch of track that was level and smooth, he heard Sheila breathing steadily beside him, not breathing in sleep, but breathing like a girl waiting. Yet his deep and troubled concern kept pulling him back to the city he had left. "I'm not old, I'm young and going away, and whatever happens to us we must be happy, and God knows tonight I shouldn't be feeling like this, yet I lie here and am still and I might just as well be old too with the sadness in me." Suddenly he raised the window shade and looked out at the landscape rolling by on that warm summer night. They were crossing the low land with lighted farm houses and rising into the dark mound shapes of hills. Soon they would be high in the mountains of Pennsylvania, the lights of the day coach gleaming in the dark of the mountain night. In the morning they would see the mist on the marshes and the flat land of Jersey. Then they stopped at a small station and there was a profound silence; then the brakeman shouted along the track, and a trainman passed the window swinging his lantern, the wheels creaked, and then screeched and the train was moving again, then gaining speed, bumpa dumpa, bumpa dumpa, bumpa dumpa, rising slowly into the hills. The slopes of the hills sometimes gleamed bright in the moonlight. Great clumps of trees began to swing past the window, dark blotches against the steady moonlight. "Tomorrow there'll be another city and new faces, a great city with a harbor on the sea," he thought.

Though Sheila was still silent, he felt her beside him as he had never felt her before, and she was calling him out of the life they had left in that other city, calling him with the warmth and loveliness of her firm body and the new ardor of her soul. Then her hand touched him and she turned to him, and he turned to her, and his lips were on her lips and her breast was against him, and she was whispering, whispering so softly, giving all of her love to him. While they were young and warm, he thought, this was the way it must be.

Thirty

MIKE WAS getting Anna her breakfast one morning when she said, "I think I feel it happening, Mike. I didn't say anything a little while ago when I felt the pains the first time, but I feel them again now."

It was very hard to believe it was happening at last, and they both stared at each other. It was only when Mike realized that Anna's head kept bending down till he could hardly see her face that he said, "Are you pretty sure, Anna?"

"They're just little pains, but they keep rising and falling. That was the way Ross said it would be."

"Then we'll get ready," he said, and his voice was suddenly casual, as if he had been preparing for this one moment all his life.

"It may not be for a long time, Mike."

"We'd better get to the hospital anyway, and we can wait there," he said.

She moved slowly while she dressed, and when she saw how grave he had become, and felt his care and tenderness in the way he helped her put her clothes on, she smiled broadly. But he didn't like that smile. It made him feel that she was really very frightened.

When they were out on the street in the early morning, with people hurrying to work, Mike wondered why no one even looked at them. What was happening to them was so tremendous that he felt lifeless in wonder and could hardly move his legs, yet for the rest of the city, evidently, it was a simple, unimportant little thing.

"I'll call a taxi," he said.

"Maybe we could go on the street car. I think it'll be all right," she said.

"We can afford the taxi this once."

"And to come home in, maybe," she said softly.

"To come home in. Oh, Anna, don't say it like that."

"I can't help it, Mike. I want very much to come home," she said.

In the taxi they hardly spoke. They sat beside each other and he held her hand tight. Once when the clear, early morning, city sunlight swept into the taxi she smiled in that old way that made her face glow in its loveliness. But they didn't speak. They just sat there, close together.

At the courtyard of the hospital Mike helped her out of the cab, and when she had taken only a few steps, she stopped, and clenched her fists and closed her eyes, and then, as he longed to be able to pick her up in his arms and carry her, he felt he had never loved her so much. Leaning on his arm, she shook her head and made a little face as she said, "They're coming more regularly now, like a stronger beat."

Mike left Anna sitting in a little waiting-room at the end of the corridor while he went to the desk and asked the old nun for Dr. Nolan, the young obstetrician. The nun, who was a very cheerful old woman with a web of wrinkles all over her tiny face, asked the switchboard girl to locate the doctor on one of the floors. The girl kept saying, "Is Dr. Nolan there? Do you know where he is? Thank you. I'll try there." Sometimes the old nun looked up at Mike from the book she was writing in and smiled calmly. "Dr. Nolan seems to be very hard to locate this morning," she said.

"My wife is in the waiting-room and the pains have started to come," Mike blurted out.

"Probably just the preliminary pains," the nun said, without looking up.

"I don't know. We don't know anything about it."

"Those pains are nothing like the real pains. We had a woman come in here yesterday with those pains and they kept up for two days."

"But my wife's afraid, Sister. She's in the waiting-room now and it's apt to happen, and she's afraid."

"For goodness sake, why didn't you say she was in the waiting-room? We don't need Dr. Nolan to put her in a bed," the nun said, looking at Mike as if he had been making a fool of her by joking with her. She swept out of the office and along the corridor, her black robes swinging back in a wide wave behind her.

When they got to Anna in the waiting-room, and Mike saw her sitting there by herself, with her hands folded in her lap, and her face full of the surprise and timidity of a shy girl, his love and his concern were so great that he could not speak. The nun, smiling warmly, put her arm around Anna to comfort her, and Mike looked at the nun gratefully. "Don't be afraid, dear," the nun said. "We'll look after you."

A white-coated attendant brought a wheel chair, and they put Anna in the chair, and when they were wheeling her away, and Mike was going along the corridor with the nun to register at the office, Anna looked back at them and smiled shyly and waved her hand.

"She's going to be brave and sensible," the nun said. "She's a fine girl. I can tell as soon as I look at them."

"I hope they don't hurt her," Mike said.

After he had registered for a semi-private ward he went up to the maternity ward, and when he was standing at the desk of the nurse who was on duty on that floor, feeling lost, Dr.

Nolan came along the corridor and stopped and shook hands with him. The doctor was a young, slim man with his hair clipped tight like a Prussian officer, and he had a pair of cold hard blue eyes that were in strong contrast to his easy, good-natured manner. When Mike first shook hands with him, he was uneasy, but by the time the doctor released his hand, he was a bit puzzled and yet sure the doctor was very steady and could be trusted. The only thing he didn't like about him was his winged collar.

"Have you seen my wife? How do you think it will go, doctor?"

"Not bad. I just took a look at her."

"How does she look to you?"

"I don't know. Her measurements are pretty good," the doctor said in his slow assured way. "And the pains seem to be increasing regularly enough. It may be sooner than you think."

Then they began to talk about Ross Hillquist. "You're awfully good to us, doctor," Mike said.

"That's nonsense. Ross would do a thing like this for·me at any time. He's a very good fellow. I'm glad he is my good friend. He'll make a very fine surgeon. When is he going to New York?"

"He went about two weeks ago."

"Good. He's married to your sister, isn't he?"

"Yes."

"It's a pleasure to help you in any way."

"Ought I to sit down here and wait?"

"No. Go out and eat an early lunch and don't worry. There'll probably be nothing doing for about six hours."

"Will I wait here when I come back?"

"There's a little waiting-room at the end of the corridor. I'll drop in on you from time to time and tell you how it's going," the doctor said.

Mike went over to the restaurant opposite the City Hall and

read the papers, just as he might have done on any other day. After he had had some lunch and some coffee, he left the restaurant because it seemed no good sitting there, and he walked through the department stores for a while, and then along the street aimlessly till he realized he was getting closer and closer to the hospital. In a little while he began to feel it was silly to be walking in the street when he could be in the room at the end of the hospital corridor, and he went back to the hospital and sat down in the waiting-room. Three other men were sitting there. One was an enormous Italian with a rosy, benevolent face and long black moustaches. Another one, the one wearing his derby hat, had precise, jerky little movements, and he had taken out his notebook and was making accurate and shrewd calculations about some business matter. The third one had sad watery eyes and absolutely no expression at all on his face. They were all poorly dressed. But they all sat there together in the pleasant little waiting-room with its palms and rubber plants and the big windows looking out over the courtyard, and the church steeples and the store roofs, over the city and far down to the wide line of blue water beyond the harbor that was the lake. From that window high up in the hospital the whole city was spread out below in the soft gray light of the early afternoon and sometimes the sun gleamed on the gilt of spires and towers.

The big Italian rubbed his mouth with his palm and looked around, grinning, and he said to Mike, "Your first one?"

"The first for me," Mike said.

"I've had five. You won't feel that way about the second one, son. Ask these fellows," and the Italian beamed and shrugged and laughed and tried to draw the man with the derby hat and the pencil into the conversation, but that one only looked at the Italian thoughtfully and then made a few more figures in his notebook. "We feel it, we feel it, no doubt about that, eh?" the Italian said, sighing, and when they all looked up at each other and nodded their heads, Mike began to feel that he and those men were really having the babies there in that little room, and that the wives were outside, waiting for them.

In a little while Dr. Nolan came in and sat down beside Michael and whispered that everything was satisfactory. "But I don't quite know why it goes so slow," he said. "Her measurements were all good. She's a pretty good type, I mean she's very feminine. Dilatation began quite a while ago. The baby's evidently a little out of position."

"What would that indicate?"

"It's probably to one side. I don't want to use the instruments unless I have to. I'll let nature do it if your wife can stand it. We can't say for sure. We just have to wait," the doctor said. He spoke in a gentle, worried way. He was a quiet, modest man with great confidence in himself, but he had tried to strip his profession of all its pretenses, and he made it plain that when a woman was having a child, it was a natural process, and he could be expected only to ease the pain a little, unless it was absolutely necessary to use the instruments. Once he started to use the instruments he had extraordinary assurance.

Mike was looking at the doctor with such an infinite trust and faith in his eyes and such a willingness to subjugate himself completely to his will that the doctor began to fidget uneasily. It seemed a marvelous thing to Michael that the doctor should be sharing his concern for Anna, that they should be joined together in this deep concern, and he smiled at the doctor, and looked as if he was going to jump up and embrace him and call him Brother.

For some reason that he did not understand, Dr. Nolan was deeply moved, and he said, "You may be sure I'll do all I can. I won't let her have too much pain. But dilatation has begun, as I said, and from now on it may go along all right."

Then a tall, good-looking nun came into the waiting-room and said, "Which one is Mr. Aikenhead?"

"Here he is, Sister," Dr. Nolan said.

"Should I send a priest to your wife?" the nun whispered.

"What's the matter? Why are you asking me that? What's happened?"

"It's all right," she said, smiling gravely. "If they're Catholics they like a priest, that's all."

"What do they want a priest for?"

"In case of death. If it gets too hard, the priest anoints them."

"There's nothing wrong with her, Sister? She doesn't want that?"

"What religion is your wife?"

"I don't know," he said, smiling apologetically.

"She's such a lovely girl she ought to have some religion. What nationality is she?"

"She was born in this country. Her parents were Ukrainians. I don't think they were religious."

"What a pity," the nun said, and she spoke with such a true sorrow, as she fingered the big wooden beads of her rosary and looked out the window, that Michael felt that something terrible had surely happened; he felt that something they could not understand was happening, while they waited, that made Anna utterly alone, and he seemed to have rebuffed the sister, who wanted to help her.

"Is there anything you can do, Sister?" he asked.

"Would you mind if we baptized her?" the tall nun said with the eagerness of a girl.

"That would be all right. I don't think she'd mind that. That would be splendid," Mike said. "And it won't hurt if it's been done before, either."

Yet the way the nun turned and went noiselessly away, floating along the corridor with her great black robe hardly fluttering, reminded Mike of death, and he was full of terror, and he stared at the men who were waiting with him for the birth of their children, and he began to mumble to himself, "I'm thinking of death and I'm waiting for birth." And from deep within him, as if it had been waiting a long time to burst out, was the unuttered cry, "What right have I to bring life into the world? Death has been growing in me. Death has been all around me. I can still hear Dave. I can hear him crying now, 'Mike, oh, Mike, help me.' Yet I let him go, and now I stand here waiting for my own child to come into the world."

Turning to the doctor, who had been speaking, he said, "What's that you're saying?"

"You're mumbling to yourself, man."

"I was thinking it's a terrible responsibility to bring anyone into this world."

"These men sitting here don't seem to think so. Look at them." He, himself, smiled at the Italian.

"Nothing has ever happened to these men here," Mike whispered. "They're vegetables, and like vegetables, they go to seed and then there are other vegetables."

"Maybe, but it's not a new thing to have a child. Children are born here every night."

"I wasn't thinking of them being born. I was thinking of death."

"And people die here every night, too," the doctor said calmly. "And they don't want to die either, but they die, and then it's all right."

"You get used to it, doctor. You see it happening, but you understand that it's not in your hands, and that you're not doing the disposing."

"That's true. Then what are you worrying about?"

"I don't know. I guess I'm getting excited. I'll go out on the street for a while. Good-bye, doctor," he said.

It was a long time since they had gone into the hospital, and now it was dusk on the street, dusk and the beginning of a summer night in the city, with the lights coming on and the people flocking out to look in the store windows. And every time Mike looked at another woman, he thought of Anna. He looked at automobiles, new models for the year in the show windows gleaming bright, and he stared at them so intently that salesmen, seeing him there, came over to the door. Mike looked up and said to himself, "Anna," and walked away. He listened to the cries of the newsboys shouting, "Extra, extra, extra, all about the big fire," and he wondered where the fire had been, and then he thought, "Anna." In the great store windows were slim manikins wearing the sheerest silk stockings and he looked at them a long time and thought, "Maybe I'll never see them on her again. It would be terrible to be forever looking at people in the streets and things in the windows and hear voices or read the papers with her gone." Then he grew very frightened, for he began to believe that he was about to be given some final justice that would take Anna from him.

When he went back to the room at the end of the hospital corridor, there were no men waiting. He thought he would sit there alone and close his eyes, and he did sit down, but in a moment he was on his feet again, walking the length of the corridor slowly. His heels sounded loud on the tiled floor. Nurses kept passing while he hovered near Anna's room. Once he heard a low groan that he knew came from her. That groan bore in to his bowels and terrified him. He had never believed such a sound would come from her; he had never believed he could feel the deep dread that he was feeling. A nurse hurried out of the room. Following her, he begged, "How is it going, please?"

"I'm phoning the doctor," she said.

"What does that mean?"

"That we believe there's been good progress," she said.

And in a little while they were wheeling Anna out of the room to deliver her. They had just got her to the end of the corridor when Dr. Nolan came along in his dinner jacket, and he looked at Anna, and made them wheel her back. Michael waited, while the doctor remained fifteen minutes in the room with Anna. When the doctor came out, he only said, "Nothing has changed much. The dilatation still goes on. That's all I can say."

"But they were wheeling her to the delivery room."

"I don't know why the hell they were," the doctor said savagely. "The nurse phoned me that she was ready. She's seen enough of them and she ought to know better, but she doesn't, that's all. I'll come back in an hour. If she's not ready then, I'll use the instruments. In any event, remember it will be all right. I've done it hundreds of times. If you'll forgive me for saying so, I'll tell you I'm very good at it," and he slapped Mike on the knee and went away.

Mike was alone in the waiting-room, looking over the city in the night, where the lights gleamed in regular patterns against the darkness. On that summer night the underlying hum of traffic floated up to the hospital window. Looking down at the streets, Mike was able to see the crowd moving along slowly, and then men separated themselves from the crowd and moved on alone, going their separate ways, living souls of his own city keeping locked within them whatever they knew of warmth and love as they went their separate ways. All the remorse in his own soul welled up in him, and he mumbled, I'm sorry, Dave. I know how you wanted to live. I know how wonderful it is just to go on living, and that that was all you wanted. Wherever you are now, Dave, I want you to know I'm sorry. You can hear me. You know I'm afraid now. You know I'm yellow now and I can't stand it if she dies." He talked like this because when he looked down there at the streets where there was light and where people were alive and moving, he felt absolutely sure that what was left of the flesh in the earth and the bones and the worms, all under the head-stone on the earth, no longer belonged to Dave, and yet Dave was not dead, and could know now what he was thinking. "I didn't know anything about death," he thought, "It was just something proud and aloof and pretty cold. Anybody can think of dying. Anybody can say they don't mind dying. You go ahead or you don't go ahead. You're like a brave sound, and then maybe you become an echo of a sound. But I'm afraid because I love her, and that makes it different." All the ways of dying were in him then while he waited; the calm old man waiting in the winter, waiting patiently and smiling, the heroic bright willing deaths of martyrs that were not deaths, the beautiful deaths, the celebrated deaths, the gasping, choking, futile deaths of soldiers in the mud. His own mother's death was like a creeping blindness; and there were the nice, quiet deaths that made them all say gravely, "He died a beautiful death in the consolation of his religion." All such ways of dying, no doubt, had a high, proud place in the hierarchy of death; but they were not the same as the death of someone young dying in the early summer, in the time of the roses and the green grass, for whom there could be no consolation, and who cried out, "I don't want to die, oh, God, I don't want to die," and yet died while the warm winds were blowing from the south. "Anna wants to live. She wants so much to live. We love each other." But then he repeated in a dogged, dutiful way, "Dave, too, didn't want to die. He was young, too, and his voice was wild."

While he listened, as if he would hear the precise quality of every small sound, the terror grew in him, and he began to remember how he had pressed his ear against Anna's flesh, night after night, listening for the smallest sound of the life growing within her. Those months had been such a lovely preparation. He thought of them taking the child from Anna in the delivery room, and he pressed his fists against the glass, feeling himself being swung out precariously in the eternity between life and death. "I can't stand it. I bring life into the world. I send life out of the world. I give and I take away, and I give and I take away. I'm not God. I say I'm not God. I'll go crazy. Just the same I bring, and I send away," and he stared down at the lighted city, mumbling, "Just like God. Is there any justice in that? I didn't mean to use the word justice because I realize that I do not understand at all what it means. Just the same I'm like God. Somewhere down there my father walks along the streets, and he wants only justice, but I've been over all that, and I don't know what it means, I only know that Anna will have to die, and it won't be unjust. But I don't want justice. Who on this earth ever really wanted justice?" And then he stopped thinking, and he was still, and he whispered, "My God, have pity on me. I don't want justice, I want mercy. Have pity on me."

When he heard a sound along that endless corridor, he turned, and he saw two nurses hurrying into Anna's room. In a little while they came out, wheeling Anna with them. He ran after them and he could just see Anna's face, so set and white. A soft moan came from her. He knew that he felt her suffering, he knew that his compassion was very great, but suddenly the sympathy, the tenderness, the concern of anybody put up against such suffering seemed detached and a poor mean thing.

The head nurse was saying to him, "Will you please sign this paper, Mr. Aikenhead? It is an instruction to operate if necessary, that's all."

His fingers were numb and the pen shook. The nurse smiled a little and said, "The husbands always feel it more."

"Like hell they do," he said. She didn't like that and swung away from him quickly.

The time they had been waiting for for so long had come, and he stood there alone and closed his eyes. He thought he could see a stretch of water in the night. He thought he could hear the lapping of water. He was sure now that she would not live. She would die that night and die apart from him. Nurses passing were puzzled by the calmness and the stillness in his face as he walked so slowly along the corridor. He didn't seem to know where he was. He was simply trying to get used to the notion of Anna dying, of Anna being dead. And then he stood still, and he longed to be able to pray. His soul yearned to make one simple little prayer, but it was very hard to know whom to pray to, for they all seemed so far away, even though he was willing, and knew the names of saints, and of Jesus Christ; they all seemed to belong to another time that wouldn't be interested in him. Yet he had to start praying, and he began very slowly, for the words were strange; he spoke each word with a dreadful slow hesitancy, as if he must test every word to see if he honestly believed it and appreciated its full meaning. "Our Father, Who art in heaven, Hallowed be Thy name. Thy kingdom come, yes, yes, Thy Kingdom come, Thy will be done," and he nodded his head slowly to that, too. As he repeated those praying words, the city noises came through the open window, and a woman groaned at the end of the corridor, yet he never heard these sounds, for there was an absolute silence within him. When it was done, he felt he had accepted whatever there had been of life, and what there was to be of death.

Dr. Nolan had said he would phone the nurse on duty at the end of the corridor. Michael had forgotten about her. She came along the corridor on her rubber-soled shoes, and she touched him on the arm before he was aware she had come. "Dr. Nolan is on the phone," she said.

There wasn't a single hope in Mike as he went to the phone. He said quietly, "Yes, doctor." The doctor said, "It's a boy. She's all right. We'll be back there soon," and he hung up.

They let him see the baby first. While a nurse held the baby in her arms, he looked shrewdly at the red, angry face and at the chin and the shape of the head particularly, like an old, professional father, and then he nodded his head calmly to show he was satisfied.

When he saw Anna, she was weak and drowsy from the ether, and every line of her face had been pulled tight. She lay there under the bed clothes as she might have lain a year ago, with the heaviness all gone out of her body. Her voice came in an unbearable whisper as he took her bloodless hand, "It's all right, Mike. Did you see the baby?"

"I saw him."

"Wasn't I right saying it would be a boy?"

"He's got such a lovely head, Anna."

"We'll call him Little Mike," she whispered.

Then he had to leave her, and he took the elevator down to the street. As soon as he got outside he wanted to run. The delight and wonder kept growing in him and he wanted to drift lightly along the street. This new, peculiar happiness was so delicately balanced in him, so close to happiness and ecstasy on one side, and sadness on the other that he felt the slightest jar would push it to a breaking point and he would not be able to stand it.

Even when he was home in the small apartment, thinking it was a vacant place without Anna, he was still holding the delicately poised and fearful happiness in him. He was hungry and got himself something to eat, and then couldn't eat. He was dreadfully tired but he could not sleep. He lay in bed and the lights outside filled the room with shadows, and he put out his hand from time to time and touched the place in the bed where Anna had so often lain beside him.

Thirty-One

THERE seemed to be nothing to do but watch Anna from day to day. She was contented with her child, and she had many tasks that kept her busy. Whenever she spoke to Mike he listened patiently, never smiling, yet showing he was willing to help her in any way he could. His grave, thin face was sometimes puzzled. There were times when she spoke to him and he didn't seem to hear her, then she was disturbed and watched him and worried a little. She began to feel the stillness and the sadness that was in him, and was sure he was sick in some way she could not understand, so she did not mention the grocery bills or the rent to him. As she moved around the room she knew he was following her with his eyes, and when she turned suddenly and he smiled shyly his face seemed to her to be calm and beautiful and full of childish surprise.

He got two weeks more work with the Lake City Light, Heat and Power Company, and there was a promise of more work to come.

When he was alone in the apartment, minding the baby that lay in the basket on a trunk in a corner of the room, a basket they had got from the butcher store and lined with old dresses, he sometimes lifted the basket down and let the child sprawl on the rug on the floor. Then he sat cross-legged, watching his son rolling and kicking his fat legs and banging his red, clenched fists against his angry face as he shrieked for Anna. All one afternoon Mike sat there, meditative, watching his child, leaning forward sometimes and frowning when the child squirmed and yelled.

Anna was out at the store and when she came in and saw him sitting there gravely, rocking back and forth on his haunches, she was afraid, not only because he was so white-faced and quiet, but he was making no effort to soothe the shrieking child.

She rushed over to them and sat down on the floor and picked up the baby that was hungry, and as she opened her dress and put his head against her breast she said, "Mike, darling, what's the matter with you these days? You just look at me when I speak and you smile a little. In some ways you are lovelier than you ever were, but why are you so timid? Things will get better, Mike. I'm not worrying. There's no use you worrying. What were you thinking of, sitting here?"

"I was just figuring something out."

"What were you figuring?"

"I was wondering why people want to suffer," he said earnestly.

She smiled brightly, hardly hearing him, for the child had ducked its head hungrily into her breast and had begun to feed, and while her chin was turned down against her own chest, with her eyes on her baby's head, and she made a low, soothing noise, there was no life nor any other world for her than the world made between her and her son as he pulled at her breast. But when it was going ahead all right she looked up and said, "What were you saying, Mike?"

"It's astonishing," he said. "I know why men deliberately suffer. They say suffering draws men to God. Maybe it does, only I think it works out like this. God becomes aware of us when we suffer. That's why it may be good for us to suffer. Otherwise we may be forgotten. We have to remind God that we exist. If we suffer, God gets interested in us and has compassion and maybe we are consoled. Suffer and you have a chance of finding God. I figured it all out watching Little Mike. When he's in great pain he shrieks and wants you, and you run to him and comfort him. Sometimes he deliberately hurts himself. You're God to him and he wants your attention. Then he's a little mystic. You'll see how he keeps it up as he grows older. He'll always know how to get your love. Some day he may get pretty ambitious and want God's love, and then he will try and get a little attention by suffering."

Anna was putting the baby back in the basket and carrying it over to the trunk, and when she had finished, she turned and asked simply, "Why do you talk like that, Mike?"

"I don't know," he said.

"Are you serious?"

"I don't know."

"It doesn't sound like you. It's cynical and worried, yet you do look so serious, Mike."

"Maybe I was kidding, half kidding, maybe, but I get pretty mixed up anyway these days. I talk to myself and half the time I'm kidding myself." He knew she was worried and he was boyish and timid and almost servile in his eagerness to make it right with her. Getting up from the floor, he began to help her set the table for dinner, but when it was only half done she went over to the window and stood there by herself watching the evening fall over the city and her face was solemn and wondering. Suddenly she said, "Do you believe in dreams, Mike?"

"I don't know about dreams. Why should you ask me about dreams?"

"Do you believe in dreams at all?"

"Yes, I believe in dreams, but I'm not a Freudian."

"Last night I dreamt I was in a house we used to live in in Detroit and there was a fireplace and a mantel in the room, and my father's head kept rising out of the fireplace and he was trying to say something to me."

"What was he trying to say?"

"I don't know. He was trying to tell me something."

"You must know what he was trying to say."

"No. I don't. I've had the dream three times. And always he's trying to say something. What does it mean? Oh, he looked so worried, Mike."

"Dreams go by opposites. You can't go by dreams."

"But he looked so worried. Maybe he's sick."

"He wouldn't be sick."

"Maybe they need me at home."

"It didn't mean that."

"Then what did it mean?"

"How should I know? You can't go by dreams. We're a race of Freudians, that's the trouble."

"Mike, I've a feeling there's something going on around here that I don't know about. I feel there are things I ought to know."

"Why do you talk about the dream?"

"I feel it's all in me. I think of my father because he was always so close to me, and I would want him to tell me if he could."

"Anna, keep quiet. I won't go on talking in this silly way. I won't talk about your dream. You shouldn't have such dreams. I'm sure they're bad. You've been worrying and watching me, haven't you? Why have you been worrying? I've done nothing to worry you, Anna." Putting his hands on her shoulders, he held her against him and he was so agitated she was startled. She tried to laugh, and then she went on laughing in a false, wild way, till he grinned sheepishly.

The uneasiness they had touched so swiftly remained with them all evening, and made them silent, yet it was not until they had gone to bed and the light was out and the baby asleep, with a little moonlight in the room making a patch on the end of the bed, that she said, as if they had not paused in their conversation, "There's another kind of dream, Mike, a day dream, that comes out of love. I don't mind it because I know it comes out of love. Only it seems too bad that the more you love the more you have to fear. I sit day-dreaming and see Little Mike falling out of the basket, and then I shiver, and I wake up. Or I see you coming along the street and you're not crossing the road carefully. You're walking with your head down and something is going to hit you, and I feel it terribly. Sometimes I see the three of us together up high, and then we begin to fall. I see things happening to us, striking at us. It's a shame to worry like this about things you love, isn't it? Then sometimes I'm like a little girl and I see myself doing proud, bold things, saving you and Little Mike from disaster." Then she was silent, then he heard her laughing softly. "You don't mind those kind of dreams," she whispered.

"No, they're lovely dreams," he said.

"I know they are," she said. "I often have very good ones like them. Good night, Mike."

"Good night, Anna."

He lay there, waiting for the night to grow longer, full of fear of the night, and the thoughts that came with the night. He had acquired a routine for these sleepless nights. First he lay there remembering little things that had happened during the day, like the time when he had looked out the window in the morning at the sunlight and had thought that some day he would walk in the park with his son, and now, when he thought of it again, the picture that had been so good faded out; as a thought it was not particularly good at all. Then he thought of Anna's soft laugh before she had fallen asleep, and even that, when he kept thinking about it, was not good. He tried hard to remember something that would be bright, something that would shine and live in the night, but nothing he could think of among living things remained substantial or good. Nothing lived for him at night and he kept saying of one thing after the other, "It's no good. That's no good either."

His body felt tired, and he was weary, yet his eyes stayed

open. By this time he was midway in the routine of the dark night world of his despair. He began to go over and over familiar thoughts, as though rehearsing them, "No matter what I do, no matter how much willingness there is in me to work with people and hope with people and join with them or to forget myself, I can't do it while there's strife in my own soul. I'm alone."

He began to think of all those he knew in the city who were in some way like him, because their souls were restless and there was a break within them. He could see Nathaniel Benjamin, the Christian convert, smiling happily; then he heard him suddenly shout in anger and yell, and then Nathaniel was weeping within himself, knowing he stank with pride. And the other day he had met Huck Farr on the street, and Huck had said, "In God's name, where have you been, Mike? I haven't seen you in a dog's age. Let's go some night and get the oil changed. How's that bimbo, Anna's what's-her-name, that was trying to make you?" It was easy for Huck. He had found the brotherhood of man in the desire for women. Then there was Bill Johnson, the revolutionary. It was hard to say about Bill; sometimes he seemed to have control and a lot on the ball and he stuck in there pitching. But he was sure about Bill's wife, for she jumped like a grasshopper from one cause to another, and it was very funny thinking of her as a communist, because she had been one thing after another, and wasn't through yet. They all tried pretty hard not to remember. Maybe young Dave Choate knew why he was drinking, but that way in this time was too easy. They were all like himself, only some of them became Catholics and some became communists, and then it was too bad for Catholicism and too bad for Communism, for such people as these in this generation only heaped the chaos in their own souls on whatever they touched. Such people were all like him in this, that they couldn't know peace or dignity or unity with anything till they were single and whole within themselves.

Then he turned his head on the pillow and saw how the bit of moonlight touched the side of Anna's face and a little bit of her head and showed the mound of her body underneath the clothes. Rising on his elbow, he peered down at her face. "How sweet and soft she sleeps tonight. No bad dreams tonight," he thought, and his soul grew full of longing as he watched her white face in the shadows. "She's everything I'm not," he thought. She went on from day to day, living and loving and exposing the fullness and wholeness of herself to the life around her. If to be poor in spirit meant to be without false pride, to be humble enough to forget oneself, then she was poor in spirit, for she gave herself to everything that touched her, she let herself be, she lost herself in the fullness of the world, and in losing herself she found the world, and she possessed her own soul. People like her could have everything. They could inherit the earth.

Then he whispered to her, without waking her, "Ah, Anna, I can't stand it this way. I don't know what's going on in me. I try to hold on to you, yet I'm losing you day by day. I'm afraid of myself. If I go out of my head I've lost you forever."

Thirty-Two

H<small>E WOKE</small> up and was startled one night, for he was sure Anna was not beside him in the bed. It was hard to see in the dark of the room. Then he heard her moving quietly, the tread of her bare feet, and he stared at the corner where he had heard the sound, and after a time, when his eyes grew accustomed to the light, he saw her bending over the basket. For a while she did not move and she frightened him by her silence.

"Anna," he whispered. "What's the matter?"

She came tiptoeing back to the bed and got in beside him. "Nothing's the matter," she said.

"Why did you get up? Was there something wrong?"

"I sometimes wake up in the night," she said. "I listen to hear him breathing and when I can't hear him I keep thinking he may have smothered. It would be so easy, wouldn't it? I listened tonight and couldn't hear him. He might die over there in the basket and I wouldn't know it. I got up to see if he was breathing all right. I've done it before."

"Was it all right?"

"It was all right. Now I'll be able to fall asleep."

When she put her arm around him and lay close beside him, they seemed so close together he could no longer endure holding anything apart from her. He felt a desperate need of destroying the last barrier between them, for the sake of their own peace, and he said, "Anna, I can't go on like this. I'll die one way or another if I go on like this. Anna, you're so good, you must listen. You mustn't leave me. You must go on loving me. It will be all right if you just say you can keep on loving me, no matter what happens. If I could be sure of that it would be all right, no matter what else happens."

"Oh, Mike, you're frightening me. What's the matter?"

"I can't stand it any longer."

"I don't know what you mean, Mike. You're frightening me."

"It's about my father and Dave Choate, the boy who was drowned. I've let my father be blamed, and I've let him be broken, and I'm to blame because I let Dave drown."

"You don't know what you're saying. You've been sick."

"I know what I'm saying. I've been trying for so long not to say it."

"Mike, you're teasing me. It's not good to talk like that."

"Let me talk, Anna. Can't you see I must tell you? Dave wouldn't leave Sheila alone. He didn't want her to marry Ross and he told her our mother was mad. I went out in the boat with him, but I only wanted to talk with him."

"You mean it was an accident, Mike."

"I wouldn't go back to the shore and he jumped out of the boat."

"He jumped out himself."

"But I wouldn't let him swim to the shore, and he turned and went the other way."

"What did he do?"

"He laughed."

"It was all right between you if he laughed."

"I can hear the way he laughed. I can see the light shining on his head as it rose up out of the water. Then he was gone in the dark water."

"It was all right, Mike, if he laughed."

"He cried out in such a wild, frightened way. I couldn't see him but I heard him cry and I sat there full of hate. I let him drown. You don't understand the hate that was in me for him and his mother and my own father, too."

"You weren't beside him. You couldn't have saved him. You know it yourself."

"I let him drown, Anna. I didn't move to help him. I didn't want to move. I know what was in my heart."

Then she believed him and she sank back slowly on the pillow, with her head turned away, and just that bit of night light on the side of her head. It was done, and his heart ached as he watched her. In a timid way he put out his hand and touched her head gently, as if he might never be permitted to touch her head again, but she did not speak or turn, or look at him; she only wept softly. "It'll break us, I know, as it has been breaking me," he said. "Poor Anna, I didn't know what to do."

"Why didn't you tell me before?" she whispered.

"I was afraid of losing you."

"Then why do you tell me now?"

"I felt myself losing you bit by bit. You were slipping away from me, because I kept thinking I was going out of my head. I didn't mind telling the police. I couldn't bear to tell you, because you're so good." He went on talking brokenly as he lay in the dark beside her; he spoke quietly, pausing for a long time, maybe waiting for her to answer, and yet she hardly seemed to hear him. There was no stir in her. Once she sighed. Then she got up slowly and turned on the light and stood there stiffly in her nightdress, staring at him.

He was lying with one arm behind his head on the pillow. His eyes were wide open, and his face, though it looked terribly tired, thin and white, was relaxed and almost calm in its expression of utter abnegation; he looked utterly beaten, yet somehow content, as if in losing everything and expecting nothing, he had found some kind of eternal peace. Then his head turned just a little and he said evenly, "Why did you turn on the light? You'll wake Little Mike."

But she could not answer, she only nodded her head, and when her hand went up to her cheek it was trembling.

"Don't stare at me like that, Anna, please," he whispered.

"Mike, Mike, I can't stand the way you're lying there with that look on your face, Mike. It's not like that. Oh, nothing in the world can be like that," she said, for she had begun to feel all the misery and terror and shame that had been in him for so long; yet even now, when he looked as if he would never have any pride again and never know hope, he seemed content at least to be rid of his wretchedness.

"Turn out the light," he said again.

"All right," she said, and when she got into bed and was warm beside him, she was a little afraid of how she should touch him, she was so full of pity and love.

"You understand it was just that I was afraid of losing you that I went on," he said.

"Losing me?" she said, sitting bolt upright. "What do you intend to do, Mike?"

"I must go to the police, so my father will be cleared of this and be able to live again."

"You'll say you did it?"

"Yes."

"Mike, I won't let you go to the police. Don't do that."

"I've got to go," he said.

Pressing her head against him, she kissed him lightly and whispered, "I know you better than anyone does, Mike. I swear I know your soul. I swear you're loving and kind and want to do good. Whatever happens to us can't make me feel different about that." Still he did not stir, and she kissed him again.

Then he began to whisper in the dark. "You don't know how good you are, Anna. You can never know the goodness I've felt in you and how I've hungered to feel it more and more."

"Don't think about me, Mike. Put your arms around me

and I'll know you weren't wrong." But then her voice broke, because she could not bear the way he was weeping beside her. "Darling, darling, I love you," she said.

"Anna, I'm sorry," he said. "I'm very sorry. You've been wasting it on me."

But in a little while he began to talk almost eagerly, now that he was sure of her love; he talked like a child, talked about his family and his childhood, and his mother and father and Mrs. Choate and Dave. His anxiety to state it all accurately increased, and sometimes he groped for the precise words, though his voice was never raised above a whisper. When he was finished, and could say no more, he said, with that desperate eagerness, "I'm not afraid at all, Anna. It's a simple matter now. Tomorrow I'll talk to the police."

Then her voice broke with anxiety as she said, "Don't be a fool, Mike. Why do you want to talk to the police? Who are the police?"

"I'm thinking of my father."

"What have the police to do with justice and you and your father? How does it concern them?"

"It's the only way there is of doing it. When they know, the whole city will know. It's time I did it. I won't feel free till it's done."

"They'd never believe you. It's just your own story. You were away off when he drowned."

"They'll believe me."

"Mike, you want to be just. Giving yourself to the police doesn't mean anything to anybody. It's stupid. It's meaningless. It's a senseless gesture. Don't do it, Mike," she pleaded.

"It's the only way there is of squaring myself with everybody."

"It was the hate in you that made you feel so full of guilt. Nobody will understand your guilt. Nobody but you. You said he laughed and swam away. Nobody'll believe what you say. Mike, darling, please, please, please, don't do a foolish thing."

"What else can I do, Anna?" he said. There was such a passionate compulsion in her voice that he wavered a little and looked at her helplessly.

"The only justice you owe is to your father," she said, smiling eagerly. "What has organized justice to do with the feeling that's in your heart? What have the police to do with justice, and you, and your father?"

"I let him be broken by malice and gossip and I did nothing to stop it."

"I remember your father. I remember meeting him in your room. He was a good man," she said. She hardly gave him time to answer. Her face was pressed close to his ear. Words flowed out of her, making a passionate promise that there could be no other way than her way. "Promise me you'll go to your father first. You must tell him, and then do what you want. Promise me that. Oh, do this for me."

"I'll promise. I ought to do that first anyway."

"Go to him like a son and tell him. Tell him you've been wrong and you want to make it right for him."

"I'll go to him and I'll ask him to forgive me. It's not late even now, Anna. It's not midnight yet. I know where he lives. Sheila gave us the address. I'll go now. If he's asleep, I'll wake him," he said, and he got out of bed and turned on the light.

She was crouched on the bed, uncovered, her face still eager from pleading with him, and her eyes shining bright, and her nightgown was twisted all around her body, and the light gleamed on her bare shoulders and her white breast. Her breast kept rising and falling steadily, as she tried to smile. Then she called softly, calling him to her, with her eyes full of longing, "Mike, don't go now."

"I might as well go now and get it over with."

"Wait till the morning, Mike. Let's be together tonight. Ah, stay with me this one night," she said. "It's just a little while, and then it's over."

He went back to her and lay beside her and she turned to

him, and they touched each other, and he pressed his body against her and she held him tight. They made love to each other, wanting all the warmth and softness they could get from each other. They made love as if it was their last chance to get all they could of life on this night that might be their last night together.

Thirty-Three

IN THE morning Anna would not stay at home, and she went along the street with him, carrying the baby. She had asked only that she be allowed to walk as far as his father's place with him. She wore no hat. She wore a little blue print dress. They were silent and white-faced as they walked along the street. Once Anna looked up at Mike and tried to smile, and he pressed her arm. It was a beautiful summer morning with sunlight flooding the streets.

"Let me carry him," he said.

"No," she said.

"You're walking much slower, Anna."

"That's all right," she said. "I'm not tired."

When they came to the apartment house they stood on the pavement and looked up at the windows. They blinked their eyes in the sunlight that shone upon their upturned faces.

"I'll go in," he said. "You go home, Anna."

"No, I'll wait here."

"You'll be tired. Please go home."

"No. Let me wait, Mike. I couldn't go. I'd keep coming back. I'll do nothing but stand here. Nobody'll notice me. I'll say nothing. I'll just wait."

And when he went to go, she called, "Mike."

"What's the matter?"

"Oh, Mike, I don't know."

"Then let me go," he said.

She reached up and kissed him as they stood on the sidewalk. "It'll be all right, darling," she said. "Whatever happens it'll be absolutely all right. Just let me wait."

On the way into the apartment house, he turned and saw her with her head turned up just as it had been when she had kissed him, for she had moved in no way at all. When she saw him turn, she only nodded her head, for she was unable to smile.

Though Mike's heart began to beat loudly as he went up the stairs, he felt very calm, and his thoughts were dreadfully clear. He was remembering how he had felt that time before when he had gone to his father's place in the country; he remembered his own arrogant aloofness, his unwillingness to return. He knew now that when he had left his father's house years ago, and had gone off to live by himself, he had left because he had felt he would not be loved. And wherever he might have gone, in whatever countries, and whatever he had sought, he was always wanting the one thing, to be loved, which would satisfy his pride and console him for his independence. But since that time, out of the things that had happened to him, he had learned at least to love. He felt very humble, full of sorrow for his father, and eager only that he be forgiven, as he climbed the stairs.

He rapped on the door, and without waiting for an answer he turned the handle and walked in.

His father, who had been sitting in a chair by the window, jumped up in a hurry, and began smoothing his hair, patting his white hair down at the back of his head. The strong morning sunlight slanted brilliantly from the window to the corner of the room, and that shaft of sunlight cut across his father's body.

The last two months Andrew Aikenhead had had a little hope and eagerness in his life, because he had got one letter from Ross Hillquist and one from Sheila; for a while he had thought it was going to go like he had wanted it to go, that these letters would strengthen him, and bring him joy. But in the last three weeks there had been no letters, just a card from Sheila. Every day, when it was time for the postman to come to the apartment, Andrew Aikenhead would find some excuse to be on the stairs, and he would ask for mail and look incredulous when it did not come. It did him good just to ask for mail and stare resentfully at the postman, standing there looking puzzled and unhappy, yet able at least to feel disappointed.

"Eh," he said suddenly, staring at Mike. Then he actually looked shy. "Is it you, Michael?" he said. But instead of coming forward, he waited for Michael to cross the room to him. Then he smiled and his face lit up with joy and he rushed forward and took Michael by the hand and said, "Sit down, son. It's not much of a place here. It's awfully good to see you. I'm not quite dressed. That doesn't matter." He pushed a chair over to his son and fussed around it, smiling his welcome all the time.

It was so hard for Michael to get used to the frightened look in his father's eyes, that he only stood there and could not sit down, and his father's flustered movements, his nervous excitement, his shy pleasure were so upsetting he could not even speak. When he had come along the street, silent, and thinking steadily, he had the picture in his mind of his father as he had been years ago; it was the picture of the father of his youth; and while he walked along the street, seeing his father's face and imagining he could hear his voice, it was always his father of that time when he, himself, was a child, when his father was assured and strong and laughing, or stern, his father of the time when his own mother was alive. Whenever he had thought of his father these last months he had felt the respect and the sympathy that had belonged to those earlier days; he could hear his mother's voice saying, "Now, help the boy, if he's asking you to. Tell him how to do it." That was the time he had had to make a speech at school, and his mother had tried to coach him, and then they had waited for the father to come home, waiting for the father's easy voice and his flowing words and sure gestures, and his laughter, to make everything plain. It was hard for Mike to see in this thin, nervous man with the frightened blue eyes and such an unrestrained eagerness, an image of the father of his youth. There was such sorrow in him and such shame he still could not speak, and he sat down opposite his father and said, "You don't know why I've come. I should have come a long while ago. I wanted to come."

"Nonsense. Nonsense. That doesn't matter at all. I'll get you a drink. Then we'll talk, eh?"

"I don't want a drink. I want you to listen to me. I don't know how to begin, dad." He looked up with such simple candor, so much like a son wanting his father's confidence, that the father was startled.

"What is it, Michael?" he said.

"I want you to forgive me."

"Forgive you for what?"

While they were staring at each other, the father had some intimation of his son's shame and humility; and what he became aware of, as they looked at each other directly in this strange way, made him so uneasy that he said in a whisper, "Why did you come here now, Michael?"

"I've let you be blamed, and I've let you suffer when I was to blame. Dave Choate drowned when he was out in the boat with me. He didn't want Sheila to marry Ross, and he told her our mother was insane. I just wanted him to leave her alone, but he jumped out of the boat and he swam away, and then he cried out and I did not go to him."

While Michael spoke, his father watched him, his pale blue eyes staring as if they saw nothing in the room. The fist of his father's right hand was lifted slowly, and it fell into the open palm of his left hand, with a slow, heavy, mechanical motion, repeated again and again. Then his eyes were closed. Still the fall of his fist into his open hand went on, rising and falling hopelessly, as if this single motion of his body would have to go on even if his spirit was dead.

"Why did you let them blame me?" he asked.

"I felt you were to blame for the bad things that had happened to us all. It was hard to think of you as my father. I couldn't feel like a son."

The father muttered to himself, "My own son," and his eyes were closed again and there were tears in the corners of his eyes. When Michael saw his father's tears he wanted to cry out, "God help him. He's an old man, and I can do nothing," yet he said quietly, "I wanted you to forgive me, but I can't ask it now. I know I don't deserve it. But I wanted to tell you I'll make it all right for you. I would have gone direct to the police but my wife asked me to come to you first. I'm glad I came. It will be all right."

Nodding his head, his father made that curiously emphatic, yet entirely lifeless, motion of dropping his fist into his open palm.

"I'm ashamed to ask you to forgive me."

"It's all right."

"I wanted to speak to you and tell you myself. Now I know there's nothing I can say."

Michael watched this man who was crouching in the chair with his head down and his body leaning forward, this man who was his father, who never spoke and never moved. Timidly, like a child, Michael went over and put his hand on his father's shoulder, and he said, "I'm sorry. It'll be all right. I'll go now. My wife's waiting for me outside. It'll be all right," and he could say no more, and turned and hurried out.

Thirty-Four

W HEN Michael had gone Andrew Aikenhead still sat there, and that slow swing of his hand became like the slow swing of time. Then he looked up and he saw that he was alone, and when he saw that he was alone, as he had been for so long, all he could think of was that his son had been in the room, and he had let him go, and he was alone again. "He was like a son," he said. "He spoke to me and asked me to forgive him. He wanted to be just to me."

He went over to the window and looked down at the sunlit pavement, and he saw Michael taking the arm of the woman who waited, holding a child in her arms. Michael and the woman stood together a moment and then they turned and raised their faces together, looking up at his window. Andrew Aikenhead drew away quickly, yet he was still watching. The sunlight shone on their faces as they looked up at the window. "I remember that girl's face. I remember her the night I went out to find Michael and how she smiled and how warm and lovely she was." The girl's face was still turned up, only the joy was gone, it was a white and wondering face, turned up in the way a face looks up fearfully at the heavens on a wild night, yet it still shone with eagerness; it still was alive with hope. Then the two figures linked arms down there on the street and walked away slowly, with Michael staring straight ahead and the girl's face turned to him full of anxiety, begging him to tell her what might have been said.

As he watched them going along the street, Andrew Aikenhead was desolate and yet stirred by his deep and utter loss. He turned away, worrying, and still thinking of the way the two of them had looked up at the window. "He'll do what he said. No one will suspect me of anything. I'll be free. I'll be an honorable man. No one will ever touch me. It's only just it should be that way. But then what will I have?"

He sat there alone, having these thoughts, remembering how his son and the girl had gone away, and then a longing for home rose in him, and it seemed terrible to be sitting alone and having such thoughts. "He was so much like a son, and he said, 'I'm sorry' humbly, like that. He touched me on the arm," he thought.

Smoothing his white hair back from his head, he grabbed at his coat and he put his hat on, and hurried down the stairs. When he was outside on the pavement, breathing the fresh air of the sunlit morning, he looked eagerly along the street. Not so very far ahead were the two of them. They were standing at the corner, waiting to cross the road. He wanted to run, but he was content to take those short rapid steps, his head craning out and his hand reaching up time after time to put his hat more firmly on his head, as he thought, "I'm his father and I mustn't let him do anything foolish." The street was so bright and alive that morning, and he looked up innocently and smiled at a cop on a horse, who was leaning down and talking to a Negro, and the Negro, bursting out in laughter, said, "That's an Irish joke, a low Irish joke," and he doubled up with laughter while the cop looked pleased and the horse began to swish its tail and back up. But his son and the woman who walked with him were only a little way ahead, and he called out eagerly, "Michael," but Michael neither heard nor turned and it made him want to run after them. He passed a Jewish merchant and his wife and their small boy, who were standing in front of the restaurant on the corner, and the merchant was saying, "Want some coffee?" and the woman said, "Naw," and the merchant walking into the restaurant alone, turned and came back and said to the little boy, who was eating a sucker, "Here, give me a kiss," and the boy took the sucker out of his mouth while the merchant kissed him and then waddled away. Andrew Aikenhead smiled at them. Those voices, this glimpse of living people, everything he saw on the streets this morning, was alive and distinct and fresh and immensely pleasing.

But when he was quite close to the two who were ahead he slowed up, for he felt it would not be good if they saw him looking so flustered, and he fixed his tie and pulled his coat by the lapels, and he tried to get his breath, and then he began to walk more slowly and with dignity.

He followed them almost as far as the apartment house that was near the botanical garden, and there he saw Michael put out his hand to open the door, and then he grew alarmed, for in a moment they would pass out of his sight and it seemed to him they would be lost to him. "Michael, Michael," he cried out. "Wait a minute."

They turned around and watched him with frightened, wondering faces; they watched him with their heads bent toward him as he hurried up with his face so full of anxiety. The girl tried hard to show a little confidence by nodding her head and smiling at him.

"You hurried away, Michael," he said.

"Yes, my wife was waiting."

"I didn't have a chance to say anything to you. Is this your wife?" he asked. He put out his hand and took hold of Anna's arm, and then he smiled at her, for hers was the face he remembered and loved, and while he got his breath he watched his son, who was staring at him calmly.

"Michael," he began earnestly, "you mustn't do anything foolish. You're my son."

"I haven't been much like a son," Michael said simply. "Anna knows what I'm going to do."

Then the father turned to Anna and pleaded with her as though he had known her for a long time, "What can he do for me now? If he'd only listen to me, that would be all I'd ask. I've been alone. A little while ago he came to see me and when he had gone I realized I had found my son. I don't want to be alone again. You're his wife and I'm his father. We mustn't let him do anything foolish. We couldn't bear it, could we?" he added, joining himself to Anna in this way. Then he said firmly, "I won't stand for it, Michael."

While his father was talking to Anna, Michael listened and watched him and was full of incredible wonder; when his father suddenly smiled and his voice sounded so firm, he was like his father of old with the eagerness shining directly and purely in his eyes, and the warmth Michael felt was made so much more intense by the anxiety and care that still showed in his father's face.

Anna saw that Michael was so moved he could say nothing; she saw his father growing flustered by his own eagerness, and her face lit up with joy, and she said, "Come on in with us, Mr. Aikenhead. Let's all go into our place."

"Let's go into your place," Andrew Aikenhead said eagerly.

They went in and began to climb the stairs, and there was no sound but the scraping of their own feet on the stairs, and they could say nothing on the way up, for they all felt a little shy with each other.

Afterword

BY RAY ELLENWOOD

Published in 1934, *They Shall Inherit the Earth* is set in the period of the Great Depression, and so images the novel presents of a society in agony are not surprising. Masses of people are out of work and worried about their future, wondering what can be done to save their dreams and aspirations. Not only individuals, but whole groups have a bitter sense of disinheritance. Rich and poor, passive victims and would-be activists, are all trying to wait out the dead season, hanging on to whatever optimism, or dignity, they can muster. The book is not specifically about the Depression, but we are always aware of it through brief descriptions of people in the city, or through vignettes involving minor characters. There are arguments between Michael Aikenhead and his disenchanted friends seeking guidance through religion (Nathaniel Benjamin), or through political utopianism (William Johnson); there is the quiet struggle between Anna Prychoda's hunger and Huck Farr's lust, going on for the benefit of spectators in their rooming house; there is the gulf between wealth and poverty, which Michael sees in the "smooth, young, spoilt and dissipated faces" of Dave Choate and his two "bond boy" chums, whose insouciant way of life mocks the distress all around them in the city.

This Depression backdrop is rich in itself, involving

characters and situations that obviously continued to fascinate the author, since he worked them over in later books. For example, the little vignette of Dr. Albert Tucker's shoes, in chapter 28, is probably the seed for conflicts between stubbornly honourable gentlemen in "The Man with the Coat" (1955) and its later version, *The Many Colored Coat* (1960). The struggle between Anna Prychoda and Huck Farr, complicated through bumbling interventions by Michael Aikenhead, with all its unresolved questions about sexual exploitation, innocence and generosity, social ostracism and repressed violence, is a prototype for the various entanglements of Llona Tomory and Jay Dubuque in *The Enchanted Pimp* (1978) and *Our Lady of the Snows* (1985).

The story of the Aikenhead and Hillquist families is obviously related to this social and historical setting. They are the privileged whose comfort is threatened, but they are not presented as either pathetic sufferers or heartless villains. There is a strange, timeless quality to the situation and events surrounding the death of Dave Choate, with its love-hate struggle between parents and children full of jealousy and fear and paralyzing guilt. Marthe Choate takes on some of the fury of an archetypal witch-mother, qualities that Callaghan emphasized in the stage play he wrote later, based on this story. A first adaptation, entitled *Turn Again Home* (note how "home" and "house" are repeated throughout the novel) was done in 1939 with a view to a New York production that never materialized. The script was later reworked and produced by the New Play Society in Toronto as *Going Home*. This, along with another drama, *To Tell the Truth*, made Callaghan a Toronto theatre sensation in 1949 and 1950, the plays enjoying sold-out houses, extended runs, and two options bought by New York producers. The last version of *Turn Again Home*, published in 1976 as *Season of the Witch*, makes for interesting comparisons with the novel.

Despite the violence that takes place, ironically, at the

idyllic summer home of the Aikenheads, the prevailing mood of *They Shall Inherit the Earth* is one of longing and inertia. There is a malaise in the family and in society for which nobody is clearly responsible. People are waiting for something to happen, dreaming, like Andrew Aikenhead, of a return to the better times they remember, or, like Michael Aikenhead near the end of the novel, "thinking of death and ... waiting for birth." Of course, for Michael, the specific death in question has already happened with the drowning of Dave Choate, but there is also for other characters in the book an oppressive feeling of doom, as in the "stillness of death" that Ross Hillquist finds in a demoralized Andrew Aikenhead, or the different kind of demise seen in those ridiculous "friends of France" who gather to speak French and discuss the impact of Dostoevsky's novels on French literature, prompting Michael to say to Anna Prychoda, "death is in the next room. Listen to them. They are the dead. Listen. You didn't know death was such a nice gentleman." Is there an echo, even light parody, of T.S. Eliot's *The Waste Land* in those words? Certainly, Eliot's poem and this novel are both concerned with a time of moral and spiritual drought, waiting for rain and rebirth, when people grope blindly for any kind of faith.

Faith is a key word in most Callaghan novels, but here, as usual, it opens a Pandora's box of ambiguities because it is applied in so many ways by different characters. Nathaniel Benjamin, a convert to Christianity, describes Michael Aikenhead as "the modern man, no hope in anything, no faith in anything." He is certainly right, but he is himself a dubious alternative. Jay Hillquist, for whom "there was really only one kind of death, the failure of his business," is described by the narrator as "a man of simple and profound faith" whose workers hope he will "restore their security and their salaries and the faith of the old boom-time days." William Johnson has as great a faith in Communism as Hillquist has in Capitalism. And all of these people use the word or the concept for their own self-justification, so promiscuously that it loses all virtue.

Although *They Shall Inherit the Earth* seems to end on an up-beat, with a birth and resolution of family conflict, a triumph of love over death, we should beware of any simplified, moralistic, or pietistic reading, such as the one that sees Anna as representing some kind of "grace" that Michael finally recognizes. There was a tendency in early studies of Callaghan to emphasize what were seen as moral fables and a certain Catholic sensibility by people who assumed they knew the author's intent. This seems to have led more recently to misconceptions of Callaghan as an author who tells people what to think. True, his narrator often appears to interpret for us, but should we necessarily believe what we are told? Are we supposed to accept without laughing that account of Jay Hillquist in chapter 3, especially his "simple and profound faith?" And if we cannot, why should we necessarily take seriously the "pity and shame" that Michael eventually feels for his father? Even the down-and-out citizens "waiting to inherit the earth" in chapter 28 may not be the meek referred to in the Bible and in Callaghan's title. At least, before we jump to conclusions, we should consider Michael's thought in chapter 31, that "people like [Anna] could have everything. They could inherit the earth." Is Anna meek? Is she innocent? Are those really virtues in Callaghan's universe? In short, I would urge any reader of this novel to keep in mind a statement by Milton Wilson: "The special talent of Morley Callaghan is to tell us everything and yet keep us in the dark about what really matters. He makes us misjudge and rejudge and misjudge his characters over and over again." This is not to minimize the importance of political, moral, and, indeed, theological concerns in *They Shall Inherit the Earth*, but to insist that the book is full of irony and ambiguity, raising many questions and answering none.

There is not much high melodrama here. Everything,

including Dave Choate's death, Michael's evasion of moral responsibility, and the decline of Andrew Aikenhead into a pathetic outcast, is handled with understatement. Anyway, who could sniffle for a man who has been a florid-faced manipulator most of his life, or for a son who cannot even make the grade as a villain? If you want good, old-fashioned romance, you will have to look elsewhere.

By the same token, this book's style lacks the rolling, resonant gush that some people enjoy. Callaghan was very careful about his effects, explaining in *That Summer in Paris* that a writer's words should be "as transparent as glass," and that "every time a writer used a brilliant phrase to prove himself witty or clever he merely took the mind of the reader away from the object and directed it to himself." A recent, detailed stylistic investigation has shown that Callaghan actually did practice the plain style more assiduously than even Sherwood Anderson, Ernest Hemingway, or Gertrude Stein. Now, one could argue about the candour of any literary style that declares itself transparent, but an important truth comes through in *They Shall Inherit the Earth* and other books by Morley Callaghan: deep human emotion is often expressed in very banal ways. No great fireworks, no eloquence. At truly critical moments (such as at the end of this book, where there is a highly charged return home, but not, this time, to the father's house), the only words that come are simple ones, usually clichés, certainly nothing literary or witty: "Let's go into your place."

BY MORLEY CALLAGHAN

AUTOBIOGRAPHY
That Summer in Paris: Memories of Tangled Friendships with Hemingway, Fitzgerald, and Some Others (1963)

DRAMA
Season of the Witch (1976)

FICTION
Strange Fugitive (1928)
A Native Argosy (1929)
It's Never Over (1930)
No Man's Meat (1931)
A Broken Journey (1932)
Such Is My Beloved (1934)
They Shall Inherit the Earth (1935)
Now That April's Here and Other Stories (1936)
More Joy in Heaven (1937)
The Varsity Story (1948)
The Loved and the Lost (1951)
Morley Callaghan's Stories (1959)
The Many Colored Coat (1960)
A Passion in Rome (1961)
A Fine and Private Place (1975)
Close to the Sun Again (1977)

No Man's Meat and *The Enchanted Pimp* (1978)
A Time for Judas (1983)
Our Lady of the Snows (1985)
The Lost and Found Stories of Morley Callaghan (1985)
A Wild Old Man on the Road (1988)

FICTION FOR YOUNG ADULTS
Luke Baldwin's Vow (1948)

MISCELLANEOUS
Winter [photographs by John de Visser] (1974)

New Canadian Library
The Best of Canadian Writing ‖NCL

NCL – A Series Worth Collecting

New Canadian Library
The Best of Canadian Writing

NCL – A Series Worth Collecting

New Canadian Library
The Best of Canadian Writing

NCL – A Series Worth Collecting